THE DEADMAN'S TRIBE  BOOK 3

never ENOUGH

NICOLE CRAIG

Ebook ISBN 979-8-9892144-4-0

Paperback ISBN 979-8-9892144-5-7

ASIN B0CZ339NWF

Developmental Editing by Sara-Jane Higgins

Editing by Steph White (Kat's Literary Services)

Proofreading by Vanessa Esquibel (Kat's Literary Services)

Internal Formatting by Kat Wyeth (Kat's Literary Services)

Cover Design by Deranged Doctor Design **www.derangeddoctordesign.com**

Nicole Craig

Visit my website at https://nicolecraigauthor.godaddysites.com/

Join my Reader's Group at https://www.facebook.com/groups/362438775111170522

Printed in the United States of America

First Printing: December 2024

DEDICATION

For my father...

Unlike Haskell's father, you encouraged me to be whatever I wanted when I grew up. You encouraged me to forge my own path, yet you were always willing to share your wisdom. I've always been thankful for that.
I love you, Wilbur!
Your daughter, Charlotte.

SEPTEMBER 21, 2018

Haskell

Haskell plastered herself to the side of the Dolder Tower in the narrow alley between the tower and the house no more than four feet away. The gate at the base of the tower, the original from the thirteenth century, was currently lit by neon-green light. Despite its age, the structure still had security cameras and two security guards, especially now with its visiting treasure inside—the Jupiter Diamond. However, she had no intention of entering the tower through the main doors at its base.

Riquewihr was a quaint village near the northern German border of France. Each year, millions of people traveled to the famous "wine road" to enter the medieval gates of the still-populated towns and take in the villages that seemed to have never left the times of lords and vassals. Tightly crowded homes made of timber and plaster still housed just over one thousand residents. Considered an open-air museum, the town housed several formal museums of historical significance, quaint shops, open-air cafés, alehouses dating back to the fifteenth century, and cobbled streets.

A clang sounded behind and around the building. She froze. After counting for seven minutes with no further noise, she unfroze her muscles. Scanning the darkened streets, she gave the front side of the building one last look.

Chalking her hands from the pouch at her lower back, Haskell searched for the climbing path in the building's brickwork she had scouted earlier today. With one last glance down the deserted streets, she began her ascent. Each foot she placed on a precariously tiny toehold, each fingertip she gripped into the raised bricks and chipped mortar, brought her one step closer to her goal.

The tower was roughly eighty feet in height and the tallest structure in the village. At its inception, it had been the fortified entrance to the city, its top floor housing the bell to toll out the time for the opening and closing of its gates, warning the vassals to return to the safety of its walls. Those bells were still rung daily and were still rung by hand as a testament to an era that seemed to have been locked in time, a stalwart refusal to age. This was also to Haskell's advantage. Minimal modernization meant it was easier to sneak in, take her prize, and sneak out.

Once she reached the top of the arch, climbing became more precarious but not impossible. More chalk. More patience. She had hours before the sun would rise and illuminate her silhouette on the outside of the building.

The third floor, which was really the first actual floor people could walk on, had two narrow windows on the tower's inner facing with window boxes beneath them displaying brightly colored flowers. She probably could have squeezed through one of them because of her childlike size, but it was better to continue upward until she was as far out of the reflective reaches of the archway light as possible.

The fourth floor held two sets of double-paned windows above their flower boxes.

The fifth floor held one triple-paned window that did not open.

The sixth floor held two square windows on the far left and right sides. Both windows flanked the town clock, which was unlit by modern lighting and covered by a steep wood awning.

The remaining twenty feet of the climb was the most dangerous. The wind and elements had been harshest to this portion of the building as there were no taller buildings to offer protection, creating thinner toeholds and fingerholds. It was here that she had to cross the face of the building, traverse the top of the awning, and hoist herself through the uncovered belfry window. Once inside, she would take the ancient wood staircase down to the sixth floor, where the Jupiter Diamond was on display as part of the city's fall celebration.

Slowly but surely, Haskell slid her way the two feet to the corner of the building that had her on a ninety-degree angle to the inner facing of the tower. She paused at the corner, taking a few minutes to calm her breathing and concentrate on how to make the turn.

After making the turn around the corner, Haskell was able to shuffle-slide the short distance to the awning. Once the awning was within reach, it was all about arm strength. Pushing up on her tiptoes, she managed to grasp the timbered ledge and then pull herself up to the belfry window. Hoisting herself into the window, she threw her torso across the ledge, legs hanging out the window, and everything else inside.

Suddenly, she was yanked unceremoniously through the window and found her back crushed against the front of a hard-muscled body. A hand quickly clamped over her mouth while a band of steel cinched tight around her torso, just under her breasts.

A warm breath with a hint of something sugary to it whispered in her ear. "Well, well, well, if it isn't Le Chatte Noire."

SEPTEMBER 21, 2018

Nemo

Hearing scraping noises outside the building, Nemo flattened himself against the wall just to the left of the window facing the courtyard. Given the prize downstairs, he knew without a shadow of a doubt who it was. His body vibrated in anticipation.

"We've got company, Midas."

His twin brother, older by eight minutes, was on the other side of the communication system that ran through his watch. "Yeah, I saw her start up the north face when you were already in."

"And you didn't think it was a good idea to warn me, fuckstick?"

"So sue me. I wanted to see her in action again."

Nemo grimaced to himself. He was going to strangle Midas. Most of the time, working with his brother was a blessing. Tonight was not one of those times.

The interloper was Le Chatte Noire, or The Black Cat. She was the most notorious cat burglar in Europe and possibly even worldwide. Not much was known about the thief except that she was tiny and very, very good at getting into impossible spaces. She had yet to fail at a job.

But you know some things about her.

He grinned. If he had his way, he was about to know even more.

For the past week, Nemo had been doing reconnaissance in the quaint little town of Riquewihr. Tonight, all of that work led to liberating ninety-five moonstones—small diamonds that were part of the Jupiter Diamond display meant to mimic the ninety-five moons of the planet Jupiter. Allegedly, they were the rightful property of an Italian family who had hired Tribe, Nemo and Midas' employer, a mercenary group hiding out as a corporation, to reclaim the stones. Currently, said stones were in his pocket.

A little under a year ago, the Saturn Diamond had been stolen from its permanent display in Gabon, and it was believed to be Le Chatte Noire's talents that had made it disappear. If that was the case, it didn't take a genius to figure out that she'd be tempted by the Saturn Diamond's partner, the Jupiter Diamond.

How he had not run into her or even gotten a glimpse of her in the last week was unreal to him.

Realizing she was about to come through the window, he whispered, "Muting," and tapped his watch, closing the line to prevent her from hearing him. He also figured it would be a good idea to keep the initial conversation with her from his brother's ears. Energy fizzed through him. As he waited for her entry, he worked to slow his breathing down, not only to prevent giving himself away before she made it through the window but also in an attempt to calm his heart rate.

Told you we'd meet again one day, kitty cat.

Shuffling noises were followed by the slap of hands on the window ledge. There was a soft grunt of exertion as a petite figure pulled itself up through the open window to lie across the ledge. Once he was sure she had her balance, he grabbed her by her armpits and dragged her all the way into the room. She squeaked in surprise as he plastered her back to his front, one arm banding around her middle and his other hand over her mouth to prevent the hissing and spitting that was about to occur.

Mouth next to the balaclava-covered ear of his captive, a soft laugh underscored his whispered, "Well, well, well, if it isn't Le Chatte Noire."

He felt the tension in her body ratchet up a level as she realized who held her in his arms. An exasperated, muffled scream of frustration came from her covered mouth as she tried to elbow him in the gut, but he held her too tightly to his front for her to gain any space to connect. He let her struggle for a minute or two until she realized she wasn't getting away, then felt her relax slightly.

"I'm going to move my hand, kitty cat," he warned her. "It will be to both of our advantages if you don't scream, but I think you already know that. In two seconds, my communications go back on, so just remember everything you say is going to be heard by my brother."

Without missing a beat, she hissed, "Let go of me."

"Say please," he teased.

She huffed. "Please," she uttered sarcastically.

Why does a British accent make everything sound so much sexier?

"See? Was that so hard? I'll do as you ask. But I warn you, kitty cat, try anything, and I'll have you up against the wall screaming my name before you can hiss at me."

Nemo released the sprite in his arms, and she whirled around to face him. He held a single finger up to his mouth in the universal "Shh" gesture, then pointed between her mouth and his ear, again reminding her that they weren't completely alone in the belfry.

He tapped his watch again, unmuting it. "Back online, Midas."

"What's going on, lil bro?" The voice was concerned.

"All good. Just took in our little stray."

"Shit. It's her?" his brother asked.

The two burglars were dressed very similarly. Black balaclavas, long-sleeved black shirts, black pants, black climbing shoes. Both had climbing belts around their waists that had assorted pouches and clips with tools of the thieving trade.

"What are you doing here?" she spat at him.

Still feisty.

He grinned beneath his headgear. It was good to know some things never changed. "Needed to get a few items on my shopping list," he joked. He heard her curse under her breath, and then he saw her eyes dart to the stairs leading down two floors to where the Jupiter Diamond sat in its case on display. "It's still there, kitty cat. Unfortunately, *you* will be leaving empty-handed."

"I'd like to see you try and stop me."

She bolted.

He cut her off, his arms banding around her waist, and he swung her around so that he was between her and the stairs. "Ah, ah, ah," he chastised. "Even if you got past me, kitty cat, I'd still catch up to you before you managed to snatch it."

Her fists clenched, and her lips pursed in frustration. "I'm taking that diamond," she warned him.

"You can try. But even if you manage to free it from its case, I'm bigger, faster, and stronger. You wouldn't make it twenty feet before I wrestled it from you."

She stamped her foot in anger. "If you didn't come here to steal it, why do you care if I take it? I need it," she insisted.

He crossed his arms over his chest. "And I don't want you to have it. What's stronger? My wants or your needs?"

"Quit flirting, lil bro. We're on borrowed time here. One of the guards must have heard something because he's pointing up and talking to his partner," Midas warned.

Nemo smiled to himself. "Sorry, sweetheart. I've got a timeline, and you're interfering with it."

She snorted and rolled her eyes. "And how are you going to stop me from interfering further?"

"Kitty cats get leashed."

Before she could move, Nemo had her in his arms, hands grasped behind her back in one of his. He gave her credit. She fought hard. At the last second, he felt her knee start to come up, and he barely moved to the side, taking the knee to the inside of his thigh. He grunted. That was going to leave a mark. He felt his grin get bigger. He'd wear that bruise with pride.

"Arrêt! Police!"

Nemo and the little cat burglar froze.

"Reunion time is over, Nemo. There are gendarmes everywhere. Time to get swimming," Midas warned.

"Dammit," Nemo ground out. "Okay, kitty cat, this was fun, but we've got to go." He gave her a gentle shove away, then ducked his head out the window.

Down below, two police officers stood at the exit of the archway. Three quick steps to the window on the opposite side of the building he had come through, and the way was clear. But as soon as he ducked out that way, even if he fast-roped all the way down, he'd likely be caught at the bottom.

"This is all your fault," she accused, looking out the front window.

He turned back to her. "How the hell is it my fault? They didn't show up until you did."

"Well, I know I was quiet as a church mouse, so they didn't hear me. You're such a big oaf; they probably heard you stomping around the building or clambering up the side."

Midas hooted laughter in his ear. "Oh, I like this girl."

"Shut up, Midas." He shifted his attention back to his cat burglar. "No one heard me. I'm no novice at this." He looked out the window again, gauging the distance across and down to the nearby roof.

It's a long way. Only about four feet across but at least thirty feet down. And probably a noisier exit than fast-roping and running. Shit!

Suddenly, she was pushing her way into the side window with him, gauging the possibility of exiting that way as well. "Bollocks," she whispered.

"Would you rather," he began, "fast-rope to the bottom and sprint for the gate on the far end of town or roof-hop across town and risk falling several stories?"

"Nemo," Midas interrupted, "quit thinking and get running. Time's up!"

"I agree," he muttered. He looked at her. She looked at him. "Trust me?" he asked.

"No."

His eyes twinkled. "Well, too bad, kitty cat. We're stuck together for now. I'm heading down and hopping to the roof of the building next door. I'll wait for you at the bottom. Leave the rope. No time to collect it."

"You've got about sixty seconds, bro," Midas warned.

Heavy footsteps stormed up the stairs. Both heads whipped around at the sound. "Fuck! Change of plans." He turned, grabbed her slight frame, and slid her through the side window he'd come through earlier. "Go! I'll be right behind you."

Her eyes locked with his, then she was gone, sliding down the rope. When she was even with the roof of the building next door, she pushed hard with her legs, sending her sailing over to that roof and dropping down onto it. As soon as the rope was in his grasp, he pitched himself out the window and down the rope. As he swung over, he noticed that she was already running into the distance. He smiled. The chase was going to be so much fun.

You're not getting away from me this time.

"Head east," Midas advised. "The gendarmerie are converging on the belfry. They haven't noticed you up top yet."

Nemo took off after Haskell's running figure, his eyes watching her as she raced sure-footed up and down the pitched roofs, jumping from building to building. Her reputation was well-earned. She definitely had better skills than he did, although his weren't bad. He wasn't a big guy, but he clearly outweighed her, which slowed him down some.

She went down a pitched roof and was out of sight briefly. When he crested that same roof about thirty seconds later, she was nowhere to be seen. However, his frustration at her ditching him was soon replaced by fear grabbing his heart. Hanging from a roof edge by one hand, her feet kicking wildly forty feet above the street, was his little kitty cat. He ripped his balaclava down around his neck. "Hang on!"

"Nemo, what the hell is going on?" Midas yelled over the airwaves.

The man in question slid down the pitched roof on his ass, his right leg outstretched to brace himself when he hit the lip of the roof. "Thank you for calling. Saving the girl. Leave a message!" He anchored himself with his left foot, then reached down to grasp the dangling cat burglar. "Gotcha!" he cheered as he clasped her wrist. "Give me your other hand, kitty cat."

He watched her glance down at the ground, then up at him, fear in her eyes and a whimper in her throat.

"You know better than to look down. Scratch and claw, tiny. I've got you!"

She tried to swing her arm up to reach for his grasp, but she kept missing his outstretched hand. "I can't!"

"You can, kitty cat! Le Chatte Noire isn't losing one of her nine lives this way."

With a gasp and a grunt of sudden energy, she swung wildly and managed to get the dangling arm up above the eave. Nemo grabbed her forearm and leaned back with all of his might, working to steady her swinging body. Under one hundred pounds or not, she was deadweight, and he could feel his shoulders and arms burning with the effort to keep her from slipping.

"That's it. Hang on!" Slowly, he managed to pull her up over the edge and brought her slight form on top of him on the pitched roof. Just in time, too, for, as her feet came over the edge, the gendarmerie rounded the corner of the narrow alley below.

Voices gathered in the streets, whistles blasting. They lay there, trying to gain control of their breathing and calm their pounding hearts as the police gave chase through the streets below, looking for the shadowy figures they had seen slide down the side of the tower.

When the voices and whistles diminished, Nemo remembered to check in with the squawking voice over the airwaves.

"Thank you for holding. Nemo is back in the office. How may I help you?"

"Cut the jokes. Are you two all right?" Midas asked, his voice in a panic.

"Nothing a good beer and some NikNaks won't cure," Nemo assured him. To the woman beside him, he said, "Well, that was exciting." He raised his head just enough to glance into the alley below.

The small woman lying on his chest stared at him wide-eyed. "You didn't let me fall."

"Nope. Do I get a prize?" His eyebrows pitched up and down.

Instantly, her eyes became guarded, and her body froze. "What do you want?"

"Just to see the pretty face that goes with the pretty eyes of Le Chatte Noire." His hand reached up and pulled the balaclava from around her head and neck.

Just as beautiful as the first time.

In the moonlight, Nemo could just make out the gray storm clouds in her wide blue eyes. He swiped a gloved hand through her springy curls that popped out from under the hood, and his hand brushed the hair behind her right ear where an industrial piercing glinted.

New metal. Wonder what else is new? Maybe some more ink?

He suppressed a shudder of heat and need at the thought.

"Still such a pretty kitty," he crooned.

"Stop calling me that," she groused, grabbing wildly for her hood. "And give me that back."

He held it out of reach and grinned. "Is that any way to treat the hero who saved your life? Again."

She rolled off him and scooched out of his reach. "While I'm thankful for the assistance, I can't say I would have done the same."

"Hissy tonight, aren't we?" He winked and shifted his focus. "Midas, are you still there?"

"Where else would I be? Quit fuckin' around and get out of there. The gendarmerie is moving in the opposite direction still, but it won't be long before they realize you're behind them and decide to double back. You've got maybe two minutes."

"Copy that." He looked at the pint-sized thief next to him. "We gotta go. Unwanted guests in two minutes." He tossed her the balaclava he'd torn from her head and pulled his own back up.

"How do you know we've got two minutes?"

"My eye in the sky has a drone. He can see all of our little friends running around. C'mon."

He helped her pull her hood in place, then he stood and grabbed her hand, leading her toward the back side of the rooftop. They both looked down over the side of the roof, gauging the distance to the next building. "Too far to jump this one. Gotta go down." He whipped his head around and scanned the wall below. Finding a rain pipe, he bent down and gave it a quick tug to test its strength. "Gonna be iffy. You go first. Should hold you no problem."

"What about you?" she gasped.

"That's why you're going first, kitty cat." He smacked her on the ass.

After planting his feet shoulder-width apart and making sure his center of gravity would keep him from pitching over the edge, he grasped her wrists like a trapeze artist. She reacted with a soft squeak as he lowered her down around the corner of the building, his muscles bulging and burning as he moved her. "Grab it and go, kitty cat!"

With a huff of indignation, the woman let herself down the pipe in a controlled slide. When she reached the bottom, he swung himself down to hang off the edge. The metal of the pipe was thin, and he was pretty sure it wasn't going to hold. He took a quick look around at his options, decided there weren't any, and then let himself begin to slide down the pipe.

Sure enough, it began to groan at his weight and collapse underneath him. He was barely twelve feet down when he had to let go and aim for the wrought iron shop sign on the corner of the building to keep him from falling the remaining twenty-plus feet and breaking his legs. Luckily, his hands managed to catch the bar of the sign. While his shoulders definitely felt the yank of his weight's sudden stop, at least now he was only about ten feet from the ground instead of twenty. Still iffy but not nearly as bad.

He heard metal grind and squeaky wheels. Glancing below, he saw his little cat burglar wheeling a dumpster to below his feet. "Come on, blondie, let's go!" she whisper-shouted.

"Well, I'll be an elephant's uncle." He dropped down to the dumpster, a huge clanging when his feet hit the lid. Quickly, he hopped down to the ground. Grabbing her by the hand, they took off down the alley.

3

SEPTEMBER 21, 2018

Nemo

Several twists and turns later, they turned the corner into a back alley behind the houses. Nemo hauled the pixie into a darkened doorway to consider their options. "Midas?"

"Congratulations. You're about to be boxed in. *Idioot!*" Nemo didn't take offense. The more stressed Midas got, the more likely he was to slip into their native Afrikaans. Nemo also understood that it was equally possible that Midas was calling himself an "idioot" for allowing Nemo to get into this position in the first place.

Nemo looked down at the woman he had corralled into the corner of the doorway. "We're in a bind, kitty cat."

She looked at the nameplate on the door behind her, then back at him. "I can't get to mine. Do you have lockpicks?"

He scowled at her. "Does a duck quack? Right pocket."

He felt her sigh and pause before sliding her hand into his

pocket. When her hand met with a hard object, he grinned. He just couldn't help himself.

"*Your* right, sweetheart, not mine. That particular key you're holding opens up very different doors."

Midas moaned. "Oh my god, bro. You didn't."

"You're a dick," she told him.

"You did." Midas groaned.

"Dick or not, and I'm guessing that your pun was unintended, it doesn't change the fact that the picks are still in the other pocket. How the hell are you such a good cat burglar when you don't know your left from your right?"

She reached into his other front pocket and snagged the picks, then dropped to her knees to attack the lock on the door.

"If I'd known that's all I needed to do to get you on your knees—"

"You're such a cunt," she hissed. "I wouldn't be in this position if your dumb ass hadn't shown up tonight."

"Nemo, she's right," Midas confirmed. "You're being a cunt."

"Go ahead. Report me to human resources, both of you. See what happens."

A faint click sounded, followed by a quiet creak, and his little thief was through the doorway. Following her, he silently shut the door and locked it behind them. The room was pitch black, so to give his eyes time to adjust, he plastered himself along the wall next to the door. She was in the same position on the other side. Neither said a word—just listened to the foot traffic outside the door.

The gendarmes were coming from both ends of the alley now, methodically looking behind every trash can and dumpster, checking every doorway, and testing every door to see if it was locked. The handle of the door next to Nemo turned twice, but because it was locked, the officers continued down the alley. When they met up with their counterparts in the middle, they stopped to discuss their next move.

"They think we're back up on the rooftops," she whispered, translating their rapid French.

A radio squawked, and the officers received what sounded like orders if the volume and irritated tone were anything to go by.

"They know there's been a break-in. The diamonds are gone." She looked at him. "Except for the Jupiter Diamond."

He dodged the question in her eyes by pulling his balaclava over his head and considering the darkness around him. His head felt sweaty from the hood and running. He ruffled his blond hair from its matted form by running his fingers through it repeatedly. "Where are we? It looks like my ouma's attic."

"It's an antique store."

"Ah. That explains it." He shifted his attention. "Midas, what have you got?"

"I hacked into their radio frequency. You're only slightly screwed. They're fanned out all around the town. She's correct. They're definitely thinking you've gone back to the rooftops. No word yet on doing an internal building-to-building search."

"Keep me updated." He tapped his watch to mute him from his brother. Leaning back against the wall, he told her, "Midas confirmed your rooftops. Looks like we're stuck here for a little bit."

"Did you think I lied to you?"

"No, not really. But it's nice to be sure." His eyes adjusted to the room lit only by streetlamps through the window. "What is it with this town? No security force for a multimillion diamond display? No alarm system business with priceless antiques in it?"

She pulled her own balaclava from her head, her springy curls bouncing loose around her elfin face.

Damn. She's even prettier than I remembered. Love those curls and those blue sparklers of hers.

Shrugging, she tucked the hood into her belt, then began removing her gloves. "It's supposed to be 'a quaint village from a time gone by,'" she quoted one of the tour brochures. "Security systems ruin the aesthetic."

She wandered around the room in the dark, looking at the pieces she could see in the dim lighting.

"You look good, kitty cat."

Her head turned in his direction. He couldn't see her face in the shadows, but he knew what he'd see if he could. Wide-open blue eyes that sparkled, but right now, they'd be like prey—frozen when it senses a predator nearby.

"Thank you," she returned reluctantly. "So do you. What's it been? Two years?"

"Little under," he corrected nonchalantly. "I've been trying to trace you. The papers say you stole the Saturn Diamond. Was it you? In Gabon?"

"I have no idea what you're talking about."

The smile was clear in his voice. "Yeah, it was you."

The light shifted slightly as the moon came out from behind some clouds.

Yep, definitely predicted the startled look.

They stood in silence, staring at one another.

When he couldn't resist any longer, he pushed off the wall and headed in her direction as best he could with all the furniture in his way. She backed up three steps, so he stopped.

"You afraid of me, kitty cat?"

Her chin tilted up. "No."

He took another step in her direction.

She backed up another step.

"If you're not afraid, then why are you backing up?"

"Strategic retreat," she whispered.

For every measured step he took, she backed up another until finally, she was stopped by a three-drawer bureau with an attached mirror. Her butt hit the edge of its tabletop, and she instinctively crawled up onto it in a seated position, backing into the mirror when he was finally within touching distance.

"And here I thought you liked me. You seemed to when we met last time."

"I don't know you enough to like you."

"Kitty cat. Seriously? My petting had you purring, and your little claws sank into my shoulder blades so deep I have scars."

"That was a mistake."

"One helluva mistake I enjoyed. You did, too."

"Yes, well, let's make sure history doesn't repeat itself."

Hands on her knees, he pushed them apart. "Oh, I'm all about a repeat."

She gestured to his ear. "But your brother—"

"Muted."

He moved in. His hand threading through her mop of curls, he pressed his lips to hers. His other hand grabbed her hip and pulled her tight to his front, where the cradle of her hips came into contact with his hard cock. Her gasp to try and tell him something only served to let him swipe his tongue inside her mouth and flick against the roof before sliding along her tongue.

Oh fuck! There it is! That sugar taste! Fuck, how I've missed it.

Her hands were on his chest. She gave a half-hearted push to stop him, but then she groaned and gave up, allowing her hands to slide over his shoulders, up his neck, and anchor around his nape.

"This is a bad idea," she managed to puff out. When he moved his mouth to her neck, she stretched her head to the side, giving him better access to nip at the cord and follow it down to where her neck met her shoulder.

"Bad ideas are my favorite," he mumbled.

"We really shouldn't," she chastised. Her hands slid down to his waist, frantically pulling his shirt from his pants, grasping at the warm flesh underneath it.

His hand slid from her hip down to her thigh and guided it around his hip. "You're totally right. We really shouldn't." His mouth agreed, but his brain was in total disagreement. His mouth hovered at the hollow in her throat as he pulled her hips even tighter to his, his hardness meeting her softness. "Christ, you feel so hot." He groaned as he ground his cock against her core.

She whimpered. "I am so fucked." The tone was resignation, not fear or anger.

"That was my plan."

He let go of her and backed off just enough to reach behind him and pull his shirt over his head, throwing it behind him somewhere. As he was doing that, he watched her grab for the bottom of her shirt, crossing her arms at the waist, pulling it free of her leggings, and ripping it over her head to drop it on the floor next to the dresser. Her sports bra quickly followed.

While stripping off his belt, he fumbled in one of the pouches for a condom. As soon as he had it secured, he let the belt fall to the floor, and he returned his lips to hers. Their kisses were fevered and hungry, and her hands roamed over his tanned and muscled chest, dipping down to allow her fingers to trace the perfectly defined muscles of his abdomen. Foreheads resting against one another, she chuffed out her approval. "Mary, Mother of God, you're even more fit than before."

He returned the caress by palming her small breasts. "Same for you. Watching your tight ass run across those roofs was the hottest thing I've seen in a long time."

Mouths were back on each other—messy, hungry, and trying to make up for lost time—while both sets of hands were trying to help the other person lose the clothing that remained on their bodies from the waist down. He unbuckled the belt with all the tools of her trade and dropped it to the floor. Shoving his hands into the back of her leggings, Nemo dragged them and her underwear down as she lifted her butt off the top of the dresser. When they were at her knees, he pulled just one leg off over her foot, then hitched both legs over his hips.

He felt cool air on his lower half as she shoved his pants down past his ass cheeks, then the warmth of her smooth palm on his skin as she grabbed his cock and began to stroke it.

Three... two... one...

She gasped.

He chuckled. "Surprise?"

"Is that...?"

"Mmm hmm." His lips were back on hers. "Wait until you feel it inside you. You can thank me later."

"Oh god," she moaned out.

"Only me here, kitty cat. Focus."

Taking his cock in hand, he made short work of securing the condom he'd pulled from his belt, then guided himself to her opening, which was just past the edge of the bureau top and in perfect position. He swiped his shaft through her arousal, the barbell of his piercing teasing her opening, even through the latex, then dragged it over her clit and back, causing her breath to hitch and her body to shudder. Finding himself quickly soaked in a new wave of her arousal, he immediately slid himself inside her, buried to the hilt. Both of them groaned at the breach.

"Hold onto the edge of the dresser," he ordered against her lips.

When her fingers were curled with a death grip as requested, he leaned her back so that her shoulder blades were pressed against the cool glass of the mirror. One hand grabbed the heavy mirror frame while the other grabbed the opposite side of the dresser top, and he lost no time pounding into her with fast, deep strokes. Almost immediately, an orgasm began to ripple through his system. He could tell that she was in much the same situation because her legs were gripping his hips tighter than he'd ever felt, and her hips were canting off the top of the dresser to try and find the best angle.

He let go of the dresser to tilt her hips into a better position, and he knew the exact moment his piercing hit the right spot because she let out the start of a scream. Swallowing her sounds with his mouth pressed hungrily to hers, one hand went to get the needed leverage on the dresser to keep it from banging against the wall, and the other hand crept in between their bodies to find her clit. He pressed on it and began circular motions with his thumb.

Now I know what people mean when they say the earth moved!

He felt her walls squeeze him so tight, and a warm wave of fluid surrounded him inside her. He couldn't have stopped his body's reaction if he'd wanted to. For just a moment, he froze, buried deep, and felt his cum erupt from his cock. Every time he pulsed, he stroked deep, held, then retreated. When the pulsing from his shaft stopped, he switched to slow, measured strokes to ease her down through the aftershocks of her orgasm.

Hands down, the hottest fucking feeling ever. Mic drop.

Placing his forehead to hers, he gasped, "Jesus Christ, woman."

She said nothing, merely tried to catch her breath between what sounded like sobs, her hands now curled over his shoulders.

His equilibrium restored, he slid his hands under her hips and hoisted her upright, his cock still hard and buried inside her, and turned to shuffle the three steps to the couch on display behind him. He sat down with her straddling him, arms wrapped tight around her waist, his head buried in the space between her bicep and her shoulder. His lips pressed soft, wet kisses to the top of her breast, and occasionally, his tongue would flick out to taste her skin.

Fuckin' sugar everywhere. It's a goddamn drug.

When he felt her breathing return to normal as well, he leaned back on the couch, his eyes locked with hers. His arms slid from around her waist, and he glanced up her torso, reaching up to brush some of her springy curls back, only for them to fall back to where they had been.

Stubborn. Like her.

His hands had dropped back down to where their bodies met in his lap. He ran his fingers lightly back and forth from where her ass met his thighs to the bottom of her shoulder blades. Her skin was so soft. He never wanted to stop touching it.

"Well, so much for not repeating history." She sighed. Her hands rested lightly on the tops of his shoulders, and her face pinched up. "Do you spend your whole life this hard?"

He winked. "Stamina is my superpower."

She rolled her eyes. When she attempted to roll off his lap, he captured her by spanning her waist with his hands. "Where are you going, kitty cat?" He pulled her forward and nuzzled her neck. "Don't you dare move. I'm not done with you yet, woman."

In one fluid motion, he picked her up, turned her, and had her tucked underneath him—her back slouched against the couch, her ass at the end of the seat, and him on his knees between her legs. She made an effort to slide out from under him, but he buried himself a little deeper, making sure to drag the piercing at the tip of his cock across her G-spot as he went. When she wiggled to try again, he stopped her by covering a nipple with his hot, wet mouth.

"You need to stop that," she groaned. He grinned against her breast as her arms told him the complete opposite by curling around his neck and cradling his head closer.

"Not happening," he mumbled before his tongue began flicking as fast as a serpent's tongue over the nub. He let his cock slip free of her, the barbell giving a quick tap against her clit when it bounced back slightly. Removing the condom as he went, his mouth continued to track down the front of her, stopping to kiss each of the tattoos he hadn't had a chance to investigate the last time they'd been together.

She'd added to her art. The first time they'd met, she'd had a partial sleeve of skulls and diamonds. No surprise on the latter. There had also been tattoos on her back, although he'd never had a chance to look at them, and she also had a tattoo of a snake slithering around her ankle and down toward her toes.

Since then, she'd finished the sleeve on her left arm and started one on her right. She also had a couple more tattoos peppered across her shoulders, and from what he'd seen in the mirror, she'd added more to her back. But the one that caused a bark of laughter was one just to the left of her belly button—an image of Saturn. He looked up into her face, smirking as he pressed a kiss to it, then traced its rings with his tongue. "Not in Gabon, my ass."

"I happen to have a very intense interest in astronomy," she deadpanned.

He rolled his eyes at her. "I notice there's an open space here next to it. Any plans for other planetary orbs to make an appearance?"

"That's something for future consideration, I'm afraid." She threaded her fingers through his longer hair on the top of his head. "You left the Jupiter Diamond behind. That's what the gendarmes were saying. You took the moonstones but left the big prize. Why?"

He ripped his gaze away from hers and concentrated on her tattoos as he considered how to answer her question. Things had changed since he met her almost two years ago. Not that they'd exchanged much information in the past thirty or so minutes they'd been reunited. Just bodily fluids, for the most part. But the stakes were definitely higher than before for both him and her.

"I was hired to take the moonstones. Nothing was said about the other. So I left it."

She smacked him up the backside of the head. "Are you barmy? The value of that one diamond is, at minimum, five times that of the ninety-five rocks you stole. You could have just swept it up with the rest and kept it for yourself."

"Could have." His mouth drifted down to the top of her mound, pressing a light kiss to the skin. He could taste a mixture of her sweat, her arousal, and the sugary flavor that was uniquely her.

A hand slid under his chin and pulled his focus back to her. "Seriously. Why?"

He shrugged. "Knew you'd be coming for it eventually. Know it means something to you. I don't need it. I'm a lot of things but being greedy isn't one of them. At least, not for diamonds."

"You don't *need* ninety-five diamonds. You *want* those."

"It's just a job, kitty cat. Now shush. I have a much more important job to do here. Mainly, rock the rest of that missing universe on your skin."

He put his mouth on her, his tongue licking her from hole to clit, swirling around the nerve center, then repeating the action. A hand fell to the back of his head and pressed firmly as he began the third swipe across her flesh. His chuckle against her skin told her he got the message of "stay here" and proceeded to fuck her with his tongue, making her come a second time.

STILL ON HIS knees between her legs, Nemo was once again tracing her rings of Saturn, this time with his fingertip. He smirked to himself and chuckled, again struck by the Saturn tattoo.

Her hand threaded through the hair on the crown of his head. "What's so funny?"

He rested his chin on her skin just below her belly button. "I was thinking about your tattoo and how you are definitely a heavenly body yourself."

She snorted and shook her head. "Your pickup lines aren't getting any better."

"I've already had you. Twice. I don't think I'm picking you up anymore." The wattage of his smile dimmed, but it was actually more sincere. "Made you laugh. Nothing I like better than seeing your smile. Still makes me feel warm all over."

Resting her palm against the side of his face, her smile became softer. "That's sweet."

He shrugged, gave her belly a chaste kiss, and slid his hands under her waist to pull her close. "Just the truth." He thought back to the first time they made love two years earlier. He rimmed her belly button, remembering she was ticklish there, and sure enough—she giggled and tried to push him away.

I love her laugh. I love her smile. She's perfect.

They stared at one another, saying nothing, both lost in their thoughts.

Finally, Haskell spoke. "Can I see them?"

"The moonstones?"

She nodded.

He winked at her. "I wondered how long it would be before you asked." Straightening up on his knees, he looked around for his pants. He stretched to reach where they'd been dropped earlier and patted the legs in the dark. Once he found the pouch secreted in an inside pocket, he tossed it from one hand to the other. He pulled open the velvet bag, then proceeded to pour them onto her flat stomach.

She giggled. "Is this what they mean by 'dripping in diamonds'?"

He laughed, watching her as she picked up one of the stones, holding it up to the moonlight, turning it this way and that to catch the sparkle.

"So beautiful." She sighed.

She definitely loves her diamonds.

"Yes," he agreed. "Nothing more beautiful in the world."

Haskell's eyes darted from the diamond to him, seeing that he wasn't looking at the stone she held but at her with unabashed attraction. There was concern in her eyes, and he felt her retreat from the tender moment they had been immersed in only moments ago.

She has no clue how beautiful she is. How is that possible?

With a sigh, she placed the diamond with the others. "Why were you hired to take these stones in particular?"

"According to the client, they were stolen from them in the first place. Best we could tell, they were telling the truth."

He swept up the diamonds carefully in several handfuls, trying not to knock any off onto the couch or floor, and put the bag back into the pocket designed to keep items safe. However, he placed one that was larger than the others in her belly button. He admired it as it winked in the moonlight. "That looks nice."

She laughed at him. "You are such a git."

He rescued the diamond, placing it on the end table next to the couch, then slid his hands back under her. He pulled her into a sitting position and kneeled upright so that he could plaster himself to her. "Kiss me, kitty cat. I need more of that sugar."

A BEEPING in his ear woke him. He sat up, a spasm in his lower back reminding him that he'd just spent several hours fucking and sleeping on an antique couch not meant for nocturnal activities. He tapped his watch.

"Yeah?"

"Lose something?" Midas asked.

Nemo looked around. "Dammit, she's gone again!" He ran his fingers through his hair, ruffling it when he reached the ends in the back.

"Getting late, bro. Shop opens in two hours. Someone's probably going to be there soon. You probably should head out."

"Did you see which direction she went?"

"North. She didn't get the moonstones, did she?"

Nemo checked his pants pocket. The bag was still there. When he looked at the tabletop, the stray diamond was missing. "She took a souvenir," Nemo admitted. "But just one."

Midas snorted. "Luckily, that works out. We need to replace one with a fake anyway. Waters wants us tracking these stones. He thinks they're going somewhere beyond the original owners."

"Any idea why?"

"Nothing yet, but he thinks they're headed for Italy. I didn't ask why he thinks that."

Nemo began to dress. "All right. I'm on my way back to the rendezvous point. I'll let you know when I'm at the airport."

"I'll be available until I know you're there. Safe travels."

Nemo heard the distinctive click as Midas severed his connection. Once dressed, he snuck out of the shop and through the street that he'd come down with his little cat burglar in the wee hours of the morning.

When he reached the edge of town, he looked back at Riquewihr with a sigh.

Au revoir, Le Chatte Noire. We will meet again. And when we do, you will not be getting away for a third time.

With that final thought and a resigned smile, he rubbed at the low ache in the area of his chest. He slipped into the forest's edge, jogging a roundabout path to where he'd stashed his motorcycle the night before. Within ten minutes, he was back on the road and headed to the small airport where his ride awaited, his brain replaying the stolen hours during the night.

Even as he allowed himself to drift into sleep on the airplane, his dreams were filled with a mop of springy blonde curls, vivid blue eyes, and an impish smile.

4

JUNE 29, 2022

Nemo

"Would you rather…"—he dragged out his opening gambit—"only be able to have sex in the shower or on a table?"

It was pitch black, hot as hell, and Nemo was bored. It wasn't an uncommon state for him. Only thing he liked better than breaking into places and stealing shit was running. All the physical activity was part of what Tribe hired him for. It's what made him great at apprehensions when someone got the urge to flee. Unfortunately, a lot of the time, his current job required sitting and watching. Those were not his strongest skills. He could do them, and he could do them well, but he hated waiting and left those tasks to others whenever possible.

Like Steel. He was a master at waiting.

Without turning to look at him, the Latino man next to him, lying on his stomach and looking through his scope, asked, "*¿Qué?*"

Nemo scratched at his scruffy, dark-blond beard and repeated himself. "Would you rather only be able to have sex in the shower or on a table? You know. Like you could only ever do it that one way your whole life."

Steel huffed quietly. "There is something seriously wrong with you."

Nemo frowned and reared his head back slightly. "What the hell do you mean?"

"We're supposed to be gathering intel on Ka-Bar, and you want to talk about my sex life?"

Nemo snorted. "If Kubrick's brother was ever here, he's long gone by now. Loki, Gilgamesh, and Medusa reported seeing him here in April. There's no way someone would still be holding him here."

"Even if he's not here, this location could give us breadcrumbs on where to look next. I'm sure Kubrick would be much happier knowing that you were invested in finding her brother rather than wasting our time on that stupid game. And I refuse to go back to the boss man empty-handed. He'll move heaven and earth for his woman, and I don't want to be caught in his earthquake."

Shrugging, Nemo lowered his night vision goggles over his blue eyes and focused back in the same direction Steel was watching. "Okay, Hansel, we'll look for your breadcrumbs. But I'll have you know, Kubrick loves my quirky charms. I'm Mr. Funderful."

"*Jesucristo*, she called you that when she was frustrated with you. Can't you tell the difference between sincerity and snark? You're around her enough—you should know by now."

"Nope. She called me Mr. Funderful. I heard joy and happiness. You, Mr. Nonfunderful, are so negative you heard sarcasm. You gotta stop hanging around with the Cyclops and start hanging out with me more."

Steel grunted. "I wanna be there when you call TB 'Cyclops.' He'll kick your ass back to mythological times."

"Pfft. TB doesn't scare me. As soon as he balloon-dropped three hundred red balloons on me in the armory, I knew it was over. He's all domesticated now." He pretended to be annoyed, but he loved

TB's woman, Flame. She was perfect for His Royal Grumpiness, all sunniness and cheer.

"My cheeks still hurt from blowing those fucking things up. I think I collapsed a lung."

"You idiots are such amateurs. For ten bucks, you could have gotten a chargeable air pump." They lay on the hillside shelf looking down into the village of Sallum. "Now quit stalling and answer the question," Nemo prodded.

For several moments, Steel was silent. Nemo thought that his teammate wasn't going to play along, but he should have known better. They all gave in eventually.

"*Mierda*." He sighed in capitulation. "I hate shower sex. Table."

Nemo twisted his torso to face his partner, raised his NVGs, and looked at Steel with an expression of absolute horror. "That's not possible. No one hates shower sex."

"I do."

"Why the hell do you hate shower sex?"

Sighing, Steel asked, "Are we really going to get into this now?"

"Yes, we really are. It's not like we have anything else to talk about."

Nemo lowered his NVGs and rolled back into his previous position on the ground. It was quiet for about thirty seconds before he twisted back, raised his goggles, and asked, "Seriously? You really hate shower sex?"

Muttering something in Spanish, Steel rearranged himself on the ground. "If I explain it to your dumb ass, will you shut up and do your job?"

"Swear it on my sister's grave."

Steel looked at him, his cold silver eyes revealed after raising his own NVGs. "You don't have a sister."

"Details. Avoidance. Start talking." Nemo twirled his finger in the universal get-going sign.

Steel grumbled again in Spanish, lowered his NVGs, and went back to watching the village. "One, I have terrible knees from jumping out of too many planes. Kneeling on the shower floor to eat someone out is hell on them. Two, I can't stand water in my eyes. Three, one too many violent thrusts can send both of you crashing to the floor in a tangle of very embarrassing broken limbs. And four, and most importantly, I go for a while, and the water always goes cold before I finish. I detest cold water."

"There is so much wrong in that answer; I can't even begin to unpack it. But I'll address the stupidest one—you hating cold water. You were a goddamned Navy SEAL. You should thrive in the water."

"Was, *compadre*. I *was* a Navy SEAL. Besides, cold showers are a choice. Cold ocean water is natural. Very different, believe it or not."

Shaking his head, Nemo grumbled about slapping Steel on behalf of men everywhere, pulled down his NVGs again, and turned to refocus on the building in the distance.

The two men lay side by side on the ground in silence for the next thirty minutes. The building they were watching was a typical rustic structure for the area. A few weeks ago, their teammate, TB, the group's Information Specialist, had made first contact with a trio by the names of Loki, Gilgamesh, and Medusa. The two men and the woman passed veiled information that they had witnessed what appeared to be an American Navy SEAL being kept in Sallum. When the trouble was resolved with TB's woman being kidnapped by her former abuser and a sex trafficker, their boss sent Nemo and Steel to the location to find out what they could. So far, what they'd found was a big, fat zero. Ka-Bar was still out there somewhere, and there didn't seem to be suspicious activity of any sort when it came to this tiny village.

"It's been three days, and we haven't seen jack shit. We're not going to, either," Nemo complained.

"Probably, but we should wait a couple of hours, then head down and take a closer look. The same guy has locked up and left at twenty hundred the past three nights, and no one has come back until oh-seven-hundred the next day. We should be safe to take a peek."

"And if we find nothing?"

"If we find nothing, we call the boss and see what he says."

AT OH-THREE-HUNDRED, the two men crept down from their hillside hideaway. Traveling through the side streets, they worked to stay in the shadows as much as possible. Both men were experts at this, given their previous lives. Nemo and his fraternal twin had been master thieves, getting in and out of some of the world's most famous museums, banks, and other sites, never getting caught. Plus, Steel had escaped from four separate Black Sites in the years before joining Tribe. If they wanted to be invisible, they were.

Well, technically, you were caught by Waters, but that's different. And then there was the kitty cat. Different kind of caught.

Nemo tried to shove that memory to the back of his brain. All it did was make him itch like it always did. And that itch needed scratching, which wasn't happening until they got home... unless he could find himself a flight attendant on her break on the airplane out. The itch turned to a pang in his chest. He rubbed the spot, then refocused.

Arriving at the back of the building, Steel took the watch position while Nemo picked the lock on the back door.

"Not even sure why they lock this door. The tumbler is so ancient, I probably could have jiggled it open," Nemo groused.

"Look at it as an opportunity to practice your lock-picking skills. You're keeping your old self alive."

"Pfft," Nemo replied. "Lock picking is nothing. Give me something challenging."

They slunk through the open door. There was little concern of a building alarm. The building was so basic it didn't even have a sign on it naming the business. A square, nondescript, flat-roofed structure, it was the perfect place to hide a captive. Non-native rescuers would stick out like a sore thumb, so guarding someone wouldn't need to be a major production.

Inside, Steel and Nemo paused.

"Well. This is unexpected," Nemo said.

The building was basically one big open space—more like an unfinished warehouse. And stacked in neat rows, four tall, were boxes approximately seven feet long by two feet tall and equipped with computer locks.

"Look familiar?" Steel asked.

"Uh-huh. What the fuck are they doing here? Are the guys who have Ka-Bar connected to what happened with Flame?"

"Dunno. Sure looks that way, though."

The two men walked quickly and quietly through the rows of coffin-sized boxes with Steel taking pictures. Nemo was remembering the recent rescue of Flame, TB's woman. She and six other women who had been captured were put into similar boxes and had been in the process of being shipped to buyers on the dark web. These, however, were more sophisticated. The boxes appeared to have computer controls on the front doors, whereas the prior boxes just had ordinary locks.

Steel looked closer. "These aren't just locks," he whispered. "There are other buttons here. Temperature controls. Oxygen and carbon dioxide monitors. They must have been losing people during transport. Had to increase their technology to ensure survival," he surmised.

A noise came from a dark corner of the room. Quietly, both men drew their weapons and focused in the direction of the sound. The floor of the room was concrete, and the tapping that was coming toward them was not human.

Steel whispered, "Dog."

A golden-colored dog appeared in the moonlight. Just short of two feet tall from pointy ears to feet, the animal was skinny as could be. Looking at the two men frozen in their tracks, the dog lowered its head and let loose a soft but menacing growl.

"Nice doggie," Nemo breathed out.

The dog advanced two steps closer, the growl becoming slightly louder and more menacing.

"Nemo. It's a female."

"So?"

"No, dumbass. Look. She's had puppies recently."

Sure enough, her belly dragged with teats. "She's frickin' emaciated. How is she feeding puppies? Shit, shit, shit."

"Back up slowly. Maybe if we show we're no threat to her pups, she'll leave us alone," Steel said.

The dog was in heartbreaking condition. Nemo's fear seemed to suddenly vanish. He felt like he understood this dog. She was clearly here as protection of the space. She was being starved to make her mean, and protecting her puppies wasn't helping the situation. He remembered more than a few days of his life being hungry and vulnerable.

"Hey, girl," he whispered. "You hungry?"

"Nemo," Steel hissed. "What the fuck?"

Nemo holstered his weapon, then ever so slowly reached into his cargo pocket for a tube from his dinner MRE he had stashed there. He gently tore open the package and gently squeezed some of its contents over the edge of the opening. Just as slowly, he hunkered down into a crouch and extended the tube to the dog. "Hey, sweetheart. You'll like this. C'mere, girl."

"Nemo, she's gonna bite your face off, and we cannot go to a hospital when she does."

Nemo just ignored the man behind him. He squeezed a little bit more of the contents so that the dog could get a better whiff of it.

"Nemo, what is that?"

"Peanut butter. It's okay for dogs, although at this point, I don't think much could be bad for her."

The dog was still growling but less intensely. Her nose quivered. One step at a time, she came closer and closer to Nemo until she was within a long-lick's distance of the offering. Her tongue swiped out.

At that first taste of the peanut butter, her ears perked slightly. One more step closer, one more lick. That was all it took. She moved in reach of Nemo's outstretched hand and began to lick the tube in earnest as he squeezed out its contents.

"Good girl. Good girl," he soothed.

He looked up at Steel.

"No." It was the only word that came from Steel's mouth.

"No one gives a shit about them."

"Nemo, no."

"They'll die here."

Nemo's lower lip protruded in a cartoon state of sadness.

"How the fuck do you plan to get them on the plane? They have to quarantine."

The dog lay down on the concrete and rolled over on her back for tummy rubs from Nemo.

"Freakin' Frankenstein," Steel swore, using one of Flame's favorite sayings. "Even these types of bitches roll over for you with next to no prompting."

Nemo grinned because he knew he'd won the argument.

Steel sighed. "Waters is going to kick my ass. And when he's done, I'm going to help him kick yours."

"You know you love me." Nemo's grin turned to a full-on smirk.

"Fuckwitch," Steel murmured under his breath. "I'll go find the damn puppies."

Steel stalked off, once again muttering in Spanish, occasionally getting louder with the swear words and threats to Nemo's life.

"You're going to love it in Los Angeles, and we'll find good homes for your pups. Promise." Nemo looked down at the dog whose belly he was still scratching. She was starved, covered in scars, probably infested with fleas, and he refused to leave her here. "I bet you've got a thousand stories to tell, girl." A thought popped into his head. "Scheherazade. Perfect."

5

JULY 29, 2022

Nemo

Looking down to his left, Nemo smiled fondly at Scheherazade at his side, giving her a quick scratch behind the ear. He whispered to her, "Okay, now, girl, remember what we discussed earlier. No barking. We don't want to wake up Midas."

The elevator dinged softly, announcing its arrival on the eighth floor of Tribe Corporation. Nemo and his fraternal twin, Midas, shared the eighth floor of the Tribe Corporation building, which was split into two spacious apartments. Because each of the team members officially "died" when they joined Tribe, each of the team members, plus their handler, Cherry, had their own apartment in the building since it would be difficult to own homes or rent properties. There were even two guest apartments in case they needed a fast lockdown for a client.

When the doors opened, Nemo exited quickly, turning right to go down his portion of the hallway. Scheherazade padded alongside him, tongue lolling out of her mouth, ears up straight, and tail wagging like a flag. She gave a soft yip.

"Are those the same clothes you were wearing last night?"

Nemo glared at Scheherazade. "Some guard dog you are."

Scheherazade yipped again, her eyes communicating how silly she thought he was to be irritated with her.

Nemo looked up to see his brother leaning one shoulder against the wall, with one foot crossed over the other, only the toe touching the ground. The two brothers may have been born only eight minutes apart at birth, but they were nothing alike.

Nemo was light-haired and had blue eyes; Midas was dark-haired and had brown eyes.

Both men were physically fit enough to be sighed over, but Nemo was just under six feet with the sleekness of a runner, and Midas was just over six feet with the bulk of a rugby player.

Nemo was a jokester, a prankster, and always laughing or at least smiling. Midas often could tease and joke, but he had to be prodded to do so. He usually had a more serious demeanor, his brows crunching over his eyes and nose.

Where Nemo was always on the move, Midas was most often found at his chair behind his computer banks.

Probably the biggest difference, however, was that Nemo was a playboy with a near-daily one-night-stand habit of high-maintenance women in designer clothes and exhibitionist tendencies. Midas lived like a monk.

"As a matter of fact, they are. You have a problem with that?"

Midas probed further. "I thought you were taking Scheherazade out to the dog park."

"I was. I did."

"Awful long trip to the dog park. It was seven thirty last night when you left."

"So? We were there an hour or so, and then we decided to go on an adventure. Didn't we, girl?" Nemo gave the dog's ears a vigorous scratch, which brought forth another happy yip from Scheherazade.

She promptly threw herself on the floor, belly up. Her owner wasted no time getting on the floor with her, scratching her belly, and crooning. "Who was a good girl? Who was so pretty? Who deserved a treat?" And other dog-lover nonsense.

"You didn't."

"I didn't what?" Nemo asked, not looking up. He was now in the stage of play where Scheherazade was rolling ecstatically on the floor and trying to wash his face while Nemo tried to avoid her puppy breath and slobber.

"You did." His brother expelled a puff of exasperated air through his lips as he ran a hand over his closely shaved dark hair. "You met a girl at the dog park."

"I met a lot of girls at the dog park," he corrected.

"Yeah, but you fucked one, and I'm guessing you fucked her at the dog park. Dude, why can't you go to a club and hook up with a girl in the bathroom, at least?"

"Gotta live in the moment, bro." Nemo managed to extract himself from Scheherazade, stand, and key in his lock's code.

Midas made an ick face. "Make sure you burn those clothes. God only knows what you were rolling around in all night."

Nemo's door opened, and Scheherazade bounded inside. Within two seconds, both men heard a thunk, a yip, and a squeaky toy being mauled to death. "We didn't stay there all night. We took our dogs to the beach afterward."

"Great. So, instead, you're dragging sand in and leaving it everywhere. Fantastic."

An impish grin appeared on Nemo's face. "Worth every scratchy moment." He disappeared inside his apartment and shut the door, and his grin disappeared instantly.

No sooner had he toed off his sneakers when a brisk double knock came at the door.

Grin back on his face, blue eyes met a set of brown eyes when Nemo opened the door. "Knew you'd wanna hear about it. Okay, so, the tide was coming in—"

"We've got a conference call at the top of the hour. Loki, Gilgamesh, and Medusa. Don't be late, or Waters will have a shit hemorrhage." Midas turned and headed back to the elevator.

The door closed. Again, the grin disappeared. Nemo stripped as he walked, dropping clothing and creating a trail back toward his bathroom and the huge glassed-in shower. He turned on the water. While he waited for the water to warm up, he brushed his teeth. His eyes perused his body or what he could see of it in the mirror. Over the years, Nemo had treated his body like an art canvas. His left arm was tatted from under his ear down to his knuckles. The tattoos wrapped around his throat and chest, and they started to track down his abdomen. He'd recently begun the sleeve on the underside of his right arm. Lost in thought, finger tracing the date over his heart, he made a mental note to find time to go and have his sleeve worked on. He had a sun image he wanted to add and build around.

He'd made other changes during that time, too. His hair was still in the fake military haircut, the top glued with enough product to make it stand up despite its length, but in the last few months, he'd grown a beard that he kept close-cropped to his face, which aged him beyond his thirty years. He'd also gauged his ears and pierced his nipples, tongue, and cock. The pain of piercings and the tattoo gun assuaged other past pains he refused to think about.

Finished with his inventory, he moved to open the shower door and stepped inside, closing the door behind him. Bracing his hands on the glass wall on one side and the ceramic tile wall on the other, he hung his head and let the water cascade over the top of him. He hissed when the sting of hot water washed away the sand from the multitude of shallow wounds on his ass, back, and shoulders caused by the girl's nails. What was her name? Olivia. She said she was an actress. He gave a single bark of laughter. Every girl in Los Angeles was an actress. Always on the cusp of that big break, just waiting for the next call from their agent about the audition they recently nailed.

Whatever. Dime a dozen. Who are you kidding? Penny a dozen out here.

When the stinging ended, Nemo soaped up to clean himself from his and Octavia's dog park and beach adventures.

No. Olivia! Christ! You're a fucking mess. Who lives like this?

An image from the past popped into his head. One that made his chest hurt, and again, he rubbed at the numbers over his heart. Blonde mop of curls. Big blue eyes. Tight, tiny body. A smile that lit her face like it was the goddamn sun. Short, blunt nails sinking into his skin. Ink crawling up her body, particularly the art surrounding her belly button.

His skin felt itchy as he remembered the last time he'd seen her, and saliva exploded in his mouth, the faint taste memory of sugar. The same scent coming from her body. The velvet of her skin. The sound of her sighs and whimpers.

Nemo let out a roar of rage, and his fists pounded against the walls. A cracking noise sounded over the falling water of the shower, and he looked to his left. The glass shower wall was spider-webbed with cracks where his fist had hit it. He ducked his head under the water and let it wash away the sand, sweat, and shame of tonight.

By the time he had stepped out of the shower, the water was cold. He marshaled his emotions; any question of who he was and how he lived his life thoroughly shoved into a drawer in the filing cabinets of his brain, and the drawer mentally slammed shut with violence. Hopefully, this time, the drawer stayed shut.

Not fucking likely.

DARK-BLOND HAIR PERFECTLY GLUED, and clothed in his typical T-shirt, jeans, and running shoes, Nemo blew out any remaining melancholy with an exaggerated breath. Inserting his double-flared ear gauges, he whistled for Scheherazade, and together, they took the fire stairs down to the second floor where the conference room and offices were.

"Well, look what the St. Bernard dragged in," drawled TB, a six-foot-seven, two-hundred-forty-pound giant sitting in his regular seat to the left of the head at the conference table.

Midas, the big gossip, already filled in the details of his dog park adventure for them.

"Technically, it was a Belgian Malinois," Nemo corrected in imitation of a snobby dog breeder.

"Either way," Demon grumbled, "I probably need to start you on a rabies shot series after the meeting."

"Scheherazade, kill," Nemo commanded, pointing to Demon, silently imagining the dog grabbing the surfer dude by the dark-haired man bun and dragging him under the table to maul him to death.

The men in the room laughed at Nemo's fake command. Since it wasn't in Afrikaans or one of their silent signals, Scheherazade leapt into Demon's arms at the opposite side and end of the table, attempting in every way to lick him to death. "Thatta girl, Zade. Show your daddy who you love more." Demon baby-talked the dog trying to roll around on his lap.

Nemo shook his head in fake disgust. She was not a small dog, probably about the size of a pointer in terms of height and length, but there the shameless hussy was—on her back in Demon's lap, gazing at him adoringly as the grouchy medic scratched her belly in apparently all the right places. Didn't matter which of the guys was paying attention to her, she would fall apart like a cheap suit, ignoring everyone else. Heaven forbid she latched onto any of the women. They were worse than the guys when it came to spoiling her.

Although he feigned hurt whenever she paid attention to anyone else, Nemo knew that he alone was her best friend. Her devotion to him was absolute. Not a moment went by when he wasn't thankful he had rescued her and her puppies before fleeing Sallum. Hadn't been easy sneaking them out of Egypt, and Steel had been pissed at the inconvenience of having to burn three markers to get safe passage across northern Africa by land to make it happen, but it was so worth it. Those puppies were happily homed with Kubrick and Flame and were already often reunited with their sibling and mother for play-dates. Waters and TB might grouse about having dogs, but he knew they were secretly happy that the women would have someone at home with them when the men were gone.

Totally whipped. Ka-cha!

"You've got to work on your training regimen, bro. If that's what she does when you say 'kill,' I hate to see what she does when you say 'search,'" Midas teased from the head of the table behind his laptop.

"You know she only follows verbal commands in Afrikaans."

"Shouldn't they be in German?" Demon asked.

"Most are, I've heard. I don't speak German. I speak Afrikaans. My dog, my choice of language. Besides, how many terrorists do you know speak that language?"

A notification bell binged from Midas' computer, and a moment later, the telescreen at the other end of the room powered up to reveal a trio the team knew well. Loki, the face of the triad, looking for all the world like a blond billionaire CEO. Gilgamesh, the dark-haired, walking, talking poster child for a metrosexual male, looking like he stepped out of a photo shoot for sports cars. And Medusa... He had no idea how to describe her. Trademark smokey sunglasses over her eyes, dark-brown hair pulled back by a hairband, and her usual emotionless expression. A frozen Lara Croft. She even out-froze Waters in the blank stare department.

Extracting a piece of gum from his pocket, he unwrapped it, popped the pink blob in his mouth, and a brief flash of a pixie in curls hit his brain as his teeth did their first cut through the sugary confection. Instantly, he felt more grounded.

That's better.

He crumpled up the wrapper and pelted his brother with it. Midas scowled, picked the wrapper up out of his lap, and pelted

Nemo back. He grinned, winked, then spun his chair in the direction of the triad.

"Good to see you, gentlemen," Loki opened. "We've got some information for you."

"Loki," Waters acknowledged. He nodded to Gilgamesh and Medusa. "What have you got?"

"Five days ago, one of our associates was in Africa doing some sample gathering for us—"

"Thieving, you mean," Nemo conjectured.

"I prefer professional terms, but yes. We weren't invited in, and we didn't want anyone to know we were there."

"What does your 'sample gathering' have to do with us?" Waters wondered.

"She's an expert on these stones and a master... or mistress, I guess... of getting into and out of tight spaces. We found her in Great Britain. Has quite a reputation for her craft. While on her assignment, she sent us some pictures and a request for an exit contact because she'd been made. Guess who we got a glimpse of?" The telescreen split in half. On the left was the triad. On the right, a picture flashed up on the screen of three men.

"Ka-Bar," Steel answered.

Gilgamesh pointed at the screen. "Give that man a prize."

"When? Where?" Waters asked, shotgun style. "This is the closest we've been to finding Kubrick's brother."

"This photo was taken five days ago in Zimbabwe. And he was being escorted by the two men in business suits," Loki answered as he hit a button on his computer to show another photo.

"Hemeda and Pilis Kader," Waters snarled, throwing the file folder in his hand down on the table so that he could run that hand over his closely cut dark-blond hair.

"Bonus question points awarded to the Navy SEAL," Gilgamesh confirmed.

Steel, silver eyes flashing beneath his mussed black hair, shifted in his chair, leaning forward on his arms on the tabletop. "What's in Zimbabwe?"

"A defunct mining site. There are several legitimate mines in the country, but this particular area was purchased by a private investor thirteen years ago. The purchasing corporation built the compound and had begun drilling tunnels, but they suffered huge losses trying to get an actual mine built and disappeared into the jungle, so to speak, leaving everyone cutting their losses.

"Fast forward to today. As far as the civilians are concerned, around two years ago, people began filtering into the old mining area, hoping to tempt certain death and hit a lucky strike. Basically, they purchase their own individual supplies, show up, pick a spot, and make human-sized tunnels to find and follow the old diamond veins. Most of them, a decent-sized man can't even turn around in. Think Viet Cong tunnels. It's not a job for the faint of heart, and the danger level is high, but these people are so desperate they're willing to take the risks. In this location, mining is strictly forbidden, but no one is really paying attention. Even when there are accidents, the miners remain quiet about it because bringing public attention to it means bringing down the police on their illegal ventures. Or worse, losing their unlawful access to the land.

"Unfortunately, even if the police did something about the illegal mining, it would have little effect. The corruption on both sides of the color wall across Africa is rampant. In Zimbabwe, most of the officers were white Europeans until 1982, when the country made an active effort to replace the older white officers with younger native officers. But the damage was so extensive, it's hardly better than it was. Many officers are on the take, not because they are innately corrupt, but as a means to remain safe from criminal gangs, political candidates, and anyone who has power or money to hire protection. Looking the other way is an occupational expectation unless it negatively affects the police force itself.

"Those who take police officer jobs are usually young and not afraid of getting their hands dirty. The hours are long and brutal because there aren't enough officers to cover the areas they serve, and the turnover is huge. No one wants to go to work in a job where they know the likelihood of them coming home that night is less than fifty percent. Some African countries lose, on average, an officer a day to violence. The justification for being on the take allows them some supplementary income and provides a little extra insurance they get to go home at the end of the day. No guarantees, but some insurance is better than none."

"What does any of this have to do with the Kaders? Or you? Or Ka-Bar, for that matter?" Waters wondered aloud.

Medusa flicked at a piece of imaginary lint on her pants. "Mythos is always interested in illegal activities. Uncut stones are an easy way to fund illegal activities."

Midas mumbled to himself, "Well, at least I have a name for the trio now. Medusa, Loki, Gilgamesh... makes sense." Nemo watched him start to madly type information into his computer, searching for anything on "Mythos" or its members.

Gilgamesh shook his head. "Ka-Bar's connection? There's absolutely nothing in his past to suggest he'd suddenly turn on the military, his country, or his family. A Westerner like him, formidable and affluent-looking, it's likely they're using him to lend outward legitimacy to the Kaders' business. The question is whether he's being coerced or is it by choice?

"As for the mining? Simple. These individuals are primarily central Africans. Even when they find stones, the rate of return when they sell them is not even a tenth of what they're worth. Men like the Kaders are middlemen. They've organized these workers into a step above slave labor, purchasing their stones at a pittance, then turning around and selling them at value, possibly a little higher, and making a killing while they do it."

"However," Medusa chimed in, "something's changed. The individual miners who were living in the self-created camps have completely disappeared, yet the illegal output of stones in this area in the last two months has increased one hundred times what it was.

Both of those conditions caught our attention enough to take a closer look."

Waters crossed his arms over his chest, and one hand rose to rub his chin. "You think they're working the mine underground now."

"That would explain why the output increased," Steel acknowledged. "You can hide a lot more people underground. They can work round the clock with the police none the wiser. If there are no illegal settlements for the police to break up, it also means less police presence in the area. And even if someone does come around to do a rudimentary inspection of the area, there's nothing to see other than an abandoned mine compound with minimal security, like an abandoned building has a guard to prevent trespassers."

TB nodded. "Likely someone on the local force has access to the inspection rotation and warns the Kaders. That would allow them to halt operations before the raid occurs, then once the way is clear, they send the workers back to it."

Waters gave a sideways nod, chin to the left. "I hate to admit it, but they're not stupid."

During the course of the conversation, something had been nagging at Nemo. Now that the conversation appeared to be winding down, he had questions. One, in particular, was giving him heartburn. He was pretty sure he knew the answer.

"Loki, what type of mining are we talking about?" he asked.

Loki looked at Nemo. "I'm sorry. Didn't I say? Diamonds."

Fuck. Female? Great Britain? Tight spaces? Diamonds?

"And, just out of curiosity, where is this associate you were going to extract? As in, where is she right now?"

He kept his eyes glued to Loki on the screen, but he could feel the heat of his five teammates' stares.

Loki had the grace to shift uncomfortably, and then he glanced at Medusa, who was looking down at her hands as if she was studying her manicure. He then moved his gaze to Gilgamesh, who simply stared back at him. Both men turned in unison to the camera.

Loki coughed discreetly into his fist. "Unfortunately, we weren't immediately available to extract her, and by the time we could get to her, she had disappeared. There's been no contact since then, and we have no idea where she is. That's the other reason we're calling you. We're hoping you might be able to assist in finding our asset."

"So we would never have seen these photos of Ka-Bar except you need us to find your lost asset. If we're on the same side, this tit-for-tat bullshit needs to end." Nemo's hands let go of the table edge, and he placed them flat on the table. "What is your asset's name?"

The air felt supercharged. Heavy. He was sure his heart and lungs were working at their normal capacity, but it felt like he was being compressed underwater. It was all he could do to keep from yelling at the triad as they paused before answering.

It was Medusa who finally broke the silence. She raised her eyes to Nemo in the camera. "Haskell. Haskell Dawson. You'll likely know her as Le Chatte Noire."

Every muscle in Nemo's body was so tense it felt like one wrong word, one wrong touch, would cause him to explode.

All eyes were focused on Nemo.

He shoved back from the table and turned to his brother. "Find. Her. Now." He stalked to the door, giving a sharp whistle for Scheherazade to follow him. "I'll be in the gym to keep from killing someone." The door slammed behind the man and dog.

6

SEPTEMBER 9, 2022

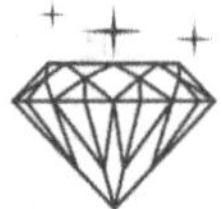

Haskell

Her cap pulled firmly over her head, Haskell did her best to meld into the crowd of people at LAX, deplaning and spilling out into the terminal. Head on a swivel, she hovered in the middle of the large group heading to the baggage carousels. She didn't have anything other than her backpack, but if someone was here looking for her, they would likely know she was traveling light and be watching the main exits for her. By pretending to have a bag to collect, she'd hopefully be going in the complete opposite direction.

"Hopefully" being the key word.

When the throng of people arrived at baggage claim, she hunched farther into her jacket, then went to stand at a carousel like any other passenger waiting impatiently for their bags. While waiting for the conveyors to start moving, she slipped a phone out of her pocket and turned it on. As it booted up, she scanned the people around her through her eyelashes. No one seemed out of place. She didn't think she was being followed, but the last six weeks had been stressful. Combined with almost getting caught in the midst of an illegal mining operation, fleeing for her life was not high on her list of things to try again. She'd had to go about things the long way to make sure she got here in one piece. Hopefully, her ride was ready to come pick her up.

Child, there's that word again. What did I teach you? You put too much faith in luck, girl. Keep it all at skill, not chance.

Glancing down at her phone, the home screen notifications showed a text from someone named "C."

> C:Be there in approximately twenty-three minutes. Red MINI Cooper coming in hot.
> Be ready to jump in.

> H:On my way.

Looking up, Haskell scanned the signs above her head to find the one for the nearest ladies' room. Finding it about two hundred fifty feet on her left, she made a show of looking at her watch, glanced at the digital display that said luggage was "pending," heaved a fake sigh, and then hitched her backpack higher on her shoulder and headed to the restroom.

Once inside, she had to wait for a stall to open up. After three minutes, she was finally able to step inside, lock the door, and change. Timing was everything.

She moved quickly and efficiently. With her backpack on the hook of the door, she began pulling items out and putting them on the shelf and door hanger. Her first step was to remove a square magnetic mirror and attach it to the door behind the shelf.

The metamorphosis began. She removed the Uma Thurman *Pulp Fiction*-style wig, revealing her real hair, a mop of Shirley Temple curls. A wet wipe was used to remove the black kohl around her eyes, the black eyebrow liner and mascara, and the ruby red lipstick. With her fresh face, she appeared younger than her twenty-four years.

Jacket and hat off. Full-length purple leggings were pulled off to reveal a pair of black capri-style leggings underneath. A two-sizes-too-large hoodie was removed to reveal a plain white ribbed tank top. Black sneakers were traded for dollar store flip-flops. A Kesha T-shirt with a ripped-out neck yanked down over her top half. Denim miniskirt with frayed edges pulled over the leggings.

The last step was to unfold the paper grocery bag that blazoned an airport restaurant on its face. Quickly, she shoved all of the clothes she had been wearing into the bag. Earbuds were plugged into her phone, and the buds themselves pushed into her ears, although there was no music playing. She zipped up her backpack, shouldered it, and exited the stall. Glancing around, she saw no one she recognized from when she first came into the bathroom. She washed her hands, dried them with paper towels, and exited the restroom at a leisurely pace.

She turned back the way she had come, went up the escalator, and made her way to the next common area and terminal entrances, where she dumped the bag in the garbage. She took the escalator down to the new baggage claim area and exited out the door marked Taxi/Rideshare. As she stepped to the curb, a red MINI Cooper swung in. Haskell opened the passenger-side door, slid into the front seat, and the car was already whipping out into traffic before she could put her backpack on the floor between her feet or put on her seatbelt.

"Were you followed?" the driver asked.

"I don't think so," Haskell replied.

The red-haired woman behind the wheel of the car didn't speak further as she zipped in and out of traffic like a professional. She wasn't doing more than fifteen over the speed limit, which seemed to be the speed of the traffic as a whole, but her eyes were constantly traveling her mirrors like she expected trouble at any moment. Perfectly coiffed and looking every inch a businesswoman, she also somehow screamed "badass." Long, fire-engine-red hair, diamond studs in her ears, and a professional quality makeup job. Designer navy-blue suit jacket, matching skirt that hit just at the knee, and white silk blouse. Stockings so sheer they had to be real silk, and Louboutins on her feet. A gold ladies' Rolex.

Cherry whipped across two lanes of traffic and exited the freeway. Only then did she seem to relax. "Okay. We should be good." She exhaled and turned briefly to look Haskell in the face, a genuine smile on her face. "Flight okay?"

Haskell grabbed the "Oh-shit" handle as Cherry slid between two semis with barely inches to spare, front and back. "Better than your driving. But I'm here, so happy to be alive. At least for now," she grumbled as they flew over another lane to the right.

"Hungry?"

"Yes."

"Great, because I am starving from the adrenaline rush. We'll stop and have an éclair with tea, and we'll figure out what to do next. The guys have no clue I'm here, so we should be able to keep your presence quiet." Cherry pulled into a coveted parking space along the café's sidewalk just as a delivery driver pulled away. She threw the car in park and pulled her keys out of the ignition. Head turned Haskell's way, she asked, "Is that still what you want? You don't want to see—"

"No!" Haskell closed her eyes and attempted to collect herself. "Sorry. I didn't mean to yell. No, I don't want to see him. I just need a night or two to rest, reassess, and get in touch with Mythos. Then I'll be on my way, and no one will be the wiser."

"If you're sure..." Cherry faded off. "He'd love to see you." She added quietly, "He misses you."

Haskell rolled her eyes. "I'm good, Cherry. I have work to do. He's filling the void just fine, and it would just be a distraction."

"You know they mean nothing to him, right?" the redhead asked.

"No. No distractions. Rest. Contact Mythos. Back to work. You promised."

Cherry nodded. "I did, and I'll keep my promise, but I had to ask."

Cherry made to move out of the car, but Haskell stopped her with a hand on her shoulder. "Thank you, Cherry. I was in a hell of a mess. You saved me out there."

"Pfft. You saved yourself, girl. You always do." Cherry clapped her hands. "I think I'm having two éclairs to celebrate a successful mission of rescuing you."

Haskell sat frozen in the car, staring at the now-empty space Cherry had been sitting in. Calling Cherry had literally been her only option, or she wouldn't have done it. As the handler of the men at Tribe Corporation, Cherry had resources Haskell didn't, which was helpful. Contacting her, though, meant that Haskell was officially in dangerous territory by being in Los Angeles and near Nemo. Oddly enough, she wasn't sure which option was worse—running for her life from the Kaders or running into the temptation of Sawyer "Nemo" Newton. Either was a recipe for disaster. And while the first might see her dead, the second would most definitely see her broken.

She jumped in her seat when the rapping knuckle came at the passenger side window. "C'mon, Haskell! Let's eat!"

Shaking her head to clear it of her conundrum, Haskell departed the car and followed the bundle of hungry energy into the café. Today was shaping up to be another crazy day.

SEPTEMBER 9, 2022

Nemo

They'd just gotten off yet another frustrating conference call with Mythos, neither side gaining any sight or sound, not even a breath of a rumor, on the location of Haskell or her alter ego, Le Chatte Noire. Nemo was starting to fear the worst.

It's been five weeks since they told us she'd been missing, but she'd already been missing for one week by then. She's good, but how did she disappear so completely? Even from Midas?

Scheherazade on his heels, he was storming off to the gym to work off his frustrations yet again, a place he was spending way too much time in when the emergency line rang simultaneously on everyone's watches. Each of the team and the women had their own ringtone so that everyone would know if there was a true emergency. Everyone was in the office, so whose code was it?

Cherry's not here!

"Fuck," Nemo whispered. "Guys! I think that's Cherry's code!"

Demon snapped. "I've got it." He clicked his alarm button and put it on speaker. "Where are you?"

"I'm at the café on Fifth and Rodeo. There's a pressure-plate bomb. It's packed here, and this is above my skills."

"Goddammit!" Demon glanced at the other men in the hallway. "You on it or someone else?"

There was a slight pause. "A... a friend."

Nemo swore he heard a cracking sound. Probably the enamel on Demon's teeth as he ground them together rather than yell at their handler.

"Okay, stay calm, Cherry. We're on our way."

All of the men began checking personal weapons as they moved with purpose to the elevator. Nemo grabbed the sweater on the back of Cherry's desk chair in the lobby, then he punched the down button while Waters alarmed the building except for the underground garage. Their team leader immediately began to dial God on his cell phone.

No answer.

What the hell? God always answers.

Demon snarled, "Cherry, tell him to remain perfectly still."

"It's a her," she corrected.

There was a pause where obvious relief showed on Demon's face, followed quickly by guilt. "Feck. Okay. How's she doing?"

"She's okay. Freaked out. Didn't believe me at first. But she's calmer than I would be."

"Is she sitting or standing?"

"Sitting. It's under her chair. I heard the click when she sat down." There was a catch in Cherry's voice. "Please get here and get her out of this!"

"We're all going to stay on the line. I need you to do something for me, okay?"

By this time, the guys were all in the elevator. Midas and TB had their keys at the ready. When the door opened at the garage level, they flew out and divided up into two vehicles. Midas went behind the wheel of his Bronco, Steel in the passenger seat, with Nemo and Scheherazade in the back. TB was behind the wheel of his Humvee with Waters in the passenger seat and Demon in the back.

"Cherry, are you listening to me? Get that tight ass of yours out of there right now, you hear me?"

There was silence for a moment. The guys in Nemo's vehicle exchanged looks all around.

What the fuck was that?

Nemo could only imagine the looks Demon was getting right now.

"I can't leave her, Demon. She's scared enough."

Waters tried to deflect. "It's not fair to ask you to stay, Cherry. If that thing has a remote on it, and it goes off, or if she shifts for some reason, you're both going to get blown sky-high. Please do what we're telling you to do."

"I'm not leaving her, Waters."

Demon came back over the line, a little less agitated, but not by much. "Clear that café as quickly and quietly as you can. Don't cause panic if you can avoid it. Remind her not to shift her weight in any way. Keep her breathing evenly, all right? Try to get her to a five-second pattern. Breathe in for five, breathe out for five. No deep breaths that are going to change her weight distribution. Just nice and easy, okay?"

"I'll try."

"Better do fecking more than try. I swear to every Irish saint, I'm going to tie you to your desk when this is over."

"Wow," Midas mouthed.

Steel had a little smirk going at the corner of his mouth. "Fucking finally."

WHEN THEY ARRIVED at the café, Nemo put the sweater with Cherry's scent on it in front of Scheherazade's nose. While this was a true emergency, and he could see Cherry from where he stood, it couldn't hurt to put the dog through a test run.

"Scheherazade, *vind Cherry!*"

Tail up, the dog put her nose to the ground and began to search. She went in circles a bit, then found a trail that led straight to the woman in question.

The outside courtyard of the café was clear except for one girl in a wrought iron chair at the far end of the garden fenced-in area. Her hands lay on top of the armrests, not gripping them, but Nemo could tell she wanted to. Nemo and Demon walked up the sidewalk toward the café while the others formed a mini-command center on the hood of Midas' Bronco.

Nemo could actually feel Demon vibrating. "Cherry, get your ass around this fence right now and into one of the vehicles."

Her eyes were blazing. "I am not leaving Haskell alone. I've already told you that. My decision is final."

Nemo inhaled sharply. "Kitty cat?" He looked closer at the woman frozen in the chair.

What are the fucking odds?

The woman's slight frame tensed, her fingers now gripping the arms of the chair. "Fancy meeting you here," Haskell quipped nervously.

Nemo swallowed tightly, his mouth completely dry. He rubbed at the spot above his heart as if touching the numbers there would somehow ease the pain and tightness.

"Cherry-girl," Nemo coaxed, "Demon's about to bust a vein if you don't move, and I've got Haskell. I'm here. She's not alone anymore."

"But..." Cherry darted a quick look at her.

"Cherry," Haskell said, "It's okay. Go."

Nemo closed his eyes, inhaled long, exhaled slowly, and reopened his eyes.

Crossing to the other end of the table, he hopped the fence in a one-handed vault and motioned to Scheherazade to back off. "*Vryheid!*" With a yip, the dog backed off her target, looked at Haskell, sniffed, gave a soft chuff, and looked at Nemo.

"*Goeie meisie,*" he praised the dog. When he looked down at Haskell, his face was sporting his patented playboy smile, looking for all the world like there was no emergency at all.

Forget "emergency." This is a total clusterfuck.

"Hello there, kitty cat. Heard you're having seating issues."

Haskell's eyes were wide, and her smile was shaky. "Yeah, I've been told I have a hot ass, but this is a little ridiculous." She was trying to joke, trying not to panic, but Nemo heard the terror all the same.

"Well, I'm just going to take a look-see and give my vote on how hot that is, shall I?" He winked at her. "Just keep breathing in and out slowly for me. No shifting your weight, and I promise, I'll be gentle."

Cherry rolled her eyes. "Really, Nemo? Jokes? Now?"

Nemo lay on his side, his head turned up to the bottom of the seat Haskell was sitting on, and began taking a series of photos with his phone. "You're just jealous I'm not staring at your 'tight ass' that someone mentioned earlier."

Demon had Cherry molded to his chest, his head tilted down to look at her. "Nemo's got this. Let's get you down to the cars, or I am going to spank that ass so hard you won't sit for a week. Move. Now."

"Baby Jesus and all the fishermen, what is the matter with you?" Cherry groused at the medic.

Nemo barked out a laugh. "Looks like someone else has been spending too many girls' book-talk nights with Sylvan. Midas is going to run out of board space for all the new creative swear words."

"Cherry, I am not going to say it again. If you don't do what I tell you to, you are not going to like the results," Demon warned. "Let the bomb guy take care of this."

"Aww, Demon, I never knew you thought I was the bomb."

Nemo couldn't resist teasing the medic as he continued to take pictures of what he was looking at.

"Shut up, motherfecker." Demon's Irish accent got more pronounced the more upset he was. It sounded like the guy was going to implode.

"Midas. I'm uploading some photos to you now."

"Copy."

Nemo looked up at Cherry. "Cherry, go. Demon's going to have an aneurysm if you don't get out of here. Besides that, I can see right up your skirt from where I am, and I'm going to be here a while, so unless you want me drooling over your pretty blue panties, go."

Demon growled, and Cherry squawked. Both backed up two steps.

There were chuckles all around on the comms that had now been activated.

Demon growled again and handed an earbud to Cherry. "You can hear everything and talk to her, but only if you go back to the cars."

Haskell spoke up again. "Cherry, listen to them. You don't need to be here for this."

"But—"

"'But' nothing. Get the hell out of here."

"But—"

"Go!" Nemo and Haskell told her at the same time.

Cherry huffed but took the earbud. "Haskell, the boys sound like dipshits, but they really do know what they're doing. I won't be far."

She stuffed the worm-looking device in her ear while Demon put one in Haskell's ear, and as soon as it was in, he threw Cherry over his shoulder. "Don't get dead, Nemo," he advised, and then he took off with the team's handler, screaming like a banshee at him and pummeling his back with her well-manicured fists.

Nemo chuckled from under the chair. "I would not want to be him."

Haskell gave a nervous chuckle. "Yeah, he seems a bit possessive. They been together long?"

"They're not together. They barely talk at the office, so his temper tantrum is going to make for great betting opportunities." He gently pushed himself out from under her chair and sat up. "Well, kitty cat, you are one hundred percent goat-fucked, as my Navy SEAL friends would say. This is the hottest ass I've ever seen."

"Hashtag life goals," Haskell mumbled under her breath.

"Hey." Nemo got serious. "I gotcha, kitty cat. Just keep breathing slow, don't shift, and we'll be out of this, and I'll be able to take your hot ass out on a date." He winked at her, then turned his focus to the dog. "Scheherazade, *vind Cherry!*"

The dog took off with a leap over the fence line and went in the direction Demon had gone with Cherry. Then he began a conversation with his team over the earbuds.

"Okay, boys, we have got a plate so hot here, it's scalding. I sent Zade out of here for safety. You get my artwork, Midas?"

"Got 'em, little bro. Downloading now."

"Your brother is still your eye in the sky?"

"Yup."

"Is the dog that was just here yours?"

"Yep. Scheherazade. Egyptian street dog. I rescued her and her two puppies while I was there and decided to train her as a working dog."

"She's beautiful."

"She is. Smart, too."

Feet came running toward them, causing Nemo to sit up and then stand. He brushed off his ass from lying on the ground, then reached to grab the small tool kit from Waters on the other side.

"Thanks. Now get the hell back. If I get blown sky-high and you go with me, Kubrick will find a way to raise us from the dead, kick your ass for being so stupid, and kill me again for being the reason you died."

Grinning, the man slapped him on the shoulder. "I would not bet against that. However, I wanted to see the situation for myself before I started making boss-like decisions."

The man walked down the fence line a few steps and looked into the girl's face. "Hello there, Haskell. My name is Waters. You doing okay?"

"As well as can be expected, I'm guessing."

He smiled at her. "Actually, it looks like you're doing great. Just do everything Nemo tells you to do and do it when he tells you to do it."

Nemo grinned. "See? You have to do everything I say. That could be fun."

Waters smacked him upside the back of the head before turning his attention back to Haskell. "Ignore his jokes. He really is very good at what he does, despite his terrible sense of humor. And timing. Do what he tells you, and you'll be out of here in no time, got it?"

She nodded. "Got it."

"All right, Nemo," Waters said. "I'm dropping back. We're all in the channel, so just yell out if you need something."

Nemo flipped him off.

Waters double-checked the hearing device in Haskell's ear. "Earbud check. Cherry, say something."

"Demon is grounded from surfing for a week."

"Good luck with that one," Steel drawled.

"I'm being grounded for what?" Demon sputtered.

"For being a Neanderthal," Cherry accused.

"Can a leprechaun be a Neanderthal?" TB asked.

Nemo could hear Demon growling over the airwaves at everyone.

"Okay. Hang in there, kitty cat. This will all be over soon."

"One way or another," she muttered.

"Hey," Nemo said, "remember, I gotcha, kitty cat. We've got a date. You can't sneak away on me after I've saved your life."

She rolled her eyes at him.

"What's the eye roll for?"

"Just... look, I appreciate the chitchat and trying to distract me to keep me calm and all, but could you just do whatever it is you need to do and try to keep us in one piece?"

"Nemo," Midas broke in, "I don't mean to bust your moves, but you've got a problem. Put the goggles on."

Nemo shook his head and said to Haskell, "You're not getting out of our date, kitty cat." Then to his brother, "What's the problem, bro?"

"Cerberus."

Opening the tool kit Waters brought him, Nemo took out several items, then dropped onto his back again on the ground. "I don't see anything. Where, Midas?"

"Bottom left as you're looking at it."

In order to see where Midas was directing him, the fit under the chair was tight. With an awkward shove to his right socket, the joint seemed to stack the shoulder on top and behind its normal placement. Now there was room for him to fit. Not comfortably, but at least into a position that was less likely to jostle the chair while he was underneath it. Using his shoulder blades and hips, he crab-walked himself back under the chair. Once he was directly under it, he put on a pair of magnifying lenses, grabbed the penlight in his pocket, turned it on, and flashed it onto the casing of the device attached there.

Sure enough, a Cerberus stamp was present.

"Well, hello there, little doggie. Haven't seen you in a while."

"Be careful, little bro," Midas reminded him.

"Yes, big bro," Nemo mocked. "I'm thrilled you care, but I got this."

Oh yeah. I got this. No problem. Bastard is the best explosives guy on Earth. How the hell did Haskell get on his radar?

"Okay, kitty cat, how are you doing up there?"

"I'm getting tired, Sawyer," she admitted.

"Well, we can't have that. All the guys will say I was a boring date, and I have a reputation to protect."

There was a mumble in the background. "Did she just call him 'Sawyer'?"

"Shut it, guys," Midas warned.

He flashed the penlight around to look for secondary triggers. He didn't see any, but that didn't mean there weren't any there. Cerberus didn't use them as a rule, and bomb makers tended to be incredibly OCD on their signatures and methods, but there was always a chance that he'd try to "grow" his skillset.

He turned off the penlight and sighed silently. Things were about to get loud. And messy.

"Waters, how far back is everyone?"

"Café has been evacuated. We're about a hundred meters back. The blue line is likely to be here quickly, though."

Nemo hauled himself out from underneath the chair. "I'm going to need something solid to get under and get under quickly. It will need to fit three of us."

"Shit," Midas breathed out over the mic.

"Relax, bro."

"You know he's watching."

"I know, Midas. Relax."

Waters broke in, "What's going on, guys?"

Nemo started rooting around in his front pocket and brought out a piece of gum. "Focus, people. We need something that three people can dive into that's fire retardant, and we need it yesterday."

TB asked, "Can't you just snip some wires or MacGyver that shit to prevent it from blowing up?"

"No, Tiny Brain, I can't," Nemo answered his work nemesis, TB, as he unwrapped the gum, stuck it in his mouth, folded the gum wrapper in half, smoothing out as many of the wrinkles in it as he could, and inserted it into the mechanism, being extremely careful not to touch the trigger hammer. "And even if I could, I wouldn't dare try." His voice was garbled around the sugary confection in his mouth.

"Okay, TB and Steel, the best thing we got right now is a dumpster in the alleyway behind the café."

"On it, boss," TB replied. Nemo could hear the sounds of running feet as the pair disappeared down the alleyway.

"Sorry, Nemo and Haskell, but you're gonna need a serious shower when you're done here," Waters apologized.

"Been there, done that, burned the T-shirt." Nemo chuckled, remembering how, during the rescue of Flame, TB's woman, he'd ended up losing a battle with a dumpster.

"What's going on?" Haskell asked.

Nemo reached his opposite hand back behind the oddly placed shoulder joint, giving it a sharp, quick yank. Now it appeared to be in its proper position. He massaged it absently as he stepped in front of Haskell and got down on one knee, his forearms leaning on the bent knee. "How are your legs feeling, kitty cat?"

"Like noodles," she confessed nervously.

"So I've got the proverbial bad news and good news. The bad news is that I can't defuse this thing. No matter what I do to it, it'll trip the timer, and I can't see how long we have between the click and the boom. The good news is that two of my friends went to grab a dumpster from the alley. What's going to happen is, once they bring that dumpster here, they're going to open it, they're going to put one of these chairs in front of it." Nemo nodded to the chair she was sitting in. "One of them is going to get in the dumpster and serve as our doorman. When the second guy clears the area, I'm going to grab you, throw you over my shoulder, and we're going to do a little dumpster diving." Nemo winked. "Nothing's too classy for my girl on our first date."

"Do you have a twitch?" Haskell asked.

"Huh?"

"A twitch. Your eye. It winks a lot."

He was stunned. Then he grinned.

The laughter on the comms was almost deafening.

"She's got your number, bro," Midas threw out.

He started clearing chairs and tables that were in the pathway of getting her directly to the dumpster.

TB and Steel came trotting in, pushing the unwieldy container up the alley. His twin gave him encouragement over the comms. "Demon's right. Don't get dead."

"No worries, bro. Not the first time I've done this."

"Yeah, but the last time, you had a lead bathtub to dive into and a lead fire blanket to cover yourself with. Now you're going to have extra weight, plus a small hill to climb."

"Relax, Midas," Nemo reassured him. "She's a tiny-ass little thing. Maybe weighs a hundred pounds, and you and I both know I'll have several seconds before the big bang."

"No guarantees on how many, Nemo, so just be careful."

TB was already in the dumpster, holding onto the open lid.

"I drew the short straw, Nutsack, so let's get going here."

"Aww, see, I knew you loved me. Together to the end, Total Butch to my Sundance."

"Fucker. Let's go."

Nemo got down into a crouch again in front of Haskell and smiled into her bright blue eyes. "Okay, kitty cat, you ready for some fun?"

"No, but I'm not ready to be dead yet, either."

"Thatta girl. When I say 'three,' I need you to go limp for me, you got it? I won't be touching you yet, so you need to trust that I'm going to grab you on the number four and get us out of here. Can you do that?"

"Yeah," she whispered.

"Once we get you out of here, we'll get you somewhere safe where you can clean up, and then you and I are gonna head out on that date."

She huffed at him.

"Hey, I'm not kidding. I'm way hungry for tacos. It's Tuesday, after all, and I can't let the girl with the hottest ass in town eat dinner all alone on Taco Tuesday."

"That sounds so wrong," TB muttered.

Nemo's focus on Haskell never wavered. "Ready?" he asked, his expression serious for the first time.

"Yes. Thank you," she said.

"No need to thank me. Just don't want you losing one of those nine lives." The words were flirty, but the expression was still serious. "Okay, here we go. One. Two. Three."

As he said three, he watched and felt her sag forward. In the space of the second it would have taken to say "four," he drove his shoulder underneath her falling form, wrapped that arm around her knees, stood, and sprinted for the chair in front of the dumpster. He heard the explosion and felt its impact as he leapt from the chair's seat, diving with Haskell's body beneath his into the garbage bags inside the dumpster, and TB dropped the lid just as the fireball was extending toward their iron box.

The concussion of the explosion lifted the dumpster off the ground a couple of feet, and it came back down hard, about ten feet back from where it had been, as well as on its side.

After the dumpster stopped moving, Haskell lay beneath Nemo's body. He raised his head to make sure she was okay. Reassured when her eyes opened, he said, "You look great, kitty cat, but we need to talk about this new perfume you've got on," he quipped.

Haskell replied, "You don't smell any better, burglar boy. But I sure as shite look better than you. What animal attached itself to your face and died? Scruffy. Yuck."

Nemo looked down into her eyes. She smiled. He smiled.

Fuck, I'm in love with a kitty cat.

8

SEPTEMBER 9, 2022

Haskell

"I shit you not, Midas. The asswipe is lying in days-old food and who-knows-what, makes a joke about how she smells, and without missing a beat, that little pint of piss ribs him about his beard."

Waters was laughing. "She's perfect for him."

TB rumbled, "Maybe, but she's totally not his type."

Waters asked, "Midas, does your brother even have a type?"

There was a snort, and Midas answered, "If it's human, and it has a vagina, it's his type."

Haskell bit her lip, a bolt of pain whizzing through her.

Child, of course he's a player. Why else would he be interested in a tomboy like you?

She was currently sitting at the conference room table in a ten-story office building in the middle of L.A. The past two hours were just about all she could take, and hearing this conversation float from an office down the hall was not helping the situation.

Barely given time to collect her scattered wits after the explosion, Nemo and his co-worker, TB, had vaulted out of the dumpster, dragging her behind them at a full-blown sprint down an alley. A Bronco had been waiting, to which she was unceremoniously thrown into the back seat. A furry missile flew in on her heels and deposited itself in her lap, followed by two hundred pounds of glorious superhero. He didn't even have the door slammed shut before the Bronco was tearing down a back street. Once it hit Fifth Avenue, the one Nemo had called Midas pulled out into traffic and proceeded to drive to this office building looking for all the world like he and his passengers were just out for a midday drive in L.A. on an ordinary Tuesday.

When they arrived at the office building, a flurry of orders began being issued. There'd been no time to process anything over the leader's instructions, the confirmations of the other men, and the squawking and growling of Cherry and Demon.

Nemo had been glued to her side for the entire time, but when he lowered himself to his knees to praise Scheherazade, a cool hand brushed down her arm. Haskell had turned to see Cherry at her right and a very grumpy medic in sunglasses just behind her.

"Haskell, let me take you somewhere to clean up."

She allowed herself to be led away by Cherry. When she turned around in the lift, she saw Nemo on one knee next to his dog, his eyebrows scrunched down and a frown on his face, but he didn't move from the spot. Their eyes remained locked until the closing lift door blocked him from her view.

A warm shower and some borrowed clothing from Cherry made all the difference. She transferred her trusty screwdriver tool to her pants pocket. She had to tight-roll the jeans to keep them from dragging on the ground, and the long-sleeved Harvard T-shirt sleeves hung so long her fingertips barely peeked out the ends, but she was clean and no longer smelled like rotting food, so she was thankful for that. Clean and comfortable, she'd been brought back here to the conference room where she waited for them to come in and question her, and she was stuck overhearing conversations she shouldn't be a party to.

It wasn't like she hadn't known she was one in a legion of women, but actually hearing it said aloud made the contents of her stomach curdle. She already had felt foolish for letting him seduce her the first time, let alone the second time they'd met. It was time to get out of this mess. She knew she was probably on surveillance of some kind, so she had to work fast.

Perusing the room, she admitted that getting out how she got in was clearly going to be a no-go. Cherry had pointed out her desk and said she'd be there if Haskell needed anything. The hallway the room had been in was one-way, with no emergency stairwell at the end. She looked up.

Whenever you're in trouble, Haskell, my child, always look up. No one ever looks up.

Haskell reached in her pocket for her trusty screwdriver, which she never went anywhere without. It had helped her out of more than one desperate situation in the past. Looked like today would be another day to add to the list.

It took less than a minute to be up on top of a chair, unscrewing the grate to the vent, and inside it. Refusing to think too hard about having no clue which way to go once inside the vent, she began crawling. As she crawled to what she hoped was safety, her mind zipped back to the first time she had met Nemo.

9

JULY 5, 2016 (SIX YEARS AGO)

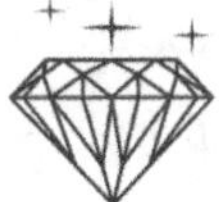

Haskell

She was in no real hurry. This tiny museum in Spain didn't currently have anything on display that she wanted, and its internal security was shite, but it did have a tricky ventilation system that kept her skills sharp. Whenever she was in the area, she liked to break in just for fun. Once she'd gotten inside, she'd take a swing through the crown jewels display and window-shop. Just because she didn't have a need to steal anything there didn't mean she couldn't look around.

As she lay in the air duct just shy of the room she wanted to come down into, she heard something unexpected. Footsteps? Couldn't be. This museum only used one guard inside the building, and he remained in the security room at all times.

There it was again. Definitely footsteps. Stealthy ones. Someone up to no good. She shifted as quietly as she could in her cocooned surroundings, her weight distributed to her hands, elbows, knees, and feet spread across the air duct framing. If she lay on the duct itself, she'd fall right through, even weighing in at just under a hundred pounds. Still unable to see anything below her, she tried to shimmy a little closer to the grate without giving herself away.

A shadow passed in the upper right perimeter. They were still too far out of her range to see exactly who was there or what was going on, so she shimmied again. Now she could just make out a figure in all black.

She was preparing to scoot back when she heard the sound of metal buckling. The figure in the room below stopped, his head snapping up to look at her hiding spot. She looked down the front of her body and saw that her foot had slipped off the frame in her enthusiasm to get a better look at the thief.

"Shite," she whispered. And then she was falling.

She tried to make herself go limp and twist, but like the cat that was her namesake, she needed more space than just fifteen feet to accommodate the adjustment. The fall seemed to happen in slow motion nonetheless, and mentally, she braced for impact.

When it came, it wasn't the bone-jarring thud of hitting the floor face-first. There was definitely a significant impact, but instead of landing flat, she hit something oddly angular. Parts of it wrapped around her and absorbed some of the impact, although her head did bounce off something hard—someone's head—causing her neck to jerk back and her teeth to clack together.

"Ow," two voices said in unison.

Whoever the guy was who broke her fall set her gently on her feet. "You okay?" His voice was low, just above a whisper.

She spun around to face him and gasped. He had the bluest eyes she'd ever seen. Poetically blue. Despite only being able to see his eyes through the black skin-tight hood he wore, she could easily tell he was smiling. Her stunned reaction to him amused him.

"I'm fine," she finally managed to get out of her mouth. "What the hell are you doing here?"

His eyebrow quirked up, and she heard a soft chuckle.

What does it look like he's doing, child? Your brothers wouldn't have said something so trite.

Lord, she hated that raspy voice in her head! Always, it tore her down. "Sorry. Dumb question. Blame it on our knocking heads, making me temporarily stupid."

"No worries," he returned. "But we are highly compromised at the moment, so it's probably best we get moving." His head nodded toward the security camera, its red light blinking steadily. "Don't think you're going back the way you came, so I'm guessing you're stuck with my exit plan."

The burglar had a strange accent she didn't recognize. Australian? Dutch? It didn't sound like either, but they were the only things she could think of.

He grabbed her hand and took off down the main hallway. In the distance, they could hear sirens. She could also hear the echoes of the radio of the security guard as he closed in on their location. The security guard had been onto them right away.

"Shite!"

"Fuck!"

Their expletives came on top of one another. The man quickly spun on his heel and gave her a push. "Second room on the left. Statue of the rearing horse. Get along the backside of it."

"We'll be cornered! There's only one way in and out of that room," she hissed.

"Go!" he urged.

As soon as she turned, he slapped her on the ass. She sputtered in indignation, but there was no time to chew him out for spanking her before he gave her a push in the direction he wanted her to go.

When she hit the statue in question at the end of the room, she slid behind it and crouched at its base. It was then that she noticed the hole. Well, not a hole. It was a metal grate that was lying off to the side, one that she could easily get through.

He encouraged her, "Squeeze in there, tiny, and crawl like your life depends on it because your freedom certainly does."

On her stomach, Haskell slithered into the narrow opening. It wasn't much larger than the air duct she had been in earlier. Slightly wider and taller, but not by much. She wondered how the man behind her, close to six feet tall and maybe one hundred and eighty pounds, was going to fit. She began crawling as quickly as she could through the heating system and prayed no one decided to suddenly turn on the furnace, especially since she had no clue where this was going to dump them out.

"Keep going, tiny." And then she heard a click, like a joint popping, followed by a grunt, and then another click and a grunt. Then there were the shuffling sounds of him crawling behind her.

After what felt like an hour, Haskell felt a cool breeze pushing onto her face. Fresh air. Somewhere along this tunnel, there was an exit to the outside.

"When you meet the first junction, go past it," the man behind her instructed. "About ten feet, there's a blind turn on the right-hand side. Take it. Then you're about twenty feet from outside. Watch out for the awkward drop."

She continued to shuffle along on her hands and knees, past the obvious turn and all the way down to what looked like a dead end. Sure enough, there was a blind turn to the right, and she could vaguely make out moonlight through a narrow rectangle in front of her once she made the turn completely.

When she reached the outer wall, she saw what he meant by an awkward drop. Normally, the vent would have opened up at ground level. But because this museum backed up to a river, the vent opened out to a six-foot uneven drop onto a muddy bank, half of the basement floor exposed at this corner of the building. This called for some rearranging of her body.

"Can you reach my wrists?" she asked over her shoulder.

She felt his body slide up on top of her legs from the knees down, his hands gripping her wrists, which she had put down by her sides. "Gotcha."

"Okay. Now take your weight off my legs so I can slide them out."

She felt the pressure of him come up slightly. "That's all I can give you in this cramped space."

"It's enough."

Like a trapeze artist in the circus, Haskell grasped the man's wrists in her own hands, similar to his grip. Using her upper body strength, she began folding herself in half, rotating underneath herself so that her legs came out on top. There was a moment where she was certain she didn't have enough clearance to get her legs over her hips, but she felt him squirm backward in the tunnel, giving her a few more inches of clearance as he dragged her back with him. Now inverted, her feet were the first to exit the tunnel.

"Neat trick," he complimented her.

"Pays to be small. Okay, I'm ready," she let him know. With a gentle push, he helped propel her out the tunnel opening. She immediately began to arch her body so that her legs, hips, back, and eventually shoulders and head came out of the gap. "Ugh. I think I know how a pretzel feels," she said, looking at her arms in a twisted version of an iron cross gymnastics move.

Once his head, arms, and shoulders cleared the opening, he glanced down. "Okay, get ready to drop. Three, two, one." He let go.

Bending her knees, Haskell was able to absorb most of the shock of the drop. After putting her hands down on the muddy bank to make sure she was balanced, she moved into ankle-deep water to get out of the man's way.

Up above her, the man was out of the opening up to his shoulders. She watched him purposefully jam one shoulder into the side of the vent, then repeat the tactic on the other shoulder. He'd dislocated his own shoulders in order to fit in the small space, then put them back in once they cleared the vent. It made her wince, but other than the initial pain, he seemed mostly unaffected by it.

In one hand, he had something that looked like a piton. He jammed it into the wall about a foot above the opening, then gave it a pull so that it extended to about a foot in length. Giving it a tug to test how it would hold in the material, and clearly satisfied that it would, he began to weasel his body out of the vent. Once his entire torso was out, he grabbed the piton with one hand, the bottom of the rough ledge with another, and propelled the bottom half of his body out of the air duct with a flip. He landed, relatively gracefully, just in front of her.

"Ready to run?" he asked.

"Whenever you are," she assured him.

They took off down the riverbed and away from the museum.

10

JULY 5, 2016 (CONTINUED)

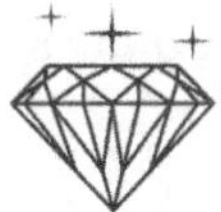

Haskell

Haskell was winded beyond belief. She had been prepared to jog back to her lodgings seven miles away, not sprint. Inside her head, she cursed her unwanted partner in crime.

Her brain focused on the man in question. She had to grudgingly admit, whoever this wanker was, he had a killer body. Wiry. Fit like a runner or a footballer. And he had those bluer-than-blue eyes, along with the mystery accent that made her insides boil.

"Oof!"

Distracted by her attraction to her running mate, she hit the ground with a thud, no time to prepare herself for the faceplant into the forest floor. It was probably better that way, all things considered. If she'd had time to prepare for the fall, she probably would have tensed up and seriously hurt herself. As it was, she'd given her ankle a severe wrench.

A pair of hands touched her shoulders and began to run themselves over her body from head to toe.

"You okay?"

"Get your hands off me, you git. I'm fine! Just tripped."

"Aww. It's okay if you're fallin' for me, tiny. I don't mind."

She heard the teasing smile in his voice, and she rolled her eyes. "Falling like a lead balloon," she muttered. "Was so busy thinking how to ditch your arrogant ass, I wasn't paying attention to where I was putting my feet."

"I've heard I have that effect on women," he admitted.

"Oh, whatever!"

He helped her to her feet, but with the first step she took, she sucked in a scream. If he hadn't had his hands close, she would have gone down in a heap.

He knelt down to feel her ankle. Even his gentle probe caused her to wince and yelp. "Already swelling. Up you go, on my back."

"No, thanks. Just give me a minute, and it'll be fine."

"Don't be stubborn. Your ankle's hurt, and we need to keep moving. Hop on. You're such a tiny little thing; I doubt I'll even notice you're there. You'll be my own human backpack."

"I said I'm fine," she ground out.

"Look, either hop on my back, or I'll pick you up, throw you over my shoulder, and carry you. That would give you a great view of my ass as a thank you for the spectacular view I've had of yours while we were running, although I doubt you're in a very appreciative mood right now."

She screamed behind clenched teeth and stamped her foot, forgetting it was injured. Tears pooled in her eyes at the pain.

"Bloody, stubborn female," he muttered under his breath. "What's it going to be? Telling me where to go or staring at my ass?"

"I'll tell you where to go. For the love of... You are such a cunt!"

He winked at her in the moonlight. "Love a girl who talks dirty, but I'd prefer to get a little farther from our friends before we explore that filthy mouth of yours."

"Oh my god, you are amazing."

He sighed. "I know. It's a cross I have to bear." He turned his back to her. "C'mon, tiny. Let's get out of here."

Sighing in suffering, Haskell knew she wasn't getting out of this forest without him carrying her. Not unless she wanted to spend the night on the cold, hard ground, hiding under bushes and praying the Policia Local didn't find her. And even then, she'd probably wake up stiff, sore, and unable to walk very fast.

"Fine," she grumbled.

Hobbling up to his backside, she launched herself at his hips, knees grabbing on like she was about to bareback ride one of the farm's horses. His hands curved comfortably around her thighs and hitched her tight. He gave them a quick squeeze before trotting in the general direction they'd been headed when she tripped.

"Where am I headed, tiny?"

She reached down and smacked his ass. "Stop calling me that. Argh! Are you always such a dick?"

"Make up your mind, sweetheart, am I a cunt or a dick? I think it's anatomically impossible to be both."

She buried her head in the back of his neck, huffing in frustration. "Neither is desirable," she replied.

"I dunno. I've heard my dick's pretty marvelous, and I wouldn't mind getting up close to your c—"

She clamped her hand over his mouth. "Don't. You. Dare." She snatched her hand back when she could feel him kissing her palm through his balaclava. She wound her arms around his neck, squeezing him like a python to show her frustration. "Just jog, burglar boy. I've got a flat across from the marina in Valencia. You can drop me off there and be on your way."

He sped up, holding her tight to his back, pinching her thigh in response to her squeezing. "If you're gonna squeeze me, use those thighs. Do a good job, and you can even suffocate me with them later when I don't have to run, and I'll promise to enjoy it."

"Are you mental?" she hissed. "What is wrong with you?"

"I'm sure you'll let me know later, but honestly? I haven't had many complaints."

Just over an hour later, they hit the forest edge of Valencia. Both of them finally felt safe to remove their balaclavas. The fresh night air felt good on her face, and the ocean breeze gave some relief to the sweat that had formed along her scalp under her curls.

He was breathing heavily but not winded. She couldn't help but be slightly impressed. His pace had been steady, and he'd only had to hitch her up higher on his back once. Then again, she'd been clinging to him tightly. He'd held onto her thighs during the run, but his grip had been more about keeping her steady than it had been about holding her.

"Where to, tiny?"

"Blue building, white shutters."

"Got it."

He took off again, sticking to the shadows whenever possible. The building in question was at the southern end of a string of quaint apartment buildings painted in bold colors facing the marina. This early, the streets were silent. No cars, no pedestrians, and while there were streetlights along the ocean road, they were soft enough to not allow anyone to see much detail.

When they reached the side door that led to her apartment, she began to try and wriggle her way down off his back, but his grip tightened. "There's no way you're climbing those stairs, and we both need to lay low for a bit."

She sighed. Of course, he wanted to come up. And, of course, he was right. The stairs were going to be near impossible with her ankle in this condition, but allowing him into her space was not a good idea.

"Just for a little while," she groused. "And no funny business."

He chuckled, opening the outer door as quietly as possible. "I only need a little while, tiny." He climbed the stairs to her door.

"Well, isn't that sad? Hard to understand why you've got time to run around free to steal shite."

"It'd definitely be fun, though. Key?"

"On the top of the doorframe."

"That's secure," he snarked.

"I didn't exactly want to run the risk of dropping my key while crawling through the ventilation system or running around in the woods. Besides, no one bothers me, and no one comes to my door. I don't have anything anyone would want."

Once inside the single-bedroom apartment and the door was closed, Haskell attempted for a second time to slide off his back, but he still wasn't having it. He reached backward and gave her a smack on her ass. "Settle down." Glancing around, he strode over in front of the futon, dumped her backward onto it, then immediately strode toward the bathroom.

After a ladylike squeak of surprise, Haskell attempted to right herself. "What the hell?!"

"You don't need to be hobbling around on that ankle and making it worse."

She could hear him opening drawers and cupboards. "What are you looking for?" she called out.

"Ice pack?"

"Don't have one."

She heard muttering in what didn't sound like English.

"Don't suppose you have a wrap bandage?"

"No. Never needed one. Never hurt myself before you barged in tonight."

More muttering.

He stalked back out to the kitchenette and began opening drawers. Finally, he found some hand towels in one drawer and scissors in another. From a cupboard, he pulled out a bowl and from under the sink, a plastic bag, then threw everything he'd collected into the bowl. His last stop was the freezer, from which he grabbed the entire ice cube reservoir.

"What are you doing?"

"Preparing to doctor your ankle." He brought all the items over and set them on the futon next to her, then dragged a kitchen chair in

front of Haskell. He motioned with his hand toward her foot. "Give it over."

She rolled her eyes, crossed her arms over her chest, and turned her face away from him.

He sighed. "Look, I can grab your ankle myself, but then I run the risk of hurting you, and I don't want to make it feel worse. Help me out here, tiny."

With an air of frustration, she turned her head back in his direction, her lips pursed, her eyes boring into his. "I told you not to call me that," she grumbled, although secretly, she felt a pleasurable tingle run through her when he did.

He motioned with his hand again. Reluctantly, she lifted her leg with both hands so that she could keep the foot stabilized and gingerly set it on his thigh. Once it was steady, she watched him smooth his hands down her calf. When he reached the tender area, his touch became even lighter, checking more to see where the swelling started and ended rather than probing the injury.

Because he didn't look at her while he was checking her ankle, she was free to check out his features in depth. His blond hair was in a high and tight cut, the top too long to be regulation, so he clearly wasn't in the military. His skin was tan like he spent a lot of time outdoors, and she wondered if he had tan lines or not. The "or not" part made her want to pluck at the neckline of her shirt to fan air down her torso. She also noticed the laugh lines around his eyes. He was clearly in his mid-twenties, but based on his banter, he loved to laugh, and the lines made him even more handsome.

"Well, I have to call you something." He began to weasel a finger in between her foot and the back of her climbing shoe.

She hissed at the pressure it placed on her swollen ankle.

"Sorry," he apologized. He glanced at her face and winked. "Your fight response when cornered and all that hissing you do reminds me of an alley cat." He nodded. "New name. Kitty cat. I like it."

She groaned and flopped against the futon's back. "I think I prefer tiny."

His grin at her frustration lit up his entire face, and it made her want to smack him, kiss him, as well as make him smile some more, all at the same time. Lordy, he was gorgeous! His grin grew further like he knew exactly what she was thinking. Then he turned his attention to her tiny foot on his leg, and as gently as he could, he slipped the shoe off. Since she wasn't wearing a sock, it was easy to see the discoloration that had already started. She felt the calluses on his hands as he ran them one last time over her foot, his concentration tight. "It doesn't look too bad. Just a moderate tear, I think."

He filled the plastic bag with ice, tied off the ends in a knot, and placed the bag draped over her foot so that it hung over both sides of her ankle. As she sat with her foot in his lap, he began to unfold the hand towels he'd pulled from the kitchen. Two of them he left folded and off to the side. He used scissors on the third to make several small snips in the ends about one inch apart each.

As he tore the towel into thin strips, he started talking again. "So, what's your name, kitty cat?"

She huffed. "Why do you need to know? Not like we're going to be besties or anything."

"Kitty cat is good for dirty talk, but when I call out your name later, I'd like it to be an actual name."

She stared at him, dumbfounded.

He laughed. "Close your mouth, tiny. You're catching flies." He went back to wrapping her ankle.

"It's Haskell," she murmured.

His eyes flicked up to hers without moving his head. "Unusual name. Suits you. Mine's Sawyer."

He continued to work on her ankle.

"I don't recognize your accent. Where are you from?"

"Jo-Burg."

"You're from South Africa?" she shyly asked.

He nodded.

"I heard you speaking another language. Was that Afrikaans?"

"Ken jy Afrikaans?" he asked.

Her eyes looked at him blankly.

"Yes. It was."

"I don't think I've ever actually heard it spoken before."

"It's not common outside of the country." He narrowed his eyes as he looked at her. "You're obviously from England but not London. Northern?"

She didn't nod, but she didn't shake him off, either. "What makes you say that?"

"Your accent is softer than the city. Definitely not the East End and not Welsh." He smiled. "So, Haskell from Northern England, you gonna let me hang out here for a while after I finish playing doctor with you?"

11

SEPTEMBER 9, 2022

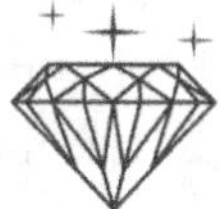

Nemo

"Jesus Christ, Midas, I know it's Los Angeles, and it's hot, but could you turn the temperature to above freezing in here?" TB groused. "It's so cold in here my balls have pulled up into my body and popped out as nipples."

"Pull up your big-girl thong and layer, asshole," Midas retorted, not even looking up from his computer monitor. "If you'd wear a shirt that was your size and not a shmedium, it wouldn't be stretched so tight you can see through it. And if those are your balls, I feel bad for Flame. I might need to stop by and see if she has any unfulfilled needs."

"Fuckwitch," TB grunted.

Nemo was sitting cross-legged on the end of Midas' desk, feeding his face with NikNaks and watching the show. He'd originally come into his brother's new office under the lure of the contraband ship-ment of snacks they were both addicted to, but then he stayed to watch Haskell on the monitor since Waters banned him from going into the conference room. Every so often, he threw a chip to Scheherazade on the floor beneath him.

"I'm not sure what's worse," TB grumbled. "The temperature in here, the lack of windows, or the fact that I feel like I'm living in Orwell's *1984* with all these telescreens."

Midas pulled up from his keyboard. "Look, my girls run twenty-four seven, and the space heats up to equator temperature. Windows allow the sunlight in, which adds to the heat factor. They'll PMS and blow up the building if I don't keep the room cold. So either put on a jacket, go buy a snuggie, or take it like a man."

He started to go back to typing, then pulled back, pointing around the room as he ranted. "And as far as the screens go, we've got a lot of shit to keep track of on-site alone. I've got one screen of thumbnails per twenty security cameras inside this ten-floor heaven we call home. Do you have *any* clue how many cameras that is? Two hundred and fucking eighty-seven! I've got an additional screen that has all the outside cameras except for the roof. That fucker has its own screen with four different views of the helipad.

"You guys want intel? That means I need to know what's going on all over this big blue marble, so I've got six different screens attuned to twenty-four-hour news channels. Do you know how annoying that is? It never stops! All the rest, with the exception of the beauty behind Nemo, are responsible for keeping tabs on whatever shit you all need me to monitor while you're off playing Doom reality-style."

"Last, but so not least, is my baby, Nova, on the last screen. She runs this harem when I can't. She watches over all your sorry asses without any thanks from you ungrateful bastards. She runs everything, from your smart watches, your navigation systems, your computer systems, and even your personal security systems in your apartments. Thanks to the glorious creation the world calls AI, but I call heaven, she's not just a watchdog spy cam program anymore like Cyclopes was. So get off my frickin' ass about the temperature in here, or I'll turn her off and see how well you all function without her."

TB squinted at Midas. "Do I need to bring you some ice cream? Cuz, I gotta say, you're acting like Flame used to when it was that time—"

"Don't fucking say it!" Midas roared.

TB held his hands up in a gesture of surrender. He looked at Nemo.

Nemo shrugged. "I don't think he's eaten yet today. Better order in." He popped another chip in his mouth.

"You mean one of these eight bajillion monitors can't do it for him?"

A projectile hit TB in the side of the head—one of the mini rubber cats Midas collected and used as stress balls. TB happened to catch it by default with a grunt. Its body was a stack of pancakes, complete with butter and syrup, and then the head, feet, and tail of a cat. "Kubrick gave you this one."

"Yes, she did, so give it back, you pathetic shitfucker."

With a snort, TB tossed the cat back to Midas, who set it back on his shelf behind his desk, making sure it was perfectly aligned with all the others.

TB looked to Nemo for help against his brother. Reaching into the chip bag, extracting a chip, and bringing it up to his mouth, Nemo reminded him, "Normally, it's me ambushing you."

"Yeah... speaking of which, neither Flame nor I are cleaning up the confetti in the garage at her house, so you'd better get over there and get sweeping."

"Sorry. Don't know how to use a broom," Nemo lied.

"Why don't you ever ambush your brother?"

Midas let out a frustrated grunt. "Because you stomp around, yell, and get pissy. He knows that if he did that to me, I'd just fucking strangle him with computer cables. Something I should have done with the umbilical cord as soon as we were out of the womb!" Midas looked over at Nemo, calmly continuing to eat his chips.

"And you! Stop eating my chips, you genetic mutant. Order your own!"

"Why?" Nemo asked with his mouth full. "You order enough for both of us."

A rubber cat designed like an ice cream cone hit Nemo square in the forehead and bounced down into the near-empty bag of chips. "There's no eating in my office! All the crumbs get in the hardware."

Nemo shrugged and showed the toy to TB. "From Flame?"

TB nodded.

Nemo tossed the toy over his shoulder to Midas, then continued to eat while he turned his attention back to Haskell on the monitor.

Waters sauntered into the office and snatched a chip out of Nemo's bag. "Thanks." He turned to Midas. "Any luck?"

Midas grumbled, "Not since the last time you asked me ten minutes ago."

Waters raised his eyebrows at Midas.

Midas sighed. "I've found plenty on our little cat burglar. As far as her heists? Since she's never been caught, the information is either news articles about what she stole, police reports on how she was able to break in and take what she stole, or sensationalist pieces with some of the craziest theories about her identity that I've ever seen. That Saturn Diamond job was a piece of artwork, let me tell you.

"As for the never-ending search on this Salieri shit we've been on for months? A big fat void, other than what we already knew, that is."

"Looks to me like we'd get better intelligence on all of that through Nemo. I mean, Sawyer," Waters quipped, snatching the entire bag of chips out of Nemo's hands.

Nemo slapped his hand. "Get your own."

Waters smirked. "Yours are here, though."

"You mean mine," Midas grouched.

"Right. Yours," Waters corrected.

Nemo leaned back on the desk to reach into the shipping container for a new bag, which he promptly opened.

Midas let loose an exhaled nonverbal sound of frustration and went back to banging on the keyboard.

Waters looked back at Nemo. "Kitty cat, right? Isn't that what you called her?"

Nemo's eyes never left the monitor. He continued the pattern of reaching into the bag, pulling out a chip, and putting it in his mouth, crunching away. Easiest way to avoid having to answer his team leader.

"Whose kitty?" Steel asked, popping his head into the room around the doorjamb, snatching the bag of NikNaks out of Waters' hands, taking a handful, and then passing the bag to TB.

"Nemo's, I think," Waters answered. "He's riveted."

"Fuck off," Nemo warned around a mouthful of chips. His attention never wavered from Haskell.

Demon was the next to slide into the room. Seeing the bag of chips, he scowled. "Those things are shit for you." The war within him lasted all of two seconds before he snatched the bag from TB and started eating out of it.

All six of the team were gathered around the main telescreen. They formed a half circle—TB, Waters, Demon, Steel, and finally Nemo, still seated on the desk, Midas behind it, watching Haskell sit in the interrogation room. The only sounds were typing and crunching.

Tired of leaning across people, Waters reached over Midas' desk, grabbed another bag, opened it, and Midas roared in frustration this time. "Keep out of my chips!"

Steel rolled his eyes. "Dude, we know you have at least five more shipping containers stashed somewhere. You can spare two bags."

"If it were only two bags, yes, but you all sniff them out and then keep eating them. I'm running out of places to hide things."

"Finding shit is kind of what we do, Midas," Demon reminded him.

"Don't you have a handler to go and handle?" Midas jabbed in return.

Demon glared at him, then reached and got his own bag of chips in retaliation.

When Waters' bag was finally empty, he shook all the crumbs into a corner, then dumped the remainder into his mouth before crumpling up the bag and throwing it in the trash.

TB watched in astonishment. "Jesus Christ. You and Kubrick really are melding into the same person."

"Jealous bastard," Waters teased.

Demon snorted. "Jealous of what? Your gut is going to rot now that Kubrick has tempted you into eating all of that shit she puts in her system. No wonder you're in the gym for two hours every morning. You need to burn off all the feckin' calories."

"That's not why I'm in the gym," Waters teased. "Gotta keep up my energy for after work."

The medic shook his head in disgust, murmuring something about still needing eye bleach.

"Be glad you weren't Midas," Waters murmured with a grin.

"Yeah, I needed more than eye bleach. I also needed ear bleach," Midas complained.

Discarding his half-eaten NikNaks, Nemo pulled a piece of bubble gum from his pocket and began to unwrap it, keeping his eyes on Haskell on the screen. The room was silent. He could feel everyone's eyes on him, but he ignored them. He vigorously chewed his gum, trying hard as hell not to moan at the sugary taste exploding in his mouth. If the team knew that his bubble gum addiction was because of her sweet taste, they would never let it go. He blew a bubble, popped it by exhaling excessive air into it, then sucked it all back into his mouth only to make it crack as he chewed it back into a blob suitable for blowing another bubble. It wouldn't be long before the sugary mess lost its flavor, but he had more in his pocket. Lots more. Some days, it was the only thing that helped him keep focused.

All her fault.

It was another solid ten minutes of bubble blowing, chip crunching, keys clacking, and stoic silence from the four standing men. Finally, Waters turned a full one hundred eighty degrees, arms crossed over his chest, and frowned at Midas. "So, nothing at all on the Salieri?"

Completely focused on his screen, Midas replied, "Nothing. Nada. Zilch. Zip. Zero. It's like Gendry, that lying sack of shark chum, made it up. They do not exist."

TB added to the conversation. "And yet, according to Loki, Gilgamesh, and Medusa, they confirm the Salieri do exist."

A snort came from Steel, the furthest left in the line. "If you call pregnant pauses and shared glances confirmation."

"Well, what would you call that?" TB snapped back. "Sometimes it's what people don't say that's most telling. Sometimes, it's what they physically do that gives everything legitimacy or illegitimacy."

"So sayeth the interrogator," Demon mumbled from his spot between Steel and Waters.

Waters broke up the impending argument. "Well, since the triad goes all see-no-evil, hear-no-evil, speak-no-evil when we try to ask them about the Salieri, we need to go to our next option. I doubt Nemo's little cat burglar has as much compulsion to hold her tongue as they do. If she works with them, she might have information she could give us, so we need to start pressing."

The guys had been so busy talking amongst themselves that they'd been temporarily distracted from the monitor. Nemo had been listening, but his attention had never diverted from the pissed-off pixie on the screen in front of him. He'd been watching her assess the room, looking for exit options. Apparently, she'd found one.

Waters had turned his attention back to the screen by now. "What the fuck?" The man's voice was soft but nonplussed.

Inside, Nemo was howling with laughter. Typical kitty cat. Go high. If her head fit through a space, she'd try to wiggle through it, too. She had dragged a chair over to a far wall, and she was now standing precariously on her tiptoes on the headrest of a wheeled chair, some sort of mini-tool in her hands, unscrewing the grate of an air vent in a room that was allegedly inescapable.

He leaned forward, hands braced on the desk's edge. The grate was hanging by the down, left screw only. Her cute little ass was just wiggling through the air vent on the supposedly impossible-to-remove grate.

It was possibly the hottest thing he'd ever seen.

When her feet slid out of sight, he rolled off the desk and made his way to the whiteboard. On it, he wrote "THIRTY DAYS," underlined it, and then listed each of his teammates' names underneath.

TB frowned. "What the fuck?"

"She's mine. In my bed, permanent. No one else." Nemo stood at the board, arms crossed over his chest, jaw set stubbornly, daring them to challenge him.

The silence in the room had nothing on the proverbial pin drop. Each man in the room was stunned. It was like someone had shot them with an old-style villain's freeze ray.

The most comical of them all was TB. If a person's eyeballs could have exploded out of their head, his would have done it. "Repeat that, please." Once he found his ability to speak.

"Thirty days. She's it. Her, or no one else, ever again."

Steel looked at Nemo, his cold snake eyes assessing the youngest member of the team. "Bet is valid under one condition. It also means no other women, dude. You're cockblocked until she agrees to be yours, even if she never agrees to it."

Nemo confirmed with a nod. "Don't want anyone else."

Demon barked out a single laugh, rounded Midas' desk, and placed his own bet on the line. "SIX YEARS. And I'm being optimistic," he added as he threw the marker back into the whiteboard tray. "Feck, it's payday. First time you set foot outside of the building, you won't last six minutes before you're up some girl's skirt."

"Nemo," Midas cautioned, "this is a bit extreme. You can't back out once we've bet on it."

"Oh, I'm taking this bet." TB grabbed the marker and scrawled his prediction on the board. "WHEN HELL FREEZES OVER."

"Not backing out," Nemo said firmly.

Waters considered Nemo long and hard before he took his turn at the board. "SIXTY DAYS." He looked at Nemo with a shrug. "I've got your back, but I think it's going to be harder than you expect. I'm actually more concerned about you staying faithful. It's not really in your makeup."

Everyone turned their eyes to Steel. The most stoic member of the group was staring at the empty room on the monitor. Then he swept his eyes to Nemo. His expression was blank, but Nemo could tell when the man was thinking long and hard. If anyone would get this bet right, it would be him.

At long last, Steel crossed to the board and wrote down his bet, "NINETEEN DAYS." After throwing the marker in the tray, he clapped Nemo on the shoulder. "You should have more faith in yourself, *amigo*." Then he went back to where he had been originally standing.

Midas looked to Waters. "God going to want in on this?"

"Who the fuck knows," Waters replied. "I don't even know where the man is, let alone when he's going to check in next."

"Maybe Cherry does," Demon suggested.

Nemo's brother changed the subject. "Umm, bro, you better get on with locating your girl. She picks the wrong turn at a junction—she could end up in the furnace."

Do we even have a furnace? This is Los Angeles.

"Nemo, your—"

"Yeah, yeah, I'm on it. Midas? Gonna need your golden fingers and Tribe's blueprints."

"On it."

Nemo looked at Scheherazade and made the signal for "stay." She whimpered but put her head down on the floor and closed her eyes.

After quickly snapping a picture of the board, he put it in a group chat so that no one could change their bet, then dug a plastic case out of his cargo pants. After opening up the case, he pulled his earbuds out and slid one in his ear, pushing it down so it would lodge comfortably in place. Not even diving into a raging ocean swell would cause it to become dislodged now.

SEPTEMBER 9, 2022

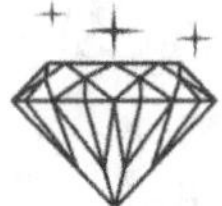

Nemo

Jogging out the door and heading into the hallway, Nemo spoke out loud at normal volume. "Nemo, table for two, and I need a window seat."

"Copy, Nemo. Need just a moment for Nova to scan the cameras and blueprints."

Nemo waited, hands on hips. He wasn't sure if he trusted this new AI program at the same level his brother did, but he did trust his brother.

Midas came over the airwaves. "Okay, here we go. You want to be creative and test the system out, or do you want to go the direct route?"

"We can give her a test run. If we run into a problem, we can always go back to direct."

"All right, bro, here we go. Nova," Midas spoke to his new

program, "guide Nemo through the ventilation system to find the subject known as Haskell."

"Acquiring target," the smooth female voice replied. "Target Haskell acquired. Nemo, access the main elevator. When inside, select the Emergency Stop button. Remove the ceiling panel directly above you and ascend into the shaft. There, you will find an access panel in the ventilation system on the southern wall."

"Whoa. That's creepy." He shook himself. "Copy that."

Nemo jogged to the elevator, which was across from Cherry's desk on the second-floor landing. She was sitting behind her desk, looking like she was hard at work on something on her screen, but Nemo knew her brain was definitely working overtime, just not at whatever was on the screen.

He tapped his ear once, muting his voice from Midas. "You okay, Cherry-girl?"

Cherry startled at his voice, then immediately fell back into her cool and collected state, which was her standard mode. "Yes, thank you, Nemo."

"You know that once they've recovered from the excitement, they're going to be on you about why you were with Haskell at that café and nobody knew about it?"

"Yes. I know. Nemo..." She bit her lip, a look of regret on her face. "Nemo, I would have told you at the very least, but she wouldn't come in unless I promised not to. I honestly don't think it meant she didn't want to see you. I think it was more that she did, if that makes any sense."

"While I certainly don't like the fact that she extracted that promise, don't stress yourself out about it. I'll deal with that problem with her. It's not your fault." He winked saucily at Cherry. "All right. If you're good, then I'm off to stalk a kitty cat."

Her laugh was natural, even if her color was still off. "I think you might have met your match, Nemo. You've heard that herding cats is impossible. Catching them is even more so."

He saluted her, tapped his ear to allow Midas to hear him again, and he punched the button for the elevator doors. They opened, and he disappeared inside.

Following Nova's initial instructions, Nemo found himself facing the ventilation shaft in question. This one was much larger than the shaft he had traversed in Valencia with Haskell. If need be, he'd be able to sit upright inside it.

"Considering the size of the exit she used in the conference room and where I am now, the system must widen and narrow in places," Nemo observed over the comms.

Nova answered his unasked question, "That is correct, Nemo. According to the building specifications, she is actually in a separate system. You are in the maintenance conduit for getting at electric, gas, water, and cable services. She is in the heating and cooling system itself. Unfortunately for her, she's actually heading the wrong way. She went south at the first junction when she should have gone east, which means she is actually burying herself farther into the building. I can direct you to a place where she will eventually work her way to you. Which do you prefer—follow her or wait for her?"

"This is really going to take some getting used to," Nemo mumbled under his breath. "I'll cut off her escape route."

"Very well," the computer voice replied. "Continue to follow the shaft to the south. When you come to the first junction, you will need to proceed upward."

Nemo arrived at the junction in less than a minute. Looking in the upward direction, he swore. "Of course, there couldn't be a ladder."

Nova apologized, "I am sorry for the inconvenience, Nemo. These conduits weren't meant for people to crawl through them except in isolated circumstances."

"Is it my imagination, or is the up shaft smaller?"

"You are correct. It is meant to be an air shaft, not for a human to pass through."

Midas interrupted, "You're going to have to use your broken fin, so start swimming."

"I am sorry, Nemo. Do you need fixing? I can recommend—"

Midas chuckled. "No, Nova. Nemo is able to dislocate his shoulders at will due to an injury at birth. The broken fin is a reference to an animated fish in a Disney movie. The fish has a damaged fin that is smaller than the other fin."

"I understand, Midas. Thank you for the explanation. I will retain this information for future communications."

Nemo rolled his eyes. After muttering a few expletives, he wedged himself into a crouch just below the upward shaft. "Okay, get ready for a big bang," he warned. Hunching his shoulders, Nemo swung his right shoulder as far forward as he could in the small space, then drove it backward hard against the wall behind him. There was a bang and a guttural interjection at the shock, but the action had the desired effect. Nemo's right shoulder was now out of the socket. "You bastards are so lucky that working like this doesn't hurt. Just gonna be sore as hell later."

"No, but I know that taking them out of joint and putting them back in does hurt," Midas mumbled, "so I appreciate the sacrifice. I'll have Cherry get in touch with the masseuse."

Nova interjected, "There are seven licensed massage therapists within one mile. Shall I make you an appointment?"

"Thank you, Nova," Midas replied. "We have one on retainer."

"You are welcome, Midas. If you change your mind, I will store the names and numbers for future reference."

Nemo cracked his neck to the left and then to the right as a way to work through the initial discomfort. "Big bro, she needs some fine-tuning. Next thing you know, she'll be ordering pizza."

"If you are hungry, Nemo, there are four pizza delivery services within four blocks—"

"No, thank you, Nova!" Nemo shook his head. "Gonna have to watch my language with her. She's as bad as that Alexa thing."

Midas chuckled. "Hey, she's beta, little bro. Give her time. She'll figure it out eventually. She's an AI, not human."

"Okay, starting up the shaft."

With only the sheer walls and his own body strength, Nemo wedged himself into the tight space, moving upward in small increments. His muscles burned with the bunching and pressure being placed against the walls as he used pressure and locked muscles to force his way up approximately twenty feet to the next junction.

"I would so kick ass at *American Ninja*," he grunted as he pulled himself into the wider conduit. "Since I can't show my pretty face, I'd wear a costume like that guy who tried to do it as a T-Rex. Or Spider-Man."

Nova popped in, "I would be happy to—"

"No, thank you, Nova!" both brothers called out.

Midas sighed, and there was the sound of a key click over the airwaves. "Definitely need to work on that. Way too eager to help without direct questioning."

BANG! A groan.

Nemo rubbed his shoulder, which was now back in its proper joint. "Don't tell me I have to do that again today. Twice is enough."

"No, little bro, I promise. You're on her level now. Move the way you were going when you first got into the shaft, then turn left. You should cut her off as she dumps out from a pseudo-dead end."

As he began moving into the cutoff position, he asked, "Can she back up or veer off this system?"

"Negative. She probably has one inch on all sides to work with. I gather she's not claustrophobic. Only one way for her to go. Gonna nickname her 'Shawshank,'" Midas joked. "I can only imagine the conversations you, Steel, and she could have."

Nemo had made it fifteen feet forward to a junction that had a grate from the air ventilation system on the far wall. There were paths to the left, right, and back the way he came in the repair shafts. He sat down perpendicular to where she would exit, his back to the wall, knees pulled up toward his chest, elbows on his knees, hands dangling between them, and waited. "Gah. I feel like I'm in that movie *Alien*, and I don't have my gun on me."

"No worries. I'll warn you if the big, scary monsters with acid saliva start moving in your direction."

There was a silence that followed between the two brothers that didn't have its normal ease. Midas was the one to break it. "So... her or no one, huh?"

Nemo listened for any scuffling sounds coming his way. He wasn't sure how far away she was, but it was clear that sound would be magnified and travel well in the shafts. When he spoke, it was barely above a whisper, but he knew the links would pick it up. "She's it. Always has been."

Midas grunted. "I knew you were hung up on her. No one could possibly be as much of a manwhore as you've been otherwise." He paused. "You know I'll help any way I can."

Nemo looked down at his hands. "What about your bet?"

"Not sure if you noticed, but I never placed one. Besides, I always bet on you. You always come first, little brother."

Nemo smiled sadly.

And there's the fuckin' problem right there. He always put me ahead of everyone else, including himself. Legal or not. Right or not. If he knew how much of my past is because of that... But I would do it all again.

"Thanks, Midas, but I'd rather you didn't help me this time around. Muting."

Normally, in these types of situations, as he waited for something to happen, he'd be running scenarios on what to do if things didn't go as intended. Since this was his kitty cat, he knew that no matter what he planned, she would always do the unexpected. She could get into anything and out of anything. He was more concerned about what she would do when she opened the end grate and saw him waiting.

He leaned his head back against the shaft wall and let his mind wander back to when he and his brother were just Sawyer and Kash, not dead men working for Tribe, and the day when a pint-sized pixie changed him forever.

13

JULY 5, 2016 (SIX YEARS AGO)

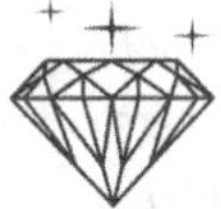

Sawyer

"So, Haskell from Northern England, you gonna let me hang out here for a while after I finish playing doctor with you?"

Kash hissed over the link. "Seriously, bro? That's the line you're going to use?"

Sawyer studiously ignored the voice in his ear that had never turned off. Just because his brother Kash wasn't physically present didn't mean that he was cutting off his lifeline to safety. He just hadn't told Haskell that the man was listening in and using a drone to inform Sawyer when to cut left and dodge right to avoid the Policia Local, who had been much too close several times during their nighttime flight through the forest. After all, he had to use everything in his arsenal to impress her.

His body language may have projected his focus was on her ankle, but Sawyer was incredibly good at focusing on things that he didn't appear to be focusing on. He'd been fooling everyone for a long time.

In this case, he was cataloging Haskell's responses to what he was doing. Her mouth winced once or twice when he touched her foot, but when he slid his fingers up to her ankle? The wince made it to her eyes. And when he brushed the top of the ankle bone? She inhaled. She was trying not to telegraph her pain, but she wasn't fooling him.

"Do I have a choice?" She huffed. "It's not like I could kick you out with this ankle."

"No, probably not," he agreed. Sawyer removed the ice bag and gently ran his fingers over her skin, making sure it was dry. "Okay, before I wrap your ankle, you probably should take off these pants."

She lowered her chin and raised her eyebrows at him.

He mimicked her face. "Will you be able to get these off over a towel-wrapped ankle?"

She sighed in exasperation, her head dropping back against the top of the futon. "No."

She's adorable when she pouts.

He stood up, careful to cradle the injured foot, and set it on the seat of his chair. Once inside the walls of her bedroom, the soft glow of a ceramic lamp lit the bedside table, allowing him just enough light to see the furniture. He went to the dresser and began opening drawers.

The first drawer revealed very utilitarian undergarments. Then he thought about the practicality of the items.

Probably very uncomfortable to crawl through small spaces wearing a string up your ass crack.

"Underwear is overrated anyway," he muttered to himself as he closed the drawer.

"Are you pawing through her panties?" Kash's voice came over his earbuds.

"No, I'm not pawing through them," Sawyer replied.

"Sounds like you are," his brother grumbled.

"Jealous?" Sawyer smiled.

Opening the second drawer, he found a few long-sleeved shirts and leggings, all black.

"Single-minded little kitten, isn't she?"

"What?" Kash asked. "What did you find?"

"Nothing to get excited about. They're clearly her work clothes. All black, totally body-covering, and meant for hiding in the darkness."

He closed the drawer and opened the third one, where he found two pairs of jeans and a couple of tops that would allow her to blend in with the tourists visiting the town during the daytime.

The fourth and final drawer revealed several too-large T-shirts and flannel pajama bottoms.

"A-ha!" he exclaimed softly. "Her bedtime clothes. Not very adventurous, is she?"

"Sawyer, you're killing me," Kash groaned.

"Relax, big bro. She dresses like a teenage boy. Very punk and grunge, actually."

"Does she look like a teenage boy?"

Sawyer snorted. "Fuck, no! Four foot ten, a hundred pounds maybe, and all waifish cuteness. She's got a few tats that I haven't seen up close, and she's pierced. Mop of springy blonde curls that would make Shirley Temple envious, vivid blue eyes. Like a smokin' hot Tinkerbell." He adjusted his growing hard-on.

Kash snorted. "Totally not your type."

Sawyer let the comment pass.

"She doesn't sound impressed by you."

"She's a hissy little kitten. She'll come around," Nemo assured him.

"We don't have time for you to get your dick wet."

"There's always time for that, bro. Besides, I need to lie low for a few hours, so I need something to do."

A quick tap to his earbud muted him from his brother. He needed to be able to hear Kash if things got dicey. However, if things proceeded as Sawyer hoped, there was no need for his brother to hear them. From the second she'd fallen into his arms, and he'd seen those wide, sparkly blue eyes, he knew he'd be trying to get some sexy time in with the little cat burglar. The sass coming out of her mouth only confirmed it.

The girls who were willing to go toe-to-toe with him and refuse to put up with his shit were always the hottest.

He pulled out a Bow Wow Wow T-shirt and a pair of green and black sleep pants. Sliding the drawer closed, he went back out to the main room. "Okay, tiny. Let's get you into something more comfortable."

She rolled her eyes as she took the clothing from him. "I'm totally capable of changing my own clothes."

"Well, get to it then."

Gingerly, she lifted her leg off the chair and brought her foot to the floor, hissing when the dead weight hit her ankle. She unbuckled the belt at her waist and threw it over to the end of the futon. Next, she reached for the waist of her form-fitting pants and stopped. Her eyes bored into his. "Do you mind?"

He grinned at her and winked. "Nope."

"Turn around."

"Tiny, you don't have anything I haven't seen hundreds of times already."

"I bet," she muttered under her breath. "Please?" she asked sarcastically.

"Since you asked so nicely." He turned slowly and showed her his back. Behind him, he heard her struggling to slide the pants over her ass and down her legs while still sitting. With every rustle of her clothing, he imagined her shedding the material. His mouth began to salivate. His little Tinkerbell was going to be fit and tight in all the best ways.

He knew the exact moment the pants were down around her ankles and that they were stuck. She couldn't bend enough to get them off without feeling pain. He almost felt sorry for her. Almost. Was he being a dick?

Yes, but I regret nothing.

He turned his head in profile to her. "Need help?"

"No, I don't need any help. You've helped enough by being the reason I've got a sprained ankle to begin with."

He chuckled. "I didn't trip you. That was the tree root."

He listened to her struggle a few moments longer before he spun around. "Stubborn little pixie." He got down on one knee and gently eased his fingers between her ankle and the pants, guiding them over the rapidly swelling and bruising joint. "There. Your virtue is still intact."

He stopped in his tracks. More saliva spurted into his mouth. His heart stuttered. His eye twitched.

Those legs!

Inside his head, he groaned. He knew it. Hotter than hot. She might be tiny, but Sawyer knew a beautiful set of legs when he saw them. They were toned like a gymnast and made her short form look long-legged, beginning at the bottom of a pair of plain white, but strangely sexy, boy shorts and continuing down to the tiniest feet he'd ever seen—size five by his guess—where they boasted pink sparkly polish on the toes.

Mentally, he gathered himself back together with an internal shake of his head. Grabbing the flannel pajama pants, he shook them out so they unfolded and slid them over her legs to just over the knees. "Lift," he ordered.

Haskell bunched her hands into fists and used them to push herself an inch or so off the futon so that he could slide them over her ass and up to her waist. The action brought him within an inch or so of her mouth.

Their eyes locked.

Fuck! Eyes really can sparkle like sapphires!

He cleared his throat, then reached for the T-shirt as he stood.

Haskell dropped her gaze and began to pull at the sleeves of her long-sleeved black T-shirt.

Sawyer wanted to look away, but the devil on his shoulder wouldn't allow it. Holding the shirt out in front of him, he turned his head as if to give her privacy, but out of his peripheral vision, he watched her change. The plain, simple sports bra she wore was no better on his heart rate than the tiny boy shorts, and he already was *envisioning being able to get those entire small but perfect tits in his mouth.*

Yeah, there was definitely a little time to fuck around.

Once she was settled, he sat back down on the chair he'd vacated earlier, took her leg back into his lap, and reached over and grabbed one of the towels, unfolded it, then refolded it in half horizontally. "This might hurt a little," he warned.

Using one of the towels from the kitchen, he began to wrap her ankle. "You'll need to stay off this for a day or two. Ice it. Keep it elevated."

Haskell was silent as he continued to wrap her up. He heard a hint of guilt when she quietly said, "Thank you for helping me tonight. I interrupted you and kept you from what you were doing. You could have left me stranded tonight. Multiple times. But you didn't." Her eyes searched his face. "Why? You could have been caught."

"Dunno. At first, it was reflex. Someone falls, you try to catch them." He shrugged. "Seemed rude to leave you behind. As for interrupting, I didn't leave completely empty-handed." He knotted the ends of one of the towel strips, holding the larger towel in place to serve as her wrap bandage. "So, what were you doing in the air duct?"

"Practicing," she mumbled. "That museum has some unique physical challenges. I use it as a practice exercise."

Sawyer began to put away all of the items he had been working with. When he returned to her on the futon, he swiped the makeshift ice bag from the floor and scooped her up in his arms. He expected her to squawk and put up a fight, but surprisingly, she merely put her arms around his neck and watched him as intently as he watched her while carrying her.

Inside her room, he set her down on the bed, her back to the headboard. Grabbing the extra pillow, he slid it under her ankle as gently as he could. Then he rounded the bed and threw himself on the other side, lying flat, his hands laced behind his head.

He could feel her stare on him as he lay there in silence. After several minutes, he turned his head to her. "What?"

"You've got balls, I'll give you that."

"How do you figure?"

"You've muscled your way into my apartment, you've taken over first aid on my ankle, and now you've muscled your way into my bedroom."

"And your bed, more specifically"—he winked—"but what's your point?"

"Does this brazen attitude work for you?"

"I don't hear you telling me to go."

She turned her head and looked straight ahead, staring at the wall opposite her. "Would you go if I asked you to leave?"

"Do you want me to go?" he asked.

She glanced at her hands in her lap. "No," she replied.

"What do you want, Haskell?"

The pause between them was heavy. "We shouldn't," she whispered.

He got up on his knees on the bed, then swung a leg over her outstretched ones so that he was straddling her. Careful not to put his weight on her legs, he cupped her face in his hands, tilting it up to look him in the eye. "Oh, we so should."

When she didn't protest, he dipped his mouth to hers. Her response was immediate—a groan and her hands fisted his shirt, her mouth pressing hungrily to his. At first, his lips were a light touch to hers. When her eyelids fluttered closed on a soft moan, her mouth opened to him, and his tongue dipped inside to flick the tip against hers.

She tastes so fucking good! Like the sweetest sugar.

One hand slid through her curls and gripped the back of her skull to keep her in place. The other hand slid down to her shoulder, curled under her arm, and then splayed against her back in an attempt to pull her as tight to him as possible. The delicate contact, the tentative touch of his tongue to hers, and then its retreat, was ramping up his heartbeat. His cock ached as it filled with blood, pressing tightly against his pants, straining to reach her.

He ended the kiss, and she whimpered at the loss of contact. Fore-

head to forehead, their breaths soughing in and out of each other's mouths, their eyes opened to gaze at the other. "Sawyer," she whispered.

"Yes, tiny?"

"I... I've never..."

He felt his heart stop for the briefest of moments, and he sucked in air. "Never?"

She shook her head, her eyes sliding away from him in embarrassment.

He was stunned. He'd never been someone's first, and he wondered if maybe he should stop. However, his mouth moved before his brain finished thinking it through, his voice low and soothing. "Look at me, Haskell."

When she ducked her head to further avoid his gaze, the hand that had been cradling her head palmed it with a tighter grip, tugging her curls at the roots to force her eyes to meet his.

"It's okay," he assured her. "We go only as far as you want, but if I don't get to kiss you again, I might just die of grief."

Her snort and eye roll showed him just how much she didn't believe that. "I'm guessing you'll survive."

He gave a minuscule shake of his head. "Need that sweet taste. You're sugar that melts on my tongue."

He touched his lips to hers again. Dropping his hands from her body was the hardest thing he'd ever done, but he knew he needed to get her out of her head, and the best way to do that was to give her something better to focus on. He backed away for just a moment and grabbed the bottom of his long-sleeved T-shirt from his pants. Reaching behind him, he pulled at the collar and brought it over his head. He dropped it next to them on the bed.

Sawyer heard her sharp intake of breath as she took in his chest and abs. Her pupils dilated, want and need flooding them.

Cool fingertips tentatively traced the ink that covered his chest. It was a mosaic of items. Things that looked like paintings, statues, jewelry, and even money. "You know, it's probably not a good idea to keep track of your thefts on your body. It's a bit like standing under a neon sign that screams 'Burglar Here,'" she teased.

He grinned. "What's life without a little risk?"

The fingers cataloging each separate item slid straight down his abdomen, drawing along the ridges of his defined six-pack of muscles. She followed the center line to the waist of his pants. When his belt stopped her progress, she looked up at him.

"It really is okay, Haskell. We don't have to."

"No," she disagreed. "It isn't. I want you. It makes zero sense. You're a total pain in my ass, but... I've never wanted something so much in my life. I just—Kiss me, Sawyer," she begged.

His hands framed her face again, his thumbs stroking her cheekbones as he moved his mouth expertly over hers. When he came up for air, they both were breathing even harder. "Don't think about anything else. Just enjoy how good it feels."

Her hands slid around his waist, palms spread wide, fingers pressing tight to his back. Her kiss became more self-assured, and her body arched to get closer to his.

Letting go of her and drawing his mouth away from hers, Sawyer slid off to her side. Careful not to jostle her ankle any more than he needed to, he pulled her body so that she was lying down. Resting on the elbow closest to her, he hovered over her prone form. Tracing her perfect eyebrows and down the side of her face, he then ran his index finger across her bottom lip. Slight pressure separated it from its top mate, and he lowered his mouth to hers again.

"Let me love you, Haskell. Let me make you feel good."

Without hesitation, this time, she answered, "Yes, Sawyer."

The words were no more out of her mouth than he had rolled over on top of her, careful to only move the leg with the unwrapped ankle so that he could lie between her legs. Her face was framed between his forearms, his hands free to brush through her hair, his hips weighing heavy just below her core, holding her in place as if he thought she was going to suddenly change her mind and run away.

Looking down into her eyes, which were focused on his own,

Sawyer realized that something was happening here that wasn't normal. At the young age of twenty-five, he'd had a good number of partners already. His naturally given good looks made sure that he attracted a lot of female attention, and Sawyer had never been one to turn away anything freely offered. Looking down at Haskell right now, somehow, everything that was past meant nothing other than it led him to this moment of knowing how to please her. It mattered if this was perfect for her. Before, all he'd worried about was if he felt good and if his partner had an orgasm. But now? It mattered that not only did it feel good but that it was something she'd happily remember.

One last brush of his fingertips through her unruly curls, he held her head in his hands as his mouth lowered to hers. Just as his lips softly pressed against hers, his eyes closed at the sugary taste of her mouth. He hummed in pleasure at the taste. "Your mouth is so sweet. Like you coated it in sugar before kissing me. I love it," he finished on a groan. He swiped his tongue across the lower lip. "Don't get shy on me now. Let me in, pretty baby."

Her mouth hesitantly opened, but once it did, her tongue immediately intertwined with his, and he felt her hands slide around his waist and up his back to pull him closer. Tilting his head to better seam his mouth over hers, his tongue continued long, languid strokes against hers. The sugary goodness on her lips continued inside her mouth, and Sawyer felt himself become instantly addicted to her taste.

With reluctance, he pulled his mouth from hers. A tiny sound of frustration came from Haskell, which he quickly dispelled with a kiss to her chin. Using his nose, he nudged her chin back so that her neck arched, and he left a series of kisses down her throat that straddled the line between a nibble and a nip. When he reached the hollow of her throat, his tongue snuck out between his lips and trailed upward to her chin. She shivered in his arms, and he felt her hips cant up instinctively to grind into his.

"Easy, pretty baby," he soothed. "I'll get there. No rush."

He began to kiss down her throat again, but this time when he reached the hollow of her throat, he sucked lightly at the skin there. Not hard enough to leave a mark, but just enough that she'd feel the skin pull between his lips. Letting go of the skin, he lifted his hips off her body and gently slid farther down between her legs so that his mouth was level with her breasts. He palmed the right one while his mouth searched for her nipple on the left through her T-shirt. She again arched into his touch and lips.

A soft rumble came from the back of her throat. Sawyer chuffed against her skin, his mouth never leaving her body as he spoke. "Are you purring, kitty cat? Wait until I get my mouth and hands on your bare skin there."

"Shut up and put up, burglar boy," she groaned.

"My pleasure," he murmured. His hands reached for the bottom of her T-shirt. "Help me out, tiny." She lifted her hips and arched her back so that he could peel the shirt up and over her body and toss it over the side of the bed. His hands returned to the cotton sports bra remaining between them up top. He slid his fingers beneath the band, pushed it gently over her small breasts, then guided the material up and off her body. The bra dropped on top of her shirt. His fingers traced the ink on her bicep that he'd only gotten a glimpse of earlier when she'd changed her shirt. Four male images peered out of a tree, one at the top, the other three equidistant from each other on lower branches.

Her family tree, he guessed. He didn't have much time to think about it because Haskell dragged her hands across his back, her nails scratching across his skin, making all thoughts disappear. "Fuck, yeah. Give me those claws, little kitty cat. I wanna feel them scraping my back, digging into my shoulders."

Immediately, her arms moved up his shoulder blades and curled over his shoulders, her short nails carving crescent shape indentations into his skin. Her head raised off the pillow, her mouth pressing urgently to his, sliding her tongue between his lips and seeking out the depths of the cavern. He gladly met each stroke of her tongue, allowing her to control the kiss and following her lead.

His hands slid inside the waist of her flannel pajama pants, spanning her waist and hips, his thumbs caressing the skin just above the band. Halting their kisses momentarily, he urged, "Lift up again, pretty baby." As her hips raised off the bed, his mouth went back to hers. However, his thumbs hooked the waistband and dragged them down past her ass and down her legs. Pulling his mouth from hers again, then kneeling between her parted legs, he eased the pants over her ankles and feet, trying not to disrupt her injury any more than necessary.

Bending at the waist, he brushed his lips against her stomach, then dragged his tongue across a tattoo of a comet that streaked across her belly. When he reached its fiery tail, he went straight down to trace her belly button. He swirled his tongue around it, tickling her. Her giggle was unexpected, as were the hands gently trying to push him away from the sensitive skin. "Ticklish much?" he teased. He darted his tongue out to circle around it again.

"Don't! Stop!" she pushed out on a giggle again.

"Don't stop? Okay." He grinned as he purposely misunderstood her instruction, circling the skin one more time.

"Ahhhhhh!" she shrieked, laughter escaping.

I want to do that again sometime.

His brain stuttered for just a moment over the idea of doing this with her in the future. Sawyer had never fucked the same girl twice. Well... maybe multiple times in a single session, but never repeated after one encounter... But then her fingers were spearing his short hair, gripping it tightly, and working to pull his mouth up and away from her torso. When his laughing eyes met her sparkling ones, he promptly forgot what he'd just been thinking about.

He let his teasing smile turn naughty, and he got caught in her stare as he watched her fun-loving smile slowly fade and turn hungry. Index finger trailing lightly from the spot between her legs, he followed a path straight up the middle of the gusset of her panties and scraped a blunt nail in a circle over where her clit lay hidden. She shivered. Her lips parted, the small pink tip of her tongue unconsciously swiping between them.

He slid back down onto his stomach, hands sliding underneath her, lifting her ass off the bed, his mouth hovering over her panty-covered mound. Without looking away, he lowered his head to swipe his tongue along the same path his finger had just traversed. The tiny mewl and buck of her hips spurred him on. Her taste exploded on his tongue, even through the material. "If I take these off, tiny, you're mine tonight."

He saw a quick flash of panic in her gaze, but then it was replaced with her eyes fluttering closed, a moan, and a roll of her hips. Then she tensed. "I'm going to regret this, but don't stop."

14

JULY 5, 2016 (CONTINUED)

Sawyer

He frowned, set her hips back down on the bed, and kneeled between her legs again. "Hey. Look at me." When her eyes remained closed, he lowered himself on top of her so that his forearms framed her head, brushing his fingertips over the features of her face, intermittently dropping a barely there kiss on her eyebrow piercing, her nose piercing, the corner of her mouth, never touching the same spot twice. "I'm not doing anything until you look at me, Haskell."

With a huff, she opened her eyes to gaze up into his face.

"There she is," he said with a smile. Watching her as he did it, he pressed a lingering kiss to her lips. "I'm not going to do this if you're going to regret it."

"Why? It clearly didn't take much to get me to agree to it. Apparently, my body has decided to secede from my head in terms of doing the smart thing."

He chuckled. "It's not like you're separating from the European

Union." His smile faded as he watched her with honesty. "I want you, tiny, but not if you're going to regret it."

"It's not like you're going to be here to clean up the aftermath, Sawyer. We both know you'll be gone in a couple of hours. This is just a fun way to pass a few hours to avoid the Policia Local."

He rolled over to the side of her that was uninjured. Sliding one hand from her knee to behind her thigh, he gripped her leg and pulled it over his. "Gotta keep that ankle elevated still." He winked at her. "You're not wrong, tiny. I do have to go soon, but I don't want to leave knowing you didn't like it or if doing this is going to make you miserable. I'd rather just make out like horny teenagers and get us off with my hands than know I left you feeling sorry you said yes."

She rolled her eyes and turned her head to look at the lamp on the bedside table.

"No, Haskell, don't do that." His hand reached to gently turn her face back to his. "I'm serious. It should be a good memory. Not a bad one."

"I'm sure it'll be a great memory, Sawyer," she agreed.

"Then what's the real issue?"

She shrugged. "I honestly don't know. I definitely want to do this, but I also know that women have a tendency to be stupid about this stuff. Which is why I said I was probably going to regret it, even though I was planning to do it anyway. Having no previous experience means I have no idea what I'll do and feel. It's just a guess."

Sawyer lay back against the bed, laughing.

He could see the irritation on her face when he looked up at her. "You're the cutest grouch I've ever seen." He leaned up and kissed her nose. "Are you always this practical?"

"Maybe," she mumbled. "It takes me a long time to process things."

He rolled them both back over, notching his hips into the vee of her thighs, his hands caressing every inch of her he could reach. "I promise, Haskell. It will be wonderful. You'll feel great, and maybe you'll miss me for a day or two, but it's not going to destroy your world. You don't strike me as the devastation-driven type." His fingers stilled at the waistband of her panties. Eyes locked, he whispered, "'Yes,' and we rock each other's worlds. 'No,' and we just cause it to tilt a bit."

Eyes flicking back and forth between his, he watched as Haskell sucked in her cheeks, lips pursed, and then she blew out the breath she'd been holding.

"Yes."

The moment the word began, his hands were pulling down her panties, sliding them down her legs and over her ankles, and then he was lapping at her between her legs to get her wet and ready for him. While he continued to drive her to the edge, he rustled around in his pockets, removing a condom from one of the buttoned pockets. He broke away from her after throwing it on the bed next to him, and he unbuttoned and unzipped his pants, shucking them off, only for them to get hung up on his shoes.

Sawyer kneeled above her, pulling each one from his feet, dropping them over the side of the bed, then removed his pants the rest of the way and added them to the growing pile. He reached for her hand and brought it to his hard cock. Keeping his hand on top of hers, he showed her how much pressure, showed her how to give it that final twist up at the top that not only allowed her to spread his precum and smooth the way but also make him shudder. Once she had it down, he grabbed the condom packet and tore the package open, dropping the foil at his side. Brushing her hand aside for a moment, he sheathed the latex over his cock.

He lowered himself back over Haskell, his heated skin pressing against her cool limbs. "Cold, pretty baby?" he asked, gathering her tightly to him.

She shook her head. "Not now," she admitted.

He smiled, then he kissed her. She was tense still, although not nearly as bad as she had been. Being nervous was normal, he supposed, but sex was fun. Nothing felt better. She'd understand afterward, he was sure. There was nothing to possibly regret except that maybe she'd waited this long.

His kisses trailed down the side of her face to her throat. Notching himself at her opening, he whispered, "Let me in, Haskell."

Without hesitation, she hitched her injured leg over his hip, opening her core to him. Sawyer began to push inside in a series of shallow thrusts. She was tight. Tighter than he was used to. Well, she was a tiny girl, so he supposed that shouldn't be surprising. She was wet, but he was going to need a little bit of assistance there.

He slid down so that his mouth was once more even with her mound. When she began to shift with unease, he put one hand on her abdomen and looked up at her. "Easy, tiny. You're such a little thing. Just making the way easier."

His tongue took a long swipe from bottom to top. Then a second. Then a third, with the tip swirling around her clit like he had with her belly button earlier. It was such a contrast to the sweetness of her mouth. Tart. Spicy. Using his fingers to separate her outer lips, he stiffened his tongue to form a point and delved into her channel, using it like he would his cock in a few minutes.

He heard her moans and sighs growing, and they quickly became as addicting as her sugary mouth and her spicy pussy. He slid two fingers inside her channel to replace his tongue, which made its way back up to flick furiously at her clit, dragging his saliva and her arousal on its way. Had he not been holding her down with one hand already, she would have shot off the bed like a rocket. Her entire body tensed and shook, his fingers feeling as if her insides were trying to strangle them as she locked down and came. With the lockdown also came an easing of the passage as it flooded itself with her arousal.

As she came down from her orgasm, Sawyer moved back into position, slipping his cock inside her instead of his fingers. Now he moved smoothly up until he hit her barrier. Tilting his head up to see her face, he felt an inordinate need to see her eyes. "Open your eyes, sugar cat. Need you to look at me."

It took a moment for Haskell to open her eyes. Something gripped inside his chest like it was tightening the space around his lungs. He could still breathe, but he felt frozen as their eyes met. He'd never felt anything like it before in his life. Unsure what it was, he searched her eyes. Was he simply sensing she was about to change her mind, and he needed to stop? That would suck.

"Haskell? Yes or no?"

She nodded.

"Need you to say it, pretty baby." He had no idea why it was so important to hear the words. She'd said yes several times.

Her eyes were soft and slumber-filled. Her body was loose and ready for him. "Yes, Sawyer. I'm yours."

"Okay. Hang on, tiny."

He couldn't seem to tear his gaze from hers as he pushed forward experimentally a few times, finding that slow and steady wasn't going to do it. He retreated until just the tip of his cock was inside her opening. He pressed a gentle kiss to her forehead, another to the tip of her nose, and a third to her lips. Then, eyes locked again, he thrust hard and fast, tearing through her hymen. He saw her eyes go wide and heard the gasp when he broke through the barrier, and he froze once he was fully seated inside her. Part of him agonized over the look on her face. It had hurt, and the idea of hurting her, in turn, hurt him.

Her fingers clutched his shoulders. He couldn't tell if she was pushing him away, trying to pull him closer, or digging through his skin for purchase. A tiny little mewl and the pinched look of her features told him it was probably a mixture of all three.

"Breathe, Haskell. I'm here, pretty baby. Not going anywhere. Just breathe through it." He stayed still inside her, feeling her walls pulse as they adjusted to his invasion. Without a conscious thought, he began to kiss her again, feeling that if he could suck the pain out of her and take it into him, he'd do it in a second.

After a few minutes, he felt her relax; her grip loosened and turned to soft caresses again. "You okay?" he whispered.

She nodded. "Yes. Move, please. I..." She seemed to rotate her hips slightly.

He smiled. "Got ya covered." He watched her face as he began a series of retreats and thrusts, taking note of how her body moved beneath his. He wondered if she realized she gasped every time he scraped the topside of her entrance. Experimenting with moving faster yet still keeping the drag on the top of her walls, he felt her begin to tighten, and her gasps became louder moans. "That's it, sugar cat. Meet me. Chase it."

His whispers sent her flying over the edge, both of her thighs gripping his hips so tight he felt like he knew how a bronco felt being ridden bareback. Watching her work through the orgasm was the sexiest thing he'd ever seen. "Fuck, pretty baby. Squeeze me tight. That's fuckin' hot." He grunted, and suddenly, his cum was releasing into the condom without warning. "Jesus Christ. What the hell?" He continued to pump them both through the aftershocks, his gaze never leaving the sight in front of him—a truly blissed-out Haskell.

Once the tremors were over, he was still hard. He thrust twice more for good measure, watching as her features relaxed and her breathing evened out. With care, he slid from her and from the bed to get rid of the condom. As he cleaned up in her bathroom, he felt an ache in his chest. His hand rubbed at the spot. Was something wrong with him? Had he pulled something during the job tonight? Maybe from carrying her so long? The adrenaline must have covered up him pulling a muscle.

Unconsciously, he reached for a washcloth, ran it under warm water, and took it with him back into the bedroom. Haskell was passed out in the soft light of the bedside lamp. He sat beside her on the bed. Feeling a little awkward but also like he needed to, Sawyer gently smoothed the washcloth along the inside of Haskell's thighs. Even though he'd worn a condom, he figured there would be a combination of her fluids and a little bit of blood. Or so he'd heard. Having never been with a virgin, he wasn't really sure. When he pulled the cloth away from her skin, he saw the tinge of pink on the material.

He felt another pull in his chest.

Ouch. That stings. Better do something about that later.

He took the cloth into the bathroom. As he ran it through cold water and scrubbed at the remnants of blood left behind to make sure it didn't stain, his face drew up into a frown. Sex with Haskell had been great. He felt weird, though. Like there was supposed to be something else. But they'd both had an orgasm, so he wasn't sure what would be missing.

When he walked into the bedroom, he picked his pants up off the floor and was about to step into them when he stopped. Haskell had rolled onto her stomach in her sleep, the pillow meant to be under her ankle kicked to the floor. Her pale skin glowed softly in the warm light of the lamp. She had the ghost of a smile in the upturn of her mouth, and the anxious look he'd become accustomed to seeing with her pinched mouth—cute as it was—no longer lingered there. In sleep, she was just as stunning.

Without thinking about it, he dropped his pants where he stood, circled the bed to the other side, and crawled in next to her, pulling the sheet and quilt up over them both. Lying up tight to her side, he placed a hand on her back, lightly brushing his fingertips up and down the tattoo of a spill of diamonds down the vertebrae. He just barely resisted the urge to kiss each one. "Sleep well, pretty baby," he whispered. He kissed the back of her head, lay his head on the pillow, and closed his eyes. A short rest would be okay. He had time.

IF ANYONE ASKED HIM, he couldn't say what woke him. It clearly wasn't her leaving the bed because her side was cold to the touch when he opened his eyes. Sun was streaming through the sheer curtains that were blowing lightly in the breeze from where the pane was cracked open. Blearily sitting up, the sheet pooling around his waist, he glanced around the room.

His clothes were folded neatly at the end of the bed, the bathroom door across the hall was wide open, and the only sounds were the muffled noise of the sea birds and the muted waves landing on the beach.

Sawyer threw his legs over the edge of the bed, stretched, and began to dress. A quick check of the internal pocket of his pants showed that the gems he'd stolen the night before were still there. She hadn't taken anything.

He frowned as he finished dressing. The pang in his chest was still there. Possibly even a little worse. A rest should have eased the muscle. He rubbed on the spot giving him trouble, but it brought no relief. Even stretching by rotating his shoulder didn't have any effect. It was as if the pain was further inside.

Glancing around, he noticed that something didn't seem right. Surveying the room, he tried to figure out what was out of place.

Her backpack. Last night, it had been on the floor next to the dresser.

He got up and crossed to the drawers. He opened the top one. Empty. The second and third drawers were also empty. He crossed to the closet and opened it. Empty. He ducked through the bedroom door to the bathroom, and the drawers there were empty as well.

She did a flit. What the fuck?

In a bit of a fog, he crossed back into the bedroom and stood just inside the doorway, his hands on his hips.

A quick search of the apartment confirmed that she had completely cleared out and left no note. Not even a "Thanks for the good time." Just gone. His hand reached up to his chest, rubbing against the pang that intensified. He had a sneaking suspicion it had nothing to do with a muscle pull.

SEPTEMBER 9, 2022

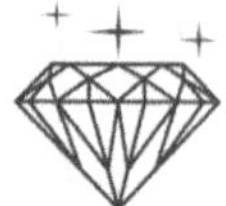

Haskell

Some days, it just didn't pay to get out of bed. She'd been crawling for approximately forty-five minutes in the pitch dark, and if she never saw another air vent again, it would be too soon. When her current contract expired, it might be time for a new line of work. Something that only required regulation doors and windows.

Stupid Sawyer. Stupid Sawyer with his stupid gorgeous blond hair, stupid gorgeous blue eyes, stupid gorgeous mouth, stupid gorgeous fit body, and stupid gorgeous little-boy charm. Then he went and got all those stupid gorgeous tattoos, stupid gorgeous piercings—especially the extra stupid gorgeous one through his cock that sent her into orbit. And now he had a stupid gorgeous dog.

Stupid girl for falling in love with him at first sight.

Stupid, stupid, stupid.

Finally, there was light at the end of the tunnel. Literally. She blamed her lack of situational awareness on sensory deprivation. It was the only reason she had for blindly pushing her way through the grate at the end of the tunnel without looking. Her handy-dandy screwdriver had her through that portal in less than twenty seconds, slithering out into the maintenance shaft, basically dumping herself into Sawyer's lap.

She sighed. "Fuck my life."

"Almost made it," he congratulated her.

She hung her head in defeat. Why? Why couldn't she catch a break?

"Sisyphus," she muttered.

"Pardon?"

"I said," she spoke up loudly, "Sisyphus."

"The guy with the boulder?"

She looked up at Nemo, her eyes wide. He knew who Sisyphus was?

"Y-y-yes?"

"Why are you saying the name of a guy with a boulder that won't stay put?"

"I'm thinking I should legally change my name to Sisyphus because every time I try to do something, it undoes itself, and then I have to start over."

He frowned. "Then stop trying to escape."

"I don't want to stay here, Nemo."

"Why?"

"Why?"

"Yeah. Why? Why don't you want to stay here?"

"Because."

"Because...?"

"Because!"

Nemo rolled his eyes. "Kitty cat, that is not an answer."

She pointed her finger at him. "That! Right there! That's why I need to leave!"

"I'm sorry... I know I'm not stupid, but I'm not connecting the dots here. What 'that' are you referring to?"

She twirled her pointed finger at him. "The stupid cute names for me. And the stupid logic. And your stupid charm and stupid niceness and stupid... everything!"

He raised an eyebrow at her. "I'm really not tracking."

Lying on her stomach in the shaft, she refused to look up. Instead, she just stayed there with her forehead on the cool metal surface and prayed to be swallowed into the first circle of hell.

"Thieves belong in the eighth circle, pretty baby."

She turned her head to look at him, sitting there all nonchalant as if he didn't have a care in the world and nowhere else better to be. "How the hell did you know what I was thinking or even know that information?"

He snorted. "You said it under your breath. These shafts amplify everything. As for the other question, I'm a thief, not illiterate, no matter what my teachers said." He kept his glance at the wall. "My feelings are a little bit hurt. I went to all that trouble to save one of your nine lives, and you took off *again*. That's three times, now, that you've done a flit on me."

She rolled over onto her back, unable to suppress a groan at the aches and pains she had now added to the ones she'd already been dealing with.

"Sore?" he asked.

"You could say that. It's been a rough six weeks."

"They called us to help look for you."

"Mmm."

"Your friends have been worried about you."

"Mmm."

"I've been worried sick about you."

She refused to respond to that comment. Couldn't respond to it, or she'd give in entirely to the stupidness that was titled "Nemo and Haskell."

"Where have you been the last six weeks?"

"More like, where haven't I been? Stumbled into an illegal diamond mine, and the fucking Kader family, joy oh joy. That meant almost forty-two days of schlepping my ass by foot, camel, back of a goat truck, leaking boat, and whatever else I could find out of Zimbabwe, into Tanzania, and finally into Jomo Kenyatta International Airport." She slipped a hand between her lower back and the floor, absently rubbing at the soreness there. "Little piece of advice. Avoid the camels if you're ever given the opportunity. Blow up the goat trucks because goat piss does *not* come out of leather. And definitely fly first class on Qatar Airlines whenever possible."

"Why did you come to Los Angeles?"

"It wasn't my first choice. More like a Hail Mary pass at survival. When I got in touch with my employers, by the time they could have gotten to me to help, I basically would have been to Nairobi anyway. One of them managed to direct me to a drop box that had some money and supplies. I had to get out of Africa, so I used my 'get out of jail free' card and called Cherry as my last resort."

"How do you know Cherry?"

"It's a long story."

"I've got nothing but time."

Haskell debated what to tell him. "Short version is that shortly after you and I met in Valencia, she found me and offered me a job. I said no. Next day she found me again and gave me her card. Said if I ever changed my mind, call her."

"You didn't exactly call her about a job. How did you know she could help you?"

"I'm guessing the conditions for even knowing what the job was were the same for you as they were for me. Open the folder, you were committed. Change your mind after that, you disappear. Correct?"

Nemo nodded. "Essentially."

"People who make those kinds of offers are people who have connections. Options. I was betting on the fact that she could help me."

Another noncommittal grunt. Suddenly, he asked, "Why did you take off?"

She barely registered the whiplash of the change in conversation. "What?"

"Why did you leave?"

Her thoughts raced. "Which time?"

"I didn't specify, did I? Let's just worry about today for right now."

Clearly, they would be returning to times one and two at a later date.

"I panicked?"

"You're not sure?"

"I panicked," she answered firmly.

"About what?" He seemed genuinely confused by her response.

She didn't have an answer for that since she couldn't tell him the real reason, so she just lay there staring at the ceiling of the shaft.

He sighed.

She waited. When he didn't say anything or make any move to get out of the shaft, she turned her head to look at him. "Why are you here?"

"Why are any of us here?"

She huffed and crossed her arms over her chest. "You know what I mean. Christ, four years later, and you're still a total cunt."

He ignored the insult. "I'm here because you're here."

She turned her head toward him again, her eyes wide at his response. He wasn't looking at her. Instead, his head was tipped back against the wall, his eyes still on the wall across from him.

"C'mon, kitty cat. Let's get out of here." He tapped his ear. "Midas, can you bring the elevator up to our level?" He gestured down the main path. "After you. This will empty out onto the top of the elevator, and then you can drop down into it."

Rolling onto her stomach and getting onto her hands and knees, she began to crawl in the direction he indicated.

16

SEPTEMBER 9, 2022

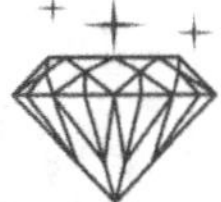

Nemo

"I think this is a classic case of misdirection," Midas said.

Midas sat at a computer directly in front of the observation room window, Scheherazade at his side, her front paws on the window frame. Her attention was riveted on Haskell, who was back in the conference room and curled up in one of the high-backed chairs at the table, doodling on a notepad she'd found. Nemo was in the middle of the line of men standing in a semicircle directly behind Midas.

"I agree with Midas," Steel said. "Cerberus is known for hitting hard targets for whatever cause he's pushing at the time. He has no history of endangering civilians when he strikes. He has no history of targeting people, period. Doing so now is out of character."

"It's been my experience that bombers have little conscience when it comes to innocent lives standing in the way of their causes," TB snarled.

His parents had been killed in the Dizengoff bus bombing in 1994 when he was seven years old. After years of abuse and neglect in an orphanage, years of being ostracized in the army for his interrogation and torture skills, and then years of self-imposed isolation due to his work on the dark web as a hired procurer, he was still a grumpy bastard. Thirty years later, TB was still bitter. Even meeting, falling in love with, and committing himself to a romance novelist hadn't quite softened him.

"Haskell is a jewel thief," Steel pointed out. "What purpose would an ecoterrorist have in blowing up a jewel thief?"

Waters' left side was leaned up against the frame of the window. His thumb and first two fingers of his right hand were pulling on his lip, a sure sign he was working through information. "We've got a device that matches Cerberus' signature down to the etching of the three-headed dog. We've got a target—a popular café over its maximum capacity in the middle of Los Angeles—which is not his usual M.O. Is it possible he's changing his game?"

Midas argued, "Bombers do practice and build their skills, but not this late in their development. By this time, he's perfected his trade. However, his motivation has always been the environment. It would take a catalyst of epic proportions to trigger him to suddenly change his methods and targets. Today's bomber is a copycat."

TB grunted. "I don't trust him, no matter what your profiles say."

Waters frowned. "Still, this feels not only purposeful but personal somehow."

Nemo looked over his shoulder at his twin. "Midas? When was the last time Cerberus was active?"

Midas clicked a few keys on his laptop. "Nova, what is the last record of activity surrounding the ecoterrorist, Cerberus?"

The polished female voice piped through the computer's speakers. "Hello, Midas. The last record of Cerberus' activity is from June twenty-second, 2021. Cerberus was given credit for damaging an oil rig in Bahamian waters. He was believed to be working with the environmentalist group SafeSeas to stop drilling in that area as they believed the rig's production was poisoning the coral reefs."

Waters stared at Midas for a moment before speaking. "I didn't realize you were so far with the program. It almost sounds human."

Midas smiled. "Needs a few tweaks yet, but *she's* coming along. Go ahead." He gestured to the computer screen and sat back in his chair, a smug smile on his face, preening like a proud new father. "Ask her what you want to know."

Waters asked, "What's its name again?"

The voice answered for itself, "Good afternoon, team leader. I am called Nova."

Waters froze in surprise at the direct address, then proceeded to shake his head as if to clear it. "Nova, how did Cerberus attack the rig?"

"I am happy to supply the information you requested, Waters. Cerberus attacked the rig using a yacht, which he programmed to function similarly to a drone. Using a home video game apparatus and the rig's own WiFi system, he deployed the craft and directed it to crash into one of the support struts beneath the rig. The blast was a low-yield explosive, meant to stop production, but not destroy the rig altogether or create pollution to an already damaged area."

Everyone stared at the computer.

Someone whistled.

Midas beamed. "Right now, she only recognizes Waters, Nemo, and me. I haven't finished uploading the voice samples into the system. When that's done, she'll recognize all of you, Cherry, God, Kubrick, and Flame as well."

Demon shook his head. "That's kind of creepy."

"Kind of?" TB echoed.

Waters pushed forward with his questioning. "Nova, were there any casualties?"

The computer responded, "Three rig employees were treated for second-degree burns they received when attempting to extinguish the flames from the explosion. There were no fatalities."

"And what is the current status of the rig and its operations?"

"With the attack on the rig, SafeSeas achieved their goal, which was to shut down drilling. However, it is only a temporary work stoppage. At this time, the only individuals on the rig are a skeleton crew working to complete repairs before the oil company can resume drilling. Current estimates put oil production recommencing in March of 2023."

"Steel and Midas are right," Nemo declared. "There's no way Cerberus is responsible for today. What cause would motivate him to hit a Rodeo Drive coffee shop in its peak hours of operation? Protesting the use of whole milk?"

There was a chuckle around the room.

Waters glanced at Nemo. "We need her to start talking."

TB asked Nemo, "What has she been doing in there by herself since you recaptured her?"

Nemo scowled. "I didn't 'recapture' her. She was never a prisoner."

TB rolled his eyes. "Let me rephrase. What has she been doing in there by herself since you brought her back to the gilded cage of the conference room?"

Nemo decided to ignore TB's taunt. "Nothing." He shrugged. "Drawing."

"Drawing?"

"Drawing."

"Drawing..."

"Yes, Turd Blossom, drawing."

"Drawing what?" TB ground out.

"She's drawn a lot of different things. Five plus pages of junk, near as I can tell. Cartoon cats. Diamonds. Air vents. Batman clouds, coffee cups—"

"Batman clouds? What the hell are Batman clouds?" TB interrupted.

"Those stupid things on the television show with the words inside them." There was silence in the room. "Christ, even we had that in Johannesburg. Please don't tell me you people have never watched *Batman*. You know... Zip! Bam! Boom! Kapow!"

"I get it, I get it," TB admitted.

"The most recent page looks like some sort of shape arrangement. I can't tell."

Exasperated, Waters pushed for an answer. "Nemo, we don't have time to analyze her artwork like a Rorschach inkblot."

Without waiting for an order, Nemo left the viewing room and walked next door to the conference room with everyone in his wake. As soon as the door opened, Scheherazade trotted over to Haskell and put her head in the girl's lap. When he reached her side, he placed a hand on her shoulder. "Tiny?" His voice was soft. "I need you to start talking."

She nodded. "Cherry should be here, too, I think."

Nemo looked up as the men filed into the room. "Demon, we need Cherry."

The medic turned on his heel and went to collect their handler. Since Haskell had selected what was normally Nemo's seat, he simply stood at her side. By the time Demon returned with Cherry, the men had all taken their usual seats, leaving her no choice but the empty seat to his right.

Waters reached for the starfish controller and depressed the red button. Instantly, the windows tinted so that they were impenetrable to light, sound, or view. The monitors changed screens to show an alarmed map of the building, with the lighting in the room moving from white to red. A deafening thunk signaled the doors had gone into lockdown mode. "Haskell, I think you better walk us through this from the beginning. You clearly know things we don't, and I, for one, am tired of being in the dark."

Haskell shared a glance with Cherry before looking around the table.

"I'm not sure what Nemo's already told you about how we met."

Nemo assured her, "Midas is the only one who knows any details, and he only knows what he overheard on the headset. Most of our time together, I could hear him if needed, but we were muted from him."

Relief passed quickly over her features. With a comforting caress to Scheherazade's head, Haskell uncurled from the confines of the high-backed chair and sat up straight. "Right. I first met Nemo in 2016 when both of us broke into the same museum in Valencia. When I unexpectedly crashed through an air duct, we were forced to improvise our exit together."

Haskell looked down the table at the handler, who nodded at her in encouragement.

"A few months later, Cherry found me in Paris. She extended me a folder with a job offer, informing me that if I opened the folder and then changed my mind, I would disappear. I had serious obligations at home, so I declined to open the offer, and we parted ways. The next day, she found me again, only this time, she gave me her number. Said if I changed my mind, I should call her.

"In October of 2018, just a few months after Nemo and I ran into each other again in Riquewihr, my personal circumstances changed. I felt that I needed out of England. That was when I found myself working for an underground group called Mythos, whose focus was on rescuing victims of sex trafficking."

"How does that work for a jewel thief?" TB asked.

"My breaking and entering skills were helpful in collecting reconnaissance on locations where victims were kept. Sometimes, if it was just one or two individuals, I would lead them to safety. Larger groups were handled by Loki, Gilgamesh, and Medusa.

"Six weeks ago, Mythos sent me to Zimbabwe to investigate a rumor about an uptick in diamonds coming from the fields around the Mzingwane Mine. I managed to get inside, but unfortunately, I was made within a couple of hours. I saw something completely unexpected, and I wasn't as careful as I should have been. In order to escape, I needed a quick exit, but Mythos was halfway across the globe and couldn't get to me in time to help. My only option was to call Cherry.

"It took some time, but with her exit contacts, I was able to work my way to Nairobi and catch a flight to Los Angeles. When I arrived, Cherry picked me up from the airport."

"And Cerberus?" Even Nemo heard the edge in his voice.

"He contracts for Mythos on occasion when they need... distractions of a loud and destructive type." Her gaze went down to her pad of paper and the drawing there. "Obviously, this bomb placement was deliberate. A pressure plate underneath a chair means it's supposed to be triggered by a person. It just wasn't meant for *me* to trigger it."

"How do you know that?" Nemo asked.

"When I was listening in on the earbud at the café, you guys were talking about the stamp on the bomb belonging to Cerberus. That's impossible."

Nemo observed her face as it heated up under his scrutiny. "And you know this because...?"

He watched her eyes shy away from his. "I've known him almost as long as I've known you."

Oh, hell no!

Nemo's entire body went still. He had never experienced jealousy before, but he was pretty sure the red-hot heat coursing through his body qualified. "You *know* him. How, exactly, do you *know* him?"

"We work together for Mythos."

He clenched his teeth. To try and school his features and verbal responses, he looked at the shapes she'd drawn on the paper in front of her.

While he wanted to rage at her for her relationship with Cerberus, he knew it was irrational to do so. She had only said they worked together. No matter how much his brain wanted to translate that into a relationship, he knew it was a ridiculous jump in logic. He also knew he had no right to be jealous. It wasn't as if he'd been celibate after being with Haskell, and it would be hypocritical to be angry with her for being involved with anyone else, no matter how much that thought hurt him.

In a sudden moment of clarity, the arrangement on the page made sense to him. "This is the layout of the café," he concluded. "The shapes are the tables and chairs. The letters are people?"

Midas used his camera to take a photo of her drawing, then uploaded it to his laptop and projected it on the telescreen. Haskell talked them through the moments from that morning. "We stopped to get something to eat, but when we arrived, the café was overcrowded. There was a long line, so I decided to go outside and watch for a table to open.

"About twenty minutes later, Cherry brought out our tray. She stopped for a moment to talk to the owner. That was when a man in a brown suit got up from his seat and offered it to me. He even politely pushed in my chair. His companion, a man in a black suit, was standing between the other chair and the table, packing up a briefcase. I thought he pushed in his chair, but that must have been when he set the pressure plate. They walked away, and shortly after that, a breeze blew through and stole the extra napkins I had brought and placed on the table, so I got up and chased them down."

Demon's voice broke through. "How did you end up in the other seat?"

"I was at least five meters away chasing down the napkins. By that time, Cherry had finished her conversation, and when she came over to the table, she sat where I had been. Both chairs were open, and naturally, she chose the one closest to her, so I sat down in the other one."

She sighed. "I'll admit, I piss people off all the time when I strike, but not enough to blow me into a million pieces."

TB grunted. "Individual threats are taken out through executions and assassinations. Bombs are for making statements. Jewel thieves don't inspire that sort of violence."

"Exactly," Haskell agreed. "So as well as knowing that Cerberus was not behind this particular bomb, there's only one group of people that I can think of that would go to such extreme lengths to remove a single person in such spectacular fashion. Not only are they willing to do it, but it's typical for them to copy other criminals' signatures in order to divert suspicion."

"And who would that be?" Waters asked.

Again, Nemo watched Haskell flash a look at Cherry.

"She's referring to the Salieri." The voice was Cherry's.

All the men stared at her in shock. TB's other half had been stalked and taken by a man from her past, a drug dealer named Gendry. His intent had been to traffic her in revenge for her running away from him years earlier. When TB and Midas had tag-teamed his interrogation, Gendry had given up the name "Salieri" just before TB ended his miserable life.

Waters fixed their handler with a stern look. "What have you been hiding, Cherry?"

She blew out a breath before answering. "The Salieri make sense as our bombers if the bomb was meant for me."

17

SEPTEMBER 9, 2022

Haskell

The room was so silent that Haskell swore she could hear her eyelashes batting.

Cherry explained her reasoning, "The man in the brown suit got up because you were headed to the table first. Had I been first, his companion in the black suit would have gotten up and offered me the seat. It was perfectly executed."

Demon grabbed her hand. "Goddammit, Cherry, why do you think that bomb was for you?"

She took a deep breath and released it slowly before delivering her own version of a nuclear bomb. "My real name is Esme Bosworth, the only child of Grayson Bosworth."

"Shit on a shingle with a side order of fries," Midas whispered.

Demon rolled his eyes. "You've been hanging out too much with Kubrick and Flame. That was the oddest combination of the two of them swearing/not swearing I've ever heard. Why can't you people swear like normal human beings?"

"You can't even pronounce 'fuck' correctly," TB teased him. "Who are you to talk?"

"I pronounce feck just fine," Demon grumbled.

"That 'u' sounds an awful lot like an 'e,' dude," Nemo pointed out.

"Feck you," Demon said as he threw up his middle finger at his teammate.

"All right, you three, simmer down," Waters warned. "Neither one of you speaks right with those goof-ass accents. Now focus your pea brains and get back to what's important." He turned his gaze onto their handler. "Now explain, Cherry. Why do you think that bomb was meant for you? And how do the Salieri, whoever the fuck, or feck, they are, fit into all of this?"

"I'll try to be quick," Cherry promised. "My father had many friends in the military even though he himself had never served. Not for lack of trying. He had a heart murmur that disqualified him from enlisting. But he believed absolutely in the military, even though they couldn't use him personally, so he turned his skills in business and manufacturing to support the service branches in another way.

"The story of the day he disappeared is public knowledge, but what the public didn't know was where I ended up and how I've made Tribe my life's quest. I've spent the last twenty years building, financing, and running Tribe from my reception desk.

"In order to do this right, I knew I had to be willing to play the long game. Success depended on relationships being fostered. I knew that would slow things down further—time that my father probably didn't have—but what other choice was there? The odds were already stacked against him being alive, so I accepted that if I was too late... if he wasn't alive... then I wanted to ensure that everything was in place to catch and punish the men responsible for his disappearance.

"It also required that I remain in the shadows. I knew I didn't have the skills to do it by myself, so I used my college years to hone my analytical skills. I learned everything I could about history, culture, finances, politics, and anything else I thought would be useful in running an operation like Tribe. Combine all of that with my family's vast wealth, and I was able to hire people who could. I purposefully scouted out the best of the best, but there was a hitch. Those individuals had to be free of family ties. They had to be people who could walk away from everything because we couldn't work out in the open. I started with God and worked my way to recruiting the rest of you."

"So we exist because of a personal need for revenge?" TB concluded.

"Justice!" Cherry sniped. She took a calming breath. "My father deserves that." She turned her eyes to TB. "Whatever the reason I created Tribe, you've all done a lot of good over these past five years. Good others couldn't have gotten done."

"We've also done some shady-as-fuck work," TB reminded her.

She pleaded with TB to understand her choices. "None of it was assisting bad people. I ensured that nothing like that ever touched any of you."

Steel brought the conversation back to the pressing issue. "What's the connection between today's bomb threat and the Salieri?"

"Years ago, when my father disappeared, I was going through his things, desperate to find clues as to who might have taken him. Buried in his personal cloud drive were folders and folders of articles relating to Mozart and his fellow composer, Antonio Salieri. Everything from research articles to reviews of numerous play performances around the theatrical world of *Amadeus* by Peter Shaffer. I nearly deleted the files because I couldn't figure out why my father would have something like that saved to his drive. He hated classical music, and live theatre was barely one step above it in his estimation."

"The articles were breadcrumbs," Waters deduced.

Cherry nodded. "In truth, I forgot about the files because getting Tribe up and running became my sole focus. When Gendry gave up the name, it triggered my memory of what I'd found, so I looked closer at those files again. They were all downloads of real articles from a worldwide database, but something about them looked... wrong. And then it hit me why." She reached for a keyboard under the conference table and pulled up her files from her computer. "What do you see?"

Silence permeated the room.

Midas' voice broke the silence. "The spacing is all wrong."

"Very good," Cherry complimented them. "I figured you would see it right away."

"Pardon my limited brain power," TB interrupted, "but what does spacing have to do with it?"

"The margins are off," Midas explained. "When you download an article off the internet and save it to your drive, it follows the same default protocols to format the file to its new location. Text centers left, right, up, down, and spaces the lines at 1.15 lines."

Haskell chimed in, "It's similar to how I configure my body in a small space or if someone played the game of Tetris. The document is formatted to use the space allotted as efficiently as possible. When you copy over text from one source to another, unless you tell it otherwise, the formatting follows along with the text. Most internet articles are formatted to Chicago style formatting—the style journalists use— where the document justifies the text so that the margins are even on both sides and words are flush with both the left and right margins. In addition, there are rules for when and where a new page can be started."

Midas picked up the explanation. "If you look at this particular document Cherry pulled up, the formatting is uneven. Also, if I were to print this document in its entirety, there would be"—he counted— "one, two, three extra pages at the end of the article that would be blank. In a professional setting, that wouldn't happen. The fact that it does here suggests hidden text to me."

Cherry nodded. "I finally came around to that as well." She high-lighted the entire article, and within the highlighting in the margins, a shadowy character like a medieval-style "S" inside a diamond appeared at the top left and the bottom right of each new page. The three blank pages that followed the end of the article showed shadowy writing in an unreadable font that was colored white and microscopic on the page.

"What are we looking at, exactly?" questioned TB.

"The authors, or the publishers more likely, used extremely low tech to hide a private message," Midas explained. "Microscopic, white-colored font. Unless you knew what to look for, you'd just assume those last pages were extra and probably ignore them."

TB rose from his seat and walked closer to the screen. "It's brilliant," he whispered. "How did no one see this?"

"Sometimes the best hiding place is in plain sight," Cherry acknowledged. "Like hiding a specific needle in a stack of other needles. Hang on." With a few more keystrokes, Cherry placed a second document side by side with the *Amadeus* article she'd used as the example for the group. The entire room could now view the new version of the document with the white text changed to blue and enlarged to size twelve font.

Haskell turned to Cherry. "Is this what I think it is?"

"Looks like gibberish," Demon complained.

"To most people, yes. In reality, it's Middle English," Cherry informed him.

"Wow." Haskell popped out of her chair and joined TB at the screen, her fingers tracing the lettering. "I haven't seen this since I read *The Canterbury Tales*."

"This is… I don't know what this is," Waters whispered.

Haskell swore under her breath. "My Middle English is rusty, but it's good enough to see that this particular file is an order of purchase. White women between the ages of sixteen and twenty-five. Clean bills of health, no underlying conditions, no history of genetic disease markers. Preferably women with few family ties and few connections to miss them." Her eyes were glassy as she turned to look at the others in the room. "Bloody hell, they wanted three hundred women."

"This is why my father disappeared. He was chasing the Salieri long before Mythos. I'm willing to bet that each one of these articles he stored in his cloud is publicly hidden communications between the Salieri and prospective clients. I'm convinced that they figured out he was closing in on them, or at least closing in more than anyone else had in the past. Now I've been poking around in his files again, as well as digging into new areas, and it looks like I inadvertently announced my presence to the Salieri." She cringed. "I've no one to blame but myself for becoming this easy of a target. I broke one of our biggest rules by eating at that café every Friday."

"Cherry," Demon groaned.

"I know, I know! No repetitions! Don't go to the same places; don't go the same routes. Haskell almost paid the price for my mistake."

Waters finished the chastising, "There's no use worrying about that now. What's done is done. But Cherry, you understand—"

"That my father's most likely dead? Yes. But I can't stop looking, Waters. This is a huge piece of information I never knew I had until Flame. It's been years without any leads, and now there are thousands of reviews, articles, and all sorts of files he downloaded off the internet. There are even some video files. I don't know what those are for—"

"Advertisements," Midas conjectured. "I bet that's what they are. Maybe for the services of the Salieri. Possibly advertisements of specific people they had for sale. There are probably embedded images inside those video files." He looked at Waters with fire in his eyes. "Each one of these files needs to be gone through and trans-lated, reformatted. Who knows what information is in there."

Waters stared at the screen. "Something tells me we need this information translated yesterday."

"I'll put Nova on it immediately and go over whatever she finds."
Waters nodded tightly.

Steel walked over to Waters and put his hand on his team leader's shoulder. "*Jefe*, we've just all had a shit ton of information dumped on us and no time to process it. Maybe we should take a break, then come back together when we're in a headspace more prone to taking on the more pressing issue at hand."

Haskell watched Waters grind his teeth, then, after a moment, his eyes closed. "Agreed. I need to... call Kubrick." She watched him come to a resolution internally as he hit the security button on the starfish, putting the room back to its normal protocol. "Reconvene at eighteen hundred. Demon, you're on protection detail for Cherry. Nemo, you're in charge of Haskell. Both of you—do not, under any circumstances, allow these women to leave this building." He ripped the door open and slammed it so hard behind him that it didn't close, just bounced back from the doorframe.

Demon took hold of Cherry's arm and guided her into the hall-way. The rest of the team followed close behind. Haskell felt a tug on her hand and looked up to see Nemo trying to help her up from the chair. "Come on. Let's get you settled in. You've got to be exhausted, but it's nothing compared to how you're going to feel in a few hours."

18

SEPTEMBER 9, 2022

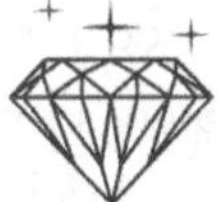

Haskell

The ride in the lift was silent, but Haskell had to admit she was more than a little intimidated. After all, she was basically crammed into a box with Nemo, TB, Steel, Demon, Cherry, and Scheherazade. The latter stood in front of her, back to the door, front paws on top of Haskell's feet, her head cocked to the side. She wasn't sure who was the biggest threat. Somehow, she thought it might be Cherry.

Demon hustled Cherry off the carriage at the fifth floor, a whispered argument starting before the doors had even slid closed.

TB snorted with a shake of his head as the lift closed and started up again. "Those two need to figure out their shit."

"Don't hold your breath," Steel murmured. "Demon has to clean his shit up first. She won't be with him unless he cleans up, and he won't clean up because that's how he keeps himself from her."

Haskell looked over her shoulders at the men. "A medic who is an addict seems a bit counterintuitive."

Steel turned his cold eyes on her.

"I see the signs. He's a functional addict, but an addict just the same."

Steel offered, "Sometimes people choose the lesser of two evils to cope with the things they've done and seen."

Holding her ground, Haskell replied, "I'm not judging him. We all have our own ways of compensating, and we do what we need to do to survive."

"We all have our coping mechanisms."

She watched as Steel directed his gaze to Nemo, who was not paying any attention. When Steel's eyes slid back to Haskell's, she saw the message in his stare, equating Demon's drug use with Nemo's own personal choices for how he coped with his choices in life.

The door opened on the seventh floor, allowing Steel and TB to exit to their private apartments. Just as the doors were about to close completely, TB stuck his hand between them. His head followed as soon as it could, and he hit Nemo in the chest with a foil wrapper. "Don't forget to wrap it up!" With a finger cocked in a gun motion, he winked, made a clicking noise with his mouth, grinned, and backed out of the doors, allowing them to close.

Nemo glanced at Haskell with a grimace, and he quickly put the packet in his pocket. "Sorry about that."

She shrugged. "Boys," she said, as if it explained everything.

The lift doors opened on the eighth floor, and Scheherazade scampered off to the right. Nemo nudged Haskell's elbow, so she followed the dog.

As they exited, Nemo chuckled. "Don't let TB hear you call him a 'boy.' The giant will likely go all Godzilla on you and destroy the city."

He keyed in the code to his door, opened it, and gestured her inside. Scheherazade flew through it, bounded over the leather couch, and yipped when she went ass over head to get to her toy box. Before Haskell could even take a step in her surprise to check on the dog, Nemo's hand was on her arm.

"She's okay," he said. "Still a puppy at heart. Look."

Haskell peered over the couch back, and all she saw were a pair of eyes and two ears pointed straight up. The mouth was totally blocked by a huge stuffed manatee. Haskell broke out into a smile that lit up her entire face, with a laugh that matched it. As if her smile at the goofy image was a green light, Scheherazade gave another muffled yip and bounded back over the couch, her favorite toy in her mouth. She made a beeline for Haskell and sat it at her feet again.

"What does she want?"

"She wants to play. Be warned. She loves that damn thing, so you'll probably be able to wring it out." He headed into the kitchen. "You want anything to drink?"

"Some water would be good," she admitted.

Haskell grabbed the manatee, making an immediate "Eww" noise, and tossed it across the room to please the dog but get rid of it at the same time. "Nasty," she gagged.

"I warned you. I've tried buying her new ones, but she just ignores them," he said from the depths of his refrigerator. "Catch."

He tossed her a bottle of water, closed the refrigerator, and then opened his bottle as he leaned against the counter. She watched him down half of it in just a few swallows. "See something you like better than the water?" he teased.

"What?"

"You haven't opened your bottle yet. All you've done is stare at me."

She shook herself, blinking her eyes several times, and looked at the water bottle in her hand. "Sorry."

He shoved off the counter and placed his bottle on the breakfast bar as he passed it. When he arrived in front of her, he took the bottle from her, broke the seal and then tightened it, and handed it back to her. One finger touched the underside of her chin and tilted her head up so that her eyes met his. "Never be sorry for looking at me, kitty cat. I don't mind. I find you difficult to look away from myself."

The silence was tense.

Nemo finally broke it. "Why did you take off on me the first and second times? And don't try that lie about you panicking again."

"That's your biggest issue with everything that was brought up downstairs? That's what you want to talk about right now?"

He shrugged. "I'll hear the rest of it later. Besides, our history is definitely not what I want laid out on the table later."

She could feel the blood rush to her face. "So sorry to know that I might embarrass you."

She began to step away from him, but she didn't get more than two steps before his arms wrapped around her middle from behind, and she was hauled up against his front. "Relax," he soothed. "That's not what I meant. Don't get your hackles up, kitty cat." His chin rested on her shoulder as he hugged her close. "I just meant that I didn't want to put you through explaining the more private details of how well we know each other. They know the basics. That's all they need."

She ripped herself out of his hold. He was too potent. It felt too good. He felt... safe.

Turning on him, she bit out, "That's not much better, Nemo."

"Sweetheart." He laughed, arms open, palms up. "I'm not sure what you're so upset about. I've been hoping to run into you again for four fucking years. Granted, saving you from being blown sky-high wasn't my fantasy of how it would happen, but it brought you back to me, so I'm gonna take it."

He took a step forward, which she countered by taking a step backward. He took another step; she stepped backward again, and he frowned. It was like the antique store all over again, and she knew the exact moment he made the connection when his smile turned devilish as he continued walking toward her. No wonder. The breakfast bar ended up cutting off her escape three steps later.

Arms braced on the breakfast bar's edge on either side of her, and his body pressed against hers, he nuzzled her under her chin. He didn't kiss her. He didn't lick her or bite her. He just burrowed in, the soft scruff of his short beard—something new and stupid gorgeous on him along with everything else—smoothing across her skin, and then she heard him deeply inhale. "Sugar," he whispered as if to himself.

"Wh-what?" she stuttered.

"You always smell and taste like sugar. I'm addicted to that smell. Took me forever to find something with that same smell, something I could have on me at all times. I should own stock in bubble gum. You imprinted on me the first time we met, kitty cat."

"Ha! That's a joke. I heard your brother. He said, and I quote, 'If it's human, and it has a vagina, it's his type.' Imagine why I wouldn't feel that you're sincere with your compliments."

Nemo backed off her, but not enough to let her escape.

"My brother is an asshole. My team are assholes as well. They think they know me, but not a single one of them has ever asked why I am the way I am. Why I chase tail on a daily basis. Sometimes multiple times." One hand moved from the countertop to her face, laying against her cheek and jaw. "It's you, Haskell. It's always been you. I couldn't forget you, so that first year, I tried to lose myself in every woman I could find just to prove that you could be replaced. You couldn't."

His thumb slid between her lips, and her traitorous tongue reached for it, wrapping around the invading digit, her eyes fluttering closed as she sucked on it.

"And then, by chance, we met again." She felt his forehead touch hers with his confession. "It all came rushing back. I couldn't have stayed away from you if I'd tried. So I let my dick take control, and I fucked you again. Not sorry in the least. I missed you. I ached for you. So, yes, I've fucked my way through as much of the female population as possible, hoping against hope that somewhere along the line, I'd meet a woman who could replace you in my head, but that's the problem. Every single one of those women paled in comparison. There is no replacing you."

She bit his thumb. Hard. A bark of pain caused him to withdraw it from her mouth.

"You need to work on your game. If you thought telling me the *hundreds of women you've fucked* mean nothing to you, I'm not going to fall for that shite."

"Nothing to fall for, kitty cat. Just being one hundred percent honest. I can't change who I was or what I've done. But now that you're here, there won't be anyone else because I finally understand. My heart doesn't want anyone else."

She ducked under his arm and fled to the center of the room. "So let me get this straight. You've comparison-shopped fucking me with the other half of the earth's eligible women that you've fucked, and that's supposed to show me that I'm the only woman in the world for you? That makes no sense whatsoever."

He turned to face her, his arms hanging loosely at his side, his posture communicating he had no fear of her getting away from him. "I'm trying to explain that there never was a comparison. I never could get you out of my system. You're like an addiction. Even though I can function when you're not around, you're always there." He turned and went down the hallway just past his kitchen. He opened a door and gestured through it. "If you want to rest before we meet up again later. Everything's clean."

She stood where she was, barely breathing. She refused to trust him. She'd tried to forget him over the years. Tried to see other people. Even tried to work her way to sleeping with a few. Cerberus was the closest she'd ever come to that, but he came with his own issues, and those were ones she *couldn't* overlook. In the end, they were made to be close friends, so he knew all about her issues with "the guy" from her past. The only guy who'd ever broken through her defenses. The only man she'd ever wanted. The only man she could never truly have. The only man who'd made her feel like a woman to be desired, not a colleague, a tomboy, or even a precocious child.

He walked back toward her, coming within three feet but making no effort to reach out to her. It was as if he could read her mind. "The room's never been used. You're the only person who's ever been in my apartment other than my teammates, and definitely the only woman. I don't even think Flame's been in here."

"Flame?"

"TB's woman. She's a romance novelist. Of the three women here—Kubrick, Cherry, and her—she's the one I'm closest to. We almost lost her a couple of months ago to sex traffickers."

"You're closest to a woman who's seeing someone else?"

"Settle down, hissy. It's not like that."

"Nemo. Look. I think I deserve to be a little hissy. I just spent six weeks moving across Africa avoiding the Kaders, and now it appears the Salieri as well. I was nearly blown up today for something that has nothing to do with me. I've been hustled into some weird-ass building that's both a workplace and an apartment building to a company that employs mercenaries, and they don't seem very prone to letting me go on my way. One of those mercenaries is a two-time mistake I've spent the last four years regretting. It's a bit much, you know?"

Nemo closed the three feet between them, their bodies so close that when they breathed in sync, they brushed against each other on the exhale. "Now there's a lie if ever I heard one."

"What's that?" she whispered.

"A two-time mistake you've spent the last four years regretting."

"I do regret it," she assured him.

"You regret that it's been four years since we've seen each other, maybe, but you don't regret me. Not even close."

His mouth was on hers before she could deny him. And truth be told, he wasn't wrong.

And then he was gone.

When she opened her eyes, he was nowhere to be seen. She whirled around to the door to the outer hall that was closing, the back end of Scheherazade and her tail wagging out of control as she followed Nemo out of the apartment. "I'll be back at just before six p.m. Get some rest."

The door closed, and she heard a series of beeps, signifying that the alarm had been engaged. Her shoulders slumped, and her head tipped back so she could contemplate the ceiling. Finding no answers there, she collected herself and headed down to the guest room he had opened for her. She figured she might as well get a nap as she didn't have the strength to do anything else right now.

Before turning into the offered room, she stared hard at the closed door across from it. Given the layout of the apartment, it was likely Nemo's bedroom. She was guessing each bedroom had its own bathroom, and a quick head-duck into the guest room showed that, yes, she did, in fact, have her own.

Her hand reached out to turn the knob of the door across the hall, her burglar's curiosity getting the better of her. But for some reason, she couldn't bring herself to actually turn it and open the door. It felt... wrong. And that wasn't something that rested easy within her. Being a thief meant her moral compass was askew. Between that and her last several years working with Mythos, snooping was ingrained in her as much as breathing. However, she did have lines she wouldn't cross, and apparently, snooping through Sawyer's things was one of them.

She let go of the knob like it burned her flesh and took a full step backward. She did not like the implications of that choice, so to avoid dealing with the sudden attack of conscience, she went into the guest room. Once the door closed behind her, she locked it and leaned against it. Shower. Bed. Deal with the rest of the nonsense later.

19

SEPTEMBER 9, 2022

Nemo

Nemo was working Scheherazade through commands in the training center when he felt TB's presence. It was hard to believe TB was capable of making his six-foot-seven, two-hundred-forty-pound frame near invisible when he wanted to. Nemo realized the man was trying not to sneak up on his teammate by leaning against the doorframe, hands in pockets. Nemo appreciated the consideration, even if it was for the dog and not for him. Scheherazade was new to training. It took very little to distract her in these early days.

Not that he wasn't distracted himself. Just knowing Haskell was upstairs in his apartment? This training session was more for him than Scheherazade. If he hadn't left the apartment, he'd be so deep in her right now that they wouldn't come up for air for days. Somehow, he didn't think Waters would appreciate that.

Twenty minutes later, he commanded *"Vryheid!"* and reinforced the command by placing his hand, palm up, down at his side.

Scheherazade yipped with excitement and ran to the far corner of the gym area to grab a ball. This would be perfect. He could throw the ball for Zade, focus on her, but still answer the questions that were about to come from his teammate without having to pay attention to the man himself.

By the time Scheherazade was dropping the ball at Nemo's feet, TB had made his way over to Nemo's side. Nemo reached down for the ball, picked it up, and chucked it hard at the far corner, knowing that when it hit, the caroms the ball would take off the corners and equipment would keep the dog entertained.

"She's looking good," TB acknowledged. "You're doing great with her."

"Thanks. It's early days, but she'll get there."

There was silence as they watched her hunt under the free weights the ball had rolled underneath.

"Listen," TB began, "I never truly said thank you for everything. You know. With Flame. I—"

"No thanks are needed, TB. She's tribe."

"But still—"

"TB. Really. It's unnecessary. Love that girl like a sister who writes porn." He grinned mischievously while TB just shook his head and rolled his eyes.

"It's not porn. It's historical paranormal romantic suspense."

"That's a mouthful. Fifty bucks says you can't say that five times fast."

"Fuck off," TB grouched.

"Porn is easier to say."

"Fuck. Off. You call it porn to her, and she'll give you a million paper cuts and pour ginger into the wounds."

"Nice. You taught her well."

TB's face went solid. "Damn straight. No asshole is ever going to take advantage of her again, that's for sure."

Scheherazade was back, ball in mouth, which she dropped at TB's feet, then sat in front of him expectantly.

TB picked up the ball and chucked it into a different corner, this one near the lockers that lined the wall. "Still. I should have said thanks officially. Especially given our contentious relationship."

"Contentious?" Nemo asked.

"Yeah. You know, the confetti cannons, the airhorns, and everything. And I was pretty much a dick about all of it."

Nemo smirked, his attention still on Scheherazade as she forgot all about the ball and engaged in mortal combat with a boxing glove she found behind a laundry bin. "Yeah, you pretty much were. But that's what makes it worth it. You are such a funsucker."

A grunt off to his side made Nemo grin even wider.

"TB, relax. I get it. And you're welcome."

Scheherazade came sprinting back across the gym, her prize firmly clamped between her jaws. She was still fighting it by shaking it, trying to show it who was boss. Both men couldn't help but smile at her antics.

TB wrestled the glove free from Scheherazade's hold. "Hard to believe this is the ferocious dog that nearly bit your faces off in Sallum." He looked closer at the glove. "Aw. It's Midas' glove. That's too bad." He threw the glove back in the direction it came from.

The dog gave a huff as if to say, "Really? I just rescued it from there!" Then she took off running to recapture it.

Nemo shook his head. "That's the seventh one she's destroyed. He's gonna flip." He paused. "You didn't come down here to thank me for helping rescue Flame."

"No, but it gave me a convenient opening," TB agreed. "So... that's her?"

Nemo's smile disappeared. "Her, who?"

TB smacked him upside the back of the head. "Don't play dumb. I don't believe you're that stupid that you don't know what I'm talking about."

Nemo shrugged. "There are a lot of 'hers' in my life."

"Nah," TB disagreed, "there's only ever been one. We just weren't smart enough to realize it until recently."

They watched the dog as she totally destroyed the boxing glove, all of its stuffing now more outside than in. Once it had finally succumbed to its inevitable death, she left it where it lay and went in search of her ball.

"Glad it's Midas' glove and not mine," he said with a smile. TB collected himself and reverted to the conversation he'd started. "If we meet the one we're meant to be with, and we're too stubborn to go after her, there are only two ways to go. The first option we have is to give up all others and become a monk. That's who I was. From the moment I was introduced to Flame, even with it being online and never having seen her, I *knew* she was the only woman for me because she was all I could think about. Option two is where we fuck everything that moves, trying to forget her. That was your route, also because she was all you could think about. And just so you're reassured, neither option is better than the other."

Scheherazade dropped her ball at Nemo's feet. He picked it up and threw it against the far wall again, up high to give it a different carom.

"Did Flame..." Nemo stopped. "Did you know she would accept you as hers?"

TB's smile was a mile wide. "Fuck no. I knew she was attracted to me. Our chemistry was explosive, but I knew I was unworthy of her. I was terrified she'd tell me to go jump off the roof, actually. That woman never did or said what I thought she would."

Nemo returned the smile. "I like that for you. Makes you less Hulk and more Bruce Banner."

"Yeah, I went so Bruce Banner I threw up after killing and disposing of the asshole who kidnapped her," the giant admitted with a grimace. "Don't ever disbelieve that loving the right woman changes you."

"She didn't change you, bruh. She just unburied your conscience. Doesn't mean you won't still do the scary shit you do. It just means that you'll mull it over a few extra seconds before doing it."

"Maybe," he mumbled. "Some things do change, though, and in ways you never think they will."

Nemo registered TB's change in tone and turned to him. "What's going on?"

He assessed his teammate with concern. TB was staring at the far wall, not seeing it or anything else in the room. "I thought someone should know. In case something should happen to me," the man finally said.

"Someone should know what?"

"You can't tell anyone. Not Waters, and definitely not your brother. We need some time to figure out how we're going to handle it before everyone tries to insert themselves into the situation."

"What situation? Spit it out. It's not like you to be so vague."

TB frowned. "Flame's pregnant."

Nemo's eyes went wide. "She's *what*?!"

"You heard me."

"No, I don't think I did. What I thought I heard was that Flame's pregnant, but that can't possibly be right."

"Well, that's what I said." TB shuffled in place, then looked over at Nemo. "This was not planned. To be honest, we're not exactly sure how it happened."

Nemo looked at his teammate in total seriousness. He placed a hand on TB's bicep and leaned in with a whispered, "So when a boy and a girl love each other very much..."

TB smacked him again, this time good-naturedly. "Fuck off, Needledick."

Looking at each other like two naughty little boys, both were grinning.

"Are you good with it?" Nemo asked. "Cuz you look good with it."

TB smiled. "Yeah. Yeah, I'm good with it. Freaked the fuck out, but good."

"And Flame?"

"She's scared. Thinks it's going to change things or some stupid shit. I told her, of course it's going to change things, but not the way she's imagining. She's worried it's too soon. The woman already wears my collar, so she's as tied to me as it gets. A baby's not going to make me stop wanting her or loving her."

"Happy for you, man." Nemo saluted, a smart-ass grin on his face. "Consider me informed and on duty to protect, aka babysit, if needed." He didn't bother to tell TB there was nothing to worry about and that everything was going to be okay. In their line of work, you couldn't make those kinds of promises. "You're not thinking of leaving Tribe, are you?" Nemo asked.

Blowing air forcefully out of his lungs, TB shook his head. "It's not what we want, but the concern is that it's not like I can exactly be a visible part of the child's life in the traditional sense since I'm 'dead' and do what I do. The child and Flame would be too vulnerable. I mean, I'm off the grid now, but Flame isn't. I suppose she could be, given that she doesn't spend a lot of time outside her house other than The Library with me. It would probably be safer to go live some-where outside the States. She can write from anywhere, and retire-ment for me has a nice ring to it now that we're together. More importantly, I'm not sure if I can keep at this if I'm suddenly going to be responsible for a little Flame."

"Sparks." Nemo snorted. "That's what we'll call her." He became thoughtful. "What if it's a little TB?"

"Fuck, I hope not. The world doesn't need more of me in it."

"Are you sure? Raising a little girl might be okay now, but how about in sixteen years when a little Nemo shows up to take her on dates?"

Horror crossed TB's face. "Shit! I didn't think of that." His face and body showed resolve. "Nope. Not happening. She's having a boy."

Nemo laughed out loud. "Don't think it works that way, big guy."

"Nope. Abso-fucking-lutely works that way. If it's a girl, I'm shoving it back in there until it cooks all the way and pops a penis."

Nemo doubled over with laughter at the despair his teammate

was now in. Wiping the tears from his eyes, he clapped TB on the arm. "Good luck with that. You try to shove a baby back inside Flame, she's going to stab you with one of those pencils she holds her hair up with. You won't even know what hit you."

TB groaned. "I'm not meant to be a father. I don't suppose this is a sick practical joke you put together with fake pregnancy tests?"

"I would never, ever joke about pregnancy. Even with you," Nemo promised. "TB, other than Waters, who is going to be jealous as fuck, by the way, I can't think of anyone more worthy," Nemo assured him.

TB agreed. "He can't even get Kubrick to entertain the 'M' word, much less have babies. Although, how any of us can get married is a whole other issue." TB pleaded one more time for secrecy. "Look. Just... just don't say anything yet, okay? I'm going to tell him and everyone eventually. We'd like a little time to let ourselves process it."

"My lips are sealed."

Scheherazade collapsed at Nemo's feet, tongue lolling out of her mouth as she panted hard from all the exertion. Nemo dropped to his knees, which was her cue to roll over on her back for belly rubs. Nemo made sure to fulfill his end of the bargain.

Still standing behind him, TB asked, "What are you going to do about Le Chatte Noire?"

Without looking up, Nemo contemplated his options before speaking. "Truth? No fucking idea. I can't let her get away again, but she's proven to be a runner, so I've probably got less time than I think to make this happen."

"I could tie her up for you. She's not getting out of my knots. Would keep her in one place."

They stared at each other. Imperceptibly, a twitch occurred at one corner of TB's mouth, and that was all it took before both men were laughing.

Nemo glanced at his watch. It was quarter to six.

Time to go wake her up from her cat nap.

Nemo stood. "I'm going to go collect Haskell. See you in a few."

TB nodded. "See you in the conference room. And Nemo?"

Nemo waited expectantly.

"If she's it, don't let go. Even if she runs again, go after her. Bring her back. And if she keeps running, keep going after her, and keep bringing her back. It'll be worth it. She'll figure it out eventually."

Nemo nodded, then walked off to the elevator with an exhausted Scheherazade in tow.

If she runs, there's nowhere she can go that I won't find her.

20

SEPTEMBER 9, 2022

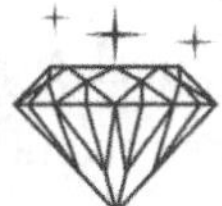

Haskell

At six o'clock sharp, everyone was back in the conference room, but this time, they all sat around the table. Scheherazade lay across Haskell's feet. Waters wasn't quite as high-strung as he had been when he'd blown out of the room earlier. Considering he was wearing a different shirt than the one when he'd left and had slightly damp hair, Haskell figured that this Kubrick, whoever she was, had used the one thing guaranteed to calm down most men who were about to lose their shit.

Those thoughts immediately made her think of sex with Nemo, and she felt her face flush. Eyes wide, her gaze flew to where the man in question sat next to her. As if he knew exactly what she was thinking, there was a smile on his face, and his eyes seemed to light up with laughter at catching her.

Rolling her eyes, she shifted her gaze back to Waters and worked very hard to ignore Nemo.

"Midas, what do we have?"

"Not a lot. I did manage to track down Loki and company. I'll patch them through in just a minute. Be advised. They've got a friend with them."

She noticed the word "friend" had some edge to it. There were two people it could be, and only one was plausible.

The telescreen flashed to life. In a large rectangle across the top half sat the three Mythos members—Loki, Gilgamesh, and Medusa. The bottom half of the screen was a long rectangle. One revealed a single male with auburn hair, black horn-rimmed glasses, and vivid blue eyes—someone Haskell knew well.

"Loki," Waters began. "As you can see, we've found your contractor."

Haskell gave a cheeky finger wave at the screen.

Loki flashed a smile. "Glad to see you haven't used up all of those nine lives, kitten."

There was a rumble of irritation from next to her.

"Nice to have them all intact, Loki," she replied. She flashed a look at Nemo sitting next to her, who now had a scowl on his face. "What's your problem?"

"He called you 'kitten.'"

"Yeah. You call me kitty cat. So?"

"You need a new nickname."

"Fine. You can call me 'goodbye.' As in, you can go away."

"Not from me. From him. He needs a new nickname for you. No one calls you 'kitten' but me."

"Maybe," she piped up, "we could just call me 'Haskell' and ignore the nicknames altogether."

A resounding "No!" came from everyone except the solo man on the screen.

Waters explained, "Nicknames keep you as anonymous as possible, which means safety if we need to talk about you over comms. No sense drawing attention to you by using your real name if anyone is listening in." Haskell noticed the slight edge of panic that Waters and everyone else in the room let creep in. Then, after his explanation and a calming breath, it ebbed out like the tide. "As entertaining as this all is," he continued, "we really do have shit to do. Nemo. Loki. You two can piss on your territory later when we're done with real-world problems." Waters took a long, hard look at the guest they brought with them. "Who are you?"

Before he could answer, Loki made the introduction. "Midas informed me of your situation earlier today. I thought you all should meet. This is Cerberus."

With the exception of Haskell, everyone on Tribe's end of the call eyed the newcomer with even more suspicion.

"Cerberus, these are Tribe's deadmen. Waters, the team leader. Midas, their cyber specialist. TB, their interrogator. Steel, their over-watch. Demon, their doctor. And the pretty boy over there shaking his tail feathers at Haskell is Nemo. He's in... acquisitions."

Cerberus seemed to look at Nemo just a shade longer than the others before he nodded his head at the group in general. "Loki said you had some work done near you with my signature on it. I've been in Sri Lanka for the past two months, so it's not my work. However, I am interested in what occurred and how you think it's mine."

Waters relayed their adventurous morning. "A pressure-plate bomb was engaged at a coffee café this morning. Haskell initiated its protocol when she sat down. We were able to observe it before it went boom."

In anticipation of Waters' order, Midas put the photos of it from Nemo's phone on the screen. "As you can see, we also managed to keep it from taking out the women, as well as any other café patrons. We have not been able to secure any forensics since we're not exactly on the up-and-up with the blue line."

Cerberus made a few clicks on his computer screen, his eyes scrunching up as he looked at the array of photos that had been taken. "It's a really good copy, but it's not mine. See the bottom left dewclaw? All the other claws are present. If it's mine, this one will be missing on the signature." He pulled up a sample of his work on the screen so that Tribe could see the differences between the two devices.

"Why?"

Cerberus flashed his left hand at the screen, where everyone could clearly see his thumb on his right hand. "Art imitates life. Massive scarring from my early years. Still, even if the signature had been accurate, it would never have been my work."

"Because...?"

"I don't blow up people, no matter how much they might piss me off with their stupidity."

"So, if it's not your work, Haskell suggested it might be a copycat from the Salieris." Waters swung his chair in an arc to survey all of his people before turning back to those on the screen. "People, this name is coming up way too many times of late, and no one is sharing. I want an explanation of who, or what, the Salieri are and why they are coming after my people."

The men and the woman on the screen sat quietly for a moment, soaking up the pronoun "my." It was not going unnoticed that he was extending this description to Haskell.

Finally, Medusa spoke up. "The Salieri," she began, "can be traced back as far as the Crusades, but it's likely they go back far longer than that. They are the original organized crime family."

"Never heard of them," TB interrupted. "I've been scurrying around on the dark web longer than Midas, and there's been no whispers of that name crossing my path. I'm pretty sure I would have at least heard of these players if they existed."

"You probably have run across them. In fact, *you've* probably worked for them at one time or another. Possibly many times. They use individual players mid-level on the chain to hire out a lot of grunt work, including targeted hits, which is why no one ever hears about them as a whole. But they haven't gotten to be who they are and as powerful as they are by letting their name slip through the cracks. While Flame's kidnapper worked for the organization, he should never have known about them yet. He was far too low on the totem pole."

The people on the screen all shared looks again.

"People," Waters broke in, "weighty looks make for great drama in movies. However, in real life, we have two women who were targeted today in a very public place. We recently interrupted a very sophisticated prototype of a distribution center for human trafficking; two of my team members found a huge increase in technology for that trafficking scheme, and my woman's brother is somehow smack-dab in the eye of this clusterfuck. Will someone please read us in?"

Haskell watched Medusa closely, noticing she didn't respond like the others. As long as she had known the woman, she more than lived up to her name. All of her—from her hair ends flipping up like forked snake tongues, the lightly shaded sunglasses over her eyes, and the stone-faced expression—she more than fit her name.

Therefore, it was surprising to her when Medusa chose to volunteer information. "What Gendry knew, or thought he knew, is immaterial since he's now shark chum." She directed those words to Waters. "The brother? We'll deal with him eventually. He knows to be patient, and the cavalry will arrive."

It took a moment for the last statement to sink in. It was Steel who spoke. "Does that mean that Ka-Bar works with you?"

Loki responded, "On occasion, our paths do cross. He was vetting a source for us in Egypt."

"Zahra." The light bulb answer came from Waters.

"Yes," Loki confirmed. "She had information we wanted, and given their past history, we sent Ka-Bar in to handle the asset. He managed to get her talking about her family's involvement with our target, and during that time, they clearly reestablished their relationship."

"You've known all along where he was? You've let us waste all this time and resources looking for him? His sister has been worried sick, which, in turn, upsets me."

Loki admitted, "Obviously, we knew who he was with, but we've always been a few steps behind on the where. The sighting we gave you a few months back was the last we had until the photographs from Haskell, and when we received those, we were under strict orders not to share that information yet. Since he was our contractor, the hope was we could handle it on our end. We broke protocol when we ran out of options looking for Haskell, so when we called you, we used it as a bargaining chip, yes. All of our asses are going to be on the line for going against orders. While I appreciate your concern for Kai Serrano, that is not our problem. Our endgame is not yours."

Haskell piped in, "Everybody needs to calm down. Before Ka-Bar disappeared, he told me that the Kaders were using an abandoned Mzingwane mine as a means to fund their new pipeline. Originally, they were manipulating the illegal surface miners to surrender their finds for extremely low returns. However, with their new discovery in the mine itself, they've since expanded to extorting the miners to abandon their individual tunnels at the surface level and work in the abandoned tunnels. No method of coercion is off the table—threats of arrest, torture of the miners, their families, you name it."

"All things we suspected," Steel said.

Gilgamesh added, "We've recently identified their source on the police force who warns them when a raid is coming. They bug out until the police leave, then start back up again. Getting in front of them and their work has been near impossible." He gestured to Haskell. "Go ahead and show them what you found, Haskell."

Haskell reached into her pocket and extracted a small packet of wax paper. She laid it on the table and opened it to reveal two dozen pebbles in various sizes. "I found these running in three separate veins that were within three feet of each other."

Cerberus explained, "Those stones are the key to a disaster of epic proportions. If they're allowed to continue mining for those stones, they'll be nearly impossible to stop financially. And not only that, but they're doing irreparable damage, raping the ecosystem there with their operations."

"Fuel pollution?" Steel asked.

"For starters. They're contaminating the water table. Illegal mining operations are not concerned about operating within safety standards regarding the chemicals and techniques they use. So not only is the land dying due to poisoned water but so are the cattle and people who draw water from that table, whether it's for everyday living or crops. The effects are far-reaching down the line, and who knows how much damage has been done once those contaminated waters hit the Limpopo and eventually the Indian Ocean. You can guarantee the Kaders aren't big proponents of reclamation."

Nemo was sifting through the pebbles with the tip of a pen. "Some of these are diamonds, but I don't recognize these stones. What are they?" he asked Haskell.

"Tanzanite, mostly. The largest one is taaffeite."

His head shot up. "Shut the fuck up!"

She shook her head. "I know, but that's what they are."

"I've never even heard of taaffeite. Why is that such a big deal?" Demon asked.

"Taaffeite is one of the rarest natural gems created on Earth. Even more rare than tanzanite, which is only found in Tanzania, hence its name," TB offered.

Nemo added, "Taaffeite is also found in Tanzania and Sri Lanka only, at least as far as we knew."

TB reached across the table and picked up one of the pebbles. He held it up to the light, his fingers crushing some of the packed dirt around the stone. "This little thing right here is worth tens of thousands uncut."

Everyone stared at the unassuming piece of pebble in his hand.

"That means," Loki began, "that if this mine happens to host all three of these rare gems, the Kaders have found themselves a possibly never-ending financial boom to fund their activities. Those stones are heavily monitored by their respective commissions. Finding all three of them in the same location? That should be impossible. Something catastrophic happened at that location in the distant past to allow for that."

"Why is that?"

Haskell spoke up. "Because the mine isn't all that deep yet. The original owners gave up on it early."

Nemo explained, "These three stones are all formed at various levels in the earth, and each has unique chemical compositions required for them to form. It's part of what makes them worth so much."

"If the Kaders are in control of that mine," Medusa added, "unlimited funds equals unlimited resources and power."

"Which means they'll be near impossible to stop." Nemo looked to Haskell. "What are you doing chasing these stones, kitty cat?"

"These days, my skills are used a lot more widely." She reached into her pocket again and pulled out another packet. She opened the packet to reveal several larger stones. "Black diamonds. These are what I originally thought I was going to find. Clearly, I did. But when I ran across the other stones, I realized something bigger was going on. Mythos hired me to go into the mines and see what was what. While I was able to gain access to the mine, I ran into trouble and had to abort the assignment or become a permanent resident of the mine. Six weeks later? Here I am."

Loki focused in on Haskell. "Haskell—"

Haskell put her hand up to stop him. "No need to ask, Loki. You know I never quit. This was just a necessary retreat. I'll regroup and head back out."

Loki nodded.

"Oh, hell no!" Nemo slammed his hand down on the table. His eyes shot daggers at Haskell. "You are not going back into those mines. Do you have any idea how dangerous that is for you, especially since you were discovered once already?"

She looked at him like he was a small child. "Nemo, you have no say in where I go or what I do. I've been taking care of myself for a long time. I know exactly what I'm getting into."

"This isn't like breaking into a museum," he argued, rubbing his chest where his heart sat. She noticed he did that regularly. While she was touched that he was concerned, he clearly was overinvested if her actions were giving him palpitations or other physical pain. It also didn't squelch her anger at being told what she could and could not do. She'd had enough of that nonsense in her life already.

"No, it isn't," she agreed. "But every site comes with risks. Some are riskier than others. I get that. I'm not stupid," she spat back. "Just because I recently needed help temporarily does not give you permission to be the Grinch to my Cindy Lou Who where you pat me on the head and send me on my way. Everyone needs help sometimes, and I'm not the too-stupid-to-live girl who refuses to take help when needed. So I suggest you take all that alpha male shite that's overloading your brain and stuff it back down. Considering you house your brain in the cock you so often seem to be stuffing back in your pants, you should be well-practiced at that!"

A low whistle came from Demon. "Feck, that was low."

"But frighteningly accurate," TB commented.

The stare-down between Haskell and Nemo was hardcore. She refused to give him so much as an inch. When her voice came again, it was softer but no less firm. "This is what I do, Nemo, and I'm fucking good at it."

Nemo pleaded with her, "Kitty cat, I'm not saying you're not capable. I'm saying it's too dangerous to do this on your own."

"Which is why you're going with her," Waters injected. He looked at Haskell. "We all are."

21

SEPTEMBER 9, 2022

Nemo

"How many times do I have to tell you people?" Demon bitched. "If you use the last of something in a first aid kit, replace it immediately! If I had opened this out on a project, someone would have bled out because the kit didn't have a tourniquet."

From his worktable in the armory, TB responded with a bored tone as he laid out his weapons and ammunition. "Relax, Florence Nightingale. You're so anal-retentive, you check all of our work three times before you let us pack it in the vehicles. Then you check it again before we pull out. And then you check it again when we arrive. There's no way we would have ended up anywhere without a fully stocked kit."

"That's not the point, fecker. I shouldn't have to check all those times. You're all adults. Check your goddamn kits and make sure they're stocked." He slammed the lid down on one of the metal box kits the SUVs had underneath the front seat on the passenger's side.

"Think how much time I'd save if I didn't have to check everybody's work."

TB shoved his primary gun into the holster at his right side. "Seriously? Even if we never ever forgot to stock our kits, you'd still check them five times. Fuck, pop a pill, would you? It would improve your mood."

Demon stomped away, muttering in Gaelic. Nemo didn't know the language at all, but he definitely knew that the medic was either calling TB's parentage into question, or he was calling down pagan curses on the man. Maybe both. Nemo smiled to himself, then went back to inventorying all of his standard tools that he'd laid out to make sure he had everything.

The air-conditioning blew a sugary wave in his direction, and the skittering of Scheherazade's toenails followed. He inhaled deeply.

"Hey there, kitty cat. Wondered when you'd get here."

Haskell stepped up next to him at the table and looked at the contents, divided into a grid system with two of whatever was in each box. "What's all this?"

Without looking at her, Nemo replied, "This is my supply kit."

Out of his peripheral vision, he watched her categorize each item one by one.

"Why are there two of each item?" she asked.

"I figured you were traveling light and probably didn't have your supplies, so I just put together a second set for you."

In the silence that followed, he could feel her gaze burning through his brain.

"Why?" she eventually asked.

"Why?" He frowned.

What is she confused about?

"Yes, why? Why would you do that for me?"

"I just said. You're unlikely to have your own stuff."

"You're not responsible for me."

He shrugged. "It's not rocket science. You can't go into this with no tools to work with. If you have to steal something, you need your bag of tricks. If you get stuck in a ventilation shaft, a conduit, or some-where else, you'll need tools to get out. It would be irresponsible of me to put my partner into a dangerous situation."

"Is that what we are? Partners?"

"For all intents and purposes for this project, yes."

"Why are you and your friends helping us?"

Nemo leaned on the table's edge, elbows locked, as he paused and thought about how to frame his words. He replied, "A few reasons, actually. One, a couple of months ago, your employer helped us rescue TB's girlfriend. So we owe them a favor. Two, these guys you're dealing with are up to their necks in some serious shit. Plus, they're using Kubrick's brother to do it. We've been searching for him since February, so we're not going to pass up the lead. Three, you're not going to stop pursuing them, are you?"

"No," Haskell agreed.

"Right. So since Waters knows I would follow right after you to help you, he's going to put Tribe behind you as backup."

"Backup?"

"Yup."

"Not protection?"

"From what I've seen, you can handle yourself pretty well. You don't need protection."

He watched her scan the table, but it was clear she was consid-ering his words. She picked up the mini-dispenser of sticky note, flag-style, double-sided tape. "You carry this tape, too?"

He wondered if the non sequitur was her way of avoiding the implications of what he wasn't saying.

"That's the stuff you used to reset the top of the Saturn Diamond's showcase, right? I read about the theft in the local news-paper. The authorities found residue from what they assumed was double-sided tape on equidistant points of the lid. Thought it was pretty smart. I used to carry a collapsible bar that had multiple joints that I used like a pry bar to lift off the tops of display cases or whatever."

Haskell looked around the table. "I don't see a pry bar."

"Nope. When I saw what you used in Gabon, I thought it was ingenious, and I retired the pry bar. Your option is way better."

"How do you know I used that in Gabon?"

"Midas. Well, Nova, his AI program, figured it out. She borrowed the files from the local police, analyzed them, and came up with a number of solutions as to how you did what you did. Then I went through and made notes of which version I figured was most likely. I particularly loved the Spider-Man-style crawl across the ceiling to lower yourself upside down into the display case. Genius."

"So, you looked at something I did, figured out what I used, and then threw away things you've been doing for however long to use my version?"

He shrugged. "No ego here, kitty cat."

She snorted.

He admitted, "I can recognize when someone does something well and be smart enough to change my ways to be better. Refusing to adapt could get me caught. Even killed."

She shook her head and went back to studying his table. "Every time I think I have you pegged, you surprise me."

Nemo ignored the loaded comment. "See anything I've missed or that you want?"

"No, you have pretty much everything I used," she admitted. "Are we leaving soon?"

"Waters said we're rolling out at oh-four-hundred tomorrow. Medusa is going to take us by helicopter to a private airstrip, and then she'll fly us by Mythos' jet to Mozambique, where we'll create a safe house. From there, we'll head into Zimbabwe. We're going to meet in an hour or so to come up with a plan of attack, then we'll get a few hours rest before we pack up and head out."

He turned to her and leaned his hip on the table's edge, his arms crossed over his chest. She was chewing on a thought. Hard. He could almost hear the wheels turning in indecision. He was worried that her teeth were going to bite straight through her lip. Finally, she reached into her pocket and removed a tool from it. She clicked a button, and a metal rod extended from the end of it. She handed it to Nemo.

"This is my get-out-of-all-disasters tool. I never go anywhere without it. It's even more important to me than a cell phone, so I'm trusting you not to lose it."

He didn't even look at the item she held out to him. He stayed focused on her eyes that wouldn't meet his. "Why are you handing it over to me, then?"

It was her turn to try for nonchalance. "I have a spare upstairs, and I figured maybe you'd want one of your own. If you get stuck in a ventilation shaft, a conduit, or somewhere else, you'll need tools to get out. It would be irresponsible of me to put my partner into a dangerous situation."

It felt like all the oxygen had been sucked right out of his lungs. As quietly as possible, he tried to suck in air so he could breathe again. He unfolded his arms from his chest, and with one finger, he tilted her chin up so that she would look him in the eye. Then, slowly, he bent down and placed a barely there kiss to her cheek. When he pulled back, he didn't take his eyes from hers. "I'll guard it with my life."

"Hey, you two!" TB's bark came from across the room. "Save that shit for in private. Some of us don't have our women here to canoodle with when we've got work to do." He chucked a box at Nemo, nearly hitting him in the head.

Nemo was thankful his back was partially to Haskell when he made the catch, as it allowed him to hide the box of condoms. Nemo rolled his eyes, mouthing, "Fuck you, asshole," at his teammate. Then, out loud, he muttered, "As if you'd ever let Flame be around me alone."

There was a chorus of chuckles around the room, and TB agreed. "She'd be safer in private with you than in public. Either way, I don't want you anywhere near her to work your voodoo on her."

That comment actually caused Haskell to flinch. Nemo looked

around the room, but everyone's focus was on whatever they were doing. He pressed his index finger against her lips. With a shake of his head, he replied, "I would never do that to you."

Anyone listening would think he was answering TB. Anyone watching would know it was a promise to Haskell.

22

SEPTEMBER 9, 2022

Haskell

Oh my god, it hurts so bad!

Haskell was holding her sides, tears streaming down her face, she was laughing so hard. Next to her, Nemo sat, both hands filled with marshmallows, and he was making all sorts of melodramatic, pantomime trash-talking faces and gestures at the red-haired Rapunzel across the table from him. Flame, TB's girlfriend, who also held two fists filled with the spongy sugar concoctions, made faces right back at him, only hers were like a twelve-year-old boy, her eyes crossing. Haskell was sure that she'd be sticking her tongue out at him except that the eight marshmallows currently in her mouth were preventing that from occurring.

"Nemo! Dude, do not encourage her!" TB threatened. "Somebody take those away before one of them chokes to death." TB attempted to wrestle the marshmallows in her fist out of her hands, but Flame was tenacious and seemingly unbothered by the giant's attempts.

Demon agreed, "Yes, please, I don't want to be doing the Heimlich on her. He'll kill me with a spork."

Kubrick, sitting in Waters' lap at the foot of the table, blew a raspberry at Demon. "Alpha funsuckers. That's what you all are."

"Rule six, Kubrick" Waters growled. Then he kissed the side of her head.

"Oh, for the love of Pete... Seriously? I don't have any money on me for the Rule jar."

"Guess she'll be paying in sexual favors tonight," Midas quipped to Steel.

"Total Brontosaurass over there is just grumpy cuz he's already out of the game." Kubrick pelted the man in question with a marshmallow.

Midas laughed. "Not only are you out, big guy, but you were the *first* one out. With your big mouth, how could you not get past four marshmallows? Bruh, the dog could beat you at that number."

"You know, it's not surprising he lost so early." Haskell looked at everyone at the table with a completely serious expression on her face. "Dinosaurs need to be marshmallow-free. It's why they died out. They can't digest fun." Haskell popped a marshmallow in her mouth, chewing innocently.

There was an explosion of laughter, resulting in TB throwing a marshmallow at Haskell, a smirk on his face. She tossed one back good-naturedly. Suddenly, a flurry of marshmallows flew from all angles of the table, resembling an epic snowball fight. Alliances were quickly formed. Kubrick dipped her marshmallows in barbecue sauce before throwing them, which basically turned the snowball fight into paintball. People were ducking under the table, using the chairbacks as shields, and reaching up blindly for ammunition. Scheherazade was barking at the marshmallows as they flew through the air and ran around the table, pulling on people's shirts and pants to keep them from attacking her dad. Meanwhile, Steel belly-crawled, completely unseen, to the foot of the table and managed to upend Waters out of his chair to steal his marshmallow stash when his own ammunition ran dry.

Haskell had eaten most of her marshmallows, so she opted to turn her chair so that she could curl her small frame up behind the high back and stay out of the mess. Her stomach and sides were beyond hurting from all the giggling, but her head and eyes were always drawn to the blond man at her right. Even with a mouth overstuffed with the fluffy treats, he was beyond gorgeous.

Her smile was tempered suddenly by Da's voice in her head.

He's no good for your heart. Don't get distracted, child.

Once everyone had run out of ammunition, and Haskell noted it had taken a while for that to occur as there were *a lot* of marshmallows on the table, everyone surveyed the fallout. The room looked like a literal war zone, barbecue sauce everywhere, like blood, with the conference room table as the front lines.

"God's going to have a total shit hemorrhage if he sees this." Kubrick grinned at everyone. She must have felt the trickle of barbecue sauce trailing down from her eyebrow because she started to reach up to swipe it away. She was prevented from it by Waters leaning over to lick it off.

"No worries, babe. We'll just send you to him when the cleaning bill comes. He never gets mad at you." He gave her a loud smack on the lips.

There was a snort to her right, and Haskell turned just in time to see Nemo involuntarily spitting a volcano of liquified marshmallow out of his mouth and onto the paper plate in front of him because he was laughing so hard. He grabbed the bridge of his nose. "Ow. No laughing with marshmallows in your mouth. It hurts when they try to come out of your nose."

The room of people erupted into laughter as Flame, chewing through a mass of sticky marshmallow residue in her mouth, jumped up from her seat with her arms in an upraised vee position. As the tiny woman whooped and hollered her victory in the pudgy bunny war, Haskell noted there was something incredibly at odds with the ethereal woman, a mouth full of white goop, running around the table as if she'd won a gold medal in the Olympics. There were marshmallows stuck in her long red hair, and Haskell was pretty sure there were several in the cleavage of her corseted top. Luckily, the woman had kicked off her heels earlier because Haskell didn't think anyone would have been able to run in the five-inch monstrosities without turning or breaking an ankle.

As Flame came around behind them on her victory lap, Nemo snuck out of his chair, curled an arm around her waist, and threw her over his shoulder. "That's it, you little pudgy bunny cheater! I'm claiming my reward!"

Flame was laughing so hard now she was hiccuping uncontrollably. "Nemo, put me down!" she screeched.

"Nope. You cheated!"

"How could I have cheated, you goof? My mouth was full. I didn't make you laugh. Blame it on Gem!"

Nemo slid Flame off his shoulder, where she was quickly collected by TB, his large frame dwarfing her foot-and-a-half shorter one. "Gem?" he rumbled.

"Yeah. Gem. She's a jewel thief, right? Gems! And when she laughs, her blue eyes are so bright, they sparkle like sapphires in the light." Flame shrugged. "She needs a nickname anyway. Gem!"

TB chuckled. "Why do I have a feeling your next female main character is going to be a shifter cat who steals diamonds and is named Gemma?"

Flame turned around in his arms, her hands sliding up his forearms to curl around his biceps. "Hmm..." She pretended to think. "Do you think that would make a good main character?"

Tenderly, the man picked a marshmallow out of her hair, where it was trapped by all the flyaway strands. "Just make sure she understands what kinds of books you write before you use her likeness, physically or in print." He dropped a kiss on her upturned nose, then threw the marshmallow on the table. "All right, pudgy bunny champion, it's time to get you back to your computer. You're about 3k short of your 10k goal today, and if I want any hope of time with you before I leave, we need to get you back at it." He looked at Waters. "I'll be back to help clean up once I get our gold medalist behind her laptop."

"Don't worry about it." Waters waved him off. "See you in the morning."

TB nodded his thanks and hefted Flame up over his shoulder. When she squawked, he simply gave her ass a smack and headed for the door. Smiling, Flame waved goodbye to everyone from her upside-down position.

"Now she's in trouble." Kubrick snickered.

"Somebody's looking for a punishment," they heard TB rumble as he stepped out into the hall, to which Flame retorted, "It's not punishment when it's a funishment!" The group listened to the couple as they continued to banter back and forth all the way to the lift. Haskell surveyed the room and saw everyone smiling to themselves as they went about starting to clean up.

Nemo flopped down into his chair at the conference room table and dug for the last rib on the plate in front of him. After rooting around and finding a plastic knife, he began to trim the meat off the bone.

She watched him work. Hesitating because she worried how he'd interpret the observation, Haskell bit her lip. The words flew out before she could stop them. "You're really fond of Flame."

"Yep, I am." Nemo tore the last chunk of meat off the rib bone and tossed it in his mouth. He winked at her as he finished chewing and washed down the food with a sip of water from his bottle.

For a moment, his smile was tempered with something she couldn't quite put her finger on. It wasn't regret or even sadness. Just something poignant.

"She was partly my responsibility when she was taken," he admitted, "so I feel extra responsible for her. TB was head over heart for her, so that made her even more important."

"That's sweet."

She watched as Nemo wiped his hands on a clean napkin, then turned sideways in his seat. The next thing she knew, his hand was turning her face in his direction. "What's going on in that head, kitty cat?"

"I just..." She looked around the room, nonplussed as to how to communicate what she was seeing and feeling.

Someone had called the local barbecue restaurant and ordered enough food for an army. Ribs, chicken, brisket, pork... and those were just the meats. Corn on the cob, seasoned potatoes, coleslaw, buns, biscuits with butter and honey, and several kinds of potato salad. When someone wanted something to drink, they just walked a short way down the hall to the office's break room, where there were pitchers of sweet tea, bottled beer, bottled water, and about twelve kinds of soda. It also looked like a paper products factory had exploded because there were hundreds of plates and napkins everywhere.

She shook her head. "I don't know. I've just... I've never had this."

"This." It wasn't a question, but he was clearly asking for more information.

"This." She gestured around them, still unsure how to put it in words. "Friends that pour into a room and create a demilitarized zone with marshmallows and barbecue."

His smile went ear-to-ear. "Family," he corrected.

"My family was not like this."

"Not a blood family. The family you choose. Blood family is important, sure. But 'this,' as you call it, is of more value than anything on Earth. And, of course, you have it," he scoffed.

"No, I'd remember something like this."

His hand reached up to tug an unruly curl. "You have it now," he said quietly. "No matter what, these people will always love you."

She looked at him with incredulity. "Why?"

"Because I do." His smile was smaller now but no less genuine. He tugged the curl again, then shifted gears so rapidly her head spun. He reached for the bone from the last rib he'd eaten and handed it to

Scheherazade, who gnawed it daintily in her spot between Haskell and Nemo's chairs.

"Nemo!" she gasped, attempting to grab the bone.

"Relax, kitty cat. It was a plain one. No sauce or seasonings. She'll be fine."

"But—"

He stayed her hand. "It's fine. I took her off the streets of Sallum. She can eat a lot of things technically dogs shouldn't since she was living off garbage to survive when I found her. But I wouldn't tempt fate because of that. I take care of my girl."

And he did it again. Made a comment that sounded like one thing but really meant so much more.

Child, do not fall for that shite.

Nemo pushed back his chair and began to pile garbage up. "Let's help with cleanup, then we'll take Zade for a walk, yeah?"

She nodded.

23

SEPTEMBER 9, 2022

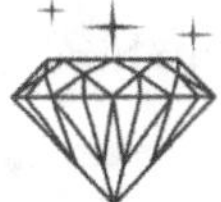

Nemo

Ninety minutes later, the conference room was clear of all garbage and as clear of barbecue sauce as it was going to be until the special cleaning crew came in the next day to scour the carpeting, furniture, and walls. During that time, he had watched the others interact with Haskell, and he took mental notes on her reactions to them.

It didn't take long for her to be won over by Kubrick. He snorted. That shouldn't have been a surprise. Kubrick begged Haskell for trade secrets about her past heists and how things were done. Haskell traded information with her, one heist secret for one filming secret. She even weaseled an invitation onto a movie set in the future. Not that she'd had to work Kubrick very hard.

Coming up on her from behind, he wrapped his arms around her waist and rested his chin on her shoulder. "Kitty cat, you smell divine, but if I take you to the beach smelling like braai sauce, you're going to get mauled."

"Huh? What's braai sauce?"

"Barbecue. It's all over your shirt."

She looked down at her shirt and saw the long-set-in stain on her T-shirt. "Bollocks! I love this shirt."

"C'mon." He gestured. "We'll go upstairs; you can change, and the laundry service can get that out of there for you."

"It's barbecue sauce. It's not coming out."

"Trust me. It'll come out. I had a guy bleed out on a white T-shirt I wore one time. You'd never know."

Slowly, she turned around on him.

He noticed her appalled stare.

"What?" he asked.

"You had a guy bleed out on you."

"Yeah?"

"You're just going to drop that there like it happens every day."

He was nonplussed. "How am I supposed to say it?"

"That's horrific! That doesn't happen to people on a regular day! What the hell is it you people actually do?"

"I told you about Flame being taken. You work with Loki, Gilgamesh, and Medusa. You think no one has ever bled out on one of them? Christ, I've got the highest body count number on Medusa for the betting pool."

"Huh?"

"Sweetheart, the people you work with don't make appointments with the bad guys and sign negotiations after a seven-course meal."

"I know, but... It's just... They've never said..."

"No, they probably wouldn't. Why do you think they're so upset about you running into the Kaders? Why do you think they were in a panic trying to find you when you went up in smoke on them? Breaking into that mine was dangerous, but when you stumbled into that clusterfuck, that ramped things up to a whole new level. Your jobs for them, I'm guessing, have been like..."—he searched for a comparison—"like Cherry going on a stakeout. They're jobs they could do, but they're low-level enough that the danger is minimal in the grand scheme of things, and they farm it out to you." He could tell that comment hurt her pride, but she clearly was unaware of what she was involved in.

He waved goodbye to Waters and Kubrick, then led Haskell out of the room toward the elevators. Scheherazade trotted alongside.

"Look," he continued. "You're clearly capable of more, or Cherry never would have approached you for Tribe. Let me ask you this. Why did you turn her down?"

They stepped into the elevator, and the door closed behind them. He leaned his ass against the railing that ran around the three walls of the elevator, his arms locked as he gripped the bar on either side of him.

He watched her consider her response. "Something felt off."

"With the offer?" he asked.

"No, the offer itself felt genuine. It was the condition, maybe. That if I opened the folder and I changed my mind, I'd be either dead or on the run for the rest of my life, trying not to be dead."

He nodded. "So there was a reason you couldn't risk it."

She sucked in her lower lip. "My da," she confirmed.

The elevator door opened. He gestured her out before him, and they walked to his apartment door in silence. Nemo keyed in the alarm code to unlock the door, and as per usual, as it opened, Scheherazade pushed her way through, leaped over the couch, and went ass over head for her manatee.

Haskell smiled. "She's got a short-term memory problem on that couch issue."

He chuckled at the goofy face looking over the back of the sofa at him, ear perked for the magic word *loop*.

"Damn dumb for a dog so smart, but it's kind of funny and cute, in a way. I'm guessing she never had a chance to be a puppy. She had her own before she was really out of the puppy stage." He shook his head. "Go on and change. I'll meet you back here, and we'll go."

24

SEPTEMBER 9, 2022

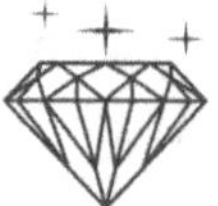

Nemo

Less than five minutes later, they were out of the apartment, down the elevator, and out on the street. Scheherazade was leashed for appearances' sake until they were on the beach. Then she was free to run. Nemo would have been more than happy to throw her manatee around for her, but she was just excited to run around and around in the surf to get the zoomies out, as well as say hello to all the other dogs.

Gem was sitting on the top of one of the picnic tables, her feet on the bench portion. The sun was starting to dip below the horizon, looking like it was setting the ocean on fire.

Damn, she is breathtaking. She's so clueless about how beautiful she is.

He sat up next to her on the table, hip-to-hip, thigh-to-thigh, his weight leaning on his forearms, which were resting on the tops of his thighs, and Scheherazade's useless leash coiled up in his hand, hanging between his knees. "So. Your da."

He heard her sigh. The breeze blew some of her curls up into her face, and she tried to move them away, but to no avail. To prevent being blinded, she looked back in the same direction he was, following Scheherazade.

They followed Scheherazade's erratic meet and greet path with all of the other dogs. He could tell this was going to be a difficult conversation, so unless she initiated eye contact, he would focus elsewhere. His girl was strong, but sometimes, conversations were easier when people didn't look at each other. If the conversation had been about them, he would have insisted she meet his gaze, but this was about her, and he wanted her to feel safe in opening up to him.

He shouldn't have been surprised when she picked up the conversation from nearly twenty minutes earlier as if they'd never taken a break from it.

"My father was known as Le Chevalier Noir. Probably the greatest jewel thief of all time. Until..."

"Until?" he prompted.

"Until he made a mistake." Gem's smile was sad. "But to understand how that happened, you have to understand who he was as a man my age. He specialized in private residences. It's how he met my mother.

"He was breaking into a castle, essentially, in Algeria. Back then, he stole items for the sheer joy of it. Along the same lines as Native Americans counting coup, if you're familiar with the concept."

"It was more the pride of getting away with it than the actual prize acquired."

She nodded.

"The way he describes meeting my mother, it was like Errol Flynn in *The Adventures of Robin Hood*. Have you seen that film? When he comes through the window and confesses his love for Maid Marian for the first time?"

He nodded. "One of the most romantic moments in film."

"She wasn't supposed to be there. He'd met her weeks earlier when he'd been posing as a guest at a public party as a way to case the place. She caught him snooping somewhere he shouldn't have been. She threatened to turn him in. He made love to her. She let him slip away.

"Weeks later, he made his move. She'd come home from vacation early, and he'd chosen her room to enter through because she was supposed to be gone. Imagine his surprise when he came through the window, and she was sitting there talking on the phone. Not exactly Lady Bess, but he swore that he fell in love that very moment. She claimed to feel the same.

"He left the castle that night with an emerald necklace and my mother. They fled back to England, sold the necklace, and bought a cottage on a hobby farm. She swore that the money, the lifestyle she'd grown up in, was nothing if she couldn't have him at her side. And maybe, for a while, it was. They lived in that cottage together for eleven years. Had four children—three boys and me. Da continued his jobs, but when I was two, she begged him to give it up. Rowan, my eldest brother, said she hated being alone and lonely on the farm with no one but four young children to talk to, so Da decided to take on a partner. That way, he could be at home more, like a regular father." She barked out a laugh. "Because being a jewel thief screams with the ability to live a legitimate life."

The sun was on the verge of totally slipping beneath the sea. Scheherazade had resorted to barking at crabs and driftwood since her new friends were starting to head home with their owners for the night. Nemo's heart hurt for the quiet beauty of the woman next to him. It didn't take a genius to figure out how this story was going to end, or how a twenty-four-year-old girl ended up a notorious jewel thief in her own right.

Scheherazade trotted over, but instead of heading to Nemo, she went straight to Gem. Standing on her hind legs, tail whipping back and forth, front paws on Gem's knees, she soaked in the scratches behind her ears that were probably as much a comforting gesture to

Gem as they were for the dog. He watched his pixie bend her face down for doggy kisses, their foreheads touching in the sweetest bonding moment. If he hadn't already been in love with her, that would have been the moment.

"What happened?" he asked.

Gem reached for Scheherazade's manatee, which she had faithfully carried in her mouth to the beach. Rearing back her arm, Gem violently flung the toy as far as she could down the sand. With a yip, the dog was off and searching.

"For years, he had worked alone. No one depended on him, and he didn't have to rely on anyone either. But he met this guy somewhere, somehow, and his fate was written. The first job they did together would be his last. He had a chance at a huge score. Some Indian prince or something. Doesn't matter in the long run. His partner buggered him at the first sign of trouble. My father fell thirty feet along a sheer cliff, and the man left him at the base. By all rights, Da should be dead. Instead, he had a broken back and two broken legs. Lay there for two days before someone saw him, and even then, that was a miracle. The only thing that saved him from prison was that he didn't have any equipment on him. He was free-climbing, and they couldn't prove he was trying to break in. So they took him to the local hospital. He recovered, and when he was healthy enough to leave, he was escorted to the border and informed if he ever returned to the country, he would be imprisoned for life.

"Ma decided enough was enough. She left her four children with my da's mum, and we never saw her again."

The breeze shifted and blew curls across her face again. Nemo reached up to smooth them back, but just like before, they immediately blew back into her face. "And little jewel thieves were born," he surmised.

Gem huffed and rolled her eyes. Scheherazade had returned with her slobbery and salty toy, plopping it in Gem's lap, her muddy paws once again on her jean-clad legs. Laser-focused on Gem, she watched as the woman picked up the toy and flung it in a new direction. Off she went, barking at every shadow in the twilight.

"You could say that. His body didn't heal properly. After the accident, he never was able to walk without pain, and the arthritis set in, causing him to lose his dexterity. He figured if he could no longer do the job he loved, then his children would bloody well learn to love it and keep his legacy alive. From the moment he returned home, there was never a moment in my childhood where I wasn't somehow being trained to be a jewel thief. Making us run across wet, mossy logs. Climbing anything and everything. Competitions to see who could hold their breath the longest. At night, he'd take us places and teach us how to break in and out without leaving a trace. And when we couldn't be outside, we were learning how to tell the difference between the different uncut stones. What the best environments were for which stones. If it could be turned into a thieving skill, we knew how to do it."

"All of you are thieves?"

"Yes, but we have different specialties. My eldest brother, Rowan, specializes in urban environments—skyscrapers, that kind of thing. He's based out of London. Gael lives on St. Kitts. He specializes in larger acquisitions. Oddities. Like, say you wanted to steal an elephant from South Africa and move it to Texas."

"He has not."

"I can neither confirm nor deny that hypothetical example."

Nemo whistled. "That takes balls way bigger than brains."

She continued, "Oscar is our version of Indiana Jones. Antiquities are his passion. No clue where he is right now. And then there's me."

"And then there's you." Nothing could have stopped him from touching her at that moment. He reached out and gently pinched her chin between his thumb and index finger, turning her to face him. "The brightest jewel in the crown."

He leaned in, stopping halfway to give her time to rebuff him if she didn't want his kiss. When she stayed still, her eyes fixed on him, he continued his slow lean. Her eyes closed just before contact was made.

The kiss was merely the placement of his lips on hers, his head tilted to adjust to her position. His top and bottom lip surrounded her top lip, the slightest of pulls to her flesh. He kissed her like that, dragging out the time from touch to pull, just enjoying her mouth beneath his. She soaked in the attention, not reciprocating but certainly not discouraging his attention.

On the fourth soft kiss, he felt a featherlight touch on his face. Her hand had lifted to touch his cheek, then curved around his jaw.

"Nemo." His name was an exhaled vocalization.

"Yes, Gem? Stop?"

Eyes still closed, fingertips still on his skin, she sucked in her lips and shook her head. "No. Don't stop."

"Good. Because I don't want to stop."

It should have been impossible to get physically closer to her, but he managed to shift the infinitesimal amount needed so that they were seamlessly pressed against one another, shoulder to hip to knee. His lips returned to hers, not changing the pressure or action. Just showing her over and over how much he liked kissing her.

The beeping of his watch interrupted the tender moment. Forehead to hers, he muttered an apology. He knew he needed to answer the text, but he remained motionless, his eyes closed, soaking up this quietness with her. The next time the notification pinged, he pulled back, tapped his watch, and saw his brother's request to call him.

Another tap to his watch, and Midas answered before the first ring was even complete.

"You alone?"

Gem gave him a smile and jumped down from the table to give him privacy, heading over to Scheherazade, who was now standing at the edge of the surf, barking at the waves.

"What is so damn important?" Nemo barked.

"Waters wants everyone on a curfew."

"What are we? Twelve? Is he doing bed checks, too?"

Midas snorted. "What would be the point? You're never in yours."

Silence.

Midas sighed. "Sorry, baby bro."

Nemo chuckled. "You're not wrong."

"This whole situation has me out of sorts. We just heard the jet's going to be coming in hot, and we need to be ready to go when Medusa gets here. Apparently, we're picking up Cerberus on our way to Africa."

Nemo grumbled, "I don't trust that guy."

"You're a bit biased. However, Loki has convinced Waters that he's a stand-up guy, and allegedly, we need him, so we're collecting him in Sri Lanka. Maybe once we're with him in person, the vibe will change." There was a pause. "How's Operation Gem in Thirty Days proceeding?"

Damn, that nickname sounds so good coming out of people's mouths.

"Was going great until my watch pinged. But no harm done. Can you do me a favor, though?"

"Have I ever turned you down?"

"I need you to keep some people under watch for me. Three males. Rowan, Oscar, and Gael Dawson."

"Gem's brothers. Already done when I dove into her background."

"You didn't tell me that."

"Believe it or not, I don't tell you everything I do. Some of it you don't need to know, and a lot of it would bore you," Midas groused. "Anyway... relax. They're all good, although I haven't been able to tag Oscar in a couple of weeks. He must be underground. Possibly literally. Last I knew, he was in the Andean Mountains."

"Does that mean you also have her father on file?"

"He passed away in 2018, shortly after you two ran into each other in Riquewihr."

"Ah. The changes in her personal life before taking the job with Mythos."

"Yeah, I'm guessing. Complications of dementia. He was in a nursing facility for his last three years."

Nemo cursed softly. "What about her mother?"

"I had to really backtrack to find her, but that's another dead end. She left her husband when Gem was two. Aneurysm about fourteen months later."

"Okay."

There was a pregnant pause again.

Nemo knew his brother better than he knew himself. Something wasn't right. "What's going on, big bro?"

"Look, I don't know how to ease into this, so I'm just going to spit it out. There's a hit out on Gem."

Nemo's heart stuttered. "Fuck. The Kaders?"

"Yeah. I'm watching it. So far, no takers, but that probably won't last long. I don't want to take it down and risk any leads we might have, but keep her close and your head on a swivel. You gonna tell her?"

"Yeah, she deserves to know. But not right now. When we're in the air, maybe."

"Good idea. Use us as the buffer for when she either flips her shit or freaks out."

"Not sure how she'll take it. She'll likely be scared, but it won't stop her."

"Nope. And what's the saying? Forewarned is forearmed?"

"Thanks for the recall to base and the warning. We'll head back now."

"Copy that."

Nemo tapped his watch to end the call. He spent a few minutes just watching Gem run with Scheherazade, allowing her the freedom and joy of playing with the dog. She had taken off her shoes and had Zade's manatee up above her head, running through the surf, laughing as Zade chased, jumped, and barked for the return of her spit-riddled toy. It made him smile to see her so free.

He pushed off the picnic table and whistled at the pair. Gem was breathless when she reached him, but her eyes were sparkling. Scheherazade was appeased as she had her disgusting toy in her mouth, rescued from the evil queen who kidnapped it.

Eww. That's going in the washing machine as soon as we get back to the apartment.

"We have to head back," he told her. "We're leaving earlier than expected. Have to make a stop to pick up the infamous Cerberus on the way."

She nodded, looked down at Scheherazade, and gave her head a solid rubbing. "This girl pretty much tired me out anyway."

Nemo clipped the leash to Scheherazade, grabbed Gem's hand, and they headed back toward Tribe. The walk was silent but comfortable. She didn't pull her hand from his, and he took that as a good sign.

Once inside his apartment, he threw the toy in the washer, and Scheherazade promptly sat in front of the front-loading machine, watching it go round and round. She'd be on guard until it came out so that she could see it was still in one piece, safe and sound.

Nemo walked down the hall with Gem toward the bedrooms. When they reached her doorway, he stopped her and gave her a lingering kiss on her cheek. "Sleep well, kitty cat. It's gonna be a bumpy ride for a few days."

"You too," she whispered. Then, with a smile, she entered her room and closed the door.

He stood there for a few moments, just staring. Giving his head a shake, he headed into his bedroom and began laying out his gear for the trip. By the time he had it all in piles on his bed, Scheherazade was barking that the washing machine was done. When he stepped out into the hallway, his throat dried up at the sight of Gem opening the door of the machine. As he expected, the dog was halfway in, pulling out Manny and then waiting for Gem to open the dryer.

"Won't sleep with a wet baby, huh?" she whispered. "I don't blame you."

Gem opened the dryer, Scheherazade put Manny inside, then settled to watch her baby tumble on low.

His eyes drew back to the woman petting his dog's head, crooning that Zade would have her baby back soon. She was wearing a ribbed tank top that cut off just above her belly button and a pair of sleep shorts that hung low on her hips. Her tattoos were out in all their glory, and it appeared that she, too, had been adding to her body since they'd last seen each other. She seemed to be almost as covered as he was, including a sleeve going all the way down her left leg.

But what snagged his eye and held it was her belly button. It glinted in the dim light above the washer and dryer in his hallway. She was pierced.

That's new.

And then his eyes narrowed.

No. Fucking. Way.

He made sure to make a slight noise so as not to startle her, then traveled down the hallway, his eyes never leaving the piercing. When he was close enough, his hands reached out to rest on her hips, and he lowered himself to his knees.

"You still have it."

"Yes," she admitted.

He looked up at her. "You put it on your body."

"Yes."

"Oh, kitty cat. I'm trying so hard to behave here, but seeing this on you? Knowing you didn't forget that night? Knowing you wanted to remember? You're making it difficult."

"So don't behave. In what universe do you think I expect you to behave and not try to fuck me? Isn't that what you do?"

Her words held no malice or judgment, but they should have. He wanted so badly to follow through with the offer, but he couldn't. So instead, he kissed just above her belly button, lingering there long enough to circle it with the tip of his tongue and dip inside to where the moonstone nestled, coaxing out the infectious giggle from the tickling sensation he created. Then he tipped his head forward to rest along her belly, hands still on her hips, his thumbs brushing back and forth across the skin.

"I can't do it, pretty baby. I won't. There will come a time when I probably can't hold back anymore because, believe me, I want you more than you can imagine. But that time is not tonight. I need to be better for you. I don't deserve you if I'm not."

"But—"

"No." He stood up, moving his hands from her hips to frame her face. "I will take some of that sugar, though." His lips touched hers again. They opened for him slightly, inviting her to match him. When she responded, he let his tongue drift into her mouth, the tip touching hers, then he slid against its entire surface with one swipe. He drew back, not prolonging the kiss. "So sweet. Nothing better. The only thing that comes close is bubblegum, and now I see even that's a poor substitute. Be prepared to be kissed, kissed often, and within an inch of your life, sugar cat."

After another kiss, this time to the tip of her nose, he let go and stepped back. "I'll take care of Manny"—he nodded at the dryer— "and I'll wake you at three thirty. Night."

She watched him for a moment. Her hand reached up to ghost along his cheek, and then she walked past him to bed. With the soft snick of the door closing, he leaned on the dryer top, his arms locked. Eyes closed, he exhaled.

You did the right thing. Making her feel good is one thing. Making her feel like she's yours is so much more.

25

SEPTEMBER 10, 2022

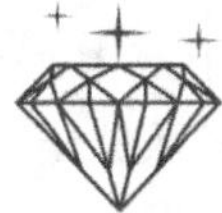

Haskell

Haskell woke up sweating and feeling crushed. There was a chuckle in the far recesses of her brain that was low and sexy. Then she was wet. Unfortunately, it was a hot, slobbery wet, and it was her face, not lower where she'd prefer.

"Eww. That better be Scheherazade, or you're losing your touch, burglar boy."

The chuckle turned into a guffaw. "She has no boundaries."

She felt the bed dip at her side, and she opened one eye to see Nemo sitting on the edge of the bed, his frame silhouetted in the light from the hallway. "Three thirty, pretty baby. Time to wake up. I started the shower for you."

She could hear it running in the background as she began to wake up. Groggily, she then eyed the dog lying on top of her. "You're lucky you don't drool, girl."

"Oh, she does. She'll just wait until you love her unconditionally before she does it." He gave her hip a pat. "Up you git. Time's a-wasting."

"Take the furry weighted blanket with you, and I will."

A funny look crossed his face but was gone almost immediately. "I'm leaving her with you for now." He stood and grabbed her bag that was sitting by the door. "There's a bagel waiting for you on the counter. We'll get real breakfast on the jet. The door will lock automatically behind you, and the alarm will reset. The lift code is zero-seven-zero-five-one-six. Press the B3 button for the armory." He stepped back toward the bed, kissed the top of her head, then was out the door with a command to Scheherazade. "*Beskerm Gem.*"

The dog immediately got off the bed and went to sit in her open doorway, eyes out, totally still.

"Okay, that's weird," Haskell muttered.

Not awake enough to give it much thought, Haskell slid out of the bed and went to take her shower. Ten minutes later, she was out the door, bagel in hand, and punching in the code to the lift. Once inside, she went to hit the B3 button and stopped.

Zero-seven-zero-five-one-six.

People often used dates as pin codes. A six-digit date? July fifth, 2016? It was the date they first met in Valencia.

Don't be daft, child. It's a coincidence.

The voice was a little bit fainter than normal. She was beginning to think that maybe Nemo was serious about her. Or at least, he thought he was. Fantasies were easy to hold onto. After a while, the blush would wear off, and he'd likely get bored. Even though she knew it would probably break her heart again, she planned to go with it for now. Fighting him was like fighting the wind, and she needed to conserve her energy for the chaos unfolding in front of them. Being distracted by all the what-ifs and does-he-or-doesn't-hes would just draw focus from what needed to be done.

She pressed the B3 button, and the doors closed. She looked

down at Scheherazade, standing at alert between her and the doorway. "Why do I have a feeling things are about to get more complicated than ever?"

WHEN SHE REACHED the armory floor, Theory of a Deadman was blaring over the stereo speakers. Scheherazade took one step out the doors, then sat down again, refusing to let Haskell by. When she tried to step around, the dog actually turned her head to look at her and growled. Rolling her eyes, Haskell let out a shrill whistle over the music. Nemo turned. When he saw her standing, stuck just inside the lift, he yelled, *"Vryheid!"* The dog's entire demeanor changed, and she went trotting around the room to see what everyone was up to. Haskell swore she saw Steel sneak the dog a biscuit when she stood on her hind legs to sniff the edge of the table.

Sliding up beside Nemo, she began to pack her supplies on her person. Some of the items went into pockets and pouches on her belt, holsters, and bandolier, but the basics were small and easily tucked away.

"Nice music."

Nemo grunted. "Demon's detoxing, so we let him pick the music rather than rage out. That means we're forced to listen to this Canadian bullshit."

"He's Irish, not Canadian."

"Yes. An Irishman with horrific taste in music, which is why you're listening to Canada's version of Nickelback-lite at an excruciating level to keep his withdrawal in line."

Haskell bit her lip. "It doesn't bother you that he uses drugs? You trust him?"

"Trust me, kitty cat. That man on something is someone I'd

rather have at my side than someone who isn't. He refuses to medicate while on a project, so yes, I trust him."

"So you cater to him and his habit, then put up with the withdrawal?"

"Yeah, basically. Don't worry. Mostly he's just pissed because he'd rather be surfing, but because he's detoxing, he's crabby as fuck, hence putting up with the shitty music. It's not worth fighting him for control of the stereo. Or the volume."

"Please tell me that you all don't fight over the music in your cars."

"Every damn time. If TB's driving, you're stuck with Flame's shit playing. Luckily, she has eclectic taste. I can handle the Toad the Wet Sprocket mixed with the Breaking Benjamin. I just pray I'm not in there when Katy Perry comes on. What's worse is Waters has adopted all of Kubrick's tastes, so it's a lot of Top 40 movie sound-track shit. If I have to listen to 'Danger Zone' one more time, I'm going to hurl all over his truck." He shook his head. "Pussy-whipped, the both of them."

"Does that mean you'll be forced to listen to my music?"

He flashed her a look. "You saying you're mine?"

She pursed her lips off to the side. "No, but based on the covert looks your teammates keep giving me, they do."

He remained silent.

"I dunno. I somehow can't see you becoming a Swiftie," she deadpanned.

The look he flashed her was absolutely horrified. "No. Just no."

"Haters gonna—"

He clamped a hand over her mouth. "I know you're doing a wind-up. Don't even try to pretend you're not. I've seen your T-shirt collec-tion, and there wasn't a single Tay-Tay shirt in there."

She grinned. "You know me too well." They worked in silence, packing up. Eventually, she couldn't hold the question in anymore. "Why is the code to the lift July fifth, 2016?"

His movements barely stopped, but she noticed the hitch. "Each of us has our own unique code so our movements can be tracked in case of an emergency. I haven't had time to give you your own code yet. Or should I say, get one from Midas."

"That's not what I asked you. Try again."

Nemo continued to pack his kit. "It's the day my life changed. I've never been the same since."

Her hand reached to grip his forearm. "Sawyer," she whispered, "look at me."

Immediately, he stopped what he was doing. The next thing she knew, she was moving through the air, and her ass landed square on the worktable. Now she was eye-to-eye with him. He was wedged up to the table between her legs, his palms flat on the tabletop on either side of her hips, elbows locked, her body caged in. "I will most definitely have this conversation with you right now if you want, but we both know you're not ready to hear what I have to say, let alone believe it. I also don't think you want me to say it in front of everyone in this room."

She searched his face. He wasn't being melodramatic. It wasn't that his expression was blank. In fact, it was the most sincere look she'd seen on him other than at the beach the night before. He meant what he was saying. He *wanted* to prove to her that what he was feeling was more than just the physical attraction they'd given into on their previous encounters. And the fact that he'd bare his soul to her —make declarations, make promises—in front of his friends without a qualm told her that this was not a ploy.

Just like his refusal to sleep in her bed last night.

"Okay." Her voice was quiet enough that only he could hear her.

"Okay?"

"Okay," she confirmed.

His eyes flickered over her face and then her body as a whole, searching for lies in her body language. When his gaze returned to hers, he nodded once. Then she was back standing at his side.

"Time to go, people," Waters called out, heading for the lift.

Nemo picked up their tool belts and gear in one hand, gripped her hand in the other, whistled for Scheherazade, and then led her to the lift with the rest of the team. Something about it felt like it was the first of many times to come.

And for the first time in a long time, Haskell felt like her world was righted.

26

SEPTEMBER 10, 2022

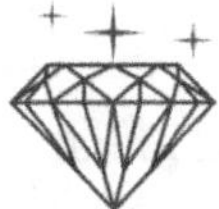

Nemo

Gem had never flown in a helicopter before. He could tell it was not an experience she was particularly fond of. Flying itself didn't seem to frighten her. It wasn't the speed or the sudden changes in direction or even the steep banking because Medusa flew like her hair was on fire. It was the noise. As someone who spent most of her time working in near silence, noise often meant complications. He understood how that was unsettling because it had been the same for him at first as well.

The dog sat on top of Gem's feet, her muzzle on Gem's knees. Nemo sat in the seat next to her and gave her a set of headphones so she could hear what was going on over the rotor blades but also to cancel out some of the cacophony. Once they were over her ears and she gave him the thumbs-up that she could hear people talking, he put on his sunglasses, put on his own headphones, and took hold of her hand. He didn't speak. He just gave her hand a squeeze and didn't let go.

When the helicopter landed at a private airstrip outside of Ramona, California, they quickly transferred to a corporate jet. As soon as their bags were stored in the cargo hold, they were introduced to the copilot, a man named Janus, and then hustled into two of four seats around a table and belted in, with Scheherazade under the table at their feet. With a cursory nod to the copilot, Medusa had switched from helicopter pilot to jet pilot, and they were off.

Seeming to sense she was intimidated by the plush surroundings, Nemo handed her a map of Zimbabwe. "Do you know where the mine was that you were at, or at least a close proximity?"

She scanned the map as Waters and Steel slid into the opposite chairs. She frowned at first, then shot Nemo a look of disgust as she turned the map one hundred and eighty degrees so it was right side up. "Cunt," she murmured under her breath.

"That's one word for him," Steel murmured back.

She looked up at Steel through her lashes, caught the twinkle in his quicksilver eyes, and winked at him. Nemo smiled. It was good to know she could interact with the men in a teasing way, even if it was at his expense.

"Just want to make sure she can actually read a map," he teased.

"Don't worry, Nemo. I won't get you lost and leave you stranded, no matter how great the temptation may be," she cooed.

Steel didn't even bother to hide his smile. "She's almost as sassy as Kubrick."

"She doesn't need any help or lessons from the sass monster," Nemo grumbled.

She opened the map to its full extension and surveyed the key. "Here." She pointed to a spot north and west of Beitbridge along the Mzingwane River.

"How can you tell? There's nothing there."

"The Zhovhe Dam is here." She pointed to a spot along the river. "I was directly west of that. If you follow the main road from Beitbridge up to Gwanda, it's about"—she tilted her head as she calculated—"two hundred kilometers, so I'm guessing the dam is approximately seventy-five kilometers from the city. That's not with any promise of accuracy since the river and the road do not run parallel."

Steel hunched over the map with a pencil. He circled the spot where the dam was located. "It's close enough. How far inland?"

"Not far. A kilometer. Maybe two. The water from the river was being diverted for artisanal mining at the site, but at the time the mine was formalized originally, they were also in competition with the locals for rights. It's part of why the whole thing was a bust, I think."

TB's head popped up from the seats in front of them as he kneeled on the seat, his arms folded across the headrest. "Why is that?" he asked.

Waters chimed in, "Alluvial deposits in the riverbed are how miners find gold. It's also how diamonds were first discovered in South Africa. Find diamonds in the riverbed, or whatever mineral you're looking for, and chances are the vein runs farther. If they're only a kilometer or two in, they're following a profitable vein."

Gem nodded. "Exactly. The mine was meant to be an alluvial site due to its proximity to the river. However, environmental studies done before the purchase of the land and after the purchase of that land showed huge discrepancies between what the projected damage to the water table would be. The owners decided it wasn't worth the pushback, so they shut down the site. It's been sitting there, unused and basically unmonitored, since the nineties."

Consulting his tablet, TB added, "Midas discovered the mine was purchased by a corporation approximately four months ago. It's a shell corporation, and—surprise, surprise—that company is owned by another shell, and so on. He's gone through twenty-two companies so far. Since its sale back in May, whoever it is has been pouring money into equipment. And bribes. I'm guessing a lot of that is going to the local police to look the other way on inspections."

Again, Gem nodded. "The Kaders are likely behind the purchase since Hemeda and Pilis are there. Not those two in particular. More likely Hemeda's father, Pharaoh. It's likely they got a hold of the prospectus from someone on the inside. Using ASM can be lucrative when done right."

"ASM?" Steel asked.

"Artisanal and small-scale mining," she defined.

"ASM might be lucrative in certain situations, but definitely optimal if you're trying to do something illegal," Nemo surmised.

Gem glanced at him.

He shrugged unapologetically. "Criminals know criminals, tiny."

He watched her process that comment. Technically, both she and he were criminals, even if their paths were a little less crooked now. She turned her focus back to Steel. "Basically, ASM is supposed to mean individual contractors rather than corporations or conglomerates. There are individuals who mine for a living, but they prefer to work for themselves. They might move locations at will or possibly even work on a limited-time contract for a small-business interest. Maybe even a larger corporation, but they want the freedom to set their time frame rather than work the corporation's timeline. Then there are people who do the work seasonally. A large number of farmers mine as a form of offseason work."

"And then, of course, there are all the illegal variations," Nemo added.

"You mean slave labor?" TB questioned.

"Yes," Gem agreed. "It's not unheard of for a warlord to use captives to mine and then line their pockets with what's brought in. Primarily men. It's more likely that women turn to the skin trade to make money in the camps rather than mine, but I've seen women working the veins as well. No one is immune."

Waters frowned as he made a decision. "Okay. So that's where we peg the Kaders. Warlords, for all intents and purposes."

Steel froze Gem with his gaze. He pointed to the spot on the map he had circled. "Proximity to the dam notwithstanding, this is out in the middle of nowhere, so we're not exactly going to be able to sneak in. How the hell did you get in there without being noticed? You don't exactly look like a local."

She shifted uncomfortably in her seat.

Now it was Nemo's turn to frown. "Kitty cat, I'm not going to like your answer, am I?"

"It won't work for the three of you. Any of you, actually. Medusa would be the only one able to get away with it."

He closed his eyes and hung his head. He tried to regulate his breathing, but he wasn't sure he was being overly successful. "You didn't." It was a statement of denial that he knew was going to be answered in the opposite.

Clearly she understood what he wasn't asking. "I did what I had to do to get the job done. And I already have three brothers who try to tell me what I can and can't do, so don't you start."

He glared at her. "Oh, I have no problem starting anything."

"You're not my mother, either, Sawyer. I've been taking care of myself for a long time and making my own decisions."

"Nor am I your daddy, but we can take it that direction if I need to get an answer from you, little kitty. Now fess up so I know how many spankings you're getting."

"Touch my ass, and it will be the last time you use that hand."

"Oh, I'll be touching that ass, and you'll enjoy every second of it, but that's for another time. Now tell me."

She huffed and crossed her arms over her chest. "Fine. I posed as a sex worker. There. Happy now?"

He began counting in his head so that he didn't lose his shit.

Steel, TB, and Waters looked at each other, then at Nemo, then back at her. Neither Steel nor Waters said anything at all.

TB, however, said it for them. "Ballsy. But when you're female, white, and blonde with blue eyes, that's probably your only option."

"Yes, it was. And there was no way in hell I was giving anything up to anyone, but I needed an entry," she admitted.

Nemo didn't know who he was more angry with—her for putting

herself at risk or Loki and company for allowing her to do it. His voice was low but measured in its delivery. "Do you have any idea what would have happened if you'd been caught? Or what could have happened if you'd been unsuccessful in getting to your target?" When his eyes opened, and he turned his head to look at her, he felt like flames were shooting out of the sockets. "Not a repeatable option," he growled.

"How else was I going to get inside? I certainly wasn't going to pass muster as a miner desperate for work. So what would your alternative have been, genius?"

"I don't know, but that option is no longer available since you've already been chased out of there once while in that role."

"No shit, Sherlock. Now I'll have to run an even bigger risk, which is to use the illegal tunnels, risking cave-ins, flooded spaces, and heaven knows what else." She looked to Steel and Waters. "I'm going to need aerial maps, a ten-kilometer radius, and eventually a plan to cut across the country. Entry is probably safest coming off the river if it isn't being diverted to the farmers. I can sneak in at night when they're deep in the overnight shift of mining. Less chance of being seen."

"No way am I letting you go across the country without me, considering they've put out a contract on you," Nemo argued.

Out of his peripheral vision, he watched her stare at him. Then she blinked once.

It wasn't how he'd meant to tell her, but it was out now, so he refused to be sorry. Maybe now she'd understand just how goddamn dangerous this was for her.

He saw her turn back to face Waters, Steel, and TB. Her voice was calm. "Well... guess I'm not surprised. I mean, I knew they were looking for me. It's why I took such a circuitous route to get to L.A."

Nemo slammed his fist on the table. "There's a fucking hit on you, Gem!"

"Nemo—"

"Shut the fuck up, Waters! It's not your woman. It's mine! Don't you dare tell me to calm down or whatever other bullshit you're going to spout. If it were Kubrick, you'd be the same way. Pissed and scared as hell."

There was a gentle touch on his forearm. He looked down to see Gem's hand there, and now he winced.

Gem asked, "Guys, can you give us a minute?"

Nemo paid no attention to the actual words behind the mumbling he heard. Instead, he concentrated on the weight of her hand, focused on the smooth skin against his, savored the soft caress as her fingertips massaged his arm. He was fucking this up left and right, but he didn't know how to stop. The thought that someone might actually take her from him was terrifying. At least if she ran of her own volition, he could just chase after her.

And that's what I'll do. It's what I should have done years ago.

"Nemo."

He raised his eyes from her hand on his arm to her face.

"I appreciate that you're concerned, but the danger is part of the gig. If you want something with me, which you seem to keep saying you do, you can't smother me. No matter how attracted to you I am, smothering me will just make me run."

"So that's why you ran the past three times? I was smothering you?"

"No. I couldn't stay the first two times. You were definitely not ready for something more back then. Not sure you are now or that you ever will be. But either way, back then, I had responsibilities that couldn't be ignored."

"Your father," he said.

"Yes. Da was... difficult at the best of times. And because I was the girl and the youngest, it was my job to take care of him, even before he became ill. When the dementia took hold, he became angry. Violent at times. Verbally abusive. My brothers helped financially, but they weren't there to deal with him day-to-day. His expectations became higher and higher for me. His ability to compromise was nonexistent. When he passed, it was almost a relief." She laced her fingers with his. "It sounds terrible to say, but dementia is an ugly, painful, exhausting disease, and not just for the victim. But he was my da, and I loved him, even when he didn't love me back. Or couldn't when he no longer knew who I was."

She shook herself. "None of this applies to what's going on right now, though. Nemo, I knew exactly what I was getting into when I hooked up with Medusa, Loki, and Gilgamesh. A target painted on my back isn't anything new. Yeah, it's a little disconcerting to know there's a monetary value attached to me now, but nothing has really changed in terms of the danger level than what was happening before."

"If you're not scared, then what was with the look? Because you looked scared."

"I was. But not because someone is gunning for me. I was scared because now it seems to matter to someone that there's someone gunning for me, and I don't like being responsible for anyone else's happiness. Been there, done that already. For years, I lived to make Da happy, and it meant I was doing things I didn't really want to do."

"But you're so good at what you do."

She chuckled. "Being good at something doesn't necessarily mean you like doing it, now does it?"

Nemo thought about how he'd been living his life. The stealing? The chase? He enjoyed those things. The women? He was exceptionally good at that, but she was correct. He did not enjoy that. It hadn't stopped him from continuing to try and drown out his need for Gem with anyone he could charm into substituting for his pixie.

He brushed the rebel curl out of her eyes, and once again, it bounced right back over them. "No, it doesn't." He traced the perfectly arched eyebrow to the small star tattoo at its end. "Rest, pretty baby. You've got heavy lifting to do later."

He started to get out of his seat, but her hand on his arm stopped him mid-stand. He sat back down, their fingers laced together again.

"Thank you, Nemo."

"For what?"

"For not trying to keep me out of the loop. For letting me do what I do."

"I know better than to try and stop a speeding train." He smiled and ran his knuckles down her cheek. "You're good at what you do. Better than me. And tinier."

Together, they laughed at his reference to his first nickname for her.

"Still. Thank you for not hulking out over it."

"Oh, I am on the inside. I can't promise there won't be moments of worry that slip out like earlier. But the harder I hold on, the faster you'll try to run. I can't have you running on me again."

"No promises, Nemo. It's not in me to make that promise. I go where my jobs take me," she warned.

"Work is one thing. Running is another. And if you run, I'll just chase you down." He raised her hand to his mouth and kissed the back of it. "Rest."

27

SEPTEMBER 10, 2022

Haskell

An hour later, she woke to Nemo's mouth ghosting along the side of her face. "Hey, pretty baby. Time to wake up."

Slowly and stiffly, she sat up with a stretch and a yawn. She knew her shirt had risen up to bare her belly button because Nemo's eyes automatically tracked to it. She wondered if he knew how hungry his eyes appeared. Probably not.

"See something you like, burglar boy?" she teased.

His eyes traveled up to her face. "Every time I look at you, sugar cat."

"Why does the name change? I'm starting to feel like I have multiple personalities," she grumbled.

He chuckled at her grumpiness, and his face lit up with a smile. "When we first met, I couldn't get over how little you were. Almost like a child. So that's why I called you 'tiny.' 'Kitty cat' is for when you get all cute and hissy. 'Pretty baby' is when you're looking all adorable."

"And 'sugar cat'?"

"'Sugar cat' is for when I want to bury myself so deep in you and kiss you so hard that you forget everything, including our names."

"Oh."

"Oh," he confirmed. He held out a hand to her. "We've got your survey of the tunnels. Time to start planning."

He helped her out of the plane seats where she had curled up for a nap and led her to the back of the plane where there was a bigger table that everyone was crammed around, except for Medusa and the copilot. There was a screen at the foot of the table where the survey map of the tunnels was projected. Since there was only one chair left, Nemo deposited her in it, then stood behind the chair and leaned on his arms on the headrest, his fingers unobtrusively combing through the curls at the nape of her neck.

Waters began to fill her in on what they had done so far. "Midas blew up the map and printed out individual pages, which we then matched up and taped together. He also forwarded a copy to Cerberus as things are going to go 'boom' at some point. While you and Nemo go in to look at the operation and see if you can find some more samples for us, he'll be doing his thing, and we'll be sweeping for people and evacuating."

"Why are we blowing up the mine?" Haskell asked.

"Orders came from Loki. He said that if these stones are truly being mined there, they want to slow down the Kaders' operations. Removing access to the stones will not only halt operations and allow their miners to go free but will also cut off some of their financial avenues."

"But it won't happen right away," Haskell warned. "The stones obviously don't come out of the mine in their final form. They have to be hewn from the rock encasing them, cut, shaped, and polished. They'll likely have more than enough stones to keep them going for a while."

"Correct, but an interruption could serve as a distraction. When people are distracted, they have a tendency to panic because their impulse is to rush to solve a problem with a metaphorical bandage rather than take their time to implement plans that focus on the bigger picture. If the Kaders have an interruption in production, even a small one, Loki thinks it might give us time to figure out how to shut them down on a larger scale. If we're lucky, the thought of no additional supply coming in will lead them to believe they'll have to be more conservative with their funds, and that means they'll have to slow down their operations. It's not optimal, but for now, it's the goal."

Frowning, Haskell bit her lip as she considered the strategy. "What about the miners? Are you sure you'll get everyone out in time? The window of opportunity isn't very large. We're going to need to get in and get out pretty quick."

"One hundred percent sure? No," Waters admitted. "There's always risk. And you're correct that the window is narrow, so it's possible that innocents could get trapped." Seeing the stricken look on her face, he told her, "No one wants that, Gem, but yes, it is a possibility. We'll do everything we can to prevent that from happening or at least minimize the damage. You've been inside. What will we be facing?"

Haskell offered up the stark reality, "Six weeks ago, the mine ran twenty-four seven. Going off that, there's no way to minimize the damage based on day or time. You're going to need a distraction to ensure the guards don't lead a shift into the mines, and you're going to need a distraction inside the mine that allows the guards to flee to the surface to save their own lives but also allows you to drive the miners to the surface. That's the more difficult one because there are only two working lifts, and each will hold about twenty to twenty-five people at a time."

"How many miners are we looking at total?" Steel asked.

"Two hundred, maybe? Unfortunately, depending on what

they've found and how well they've organized in the meantime? I wouldn't even want to take a guess."

He followed up with, "Any idea how fast the lifts move?"

"Not fast enough. Approximately one hundred miners per shift, that's two runs. It probably takes five to seven minutes to travel from the surface to the main cavern. Your best bet will be to have the guards bring a portion of the shift to the surface, then strike before they take the first half of the next shift down."

Steel looked at their team leader. "We're going to need to be super focused, *jefe*."

"Agreed," Waters replied. "We'll have to run a few different contingency plans. Start brainstorming things that can go wrong and how to combat them."

Haskell looked at Midas. "Do you have the topographic map of the area surrounding the mine site? I'll need to find several possible surface tunnels to approach the main cavern from."

"Yes," he replied. "I can zoom in or out to any width. What do you need?"

"Start with one kilometer in all directions, radiating outward in a circle. I need to look at what I can actually see versus the overview itself."

Midas flashed the topographic map on the screen. "Just let me know when to zoom in or out."

The group sat in silence, contemplating the map and her. It was unnerving. She knew she was tense. She wasn't used to working in groups. They had to be concerned she wasn't up to the task. When she worked alone, the only person she had to consider was herself. Now, the intel she offered would affect not only these men but several hundred lives. It was unnerving.

They don't trust you. Why should they? You're young. You're a woman. Just a thief. What could you possibly have to offer them? Quit putting on airs and stay where you belong.

Mentally, she shook off the voice. This was not the time to allow her da to worm his way into her head.

She blocked out their stares and the sound of them turning pages in their briefing folders. Instead, she allowed herself to feel the reassuring weight of Scheherazade sitting on her feet under the table, Nemo's warm breath in her ear, and the touch of his opposite hand that was lightly kneading the back of her neck. The man and his dog knew her tension without having to ask and offered silent support.

Haskell cocked her head, squinting at the map on the screen. "Midas, zoom in one-half kilometer."

He complied.

"Color, please," she requested.

The map went from black and white to color.

"Can you overlay a grid over the map? Red lines. Twenty-four squares. Six rows of four, labeled by letter, left to right, skipping letters I and O."

A few seconds later, the grid she requested was in place.

"Okay, without changing the scale of the grid overlay, zoom out ten percent."

One corner of Midas' mouth tipped up into a smirk as he did as she asked, and he flashed a look at Nemo. Nemo smiled in return.

"Yes. This will do. Keep the table version of the map, but can you reprint the version that's on the screen?" Her look was apologetic. "Sorry for the extra work. It will just be better if we're working on the same scale."

"No problem, Gem. I assume you want the grid overlay on the new printout as well?"

"Yes. That definitely makes it easier for reference."

She rerouted her focus back to the map. Absently, she gave Scheherazade a quick scratch behind the ear and gently pushed back on her chair. Nemo stood up straight and helped turn the chair back so she could exit the table. She walked to the telescreen and began to run her fingers across the map.

28

SEPTEMBER 10, 2022

Nemo

It was fascinating watching Gem in work mode. Nemo knew she was exceptional at what she did, but seeing her in planning mode was intense. It was actually a turn-on watching the analytical brain. He decided that sitting down in the chair she had vacated might be prudent, given the hard-on he was getting from observing her.

When the new map with overlay was done printing, Steel, Waters, and TB began to assemble it on the table and tape it together. Midas was still in his seat, but his eyes were also on the girl up at the telescreen. Since he'd been sitting next to her at the table, he was able to keep his voice low enough for only Nemo to hear him.

"Never thought I'd see her in planning mode."

"I know. She's like a whole different person."

Demon walked up between the two men and pelted Nemo with an empty cup. Confused, he looked up at the medic. "You're drooling. Medusa's gonna get pissed if she has to have the upholstery cleaned in her jet because you're having sexual fantasies about your favorite burglar. Now quit eye-feckin' her and get back to work."

With that, the medic walked away.

"Wow, he's extra cranky," Nemo commented.

"Yeah. He and Cherry had a knock-down, drag-out fight."

"Uh-oh."

"Those two are so confused over their hormones; it's like watching two teenagers figure out how to negotiate the dating game. He does crazy-ass nice shit for her to make her think he's changing, then pulls back into bad habits to push her away. She pretends his habits piss her off when really all they do is scare her to death, so she gives him impossible directives on what she requires for them to be together. Then she tries to live her life, causing him to forbid shit he has no right to forbid. He won't follow through with her because he thinks he's not good enough for her. To make sure he doesn't get her, he purposely does things that make his belief true, and so the cycle begins anew. It's all kinds of fucked up."

Unwrapping a piece of gum from his pocket and popping it in his mouth, Nemo commented, "So? That's been the everyday soap opera of the office for the past five years. Why is he more pissy today?"

Midas snorted. "Since when isn't he pissed off? I'm guessing her being a target and nearly getting blown up scared him straight? Who the fuck knows. He doesn't talk to any of us. Well... not that I know of anyway. Maybe he's talking to Steel cuz that motherfucker doesn't let anything slip when you tell him stuff, but I doubt it. More likely, he's talking to dolphins and sharks while out on his surfboard." Midas surveyed the area over his shoulder to see if anyone was lurking. "Basically, he played her. Got her all hot and bothered, then informed her she couldn't come along for the ride, and she was under house arrest. If she so much as puts a toe outside of the office, he threatened to let security tase her."

"And you know this because...?"

"The idiot forgot to turn off the security cameras in the conference room," Midas mumbled.

"Dude. Stream some porn, for fuck's sake. First Waters, now Demon?"

"Hey!" Midas got pissed. "It's not my fault Waters didn't give me the code word. As soon as I realized what was going down, I shut it off and erased the footage. As for Demon, it's not like he warned me what he was up to. I don't go looking for you all to be getting your freak on at the office. But there are women involved now who were never an issue before, so now I'm not just in control of all the computers and all the surveillance and all the intel and all the hacking, now I'm a fucking censor, too!"

"Jesus, dude, calm down. You really need to get laid."

Midas snorted. "Yeah. Cuz that's as likely as snow in hell. I leave the building less than God does."

"Wonder if there's a delivery program for women like there is for rideshares and food delivery?" Nemo teased.

"Fuck you." Midas smacked him good-naturedly, knowing his brother was teasing him. "Not my type, and you know it."

"I keep wondering what your type is."

"You and me both," his brother muttered.

Gem's British lilt rose over the mutterings of the two groups of men at the table. "Midas, zoom in on zones S and W, and if there's a way to clean out the blur, that would be lovely, please."

Midas grinned as he complied. "I love it when she begs."

She remained with her back to him when she called out, "I didn't beg. I asked politely."

Chuckling, Midas countered with, "I heard my name and 'please.' I count that as begging."

Gem turned to look at Midas over her shoulder with an are-you-serious stare, then looked at Nemo. Nemo just smiled and blew a bubble at her, winking as it popped. She rolled her eyes, then turned back to her map zones on the screen, muttering to herself. He was pretty sure she said, "Delusion runs in the family."

Waters, Steel, and TB finished taping together the new map, then grabbed pencils and highlighters and pulled their briefing folders from under the maps.

"Hey, Demon!" Midas called out. "Can you change the paper in the printer to photo paper?"

Demon grunted what Nemo assumed meant "yes," and then the medic stood by the printer, waiting for the photos to come spitting out of it. As soon as the switch was made, seven copies of each zone on the map began to collect in the tray. Once it was done, he distributed a set to each place at the table, including where Gem now stood at the foot.

She asked, "Midas, when was the last internal survey performed?"

"Nova." Midas pulled up his AI counterpart. "When was the most recent map completed of the tunnels on the Mzingwane Mine."

"Good morning, Midas. The last reported official survey of the mine shafts was completed in 1998."

"Are you able to access any unofficial surveys?"

There was a pause. "I have found an unnamed map sent from an IP address located at the Mzingwane Mine location to an IP address based in Sallum, Egypt, dated four months ago."

Waters looked at Steel. "Sallum again. Anyone starting to see the pattern I'm seeing?"

"Put it on the screen, please, Nova," Midas commanded.

"Begging, are we?" Gem teased.

"Can't beg a computer. She only responds to commands," Midas quipped.

"Don't you dare make us call you Master Midas," TB warned. "I don't want to watch you spanking the computer."

"Is that a euphemism for something?" Waters teased.

"Watch it, all of you," Midas warned. "Remember who controls all your personal security."

Gem clapped her hands several times, effectively getting the men's focus on her. "Okay, I think our best bet for a quick entry is either through zone S or zone W. There are multiple hand-drilled shafts that would allow quick access to the core of the mine as long as there haven't been any recent collapses."

The computer system asked, "Midas, who is speaking, please?"

"Nova, the new voice is Gem. She will be working with us on this project."

"Excellent. Thank you, Midas." There was a brief pause. "Good morning, Gem. Since the map was emailed, there have been two seismic tremors that have registered on the local systems. It is unknown if the surface-to-mine tunnels sustained any weakenings or collapses."

"So we're going in blind," Steel surmised.

"Well, she didn't say there *were* collapses or damage, so we shouldn't just assume the worst," Gem replied. "After all, earthquakes happen around the world all the time, and they don't necessarily cause destruction every time." She directed her attention to Midas' laptop. "Nova, what is the ground's stability factor in the area of the mine?"

"Seismic data shows minimal negative effects in the area within the last ten years."

"What about flooding? Is there danger of flooding into the mine tunnels and shafts from the river?"

"That is a negative, Gem. Currently, the area is outside of its rainy season, and the Mzingwane River is at lower levels due to drought."

"Good."

Nemo looked at her, puzzled. "Drought is good?"

"No, of course not. But a lack of seismic activity as well as lower levels in the river means that I'm also less likely to drown in the tunnels should seismic activity occur."

"So you're not worried about being crushed to death due to a cave-in, just drowning?" Nemo snarked.

She laughed. "I was trying to predict the odds of one, the other, or both. Don't get your knickers in a twist."

"Wrong gender, kitty cat."

"Oh no. You're acting like a girl right now. I had it right. But if you're going to continue being a cunt, fine. Don't get your smalls in a twist."

"He'd have to wear some first," TB argued.

"True," Gem agreed. Then blushed.

Oops. Now they know for sure, sugar cat. Sorry, not sorry.

Nemo grinned. "Nothing small about me, kitty cat, and you know it."

"Confirmation achieved," TB murmured under his breath.

He watched Gem lock down her emotions. There was no way to stem the tide of pink traveling across her features, but the shaking in her hands was barely noticeable, even if her stiff, locked posture wasn't. He gave her points for trying.

"Okay, guys, give her a break," Nemo ordered. He tried to help her by leaning over the table to rifle through his set of photographs and pull out the zones she mentioned. "So why S or W?"

Gem leapt at his opening. "They present shafts that are farthest from the point of the origin structure but closest to the river. The roads will be too open. Instead, we can hire one of my local contacts. He has a small flotilla of boats we can use as cover, pretending as if he's headed to Beitbridge. The boats have a small hut-like feature we can hide inside while he and his men navigate to the zone from the north. He can drop us off just before dawn and be on his way toward the dam with no one the wiser. Traveling by night from his location to reach the dam by dawn would raise no eyebrows."

"This contact... How trustworthy?" TB asked.

"I've used Itai often, and he has worked with Loki many times transporting slaves downriver to freedom. The only downside is that he will not be able to take us back up the river. We'll need another way out."

"Don't worry about that," Steel assured her. "We'll be coming out of there hot. Medusa will be our ride home. Loki and Gilgamesh will be the escape transportation for the miners."

"All right," Waters interrupted. "Midas, due diligence on this Itai fellow. Dig so deep; I want to know what he had for breakfast ten years ago today."

"On it, boss."

"Steel. I want maps of the river and any way on or off it in case of emergencies. I don't want surprises."

Steel nodded and flipped open his tablet.

"TB. I want schematics on the dam even though we have no intention of being near it. I want to know who works it, when, and who crosses it. Leave no stone unturned."

"Copy that."

Waters turned to Gem. "Gem. The people in the mines. Are they free roaming? Chain ganged? How are they controlled?"

"Fear controls them. Ask for water, and if the guard's cranky, he'll shoot you without a qualm. There's no need to chain them down below because there's nowhere to go. A key card is needed to operate the lifts, so they can't get into a lift without a guard. Run? You're shot without warning."

"Okay. Demon. We're bound to run into people who need medical help once we get down in those mines, but we're not going to have time to triage. Since there are guns down there, everyone on our team needs supplies for gunshot wounds. In addition, I want everyone on our team to have breathing gear in case of gas being used or some sort of disaster where they need to be able to breathe in a toxic environment or the case of a cave-in. What maximum time can we expect?"

Demon replied, "Right now, we each have a canister for a maximum of thirty minutes."

Waters rubbed at his forehead and frowned. "I want more time than that. Demon, get Medusa to connect you with Loki. See what we can do. Can't load you down too much, but you all need more than thirty minutes of time to work with in an emergency."

Gem jumped in, "You don't need Loki. You need Cerberus. He's the one with all the connections to things like that, including his own stashes. Might have to make another stop somewhere quick before Zimbabwe proper, but he'll have access."

"Got that, Demon?" Waters acknowledged.

"Copy that." Demon got up from the table and headed toward the cockpit.

"Gem. Use the maps to get a plan going on which shaft you're going to use to enter into the mine. We need visual confirmation of the diamonds, taaffeite, and tanzanite in the same location, in their raw form, so before you leave us, Midas will attach a camera to you for that."

Gem nodded. "Since this map is four months old, I'll put together several routes in case we find cave-ins."

"Excellent," Waters praised. "Nemo. I need you to run possible exit routes from all sections of the mine. Watch for dead ends."

"Got it, boss."

Waters sighed and ran a hand through his extremely short hair. "I'm going to call Cherry. We need to talk to God, no matter where he is. Can't keep him in the dark any longer."

Midas snorted as he worked. "You really think he's in the dark? I'm sure Cherry's in touch with him regularly. He just doesn't want to talk to *us* right now."

Nemo looked at Waters. "What's up with that, anyway? Do we really not know where he is?"

"I don't have a fucking clue," Waters admitted. "Midas is right, though. He probably has his reasons, but it's frustrating as fuck. I'm sure Cherry is in touch with him daily, and you can bet he's not really in the dark. But for whatever reason, he's just not available to us." Waters walked away from the table, muttering to himself.

"I thought Waters was your boss," Gem said to Nemo.

"He is," Nemo told her, "but our overall boss, God, has been off the grid for a while, and no one seems to know where he is or why. Or if they do, they're not talking." Nemo shrugged. "Not like we ever really see him anyway."

"What does that mean?" Gem asked.

"He only talks to us through conference calls. Audio only. Lives up in the penthouse apartment at Tribe, but he's never been downstairs that we know of."

"And you don't find that the least bit odd?"

"Kitty cat, my whole life has been nothing but odd since Midas and I lost our mum when we were seventeen."

"Even I've seen my boss. Bosses," she clarified. "Weird trio they may be, but I still have seen them."

"Yeah, but which one is the head of the triangle?" Nemo asked.

Gem opened her mouth to answer, then closed it with a frown. "You know, up until just this moment, I would have said Loki without a doubt. But now..."

"Now?"

"I don't know."

"Yeah. We've got an ongoing bet. Most everyone thinks it's actually Medusa who's in charge. Those who don't think it's Loki."

"Well, it's definitely not Gilgamesh. And Cerberus is a contractor, like me. Who's your money on?"

"I think Medusa is like Waters. But there's someone else pulling the strings. Someone we haven't seen."

"Huh." She thought about it for a moment. She shifted her attention back to Nemo. "None of you have ever seen your boss? Really?"

"None of us have ever seen him. Well," he reconsidered. "That's a lie. Cherry's seen him. And Kubrick."

"Why Kubrick?"

"It's kind of a long story, and it's connected to another handler we had. She was Waters' sister, and her name was Sarah. Suffice it to say, when she was killed, we all sort of lost our minds for a bit. God put down a commandment—pun intended—Thou shalt not get into a relationship. Punishment was erasure. Complete and total."

"As in... dead?" Gem whispered the last word. "But the woman wasn't involved with anyone. Was she?"

Nemo shook his head. "No. After the decree was made, most of us sort of figured God had a thing for her. You don't get that pissed off over one of your employees. None of us questioned it, and we were fine with the rule at the time. No way were we going to allow another woman to be vulnerable because of what we do. But... time changes things. And when Waters met Kubrick, well, that conference room was *on fire*. God couldn't have stopped that conflagration if he'd tried."

"Wow."

"Yeah. I've got video. It's fabulous."

She stared at him. "I don't think I want to know."

"Oh, no, you totally do."

A throat cleared off to the side of them. "Thought I confiscated all those DVDs."

Gem turned to see Waters standing behind them, hands on hips, a scowl on his face.

"I guess you missed one?" Nemo posited innocently.

"How many more are there since I'm still finding them now, months later?"

"I have no knowledge of the exact number of copies that were made," Nemo answered truthfully as he turned his back on his team leader.

He leaned over his brother's shoulder at the laptop. Out of his peripheral vision, he watched Gem roll her lips inward to prevent from laughing. Her eyes flashed to Waters' face. Waters' mouth tipped up into a smile, and the man winked at her to show he wasn't really pissed off. She let her own smile show through as she shook her head over their antics. Nemo felt a soft glow in his chest. His kitty cat fit in so well here.

Maybe when this was done, Waters would offer her a job with Tribe. Wouldn't that make life so much easier?

29

SEPTEMBER 12, 2022

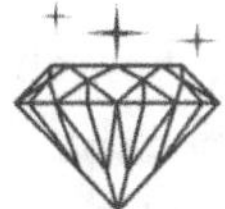

Haskell

Thirteen hours and a jump over the international date line later, the group was deplaning in Melbourne, Australia, to meet with a contact for the things Cerberus needed, as well as to collect the rest of Mythos. Loki met them at the airport. It would only be a short ride to the hotel where the group would be staying overnight before going to collect Cerberus in Colombo in Sri Lanka, then heading on to Vilanculos in Mozambique. The plan was to use a beach house there as their home base for a few days while they planned their final steps.

Before heading to the hotel, the group split into pairs so that they attracted as little attention as possible.

Medusa and Waters took the waiting truck and drove to pick up Cerberus' supply order. Once that was done, they would take it back to the airport, where Loki and the copilot would be waiting to load the items into the cargo hold for takeoff and pay off customs.

Scheherazade would be staying with the copilot on the plane so that she didn't end up quarantined.

Steel and TB went to a local bar and stayed for a meal and the bulk of a football match so that they would arrive later than the others.

Demon disappeared toward the beach for the night—surfing with Midas as his guard, having dinner, and connecting to the local WiFi at a beachside café.

Haskell and Nemo headed straight to the hotel, where Gilgamesh met them in the bar and passed them their room key.

Haskell was torn on whether she wanted to protest the rooming arrangement. On the one hand, she felt that it was presumptuous on everyone's part that she would room with Nemo. On the other hand, she knew she wouldn't be allowed her own room, given their circumstances. Being a part of a couple helped them blend in a little bit. She knew Medusa would be rooming with Loki under the guise of being a couple as well, so she felt trapped in the situation, but she had to admit... deep down, she wanted to stay with Nemo. This gave her permission to do so without guilt, although why she felt guilty about it in the first place, she wasn't sure.

'Cause you know he's just using you, child. That's all that boy's ever done. You're only convenient to a loser like him.

"I am not," she whispered to herself, trying to brush the voice aside.

"What did you say?" Nemo asked as he used the key to open their door.

"Nothing. Sorry. So tired I'm talking to myself."

Nemo raised an eyebrow at her, blocking the door.

"I'm fine, Nemo. Nothing a shower and some food won't solve."

After searching her eyes for a moment, he nodded. "Then that's what we'll do. Follow right behind me. Once you're in the room, step immediately to the left of the doorframe and put your back to the wall. Do not move until I've cleared the room. Got it?"

"Got it," she replied.

He gave her a smile, drew his weapon from under his shirt, then stepped into the room. After doing a rapid check behind the door to the hallway, he checked behind the curtains, out on the balcony, and inside the closet. He followed that with a look under the bed and inside the bathroom. Once he was satisfied no one was hiding, he told her, "All clear."

He grabbed both of their bags, placing his on the bed. Holding out his hand to her, he tilted his head in the direction of the bathroom. She laced her fingers with his, her heart thumping erratically as she followed him into the stark whiteness.

He placed her bag on the double vanity, then let go of her hand to reach into the shower and turn it on. After closing the shower door, he grabbed two towels from the alcove under the vanity and placed them on the closed toilet seat. It wasn't until then that he turned back to her and let go of her hand. The loss of contact was short-lived, as immediately both hands went to frame her face. Nemo stepped into her personal space, their bodies barely brushing against one another. His lips met her hairline in the center of her forehead.

He sighed. Against her skin, his hushed voice said, "As much as I want to get into that hot water with you and make you so clean you're dirty, I'm going to be a very good boy and go in the other room. Take as much time as you need. When you come out, I'll clean up, and then we'll find some food." With another chaste kiss to her hairline, he turned and left the bathroom, closing the door behind him, leaving a stunned Haskell standing in the center of the room, her skin already starting to bloom in the steaming heat of the shower.

Clean and clothed in something she hadn't been in for almost twenty-four hours, Haskell emerged from the bathroom and into the dark hotel room to find Nemo standing in front of the sliding glass door, legs spread shoulder-width apart, hands on hips, staring out into the night. Before she had a chance to even consider her actions, she walked up behind him, slid her arms around his waist, pressed a kiss between his shoulder blades, and laid her cheek against his back where her lips had been. His hands dropped and covered hers.

"Feel better, sugar cat?" he whispered.

Haskell nodded, knowing he'd feel the action against his body. Slowly, he turned in her arms and wound his arms around her shoulders, pulling her tight to his body. He rested his chin atop her head and breathed in heavily.

Nemo held her like that for several minutes. His first words to her when he broke the silence were nearly her undoing. "You always smell like sugar." He buried his nose in her curls. "Even your hair. Everything about you is so fucking sweet. All I want to do is warm you up and make you melt on my tongue." Nemo pulled back from her, breaking the circle of their arms. "I promised you food. Give me five minutes to clean up. I found an Indian restaurant that's open late, about two blocks away. That sound good?"

She nodded, incapable of speaking.

He smiled, grabbed his bag, and on his way past her to the bathroom, he placed a kiss on her star tattoo.

30

SEPTEMBER 12, 2022

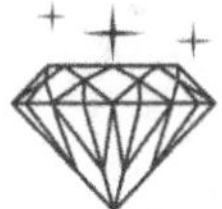

Nemo

Australia in August was mild yet, even at ten thirty at night, so the temperature was just above fifty degrees. However, there was a breeze coming off the ocean, so he used it as an excuse to pull Gem to his side as they strolled the two blocks to the restaurant.

After they ordered, Nemo took hold of the hand closest to him that she had on the table. "Gem. Can I ask you something?"

"You're going to ask me why I left both times, aren't you?"

He grinned. "I'm like Scheherazade with her manatee. Relentless."

Nemo observed closely as Gem looked down where his thumb was caressing the back of her hand. The slow and steady stroke was almost hypnotic. She was considering how to answer his question. The darkness of the restaurant, with its soft yellow table lighting, was soothing and less baring, but she clearly didn't want to talk about it here.

"Can we take a walk after dinner?"

He opened his mouth to speak, but she cut him off.

"I'm not dodging the question. Honest. I'll answer it. Just not here. Not now. Let's eat, and then I'll tell you whatever you want to know."

"Okay. But I'm holding you to that, sugar cat."

"I promise, Nemo."

WITH DINNER OVER, Nemo guided Gem over to the opposite side of the street and onto the sidewalk along the waterfront. His eyes continually scanned the area around him, and he kept himself between her and the street, his arm once again around her shoulders, pulling her tight to his side. Patiently, he waited for her to start talking.

"So. Why I left."

The only sounds were the ocean waves, the seagulls, a few distant calls from the night surfers, and randomly passing cars.

"I told you the basics about my mum, how that affected my da, and what my childhood was like. The prize he was after when he met my mum was the Saturn Diamond. He had to make a choice. He chose Mum. He'd never failed at collecting his quarry before, so despite how happy he was with her, he always felt like he let the diamond slip away. Then he got a second chance, only to have it snatched from him again."

Nemo put the pieces together. "His accident."

"Yes," she confirmed. "The entire time he was recuperating, it ate at him. And when Mum left him while he recovered, it snapped something inside him.

"The diamond became an obsession. I think, in his mind, if he'd been able to steal the Saturn Diamond, Mum never would have left him. To be honest, I think she would have left eventually anyway, but we'll never really know for sure. Anyway, he couldn't let it go. And since he could no longer do the theft himself, he set all his sights on me. At first, I was excited to have his eye. To know that he was admitting that I, his *daughter*, could be successful.

"In the beginning, I loved the work. With each job, though, the pressure became more intense. I didn't recognize that his obsession was starting to take hold of me as well.

"When you and I first met, I was on my way back from a job in Madrid. Da took on a contract job for a pink diamond being held at the Museum of Natural History. He never told anyone that he didn't actually do the jobs anymore, that it was his daughter he was sending out to collect their prizes. As I was on my way home from that job, I decided to take a detour to Valencia just for practice, and I met you."

He turned Gem down a wooden sidewalk leading out onto a pier. During the day, men used it as a place to sit and talk as they pretended to fish. At this time of night, it was deserted.

"I didn't want to like you. But despite the charm and jokes, you were honestly concerned about me being hurt and wanted to make sure I was taken care of. You were temptation itself, and I tried to use snark to push you away. You just kept coming at me, and with one kiss, you became a drug. My eighteen-year-old self would have followed you to the ends of the earth if you'd asked, but even I knew that you were out the door in a few hours. You were my first, and all I could hear in my head was Da's voice, like always, reminding me not to be a fool. Not to be distracted by a pair of pretty eyes and a fit body. I always heard him in my head—things he claimed he told me were for my own good, but now I see they were things to bind me to him. To prevent me from becoming my own person. To make me into himself. The only way he could do that was to drill into me over and over the mistakes he made with my mother, hidden in the guise of how others would use me for their own ends. The irony was, he was doing that very thing to me."

They were at the end of the pier now. A soft rumble of thunder came, letting them know that a storm was brewing over the ocean, and a bolt of lightning flashed in the distance. Nemo pulled Gem between him and the wooden fencing. Her head rested where he knew she'd be able to hear the heartbeat he felt pounding in his chest, and he buried his nose in the curls at the top of her head, breathing her in, trying to send her comfort without words.

"When I managed to steal the Saturn Diamond for him, I was on top of the world. I knew for sure that he'd be so proud of me. He'd love me best of his children. That he'd forget his bitterness toward Mum and become a real father."

"Let me guess. He got more demanding."

"What's the saying? Bingo?"

Nemo squeezed her to him just a bit tighter. "You hear his voice in your head, don't you? Telling you all the ways you're a fuckup. Telling you all the reasons I, or someone like me, couldn't possibly love you. Couldn't possibly find any value in you. Because you're just a girl, and a little girl at that, and, therefore, of hardly any use at all."

She looked up at him. Her eyes had this appearance of always being wide open or of her always being shocked. Maybe it was the crystal blue of the irises that made her always seem startled and fearful. His memory went back to one of their encounters years ago, when, in his head, he'd likened her to prey spooked by the predator. She'd been standing so still he couldn't even tell if she had been breathing, and he could see every moment of her debating with herself, deliberating running from him or remaining frozen and waiting for him. Her slight build made her more waif-like, and the paleness of her skin made her seem more fragile, but he knew for certain that his little sugar cat was anything but weak. Vulnerable, maybe. But never ever weak.

"How did you know that?"

Give her honesty or no?

He lifted one hand from around her waist to brush back what he referred to as her rebel curl, trying to push it out of her eyes as the breeze blew it across her face. It just kept flying into her eyes, making her smile at his endless fight.

"Guess my nickname should be Sisyphus, too," he whispered, kissing the tip of her nose.

They both giggled at his reminder of how she nicknamed herself after the man who'd angered the gods and was punished by being given the destiny of rolling a huge boulder to the top of the mountain, only for it to roll back down to the base once he got it there.

Then the smile went a little sad. The corners of his mouth were still turned up slightly, but his lips were otherwise straight.

"You answer him sometimes," he shared. "Out loud. In a whisper, but I hear it. I don't know if anyone else does, but like you... I've trained myself to hear noises far more subtle than most people would pick up on.

"Then there's the look on your face when you hear him. People might mistake it for concentration on whatever you're doing or looking at. But it's different. Not angry. Not sad. Almost as if you're..." He searched for the word. "I don't know. Resigned? That doesn't feel like the right word."

"That you've come to accept what you are to that person? You've come to understand that the way they think about you is how they will always think of you, and nothing you can do will change it, and that's just how it is?"

"Yeah. Like that."

Gem pursed her lips and nodded, her eyes at chest level on Nemo. "Yes. I still hear him. I tell myself that he was wrong about me. That it was when I was stealing that I was hardly useful to anyone. After all, those were things, and things don't make anyone a better human being. They don't make us more capable, more honest, more empathetic, which is what the world *needs*, and we, in turn, can be useful. Purposeful. And things don't add to the world, either. They're just... there."

"It's why you went to work for Loki and company. You needed to prove you and your talents were useful."

Her smile twinkled like the stars reflecting in the pupils of her eyes. "Exactly." Then the smile disappeared. "Lately, Da's voice found its way back in there. Even though I know his words are untrue, my failure over the last six weeks has brought him rushing back. I guess the reason I'm talking to him out loud is because I'm trying to push him out of my head since responding to him inside my head doesn't seem to be doing the trick."

Nemo tucked her head back to his chest. "He'll go away again. This was just a bump in Le Chatte Noire's perfect past. Now you see how the rest of us mere mortals survive."

She laughed, which, in turn, made him laugh. He rocked her back and forth in small sways, but even though the laughter died, the rocking did not. They simply rocked together in the ocean breeze.

"There's another reason I know what you were feeling," he admitted.

"What's that?"

"Midas." He looked out at the storm over the ocean, creeping ever closer. "My whole life, Midas has had to look out for me. When I was born, our umbilical cords got wrapped around each other and nearly killed me, and when they finally managed to extract me from my mother, I came out with two dislocated shoulders, which have since turned into a bonus for my work. Midas has always felt responsible for that, despite the fact that there was no way he was." Nemo shrugged. "Shit happens when you've got two babies struggling to get out of you. I certainly never blamed him for it, although we give each other shit constantly about killing each other in the womb.

"We had a father in our lives, but he left when we were young. Although Midas is only eight minutes older than me, he became the man of the house, and I became the irresponsible son." Looking out over the ocean, there was a smile on his face and a laugh in his voice, but his eyes and his words held sadness behind them. Regret. "I was always getting into trouble. I didn't even have to go looking for it. It found me, and often. Fights. Bad marks in school. Trouble with the police. And every time, Midas was there, bailing me out of trouble, sometimes literally."

She studied his face before she spoke. "The fights were over your brother, weren't they?"

He looked down at her. "Pretty smart for a *little* girl, aren't you?" he joked. "Yeah, they were. Midas was always so serious. A nerd from day one. Loved taking things apart, making them better, and putting them back together again. He loved books and maps, and his math skills were off the charts. Don't even get me started on anything tech related."

"So he got picked on," Gem guessed, "and your bad marks were because you were trying to keep an eye on him."

Nemo nodded. "Totally clueless about the threats around him because he was so deep into his books. It was up to *me* to protect *him*. I couldn't focus on anything because I was constantly worried he'd get the shit kicked out of him, and he probably would have on a daily basis just for being so fucking brilliant." He shook his head and looked out across the water again. "Did you know he has a master's in psychology? Did university all online, undergraduate to graduate school. He could be anything he wanted to be. Instead, he's spent his entire life getting me out of one mess after another."

"And the trouble with the law?" she prompted.

He groaned and looked back at her. "By the time our 'father' bounced out of our lives, I was already on a path hell-bent for destruction. Things just got worse. Our mother was working several jobs just to keep a roof over our heads, the lights turned on, and food in our bellies. Midas got work as soon as he could to try and help out, and it wasn't always legal. He was so good at computer shit, he had a reputation for never getting caught, and by the time he was sixteen, grown adults were paying him to do who knows what over the internet.

"The only thing I was good at was sports, and I excelled. Midas thinks I could have been an Olympic sprinter. I think he's crazy, but who knows? I had no direction. Father missing, mother working,

Midas hacking. I was left hanging, feeling like I had no skills to contribute, so I ran wild. No dare was too big."

"Nemo the thief was born," she said with a grin.

"Yeah. Something was stolen, vandalized, whatever—it was that Sawyer Newton boy. Funny thing is, over half the shit I was accused of, I never did. But I let the reputation build because with each new sin attributed to me, it allowed Midas to shine. I never even told him the stories weren't true. I just let him believe they were because it was better for him to think I was a fuckup than I was adrift. He just kept fixing shit for me, and he still does. I'm a horrific disappointment to him. He never says it, but I see it in his eyes when he solves yet another problem for me."

"He loves you, Nemo. He wouldn't do it otherwise. And clearly, you love him, or you wouldn't let him believe the lies. Sometimes, we have to mislead others in order to protect them. Midas may have been getting you out of jams all these years, believing he's protecting you, but the truth is, you are the one protecting him. Sacrificing your own self-worth so that he's able to do what he does."

Two sets of blue eyes watched each other. His heart felt near to bursting because, after thirty-one years, someone finally got him. Someone understood who he was behind the brash personality, the infantile pranks, the parade of women, and the constant fuckups. Gem *knew* him, and she'd probably seen right through him since the day they met.

At that moment, Nemo knew that he wanted to make love to this woman and show her what her own worth was, but he refused to make the first move. This time, it had to come from her. She had to want it, and whatever she wanted, she would get. He wanted to be everything to her, not just a boyfriend.

Boyfriends catered to a girlfriend's wants.

He preferred to give her what she needed, though. To be her partner because if he could fulfill all the levels of her triangle—basic to self-actualizing—then she wouldn't have any wants. If he could satisfy her needs, he was demonstrating not just the ability to provide but the ability to nurture and grow.

He almost laughed at himself. For years, he had been chasing ass —and could you really call it a chase when most of the time, all it took was a wink and a smile?—to fulfill his need for Gem in his life. Most nights, he hadn't even had to buy the girl a drink. She was ready to go. And the encounter would be over in even less time. Just a "Hello there, pretty girl," an "Oh my, you look like you have a big cock, let's go," and a "That was fun." Not that anyone wanted to be pinned to a restroom wall of a seedy bar for much longer than that, anyway, but sometimes you didn't even get the third part of that conversation.

But this? With Gem? It was different.

He felt her warm breath on his neck, and her fingertips pressed into the muscles of his shoulder blades. She sighed, but it was so quiet he barely heard her over the waves coming in on the shore. Her face tilted up to his.

"Nemo? I want you."

Instantly, his lips crashed onto hers. She wanted him! He couldn't resist that if he tried. He didn't want to hear logic and reasoning as to why they shouldn't. All he wanted to hear was her panting breath in his ear as he worshiped her. Ruined her. Loved her.

31

SEPTEMBER 12, 2022

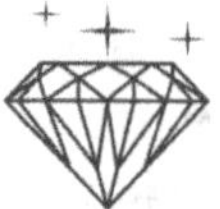

Nemo

A loud rumble of thunder and a crack of lightning shook the pier, the storm much closer than it had been when they arrived. He had one of Gem's hands in his, and he was making serious speed toward the street end of the pier. He knew she was struggling to keep up, but she wouldn't be struggling for long. When they reached the end of the pier and hit the sidewalk, he made a sharp U-turn, dragging her down to the beach toward a row of bathing huts along the divide between the grass and the sand. He picked the third one because it had a sign above it, "Welcome to the Hansen's! Make yourself at home." This one was likely to be more like a mini house inside rather than a storage shed. Within seconds, he had extracted his picks, made short work of the lock, and pulled her inside the shack just as the heavens opened up and poured down rain.

He'd been right. The family that owned this bathing hut was one that used the space like a tiny house for beach days. There were a couple of cots, some stacked lounge chairs, a table and four chairs for dining, and a bureau where they must have kept supplies. While there was no running water or electricity, he noticed they had a huge canister for collecting water, several bowls that were probably used to hold water, a large cooler, and a grill tucked in the corner.

No sooner had the door closed behind them, then Nemo had her back against it, the door relocked, and she was in his arms. His lips plundered Gem's, pressing hard until she opened for him. Once he broke through that barrier, their tongues attempted to dominate the other into submission, but neither seemed able to gain the upper hand.

Their heads turned and tilted to get better angles. Hands speared through hair, pulling strands to bring the other closer, palms cradling skulls, and fingertips massaging away the sting of pulling each other's hair. Teeth took nips at soft flesh and darting muscle in an attempt to subdue, and all the while, the rain beat against the flimsy tin roof of the hut, and occasional flashes of lightning briefly lit the darkness of the space.

Nemo pulled his mouth from Gem's. However, his lips remained close to her skin, pressing soft kisses to her face, the underside of her jaw, and her hairline. She whimpered, clutching him desperately, as she tried to drag his mouth back to hers.

"Shh, sugar cat," he soothed.

His hands went to frame her face, brushing the curls back in his never-ending quest to tame them. They were just like her. Glorious. Alive. Irrepressible. His eyes held hers, her pupils dilated to where the barest ring of blue surrounded the darkness. He began to take subtle deep breaths, then gradually let them out. After about a half dozen cycles, he felt her breathing align with his, and then a few more breaths later, he was able to ease them down completely.

Nemo's eyes never left hers as his hands curved under and around her thighs, lifting her slight weight so that their hips matched up. She'd worn a short skirt tonight, which had already risen indecently when she wrapped her legs around his waist. Pinning her tightly to the door with his body, he used his hands to pull the skirt up around her waist completely, then allowed his palms to trail down the smooth expanse of her skin from her lower back to where her legs met his body. He lowered his head to rest in the crook of her neck, the tip of his tongue tracing the cord from shoulder to ear. Meanwhile, his hands were busy unbuttoning and unzipping his pants.

Gem gasped when his naked dick brushed against her core, the piercing at its tip teasing her through her panties.

"Shirt pocket, sugar cat."

Her smile became impish. She dragged one hand down from behind his neck, around the collar of his shirt, then down the front of his T-shirt until it came even with the pocket on his pectoral muscle. If possible, it seemed as if she traced over to the pocket with her index finger even slower than she had been. She placed her palm flat along the pocket. She had to be able to feel the pounding of his heart beneath the material, even with the contents of his pocket between her hand and his chest.

Her delicate fingers reached in and pulled out one of the several foil packets he'd stashed there. As soon as he knew she had it, she started giggling. "Flavored? Seriously?"

"Huh?"

She showed him the packaging. The howl of laughter burst out before he could stop it. "Fuckin' TB threw the box at me in the armory as a joke. Motherfucker opened up the box and switched out my brand for this shit. He's so getting a confetti cannon inside his Humvee when we get home."

"Can I help?"

He laughed harder. "Sugar cat, you can bomb his car yourself. I'll be your lookout. Dare I ask what flavor it is?"

Holding up the packet to the moonlight, she looked at the label. "Cowboy Carl's Every Flavored Cock," she read off the packet. "Seriously? Who comes up with this shite?" She tore the corner off the packet and gave it a tentative lick. "Black licorice."

"Eww." He made a face. "At least they're not lubed on the inside with ginger or anything." Then he shuddered. "Ouch."

He moved to take the packet from Gem, but before he could, she ripped it open the rest of the way with her teeth and spit the top piece off to the side. She slid it from the packaging and shoved the foil back in his pocket. What happened next... his brain wouldn't wrap around it, no matter how much it tried.

When he reached for the condom, she shook her head. "Put me down."

He felt his heart rate pick up again. Hands still palming her ass, he eased his weight off her against the door and helped her slide down his body. He was frozen for a moment, but that was all the time she needed. She dropped to her knees between him and the door, and his brain flew to the moments in Riquewihr when she was in much the same position, trying to pick the locks of the antique shop.

She quirked an eyebrow at him. "Joke's on him. Black licorice is my favorite flavor."

With that final statement, Gem popped the condom in her mouth. He watched her intently as her hands slid up his legs from shin to thigh to hip. His cock pointed straight at her, a bead of precum already welling at the tip, and he used every ounce of his control to keep from hauling her up his body to slam her back up against the door. Gripping her hands at his hips, he let her surround the tip with her mouth, smoothing the latex down his shaft.

She took her time, and he felt his eyes try to roll back in his head. Her lips were rounded to the rolled material, pressing firmly to his cock as she moved down his length. After about three inches, he felt her back off him, a teasing tip of her tongue sliding along his dick to test how well the material was fitting to the skin on the underside.

Don't stop! Whatever you fucking do, don't stop!

Firm pressure on the second downstroke took the condom another inch past where she'd previously stopped, and on the way back, he watched her bare her teeth and lightly drag them along the latex.

"Fuck, sugar cat! More."

He agonized through a repeat of her actions, pushing the condom farther down on his dick, then barely dragging her teeth back up toward the tip.

"You can go a little harder, pretty baby."

On her next pass, he felt her teeth pushing the last of the material around him. He worried he was crushing her fingers as he clamped them to his sides, but her hum of laughter at his panting breaths, squeezing fingers, and twitching hips told him she was more than good with his reactions.

He tried. He really did. But his palms could no longer remain on top of hers. He speared his fingers through her curls to shape around her skull and hold her head firmly. He didn't force it, but with each subsequent stroke and glide from her to him, he encouraged her to go just a little deeper until, finally, she buried his cock in her throat, her nose pressed deeply into his skin.

"Fuck, sugar cat," he ground out. Or at least he thought he said it. Maybe it was just in his head because he knew he wasn't thinking clearly. It just felt too good being buried in the warm, wet heat of her mouth.

Gem's response was to drag her index fingers down the Adonis belt grooves leading to his cock, and then she made a sharp detour so that her hands could wrap around his ass cheeks and pull him even tighter to her. There was a humming sound that came from her, then the flat of her tongue began to massage the underside of his cock. At least, what was in her mouth and not her throat.

What the hell? She did not... Oh my god, yes, she did because she's doing it again. Marry this woman! Marry her now! Tie her up! Carry her off! Hide her in a cave!

The tip of her tongue fluttered at the base of his shaft, retreated, and then he felt her jaw drop like a cobra. Her tongue slipped past her lips and curled along the front of his balls. As he opened his mouth to thank any god he could come up with for her lack of gag reflex, the pool of saliva she had generated coated him, allowing her to bring them inside her mouth along with his dick. Between her reflexive swallows, the massaging tongue, and the incredible amount of saliva she was generating, he wasn't going to last long.

The only thing that would make this better is if there was no condom. I'm not sure whether to thank TB or spray ginger on all the cotton swabs in his bathroom.

One hand moved from the back of her skull to smooth back the rebel curl. "Make sure you get every bit of that licorice taste, woman, because I'm going to fuck you stupid in about twenty seconds," he warned.

She winked at him.

She fucking winked at me!

He chuckled. "Something wrong with your eye, sugar cat?"

He caught the naughty twinkle in her eyes as she watched him from down below, and she made a huge show of backing off his cock. The groan she pulled from him was long and low. "Please remind me to thank TB for the prank condom."

Nemo stopped her from wiping up the spit with her denim jacket sleeve. Instead, he pulled her to her feet, then picked her up and pinned her to the door once again. He made sure her skirt was completely up around her waist, his soaked cock dragging across the small triangle of material covering her mound. Meanwhile, his mouth dropped down onto hers, feeling the slickness of her skin against his face, and he made sure to drag his cheeks against her mouth to spread it on him. He groaned against her lips. "I fucking love you messy," he admitted. "Didn't get to taste that pussy, but at least I feel like I was between your thighs, sucking up all that sugar."

He backed up to the lounge chair stored along one wall and threaded his fingers into the waistline of her panties, skimming them down her legs, making sure they didn't get caught around her shoes. Before pulling her knees up around his hips, he growled, "You want control, sugar cat? Hop on."

She kneeled above him, straddling his thighs. He was about to make sure she was ready for him, but she was too fast. One tiny hand gripped his cock, she shifted slightly, and then he was buried in her, her channel so slick there was no resistance.

Nemo's hands grabbed Gem's waist. "Warn a guy, would ya?" he groaned out.

She rose up and slid back down, grinding against him. "Where would the fun be in that?" she teased.

He slid down the lounger a few inches so that his lap allowed her more room to move, and he was in a leaning-back position so that he could see more of what was happening. When she bottomed out on him the second time, he stopped her movements by gripping her so firmly he worried he'd leave bruises. Later, he'd kiss each fingerprint in apology, but he wasn't going to last very long at this rate. "Sugar cat, you've gotta stop moving. My dick is all in—in more ways than one—but I'd like this to last a little bit longer than sixty seconds."

When he wouldn't let her move, she changed her tactic. "I thought you were giving me control, Sawyer? Maybe I want it so hard and fast that it makes me believe you can't bear to be without my pussy squeezing your cock." Her hips swiveled and ground down on him as best they could. He felt his dick swell further, and her walls grip him tighter, massaging him with each pulse, each breath.

"Please, sugar cat, ease down," he moaned.

She whispered, "Why, burglar boy? Can't take the heat?" Her hands latched onto his, where they gripped her hips and pried them loose. Nemo found they were suddenly above his head, and she was curling his fingers around the top of the lounge chair as she lay on top of him, plastered to his chest, resting her mouth against his ear. "Leave them there, or I'll stop."

Nemo groaned as her lips and teeth grabbed onto his ear lobe. "Suck on that any harder, and you're going to remove the gauge."

"Maybe I want a souvenir," she quipped back.

"No way." He poured every ounce of truth into his next statement. "Souvenirs imply memories of places you once were, and I'm not a place you *once* were anymore. I'm the place you *are*."

She froze in his lap. "Nemo, I—"

"No, Gem." He looked at her intently. "Just, no. We're not talking about this now. But we will be talking about it. Right now, though, all my brain power has been removed and sent in reserve to other parts of my body, and I refuse to ruin this moment. We'll deal with the rest of 'us' when we get back home."

A crash of simultaneous thunder and lightning shook the beach shack as he gave a quick, sharp punch up of his hips, making sure he dragged himself across her top inner wall on the way, drawing a hiss of pleasure from her. He watched her eyes glaze over as her head tipped back, and her fingers dug into his shoulders hard, her short fingernails leaving half-moon indents where she gripped him. He held himself in place.

"Move, Nemo."

"That was just a reminder that I'm inside you. No way am I moving anymore, Gem. You wanted control, so you've got it. I want *you* to fuck *me*. Use me to get yourself off. I'll enjoy whatever you do simply because it's you."

The look on her face was one of uncertainty. He gave her a single nod to encourage her. "I've got you, sugar cat," he whispered.

She leaned back, hands on his thighs behind her, so that his cock was buried as deep inside her as it could get. Now upright, she began a slow up-and-down pace on his shaft, grinding his piercing against her G-spot for maximum effect. Then, once she had a comfortable rhythm for herself, she began to add a twist from left to right with her hips that helped grind her clit against the base of his cock with each dragging motion. He felt her increase her speed, struggling to maintain both the internal and the external friction, working hard to get her release.

Nemo had always been in charge of what they'd done in the past. With her blow job moments ago, she'd made a decision on her own of what she wanted, and he found it heady as fuck. Not that a submissive partner was a bad thing, and not that she didn't actively participate once he set things in motion, but she'd never made the first move on anything. Not even with prompting. This version of Gem was what he imagined her to be like when she worked a job solo. Confident. Brazen. Independent. It was difficult not to take over, but he wanted her to see herself in her glory.

She wasn't a talker, but he heard her cues in the whimpers and panting breaths she began to make. She was close to imploding, and he couldn't wait to feel it. His eyes drifted down her body to watch it move over his, and his eyes caught the wink of the moonstone piercing in her belly button.

Fuck! So hot that she put that diamond there. She marked herself with me, whether she realizes it or not.

His eyes drifted to the floor. The lightning through the back window depicted her shadow there as if she were playing out a voyeuristic scene in a movie, suggesting she was fucking someone but giving no clue as to the other party involved. Head tossed back, her throat was exposed, and he had just enough light to see her pale skin glow in the dark, shadows passing over her face and arms as she moved in the frame of the window. Leaning low in the lounge chair gave him a fabulous view of her movements and reactions, but it wasn't enough. Nemo slid down just a touch more, which brought more of her into the frame of the lightning flashes through the window.

Nemo turned his gaze back to where they were joined together. He marveled at the slickness her body created. The shine of her left behind on him. The tightness of her muscles as she gripped his cock inside her. "Fuck, that's so it. Right there." He groaned. "You squeeze me so tight. So hot. So wet. Come for me, sugar cat. I want you to come so hard you see stars."

Her breath hitched, her eyes rolled back in her head as it dropped back onto her shoulders, and he felt two things happen simultaneously. Her weight slammed down on him, and her inner walls squeezed him impossibly tight. There was a flutter he rarely felt with a woman, and his heart raced.

Nemo's control snapped, and his arms came off the chair to grip her waist. He needed to watch this bomb go off more than he'd needed anything else in his life. "Need you to get yourself off, pretty baby. Play with your clit for me."

Gem wasted no time doing as he asked. He watched the fingers of her right hand drift down her body, then slide into her pussy to separate her lower lips to reveal her clit. Creating a vee with her fingers and pressing the flesh back from her hard pearl, she used a single finger to tap it several times, then rubbed the nerve bundle in tight, fast circles. When he felt her body clench him even tighter within her walls, he used his upper-body strength to lift her completely off him. It was a little bit of a struggle because her body did not want to let go of him, but he won the battle, and she was barely an inch over him when her body completely let go.

Then she screamed, her release bursting out of her at supersonic speed and power, soaking her and him. He'd never seen anything like it.

Bet this chair has never seen that kind of action before!

He felt Gem's body begin to collapse as soon as the flood was over. He pulled her close, a hand to her lower back, the other around her shoulders as she started to shake. Then he heard the sobs. She was completely overwrought.

Gently, he moved the arm that was around her shoulders so that he could support her neck with his hand. He remained pressed tight to her body, his free hand running through her hair. "That's it, sugar cat, let it out," he whispered. He pressed kisses to the side of her hair as he reassured her. "You did so well. Just breathe. I've got you. Shit, that was the sexiest fucking thing I've ever seen. So fucking hot."

The storm outside began to lose power just as the storm inside Gem subsided. He sat up, scooped her up as he stood, turned, and straddled the chair in the opposite direction, laying her down like a baby in a crib, a hand palming the back of her head, the other under her ass. He kissed his way down her body—lips, chin, hollow of the throat. When he reached her belly button, the tip of his tongue orbited her piercing, giving a gentle tug to the moonstone gem with his teeth, and she let out a giggle as she weakly tried to fold in on herself to prevent him from continuing to tickle her there. Smiling in amusement, he moved to the top of her mound, her clit, and then he began the process of licking her clean.

When she finally regained her voice, she covered both of her eyes in embarrassment. "I can't believe I just did that."

Continuing his work, he chuckled. "Guess you should be in control more often."

She glanced at him from between her fingers, quickly tightening them back to cover the heat spilling across her face. "And I *really* can't believe you're doing that."

His tongue took a long, slow swipe between her outer and inner labia, making sure to get all of her taste. "Fuck yeah, I'm 'doing that.' Why wouldn't I?"

"Eww," she complained and slapped his shoulder. "It's gross."

He lifted his head up. "What's gross?"

"That."

"Your cum? Hell no! Hot as hell that you can do that, and there's no way I'm going to allow any of your sugar to be wasted. I'd lick it off myself if I could. I'm flexible, but not that flexible," he teased.

She paused. "Do you need me to..." She gestured to him.

"Need you to what?"

"You didn't finish."

"Oh, that. Don't worry about it. I'm good, sweetheart. I made you feel good and that's all that matters right now."

Her eyes blinked twice. "You never say or act the way I expect you to." She sat up on her elbows. "Can I ask you something?"

He ignored her stare, continuing to kiss and lick down her thigh to her knee. "Of course."

"Why me?"

Nemo began the same process but up the other leg. "Why you what?" he murmured against her flesh.

"If I listen to your team, you've slept with the entire single population of L.A. and half of the rest of the single females in the world.

So I get it—I'm single, I'm female, I'm convenient. But you keep saying these things that make it sound like I'm different."

He gave one last swipe to her clit, causing her to shiver, and then he folded his arms over her belly, laying his chin on top of his hands.

He sighed. "I'm not sure this is the best time to get into this."

"Nemo, don't dodge the question."

He stared intently at her. "You really don't know?"

"How would I possibly know the answer to the question?"

Nemo's index finger drew patterns on her Saturn tattoo, his eyes looking at what he was doing, but he wasn't really seeing what was in front of him. "Because, tiny, you *are* different. When we met, you stole every sensible thought from my head. No other woman has ever made me forget myself."

She frowned.

"You literally fell into my arms when I least expected anything to happen. You brought out all the protective instincts in me that I had never felt before. You tempted me to cherish you without doing anything other than just being you. I was stupefied by your gorgeous eyes that looked so sad, the tight little body that could bend itself into a pretzel. I couldn't have walked away if I'd tried.

"And when I got inside you." He closed his eyes, groaned, and lowered his forehead to her belly, his voice muffled. "You were Circe leading a sailor to his death. Even though I knew you would destroy me, I went to you anyway. And I'd do it again." His lips kissed her belly tenderly. "And again." Another kiss. "And again, until I was nothing but a useless shell of a man," he whispered.

Nemo raised his head to look her in the eyes again. "When we ran into each other two years later, I couldn't believe my luck. But then—poof—you were gone again. For the next four years, I searched for you in all the wrong places." He reached for her hands, laced their fingers together, and drew them to her waist, where he held them. "I wish I could take every one of them back, sugar cat." His eyes burned. "I tried to convince myself that I could fuck you away, but all it did was make me feel worse. Miss you more. I hated what I was doing, but I couldn't stop because that meant I'd have to face the fact that no one else would do. If I could take it back—"

She moved their hands to cover his mouth, and she shook her head. "I don't care if you fucked ten women or ten hundred. That wasn't what I was asking. It might seem needy, girly, whatever, but I don't understand this need you seem to have to conquer me. You've already had me. Three times now. And you don't do repeats, so it's odd to me that you'd return to the scene of the crime, as it were."

He smiled. "You're the only one who makes me feel like I matter. The only one who I really want. The only one who makes sex move the earth for me. The only one I want to commit to in every way. No one else completes me."

He let Gem free one of her hands, which she brushed over the top of his head, threading through the glued-up hair, separating some of the tangles that managed to settle in his short strands. Her fingertips smoothed down the sides, then traced around the shell of his ear and traveled to his swollen lips from making love to her with his mouth. "I think those are all lovely sentiments, but when this is done, and I go back to contracting for Mythos, you'll go back to your playboy ways. It's part of you, Nemo. It'll always be part of you. It's just... who you are. And while our paths may cross again in the future, even leading to more sex, I don't know if it's truly in you to commit to anyone but yourself and Midas. Even your friends see that."

He felt anger rise from deep inside his belly. "You honestly believe I couldn't make a promise to you and keep it?"

She smiled sadly at him. "I think you truly believe, right now, in this moment... maybe even over this short-term period... you could commit, but it would fizzle sooner rather than later. You might not cheat on me, but you would eventually move on."

Nemo extracted himself from between her legs and stood at the side of the cot. He yanked the condom off his cock, pulled up his pants, buttoned them, zipped them, and shoved the condom in his pocket. He snagged her panties from where they lay on the floor and handed them to her.

"We should head back to the hotel. We've got an early start tomorrow."

He watched Gem swallow tightly, aware that she'd hurt him, but no apology or backtracking came from her mouth. She simply stood, pulled down her skirt, and put on her underwear. Absently, she smoothed her hair back.

Silently, he headed to the door, opened it, and waited for them to pass through. Nemo and Gem walked side by side back to the hotel, but this time, there was no hand-holding, no tucking her into his side to keep her warm, whether she was cold or not. He was thankful it was a short walk.

When they got to the room, Nemo opened the door, then held the key out to her. "Phone." He held his hand out.

Reaching into her back pocket, she removed her phone and handed it over. He clicked into her contacts and added several series of numbers. He extended the phone back to her. "Make sure to bolt the door. Don't open it for anyone but a member of the team, no matter what the reason. Midas is next door. Waters and Demon are across the hall. TB and Steel are just two doors down and will come running if you text them. One of them will collect you at five o'clock."

She looked up at him, her eyes sad and filled with regret. "You're not staying?"

"No. I don't think it would be a good idea." His voice went softer, but he knew it was clear that he was still mad. "You're safe as long as you stay inside. I'm going to head to the airport. Scheherazade is probably confused without me there, anyway."

"I'm sorry, Nemo."

"Don't be," he said tightly. "You're probably right. I've always been an asshole on the inside. The pretty candy coating on the outside only covers that up. It doesn't make up for it."

"You know that's not true," she chastised. "Asshole is never a word I'd use to describe you, and I don't think anyone else would either."

Nemo shrugged, attempting to hide the hurt. "Asshole. Irresponsible. Playboy. They all essentially add up to the same thing. Incapable of being taken seriously." He felt his mask solidifying in place. "Go inside, Gem. Bolt the door. Go to bed."

She gave him one last look, then passed into the room and closed the door. He waited until he heard the bolt flip over, then he turned on his heel and went to the elevator. With each step he took, he felt colder. And when the doors closed on him and the empty hallway, he held his head high, his face expressionless. But inside, the shutting of the door was a loud thunk, closing any opportunity to have his pixie in his life.

32

SEPTEMBER 12, 2022

Haskell

As soon as the door clicked shut, Haskell felt the loss of Nemo. She leaned her side from head to knee against the door as she shot the bolt, then placed her palm flat against the door and closed her eyes.

It's for the best, child. You know what you said is true. You'd never hold his attention for long, and he'd be chasing everything with tits while you watched him do it.

"Maybe you're wrong," she whispered, a tear escaping from one eye.

She heard the lift ding as it arrived and listened to the door close, knowing that Nemo was inside and traveling away from her. He should be in the room with her, stripping her down and making love to her right now. Instead, he was heading to the airport to spend an uncomfortable night sleeping on the plane, despite the comfortable leather seating, with only his dog for company. "Stupid, stupid, stupid," she muttered.

Before she could pull away from the door, there was a quiet knock. In her excitement that maybe Nemo had changed his mind and not gotten in the lift after all, she unbolted the door and whipped it open. Unfortunately, Nemo was not standing there. Instead, it was the hulking figure of TB.

He glared at her. "What if I'd been someone who took the hit on you?"

She huffed and crossed her arms over her chest. "Then I guess I'd either be dead or carted away inside a piece of luggage. What do you want?"

"Let me in," TB ordered.

Haskell stood back from the doorway, holding the door in her hand. Once TB had cleared the threshold, she closed the door and turned to face him. "What do you want?" she repeated.

He studied her. "You okay?"

"I'm fine. Why wouldn't I be?"

TB smirked. "You're a terrible liar. And I know you're not okay because I happened to open my door while you and Nemo were saying good night, so rather than interrupt what did not sound like a happy good night, I stayed put. Then I saw Nemo leave here, and he was *definitely* not okay. He would never leave you on your own, given how he feels about you, so that means whatever happened was bad."

"Well, I guess he's got everyone fooled because he's on his way to the airport to spend the night with his dog rather than me." Even she heard the hurt in her voice.

TB was totally on the mark. She was a terrible liar. Always had been. It was part of why she chose to stand silently when people spoke to her, and she either didn't have a truthful answer or didn't know how to talk around the truth.

TB turned his head to consider the view outside the window. When he brought his eyes back to hers, he looked decidedly uncomfortable but resolved. "That man is head over heels in love with you. Has been for years. If this is about the women he—"

"It has nothing to do with the women he's fucked his way

through." She crossed her arms again over her chest. "Well, not directly. I don't care about the women themselves, but they're too much a part of his psyche. I can't compete with them, and frankly, I don't want to."

"What has he told you about them?" TB asked.

"Nothing."

TB nodded as if he expected that response. "All of them have looked nothing like you."

See? I told you he's not interested in short little tomboys like you.

Why did TB's admission hurt so much? It wasn't like she hadn't known that she wasn't really his type.

He continued, "We didn't know him when you met for the first time. He's been really closemouthed about it, so what little we know we got from Midas, and his knowledge is minimal, at best. The second time you two got together, he was on one of his first assignments for Tribe. Midas told us that he'd run into you again, and Sarah, our handler, was pissed as hell at him for letting you get away. From that point forward, he fucked every woman he could find, but not one of them was a tiny, curly-headed blonde. No tattoos or piercings. All high-maintenance, manicured, designer-dressed women who just wanted a quick fuck. He was doing everything in his power to drive you out of his brain." Now he really looked uncomfortable. "You did not hear this from me. I will deny it to my dying day. Do you know about the bet?"

"Is this supposed to make me feel better? Because it doesn't," she grumbled.

"Yeah. We're guys. We bet on everything imaginable. It's a terrible, asshole move, but I'm pretty sure it's part of a male's DNA. Anyway"—he shrugged—"when you were sitting in the conference room, he opened a new bet. Said that he wanted you or no one. He predicted thirty days to get you to agree to be his woman. We, of course, being the dicks we are, gave him shit about it. Predicted everything from months to never for that to happen.

"Of course, we were being shitheads on purpose. I think we were so surprised that we didn't know how else to respond. There's one person who said he shortchanged himself, but Steel is some sort of Nostradamus. Either way, Nemo was dead serious. So serious that he claimed you, no one else, and if not you, then no one ever again."

Keeping the look of surprise from her face was impossible, and she knew it.

TB confirmed, "He's dead serious about you, Gem. So much so that he's had several conversations with Flame about how to handle what he sees as the most delicate operation of his entire life.

"The guy who I just saw leave this hallway? He was hurting. Hurting badly. You've got a lot of power in your hands when it comes to him. If you don't want him, then, by all means, cut him off right now and keep away from him. We'll always protect you and be there if you need us, no matter what happens between the two of you since he's claimed you as tribe." TB walked to the door. Before he opened it, he looked back at her. "If you love him, or even think you could love him eventually, then believe in him. Because if there's one thing I know about Nemo, it's that he honestly believes that no one does."

TB was almost out the door when she called him back. "TB, wait!"

He ducked his head back in the door.

"Will you take me to the airport?"

TB grinned and stepped back in to grab Nemo's duffle bag. "I was hoping you'd ask. Grab your shit. Let's go."

WHEN THEY GOT to the airport, TB made sure she was able to board the plane, put Nemo's bag in the front galley, then got back in the rideshare and went back to the hotel.

Haskell crept to the back. The lights were dimmed throughout, but not enough that she couldn't find Nemo and Scheherazade.

When the dog saw her, a low whine came from her throat, and she got up and went to Haskell. She nuzzled Haskell's hand, then went to lie in the doorway of the plane as if she understood that Nemo needed his human woman right now.

Nemo lay flat on his back, the arm closest to the back of the couch thrown over his eyes. Quietly, she placed her bag on one of the seats. She pulled off her shoes, then crawled onto the sofa, weaseling herself between Nemo and the back of his makeshift bed.

His arm snaked around her waist, pulling her tightly to his side. His other hand dropped from his eyes to snake through her curls and pull her head to his chest.

"I'm so sorry, Nemo. I didn't mean to doubt you. I just don't see myself the way you do."

Nemo pressed a kiss to the top of her head. "You need to stop listening to your da's voice in your head, tiny."

"It's hard," she admitted.

"I know," he whispered. "But from now on, the only voice you should be listening to is mine. Or yours and mine."

"I'll try," she promised.

"Good. Now, get some sleep. I think we'll both sleep better now that we're together. I'll wake you up when everyone gets here."

Haskell snuggled into Nemo, and within moments, she was asleep.

33

SEPTEMBER 13, 2022

Nemo

After just a few hours of sleep on the plane, they were off on another thirteen-hour flight that got them to Sri Lanka to pick up Cerberus and the rest of his supplies. Upon arrival at a private airstrip at Bandaranaike International Airport, the group exited the plane, Nemo's hand on Gem's back, and he saw Cerberus stiffen involuntarily.

"You got something going with Cerberus?" he asked in a voice only she could hear.

"No. Why?"

"He saw us, and he went military-straight."

She paused, and he could see her formulating a careful response. "When I first met him, we were together a lot. I thought... maybe... I might see if there was something between us. We tried, but I just couldn't seem to let go enough to be romantically attached."

"He clearly still feels something for you."

"If he does, it's more of a sibling kind of thing." She looked up at him. "You should know that I did share with him that I'd been involved with someone, and it hadn't ended well, either the first time we'd been together or the second time. He's very perceptive, and it's likely he picked up on there being something between us when he saw us over the video chat. He probably figured out that someone was you. He won't say anything, though."

"No one likes to lose, tiny. This feels like more than sibling affection."

"I guarantee it's not. Even if it were, he knows it's never going to happen between us. His interests are a bit more... varied. Last I knew, he had his partners stashed away in Barbados."

He looked at her quizzically, then he got it. "Partners? As in plural?"

Gem nodded. "Yes. Last I knew, he had two women living with him. I adore him, but I don't share."

After an hour to load up supplies and grab some food, it was another seven hours until they landed in Mozambique. Everyone was exhausted and grumpy after two days of straight flying, but it was better for them to all be together to do the last-minute planning before they arrived.

They landed in Vilanculos, a popular seaside city for tourists, and traveled a short ten minutes to a house they had rented. It was large enough to house all of them, had a pool, and was just a walk across the street to the ocean. They were a couple of women short of looking like they were an honest group of friends on vacation. But most of them didn't plan to be out and about in more than pairings or small groups, if at all, and they weren't going to be at the house much in a day or two. Or at least, that was the plan.

When they arrived at the house, everyone paired up and took over their rooms, some with the intention of napping. Others began taking over the common areas.

Midas immediately began to set up his computer base on the dining room table. He claimed he didn't sleep much anyway, and given his sugar intake, it wasn't really a surprise. Nemo knew that much of his lack of sleep had to do with the conditioning from their big boss, who had Midas going almost nonstop. When Midas did sleep, he slept hard, and it took nothing short of a bomb blast to wake him up.

Cerberus took over the kitchen table to set up his workshop area. Waters gave a shout down the hallway not to blow them all up in the process, to which Cerberus merely grunted.

Suddenly, Steel was back in the room. "I'm going to pick up food. Hopefully, that's enough time because I need a shower and about twelve hours of uninterrupted sleep." A quizzical look from Nemo brought out the reason he was really leaving. "Waters is on the phone with Kubrick, and I'm not intruding on the phone sex," he grumbled.

Demon came down the hall in his short-sleeved wetsuit and flip-flops. "And TB is texting Flame, so I'm heading out to the beach." He made a stop in the kitchen, his cupped hand popping up to his mouth, then reaching for his bottled water on the counter.

"Another sexting session?" Nemo filled in.

Disgruntled, Demon replied, "You'd think he'd just call her, but no. All out of some weird nostalgia for how they met."

"At least you can't hear them if they're sexting."

"No, but I might see something I don't want to see, especially if they suddenly get too worked up."

"Same here," Steel added.

Nemo decided to poke at Demon to see if things there had calmed down at all. "You're not calling Cherry?"

Demon ignored the comment and headed out the door to find somewhere to rent a board.

"Was it something I said?" Nemo asked Steel teasingly.

Steel picked up one of the sets of jeep keys. "He did call her. She sent him to voicemail."

"Eww. Ouch." Nemo grimaced. "Cock-blocked by the cell phone."

"You're mean," Gem said as she came down the stairs, Scheherazade alongside her.

Nemo almost combusted. She was wearing her little denim skirt again, but above it, she had on possibly the tiniest bikini top imaginable. Granted, she was small up top, but he was still caveman enough that he didn't want anyone seeing her in it.

"How is making an observation mean?"

"It's hard enough knowing you're into someone, but they're not into you. You don't have to rub it in that she's not interested."

"Oh, she's interested," Steel corrected. "They just have shit to work through."

"You mean *he* has shit to work through. I doubt those were ibuprofen he was popping just now," she huffed out.

"Nah, tiny, they likely were. When we're on a project, he doesn't take that shit."

"He shouldn't take it at all," she grumbled. One look at Steel, and she huffed again. "I don't care. It's a crutch, and if he'd quit, he'd feel better."

She headed back to the pool deck, Nemo's eyes following her ass the whole way. He really wanted to sleep right now, but he supposed he could do that out at the pool just as easily as in the room. He watched her spread out onto a lounge chair while Scheherazade sniffed the perimeter.

"Hang out for five minutes while I change?" he asked Steel. "These two are balls-deep in their work. I want someone watching her at all times."

Steel nodded.

Nemo raced up the stairs, threw on board shorts and a T-shirt, then padded back downstairs and out onto the deck with a wave of dismissal to Steel.

The dog was in a position of watchfulness at the foot of Gem's chair. Nemo smiled. Scheherazade had taken an instant liking to the girl and spent most of her time following Gem around, even though Nemo hadn't directly ordered her to. He stood behind Gem's chair, gazing straight down at her head, then down the path of her cleavage to the front-closure top.

"I can hear you thinking, burglar boy," she murmured, her voice sleepy as if she'd been dozing already.

He walked around the chair and sat sideways on the one next to hers. "You're going to burn."

Eyes still closed, she waved his comment away. "It'll make me look more touristy. But if it makes you feel better, I put sunscreen on while I was upstairs."

"Damn. I didn't get to help," he complained.

"If you helped, I wouldn't be down here. I'd still be up there. Probably naked. Then again, my understanding is you don't have sex in beds ever, so maybe I'd still be down here," she teased.

Nemo leaned back in the chair. "Nope. Not since Valencia."

He heard her head turn, so he turned his as well. Her head was pulled up from the chairback, and her eyes were open in her surprised look again.

"Even when I was a teenager, it was always somewhere odd, though not necessarily public. That was more of a post-Valencia thing."

"You've never had sex in a bed with anyone except me?"

He turned his head back to look out at the pool, then closed his eyes as if settling in to nap himself. "Too intimate."

The silence was long, but he didn't hear her shift back to her relaxed position. Finally, he turned back toward her. "What?" he asked.

"But it wasn't too intimate with me?"

Is that hope in her voice?

He returned to his napping position, eyes closed, and answered as nonchalantly as he could, "Tiny, I have strange habits, I know. But I knew you were special the moment you fell into my arms. It seemed wrong, for some reason, to do that with anyone else."

The deck was silent for several minutes. Then, he heard her get up from her chair and the rustle of clothing as she shimmied out of her skirt. He looked through the barely open slits of his eyes as she took the few steps to the pool's edge. Mentally, he groaned as his dick took notice of her svelte body before she dove into the water.

The bottom of the bikini is worse than the top. Fucking thing ties around her hips, and her ass is barely covered, with her cheeks just teasing out at the legs. Not an opportune time for a hard-on. But do I give a shit? No. Am I going to take advantage of that? Hell yes.

He rose from the chair, shucked his T-shirt, and dropped it on the chair, then followed her into the pool. When he came up from the short dive, she was at the far end, where the water cut off at five feet. He hated shallow pools, but today... he might like them a little more.

His arms cut through the water until he came up to her feet. Her neck was curved over the edge of the pool, and her body floated out to the center. She gave no sign that she knew he was there, but if she didn't, she would know in a second. Gently taking hold of her ankles, he spread her legs to either side of him. Moving his hands up to her knees, he bent them and wrapped them around his waist, pressing up against her so that she was trapped upright along the pool wall.

"We should be napping."

"Mmm hmm," was all she said.

"You're going to be tired tomorrow."

"Quite possibly."

"You don't care, do you?"

"Zero fucks given."

He moved impossibly closer, wrapping one arm around her waist, the other anchoring on the pool's edge. "Put one arm around my neck, sugar cat, and hold onto the pool deck with the other. Lock your ankles behind my back."

Her eyes opened, the pupils dilated with the barest ring of blue around them. He thought she was going to refuse, but then suddenly, he felt her knees grip around him a little tighter, her ankles crossing at his back, and her fingertips reaching behind her to grab the pool's edge. He let go of the pool deck now that she was anchored by her own hold, and he dropped his arm beneath the water. His mouth found hers, his tongue sliding between her lips on the gasp she uttered as, under the water, his thumb slipped beneath the material where it covered her bare mound. Unerringly, he found her clit and placed barely there pressure on the button, lazily rubbing in circles.

"Nemo, someone could see," she whispered, ending the kiss but speaking against his lips.

He bent his head at an angle to kiss her neck just below where her jaw came up under her ear lobe. "All anyone watching can see is me kissing you."

"But it's you," she hissed, tilting her head farther to give him better access.

"Yup, so they'll wonder. But they can't see, so they won't know for sure."

His mouth traveled down her neck to her shoulder, and then he kissed a path across her clavicle to the hollow of her throat.

"Can you be quiet, sugar cat?" he murmured against her skin. His thumb continued its lazy circles. Without warning, his four fingers slid along her pussy, rubbing back and forth at the same lazy pace. "If I slide my fingers inside you, will you be able to keep from moaning?"

"I-I-I don't know," she replied honestly, her breath hitching.

He continued to stroke her under the water, continued to circle her clit, his lips on hers, his tongue slipping inside as she panted. Inside her mouth, he stroked her tongue with his, mimicking what his cock would do inside her.

He felt her hips start chasing his fingers, a sure sign that her pleasure was building. Carrying through on his threat, he slid his two middle fingers in between her lower lips and into her channel. Inside, she was just as wet as on the outside—only the consistency of that wetness changed. She whimpered softly, her eyes pleading with him.

"You want me to stop? If you want me to, I will. I'll take you upstairs and get you off there, but I'd rather not move. This feels too good."

"No, don't move."

He smiled as he brought his mouth back to hers. "Then you can't move your hips. You gotta stay still. Let me control this. I promise I've got you." He traced her teeth with the tip of his tongue and licked at the insides of her cheeks, then repeated.

She whimpered, her frustration building, but she stopped her movements.

"Good kitty," he whispered back, then covered her mouth with his again.

He lowered himself slightly in the water so that his shoulders wouldn't be seen moving. They were far enough away from the doorway and off to the side so no one could see them without physically going to the far side of the patio door or coming out onto the deck. He'd hear the latter, and he wasn't really worried about his friends catching a show. If they did see them, they'd move away. But he didn't want Gem to feel self-conscious. He wanted her mindless to everything but him like she was right now.

Nemo curled his fingers up inside her to touch the top wall, lazily stroking the rough patch of flesh. He didn't want her going off on him like she had in the beach hut. Well... he wouldn't mind. There was enough chlorine in the water to kill anything that wasn't water, but he knew that would freak her out. So he put just enough pressure there to make it feel good but not enough to cause her to release in a gush.

Her whimpering became a little more frantic, and the fingers attached to the arm around his neck began to dig her short little nails into his skin. He pulled his mouth away from hers just enough to talk to her. "You ready, sugar cat? You ready to give it up to me?"

"Yess," she hissed, her eyes going closed, her head tilting back.

"Nuh-uh. Look back at me. I want you to give up that orgasm to me."

"Take it," she whimpered.

"No, *my liefie*, I need you to relax and let it happen. This is a gift from you to me. Head up. Eyes on me."

When she tilted her head up, he pressed his lips to hers, and while the pressure stayed the same, he took pity on her and moved his hand a little faster. Her eyes rolled back in their sockets, and she pressed her forehead to his. A high-pitched, muffled shriek let him know he'd hit just the right spot. He felt her entire body tighten. Moments later, a muffled moan passed from her mouth to his as she relaxed.

He stroked her slowly through the aftermath, then slid his fingers from inside her bikini and wrapped his arm around her tightly, just like the other arm had held her through their play. Her head moved to rest on his shoulder, both arms curving around them.

"Feel better?" he asked.

"Yes," she replied quietly. "But I'm guessing you don't." She bucked her hips into his, rubbing slightly against his hard cock.

"I'm okay. You can make it up to me upstairs. Gonna need to wash off all this chlorine anyway. Ready to go in?"

"No."

Nemo chuckled. "Well, you can't stay out here. You'll fry in the sun. Can't have that cute little nose all red and peeling. Besides that, you'll shrivel up like a prune, and you're already tiny. Can't have you getting any smaller."

She giggled sleepily and made a move to get out of his embrace.

"Nope, I've got you."

He untangled from her arms and legs, then turned his back to her. "Piggyback time."

That drew a snort from her, but she wrapped around him anyway. "I remember how this went the last time."

He knew his smile was from ear to ear as he turned to look at her over his shoulder where her chin rested. "Yes, but you're a little less leery this time around."

Chin propped on his shoulder, she hummed her response. "Still leery. Just not fighting it right now."

I'll take it.

He worked his way through the pool to the shallower end, then climbed up the stairs with her still wrapped around him like a monkey. Leaving their things on the chairs, he slid the patio door open, stopped long enough for her to close it after they passed through, and then made his way to the stairs.

Nemo called out, "Scheherazade, *bly*." The dog immediately padded over to Midas and lay at his feet.

Without looking up, Midas reached down to scratch the dog's head, and he called out, "Steel's on his way back with food. Dinner in two hours. You want me to bring it upstairs?"

"Thanks, big bro, that would be great. Need to catch a nap."

"I'll bet," he mumbled. "God was right. Nothing is ever going to be the same. Kubrick tainted us all."

Nemo grinned, then climbed the stairs. Once up in their room, he noticed that the guys had left him and Gem with the primary bedroom, which had its own attached bathroom. He made a mental note to order everyone their own private order of NikNaks as a thank you.

He headed into the bathroom, opened the shower door, and turned on the water. Setting Gem down on the floor, he quickly dropped his board shorts. "I figure you've got two minutes for that water to be at its best temperature. Just how good are you, sugar cat?"

She grinned, dropping to her knees on the floor. "Oh, I'm the best, burglar boy."

She made her cutoff time with ten seconds to spare.

34

SEPTEMBER 14, 2022

Haskell

Once again, Haskell woke to a heavy weight on top of her. This time, however, she was on her stomach, and someone was lying half on top of her, biting and sucking on the back of her neck. "Your skills as an alarm clock are only slightly better than Scheherazade's, you know that, right?" she mumbled.

He let go of her neck and chuckled. "Zade's out running with Demon. I can have her come wake you up when they get back if you prefer, but then you'll probably miss breakfast."

He slipped from covering just her side to lying on top of her back, weaseling his hips in between her legs. She could feel his hard cock along her leg and poking at her folds at the apex of her thighs. She groaned and shoved her head face-first into the pillow.

"You mean I'm not already going to miss breakfast? Parts of you seem to have other things on their mind."

He rolled all the way off her on the other side. He stood up at the side of the bed, ripped back the sheet to expose her half-naked body, and slapped her quick and sharp on the ass where the T-shirt she'd worn to bed had ridden up.

"Ouch!" She bucked straight up at the contact, rolling to a sitting position on the offended butt cheek. "What was that for?"

"Since the hickey wasn't working to move you, I figured that might." He pushed down the pajama pants past his hips and walked out of the material at his feet.

"I'm not picking those up," she yelled at his back as he stepped into the bathroom. "And I do not have a hickey."

She heard him yell as he used the toilet, "I beg to differ, and it's a great one."

Haskell bounded up out of the bed and stalked into the bathroom to look in the mirror. "I don't see anything," she remarked as she tilted her head to the side, pulling the skin tight from behind her shoulder to get a better look.

Nemo came out of the separated toilet area after flushing. He put both hands on her biceps and turned her so her back was to the mirror. "Look over your left shoulder, kitty cat."

"Eww. Wash your hands."

He squinted at her. "I'm getting in the shower. That's stupid. And so are you. You'll wash off. Besides... you had my dick in your mouth last night." He slapped her hip one more time, then ducked into the shower.

Shaking her head, she looked over her shoulder as instructed. She groaned and hung her head. She had a huge bruise welling up on the back of her neck, and it would show when she went downstairs. "Asshole," she muttered. "And you were clean when I sucked your dick. I'm surprised all the taste buds didn't burn off my tongue from all the chlorine left behind," she projected over the shower water.

Nemo popped open the shower door. "Get your ass in here. Water's getting cold, and pressure is weak since everyone's probably showering right now. We got shit to do, so hustle, hustle, hustle."

"Hold your horses, stud. I need to pee."

She heard him mumbling to himself, something about she could do that in the shower, and she started laughing. "I heard that, and no way."

She stripped out of her T-shirt on the way to the toilet. When she finished, she came back into the main area of the bathroom, folded it neatly on the counter, then washed her hands. She then stepped into the shower. She was barely under the spray when Nemo had her backed up against the wall, kissing the daylights out of her.

"Double eww... morning breath," she teased.

"Yeah, you probably should brush your teeth," he teased back.

"Well, it's not my fault it's all dick breath. Keep it to yourself, and you won't have to taste it."

Next thing she knew, she was being lifted into the air. Her legs went around Nemo's waist reflexively, their bodies slippery from the water and the soap he hadn't rinsed off yet. His mouth was on her again, but this time, his tongue was so far inside it almost made it to her throat.

When he came up for air, he looked her straight in the eye. "Mmm," he hummed appreciatively. "Make no mistake, sugar cat. Nothing tastes better than your mouth. Your mouth tasting like a combination of my cum and yours that you sucked off my dick? That's fucking heaven." He gave her a wink, then a hard kiss to the mouth, before he set her back on her feet on the shower floor and began to rinse off.

Every day, he said something new that stupefied her. Apparently, this was today's comment. "I have no words for that comment."

"Good because we are running late, sleeping beauty."

He jumped out of the shower and began drying off. Through the quickly steaming-up glass shower walls, she absently lathered soap over herself, her eyes glued to his muscles as they clenched and rippled while he passed the towel over his body. Then he caught her stare in the bathroom mirror that was just starting to steam up. She thought she heard him say, "Fuck it," and then she knew that's what she'd heard because he threw the towel on the vanity, ripped open the shower door, and slammed it shut behind him.

She smiled at him. "Guess we're going to miss breakfast."

"Yup. Now, turn around and face the wall, sugar cat."

WHEN THEY CAME out of the bathroom and down the stairs fifteen minutes later, both were grinning and laughing. Nine faces looked up and over at them as they went into the kitchen to grab fruit and bread that Steel had bought at the market the night before. Nemo grabbed her around the waist and hitched her up to a sitting position on the kitchen counter.

"Dude," Steel groaned. "I just wiped that counter down."

"Knock it off. It's not like it's her bare ass."

"Thank God. Save that for your own kitchen counter." Steel turned back to look at whatever was on Midas' screen, but Haskell was pretty sure she saw one corner of his mouth tipped up. He clearly wasn't as grossed out as he'd pretended to be.

She'd just finished peeling her banana when a hand grabbed hers. Nemo shoved the tip in his mouth, then lowered down to at least halfway, bit down, and winked at her, settling between her thighs as he leaned his butt against the counter, his back to her front.

Pulling the peel down farther, Haskell asked, "Had much practice at that, have you? Maybe I should have been asking you if you wanted a hate fuck with Cerberus last night." She bit off a chunk of the banana.

"I heard that," Cerberus rumbled. "Not even for an entire cellar of Leroy Musigny Grand Cru."

Haskell sighed. "Man has bat hearing," she grumbled.

Nemo just laughed it off. "Man has expensive taste. But sorry, Gem. I don't share."

"In all of your exploits, never?"

"Let me rephrase," he corrected. "I don't share *you*. And it's not all that it's cracked up to be anyway. You just get in each other's way."

Cerberus just muttered something to the effect of, "Then you're not doing it right."

Nemo bit into a hunk of bread that he'd slathered honey all over. A drop oozed off the bread on the corner of his mouth. Haskell used her free hand to turn his head sideways, and she tipped forward and licked it off. "I don't share, either."

A chorus of "Eww!" "Gross!" and "Eye bleach!" rang out across the room.

TB offered up, "As long as we don't have to give the pool an extra shot of chlorine." He looked hard at Nemo. "We don't, do we?"

Nemo shoved the rest of his piece of bread in his mouth and grinned as he chewed.

"You're lying."

Nemo shrugged.

TB made a gagging noise.

Waters winced.

Gilgamesh gave them a long, hard look. "Nah. They didn't. Accidentally caught a bit of the show from the second-floor balcony. A little foreplay maybe, but no sex." He clapped his hands. "Okay. Time to finalize. What have we got, Midas?"

"First, Waters talked to Itai last night."

Waters leaned between Gilgamesh and Medusa at the table, everyone picking up their bowls, plates, and coffee cups when he began to spread out the map. "Itai suggested coming in from West Nicholson. We'll take the coastline north to Nova Mambone, then cut across on secondary roads to Espungabera. Once we hit the border, he suggested we redirect and take the main road to Masvingo through to Zvishavane. Shortly after that, we can cut southwest on another main highway to West Nicholson, where we pick up at the source of the Mzingwane."

"It would be faster to follow along the borderline to Beitbridge and head up," Loki observed.

"Yes, but no sense in the border patrol seeing us," Medusa countered. "You're better off going out of your way on the upswing and cutting back. There's no checkpoint where we'll be crossing into Zimbabwe, and the airport in Bulawayo is closer when it's time for me to come collect you. Plus, you don't have to cross the border into South Africa."

Haskell hopped off the counter and stuffed her hands in her back pockets. "She's right. And I'm probably posted at every checkpoint along the South African border."

"Sweetheart," TB chastised, "you're up on the wall at every border checkpoint throughout Africa. How you managed to get on a plane out of anywhere on this continent is nothing short of a miracle."

She shrugged. "Job hazard."

Waters continued, "Itai told me that the closer we get to Beitbridge, the lower the waterline is. Something to do with the aquifers being used to supply farmers with water for their livestock and a temporary restriction on the river. Normally, it only has unrestricted traffic in the winter months due to rain. Hopefully, we don't run into any patrols who want to investigate nonsanctioned traffic. However, if we do, Itai says he has the word of the farmers in question to back him up. They normally work with Itai to run interference on his underground runs."

Loki nodded in agreement.

Waters finished with, "We should be covered in case of emergency. Our biggest area of concern is if we overshoot the landing due to patrols because then we run into trouble."

"So, let's make sure we don't run into any trouble," Loki warned.

Midas jumped back into the conversation. "Second on the agenda, I called in a favor from a contact in Johannesburg. He sent up a drone and sent me the footage it came up with." He flipped the screen around so everyone could see. "There are two guard shacks on the main road in, and there's a dirt track going out toward the river. In the past twenty-four hours, there has been no traffic on the dirt road, and there's only one guard. The guard there shifts out every four hours, beginning at zero hundred. The guard does carry a sidearm and a machine gun, but so far, none of them have seen fit to take the latter off the hooks in the back of the booth. I'm guessing no one ever comes through that way, but they put a guard on it just in case. In addition, there's no surveillance equipment, according to Nova's scans, so probably more primitive contact there. Walkie-talkies if we're lucky. Cell phone at worst."

"Nova hitched a ride on the drone?" Waters asked, concern written all over his face.

"No, I put the old system on the drone. I put a burn-out on Cyclopes in case he was compromised. His program is out-of-date, anyway, since Nova is up and running. I transferred the information he brought back through a scrubber, then gave it to her through a ghost system. It can't hurt her. So far, Cyclopes is showing no signs of compromise, but if someone did try to download his software, Cyclopes'll eat himself and blow up."

Waters nodded. "I know that would suck, but better safe than sorry."

Steel cut in, "So I'm guessing TB and I will be going in the back door."

There was a pause. When there was silence, everyone looked at Nemo. He was eating a handful of grapes and studying the footage. When he realized everyone was looking at him, his face turned puzzled. "What?"

"No comment from the penis gallery?" TB asked.

"Peanut gallery, fuckwitch." Nemo popped another grape in his mouth.

"I know what the saying is," TB growled, "but when talking to you, sometimes the sayings make more sense if they change."

Nemo thought about it as he ate another grape. "Nope. No comment."

TB looked at Demon. "Better check his temperature, dude. Think he's sick."

"Har dee har har," Nemo barked out. "I don't always have to make a twelve-year-old-boy comment."

"No, but it's abnormal when you don't," Waters agreed with TB. He looked at Haskell. "You need to stick around. He becomes a human being when you're here."

With the exception of the Mythos crew, they all turned back to the monitor, blissfully unaware of the panic they'd just caused. The Mythos team, however, were all staring at her. She couldn't stay. She knew it. They knew it. Her contract wasn't up until 2025. When this was done, she was leaving with them.

Medusa shook her head at her, telling her not to address the comment. She nodded in return, then focused on the screen with the rest of them.

Steel was speaking again. "All right, so TB and I will go in the back door, take out the guard. Are we leaving someone there?"

"No," Waters replied. "We'll have you go in at the start of a shift. We need to be in and out within three and a half hours. Should be manageable." He looked at Haskell.

She nodded. "Even if I have to go through tunnel choice B or C, it'll be enough."

"And what if you can't get in through any of those choices?" TB questioned.

Haskell looked TB straight in the eye. "Then we won't need three and a half hours, will we? We'll have to abort. But don't worry. I can get in through tunnel choice A as long as there hasn't been a recent cave-in."

TB turned back to Midas.

"Okay," Midas picked up again. "The main road is a completely different story. Traffic goes in and out pretty regularly. And... no outsiders. It's all people who belong to the camp. No food vendors, no suits, nothing."

"That creates major difficulties. We aren't exactly going to pass as locals," Demon pointed out.

"Nova did take a walkabout through their limited email system. There's an inspection planned in two days."

The group shared a look around the table.

"Then we either need to go in before that check or after. We can't do it during." Haskell chewed on her lip. "I think we're better going in after. They'll be more relaxed once the inspection is over. More prone to be careless since they know they're in the clear for a while."

"Agreed," Waters confirmed. "The day after?"

"Midas, the inspection is set for the sixteenth?" she asked.

"Yes. Thirteen hundred."

She considered his suggestion. "That's Friday. New shipments of workers come in on Thursdays. Or, as of a couple of months ago, they did. That's when the other girls and I came in and when the previous week's girls were shipped out. They also brought in new miners to replace any they lost during the week."

Demon looked up at her. "What did they do with the ones they 'lost'?"

"Not sure," she admitted. "But they certainly didn't send them out through the front gate. It's possible they dumped them in a shaft in the mine, especially in a caved-in tunnel. They're certainly deep enough, and those tunnels are unstable enough that no one goes in there without prompting. No one would find them."

Demon grunted. "Sounds about right. And smart. Any gasses leaching out of the soil would cover the smell, too."

"Okay, so Saturday the seventeenth."

Haskell nodded. "They'll be extra slow that day. Most of the men will have visited the fresh sex workers, so in their off time, they won't be roaming around. They'll be in the old infirmary they've created as a brothel." She pointed to a building on the far west side of the compound with a green roof. "That one. The informally partitioned-off rooms make it perfect for the job."

She turned back to Waters. "Our best bet is to go in early morning, just after the eight hundred shift change. Workers will be coming topside, some will be heading underground, and there will be some caught in limbo in both places. Once a lift starts, you can't stop it until it reaches the top or bottom, but there will be fewer workers underneath since they will bring about half of them up before taking people down. Each lift will hold about twenty to twenty-five people, depending on size. And there are no guards in the lifts since there's no way to get on or off during the ride. Nowhere to go. No side tunnels or anything like that."

Waters gave his first set of orders. "Okay. So, TB and Steel will hit the back guard shack at eight hundred fifteen. Steel, you and TB will go clean out the infirmary. I want those women on the truck. Demon will go with you in case you need medical assistance.

"Medusa. You're going to head to Bulawayo once we hit West Nicholson. How long before you reach the facility for extraction?"

"Forty-five minutes if I fly casual," she replied. "Closer to thirty-eight if I hoof it."

"Okay. We'll want pickup at eight hundred twenty-five, so plan accordingly."

She nodded.

"Loki, Gilgamesh, you'll have your trucks at Beitbridge, timed to crash through the gates at eight hundred twenty. Don't be late."

Gilgamesh smirked. Loki just looked pissed at the mere thought of ever being late.

"We'll drop Gem, Nemo, and the trio in West Nicholson on Thursday, early morning. Medusa, Midas, and I will stay overnight in West Nicholson, but you five will have to meet with Itai during the day. He'll have a space for you to hang out. You'll be loaded onto the boats into his hut space, and you won't be able to come out until you hit the landing spot. TB, Demon, and Steel will be in the second and third boats. The huts are small, and they're going to be a tight fit. It's just over one hundred miles, so he said it will take about ten hours from start to finish without any patrol stops. He's planning to leave before first light, whatever day we indicate. After we make sure you make it into the boats, I'll circle around with Midas and set up a base in Beitbridge. We'll coordinate from there."

"Gem," Loki called out. "These tunnels are pretty narrow. Is Nemo going to be able to follow you?"

"He should be able to. The shafts I'm looking at were carved out by miners with jackhammers. They're not conventional tunnels, and they'll be tight, but we've both been in tighter spaces."

Her eyes flashed to Nemo, who was clearly holding back laughter. The smirk was impossible to hide, however. He held up his hands in surrender when he read her tight expression. "I didn't say a word," he pointed out.

"No, but you were thinking it, and that's bad enough." Haskell shook her head and rolled her eyes before focusing back on the conversation regarding the tunnels. "Many of the miners are smaller, it's true. Extreme poverty leads to poor nutrition, and that's what drives many of them to dangerous work. When you have no other options, you do what you have to in order to feed your family, but some of the miners are bigger men, as well. It takes a lot of strength to run the jackhammers for long hours. Strong constitutions to be in the dark, confined spaces. I picked this particular tunnel because its opening looks as if it was carved out by a larger person."

"But that doesn't guarantee that it doesn't narrow once you're inside," TB pointed out.

"No, but miners tend to be territorial, especially if it's a successful vein. A miner would not voluntarily leave his find. This one appears, based on the map, to be a successful vein, so the tunnel should be consistent with its opening."

She reached to the extra table the men had dragged into the room, where all sorts of maps and blueprints were being kept. She searched for the original grid map Midas had made for her on the plane and the overlay map of the tunnels Nova had found in the email. Waters backed out of the way as she scooted between Loki and Gilgamesh.

Placing the overlay on top of the gridded map, she drew her

finger along the tunnel line on the secondary map. "See how this goes all the way to the ceiling of the cavern? That means they drilled through to the actual mine area itself. A miner wouldn't bother to do that if he hadn't found a vein after about twenty feet. Maybe twenty-five."

Steel connected the dots. "So this miner hammered his way at this starting point, and by twenty-five feet in, he found diamonds. He continues to follow until the vein either runs out, or he hits the mine operation below ground since he can't go any farther without falling however many feet to the floor."

"Exactly," Haskell confirmed.

"What guarantees that we can get through that exit opening?" Nemo asked, now making short work of an apple.

Haskell grabbed it from him and took a bite. "Nothing," she said through her chewing. She swallowed. "Chances are the hole is big enough for me to get through. You? Questionable, but not impossible."

"What happens if Nemo can't follow you through?" Waters asked. "And how will you get down into the mine itself without being seen? I imagine a woman falling out of the sky would be pretty noticeable."

"We'll rappel down. Nothing we both haven't done before. And if he can't get through, he'll have to backtrack, and I'll be solo."

"Abso-fucking-lutely not," Nemo growled. "There is no way you're going solo. We've already established this. I won't stop you from going—"

"Good because you can't," Haskell interrupted.

Nemo steamrolled right through as if she hadn't spoken. "—but you're at double the risk if you go in alone."

"He's right, Gem," Midas cautioned. "That's the third thing I have to tell you all. The hit on you has been picked up."

"Do we know who?" Loki asked.

"No. It's anonymous. Bank account number only."

TB grunted. "That's how we always did it when I was The

Collector. Numbered Swiss account. Or Cayman. Those banks don't give up shit, and even if you can get a warrant, they don't even always know who has the account because backtracking it takes a long time. It's usually rerouted from there through at least six or seven accounts, if not more."

"How many accounts did yours go through?" Nemo asked.

"Fourteen. I was extra paranoid."

"You still have those accounts?" Waters asked.

"Yep. Always have a backup plan for emergencies. Plenty of cash to access." The two men stared at each other briefly. TB shrugged. "I can go under for a long-ass time if need be."

Waters turned back to the maps. "Okay. So. The five of you will be dropped off in the early hours of the morning. Itai figures around oh-three-hundred. Gem and Nemo will need extra time to navigate the tunnels and get video corroboration as well as samples of anything found on site. What's your exit plan?"

"Back the way we came would be best," Haskell answered. "We'd stick out big-time amongst the miners."

"No shit. Blonde, blue-eyed female, not to mention Captain America over here," TB snarked.

"If not, we'll have to try and exit with a lift full of miners. Risky, but not impossible," she posited.

"Cerberus"—Waters turned to the bomber—"we're going to need that distraction right on the money. What's the plan?"

"Figured your back-door guard shack might be a good starter. An explosion there would draw some of the guards away from the main camp. While they're dealing with that, we can also set a small charge loose in the mine itself. That will drive people to the surface."

"Won't that cause potential cave-ins?" Gilgamesh asked with a frown. "We don't want to catch any of the miners in the crossfire if we can avoid it."

"Not if I'm any good at my job," Cerberus barked. "There are ways to make small explosions look bigger than they are. What I'm thinking of would be more like an indoor firework."

"What about panic? We don't need the guards and workers trampling each other in an effort to get to the lifts," Demon complained.

Cerberus sat stone-faced. "It could. It's an acceptable risk. We can also save it as a last resort. Don't set it off unless we absolutely have to."

Waters nodded. "Agreed. All of this can be done remotely, I assume."

"Yes," Cerberus confirmed. "And if TB, Steel, and Demon have taken care of the guard, depending on what you want to happen to the body, we can either use it to destroy the evidence, or he can be put somewhere safely by the time the explosion occurs."

"What about topside?" Loki asked. "We need something in the camp itself, even if we don't use it."

"I don't set bombs not to use them," Cerberus replied. "Unless you want them found, they need to go boom. There's a maintenance shed near the *infirmary*." He said the last word like he had a bad taste in his mouth. "Probably enough chemicals in there to send a fireball so high it could be seen from Madagascar. I'll start with that. If it's a no-go, then I'll stick with the water tower."

Steel grunted in approval. "Blow the legs out from under that thing, you can probably put out any fire you already started."

"Exactly," Cerberus agreed. "I make the mess, and I clean it up."

"We definitely do not want these brought back on Tribe," Waters warned.

"Or Mythos," Loki added.

"Boss' orders," Medusa intoned from the end of the table.

Cerberus and Medusa shared a look, after which Cerberus sighed. "It goes against all my principles, but fine. No signature stamp on the devices. Not that anyone here would look for it anyway." He grumbled the last sentence under his breath.

"Sounds like we have everything good to go. We head for West Nicholson on the fifteenth, dropping off Gem, Nemo, TB, Steel, Demon, and now Cerberus. On the sixteenth, Medusa will head to Bulawayo, and Midas and I will head to Beitbridge. Gem and the fabulous five will head downriver to the launch point. On the seventeenth, we hit it and quit it."

"One day to get whatever rest you can, people." Loki looked each one of them in the eye. "You're going to need it. Especially those of you on the river cruise."

Everyone started to break up and head in different directions. Nemo looked at Gem and muttered under his breath. "A whole day with nothing to do. However shall we occupy our time?"

Haskell looked up at him. "I don't know about you, but I have a book."

"Kama Sutra?"

She rolled her eyes. "You're such a boy."

"I'll show you 'boy.'"

35

SEPTEMBER 17, 2022

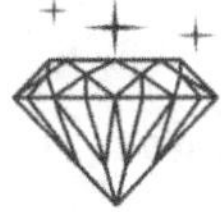

Nemo

During preparation time, Midas barely left his computer, only complying when Gem dragged him away, reminding him he'd be useless to them on the big day if he didn't sleep. Still, he was able to add to their intel daily, updating them on comings and goings. It was becoming normal to hear him talking to Nova nonstop. Not that they didn't find it a little creepy since he treated her like a real person, but it felt normal to hear the conversations. Nemo told Gem the man needed to get laid, but he kept back the information that it was about as likely to happen as hell freezing over.

The group barely saw Demon. The man spent almost forty-eight hours on the beach, probably sleeping there if he slept at all. Since they were on a job, he wasn't medicating, and that meant he was grumpier than the devil. Not that he was all that pleasant when he *was* medicating.

Waters and Loki closeted themselves with the telecommunications, finally able to get in touch with God. Waters was concerned. God had never stayed off the grid so long before, and the team leader said the man sounded strange. Almost as if he was drugged up himself. He didn't offer the distress code, so Waters was leaving it alone for the time being. They were also talking to Cherry, who was cranky as fuck, and very pointedly not asking about a certain medic. When they weren't talking to one of those two, they were bothering Midas for updates every five minutes. Waters only took breaks to talk to Kubrick, and Nemo joked that the phone sex had to be costing him a small fortune.

TB was just as bad with Flame, but at least they saw him most of the time. He spent the bulk of his time working with Steel, poring over maps and contingency exit strategies out of Zimbabwe.

The downtime they had saw the crew playing poker, napping, or reading Flame's latest book, much to TB's dismay. Apparently, it was her steamiest one yet. Nemo had read it before it was published, so he spent his off time focusing on Gem.

Nemo couldn't put his finger on it, but something had changed with her. She'd withdrawn from him just when he thought he'd been making progress. They slept together at night, and there had been some making out but no sex since the first morning. Even after replaying the conversation in the kitchen over and over in his head, he couldn't figure out what had been said that caused it. He knew he should just corner her and ask, but he was more than a little afraid of having that discussion. His best bet at this point, he felt, was to let things play out, and maybe they'd just naturally return to normal.

Before they set off with Itai, Cerberus had given them a lesson on how to set the distraction charge while they were in the tunnels. He, with the help of Demon, had also gone over how to use the oxygen masks and tanks should they get themselves caught in a situation with noxious gasses or, heaven forbid, a surprise cave-in. They'd have roughly three hours, which was very little time in the event of a cave-in, but it was better than the thirty minutes they would have had with Tribe's equipment.

On the trek down the river yesterday, she'd spent a lot of the time sleeping. He'd been reluctant to disturb her, even though it would have been the perfect time to talk in private. Distracting her would be the worst thing he could do.

Now they were on the riverbank going over the plan one more time. His head was on a swivel, constantly worrying about the hit that had been contracted on her. Out in the open like this, even in the dark of the early morning hours, snipers were still a concern. His inner radar wasn't tripping, but he did find it odd that no attempt had been made yet. The contract wouldn't have been bid on if the individual hadn't been relatively sure of where she was and how to get to her.

With Midas in his ear watching the drone footage with Nova, the six of them and the dog made their way across the lowland to where Gem and Nemo would use the tunnels.

"Good luck," Steel wished them.

Nemo looked at TB. "Scheherazade—"

TB clasped his shoulder. "I know. I've got her."

The dog looked up at Nemo, who crouched down at her side. Forehead to hers, eyes closed, he scratched her behind both ears. He whispered to her in Afrikaans. He knew the dog wouldn't understand the words, but she would understand the tone.

"*Gaan saam met* TB," he said as he stood.

Scheherazade gave a soft yip as if in agreement.

As the dog took her position at his side, TB absently petted her head in comfort and glanced one more time at Nemo. "And... the other thing?" he asked.

Nemo nodded. "Always. Like my own."

The giant smiled sadly.

Turning to Gem, Nemo saw the question in her eyes. "Requests. In case one of us doesn't come back. TB will take Scheherazade if something happens to me."

She grimaced and gave a slow, single head nod. "And you'll watch over Flame."

Nemo nodded. "All of us would take care of her without him asking, but there's a complication, so yeah, he asked me specifically to watch out for her."

"Audio check," Waters said.

"TB copy."

"Nemo copy."

"Midas copy."

"Steel copy."

"Demon copy."

"Mythos is online. Loki copy."

"Gilgamesh copy."

"Medusa copy."

"Cerberus copy."

"Gem copy."

"Waters confirmed. Good luck."

Gem and Nemo turned and began the descent into the tunnel, with Gem leading the way.

The tunnel was ragged inside since it was created by a jackhammer. Had the miner possessed the proper equipment, the tunnel would have been smoothed and large enough to stand up in. As it stood now, most of it they had to crouch or crawl through jagged rock. More than once, Nemo had to unhook her from something she got snagged on.

"Nemo, report in."

"Miss me already, Midas?" he quipped.

"Waters wants regular check-ins."

"Worried I'm eloping with Gem?"

A snort from in front of him clued him in to how she felt about that comment.

"Steel crawled in after you about twenty-five feet and took an air sample. There are some remnants of underground gasses Nova hasn't identified yet. Watch yourselves for signs of hallucinations or other weird behaviors."

"If they're in here, then they're also going to be in the mine. If nothing has been noted, we're probably okay," Gem responded.

"Yes, but the cavern is also much more open. They could dissipate and not affect the miners. Could be nothing, but better safe than sorry."

"We'll check in, Midas," Nemo reassured him.

"Cerberus is on his way to his location. TB, Steel, and Demon are heading into position for their part."

"Copy." Nemo tapped Gem on the leg. "You start feeling woozy, let me know."

"Copy," she replied.

After an hour of crawling, there was a moment of panic when an explosion went off in the mine. They knew it wasn't Cerberus' work since they had that in their packs, so it was obviously a blast to clear rock in a tunnel. Unfortunately, that tunnel was underneath them, and it caused a small shower of rocks and dirt to fall on top of them as the rock strata resettled. When the rain of debris stopped, there was a squawk over their earbuds.

"You two good?"

"Yeah, Midas. We're good. They're blasting in a tunnel beneath us."

Nemo squinted into the distance beyond Gem. "Am I seeing a light, Gem, or is that a trick of my eyes?"

"No," she replied, "that should be the exit hole into the cavern. We're close, Midas. No need to panic."

There was grumbling on the other end of the airwaves, something to the effect of "Don't panic, she says."

Gem informed Nemo, "I'm turning off my headlamp. I don't want it to shine out into the cavern. It probably wouldn't get noticed, but I don't want to take the chance.

"Copy. Turning mine off as well."

For the last fifty or so yards, they basically crawled in the dark. When they made it to the end, the opening was definitely wide enough for Gem to sneak through. Nemo would be a tight fit, but he was pretty sure he could make it.

"I need your hand, Gem."

There was a snort from one of the others on the comms. "Really? The tunnel? That's ridiculous, even for you," Steel spit out.

"I need her to cover the glow of my watch, dickhead. I do have some sense of timing, you know. Besides, this would be uncomfortable as hell."

"For you, maybe," Gem replied softly. "I'd be on top. No way I'm lying on my back on the floor of this tunnel."

There was a round of soft chuckles from everyone online. She tossed a smile over her shoulder at Nemo, and it was almost like they'd returned to normal.

She put her hand back, and Nemo moved his arm up her side so that it covered the green glow of his watch.

"Midas. Confirm oh-five-twenty-two."

"Confirmed."

"Gem," Nemo asked. "How are we looking?"

"We need to lie low for a little bit. There's a considerable amount of activity in the central cavern. They're probably waiting for the dust to settle after the blast."

"Any idea how long that might be?" Waters asked.

"Well, it's been about thirty minutes since the blast. Probably thirty more, maybe less. They're not going to supply the miners with proper breathing equipment in there, so they're going to be cautious," Gem answered.

"Will that leave you enough time?" he worried.

"Should be in and out with plenty to spare. I know exactly where I'm going."

"Keep us apprised. Midas is still watching drone footage. Cerberus has been in for approximately five minutes and is setting the charges in the maintenance shed."

"I didn't hear him check in," Nemo said.

"No," Loki chimed in. "He works radio silent, no matter the situation. He did send us a signal that he was in and good, and Midas caught him on the drone."

"Nothing like a rogue teammate," Nemo muttered.

"Don't fret, Nemo," Gem reassured him. "He's good at what he does. You know that. And he's cautious. If something even has a hint of hink, he'll be out of there."

Nemo and Gem lay in the darkness, Gem keeping an eye on the cavern as best she could without sticking her head through the tunnel opening. He desperately wanted to ask her what was wrong, but between the tenseness of their situation and everybody listening online, it wasn't the best time. After twenty minutes, he couldn't do it any longer. He had to know.

"Midas. I'm closing out communications for a couple of minutes. I'll be able to hear you in case you need us."

"Not advisable, Nemo," Waters grouched.

"It'll just be for a couple of minutes," Nemo assured him.

Nemo closed the voice channel with a tap of his finger. He patted Gem on the ankle, and through hand signals, he asked her to do the same. She scowled at him but complied. Her head turned back to the tunnel opening.

"I see guards and people starting to go into the corridor, but something..."—she shook her head—"something's not right about what I'm seeing. I can't figure it out. The miners look... wrong, somehow," she whispered.

He sucked in a big breath. "Gem?"

"Yeah?" she replied distractedly.

"What happened?" He let the breath out. The words were out there, and he couldn't take them back.

"What happened when?"

"At breakfast the other day. We were fine. Better than fine. Then suddenly we weren't."

"I don't know what you mean."

"Bullshit. You know exactly what I mean. What. Happened?"

She sighed. "This isn't the time, Nemo."

"It will never be the time," he chastised. "There will always be something that's pressing, so while we wait here for that cavern to clear, we may as well talk about it."

She turned on her side. "Fine. But we cannot get distracted by this, okay?"

"I promise. I'm distracted because I *don't* know."

Gem paused. "Waters mentioned me staying. And I can't. It was a reminder that this is temporary, and I feel bad. Like I've led you on somehow."

Nemo's chest ached. She was withdrawing. She still didn't believe he was in this, in them, despite the fact that she had come to him on the plane after their argument.

Son of a bitch! How do I fix this?

"How do I make you understand I'm not temporary?"

"You can't, Nemo." Her voice sounded small and sad. "There's too much baggage in my head right now. Too much to work through. You've no idea how hard it is to undo nearly twenty years of hearing you're not worthy.

"Besides that, I'm under contract with Mythos for several more years. I can't just up and leave. Loki could pull me tomorrow, send me somewhere else, and I'm bound to follow his direction. Just like you're bound to Tribe."

"What if I was willing to wait?"

She laughed. "You? Wait? It would never happen. You might be able to do it for a short while, but without being able to talk to me, without seeing me for long stretches of time, I don't think you could do it." She turned her head just enough so he could see her expression. "I don't fault you for that, Nemo. I really don't. I honestly wouldn't want you to wait. Nothing's guaranteed in this world. You shouldn't bind everything up in me and then have it come to nothing. What I do is just as dangerous as you. Now with a price on my head? That just makes it more likely you'll outlive me."

He snorted. "You don't think there's a price on my head? Fuck, I'm wanted in thirty-six countries for the shit Midas and I have pulled alone. I can name at least four terrorist groups that would behead me and set me on fire on sight, and who knows how many private individuals would gut me just for fun. Your reasoning is an excuse because you're scared. Scared I'm playing you. Scared because your da has filled your head with a ton of shit about not being worthy of anything, much less a man.

"I'm in this, Gem. I wanted in this when we met back up in Riquewihr, but you took off." He started shuffling up along her side. He tapped her calf. "Move over onto your side facing me." It was a tight fit, but he managed.

"Steel's right. This is hardly the time," she quipped.

"Cut it out. This is serious, Gem." He raised a hand to her face. He could see her in the dim light, and there was want and hope in her eyes but also restraint, as if recognizing that hoping was foolish. "I. Am. In. This. All the way." He kissed her lips, just a quick brush of his lips. Reflexively, he smoothed a finger across her eyebrow, then tried to push back the rebel curl. "I promise. And I don't make promises I don't keep. So push your father the fuck out of your life. I told you. Listen to me. My voice. I'm here, and he's not. You're priceless, Gem."

They both smiled at the pun.

"Wanting something doesn't mean you get to have it."

"You only can't have me if you don't want me. Is that it? You don't want me?"

"I—"

A shout in the tunnel distracted them. Gem tapped her ear to reestablish communication. She dared to look out the opening.

"Waters, the miners are back in the tunnel, and the cavern is empty. We're heading in."

"Copy. Progress report at all intervals."

"Copy."

Nemo huffed in frustration, then turned his earbud back on. At least he knew what he was dealing with. Conversation tabled.

For now.

He backed up in the tunnel to give Gem room to access her equipment as well as get his own together.

Pitons hammered in, cordage and rope attached, carabiners locked, Nemo looked on as Gem took one last glance out of the opening before pulling down her balaclava and goggles, then slithered through it. "Gem is rappelling," Nemo informed the channel. "I'm following when she hits bottom."

"Good luck," Waters said over the line.

"Stay safe," TB added. A yip in the background added Scheherazade's thoughts as well, making Nemo smile.

I love that dog.

Nemo watched as Gem traveled down, putting additional pitons loosely into the wall to loop her cordage and rope around. They were simply meant to keep their gear as close to the wall as possible. While both items were brown to blend in with the walls, it didn't pay to have the ropes hanging out free from them while they were out and about in the cavern. When they climbed up later, they would simply pull the pitons out as if they'd never been there.

The rappel down the side of the cavern was uneventful. Once on the cavern floor, they used another piton to pin the ropes off as close to the wall as possible, and luck was with them as it was behind some tractor equipment used to move heavy debris.

36

SEPTEMBER 17, 2022

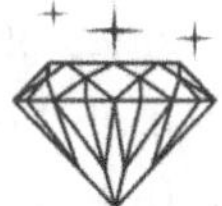

Haskell

Haskell took a quick look around the side of the bulldozer they were behind. Out of the corner of her eye, she watched Nemo tie off their ropes. She knew her answers to his questions had upset him, but there wasn't much she could do about it now. She also knew she desperately wanted what he was offering. Had since she first met him, but they just couldn't. She had commitments. So did he. And those commitments weren't going to change for some time, if ever.

"Midas. Camera check."

Over the airwaves, she heard keys clacking. "I've got you, Gem, but Nemo's is static."

She felt the man in question come up next to her. She turned her head to look for the red light on his goggles and gave the right lens a flick.

"Hey!" he complained.

"Got him," Midas confirmed.

"You were static. Everyone knows when technology doesn't work—"

"Flick it. I got it. And I heard him. I do have an earbud in. I could have flicked it myself."

"What would be the fun of that?" she teased.

She glanced around the side of the bulldozer again.

"Anything?" he whispered.

"No. Clear the opposite side."

He chanced a quick look. When he gave the thumbs-up, both slinked around the prospective sides of the bulldozer to ensure that no one was hiding along the front of the machinery. When their eyes connected again, she pointed to the pallet of crates fifty feet ahead of them, letting him know where she was headed.

He gave her a thumbs-up.

She sent the update. "Clear. Going in."

Both took off and plastered themselves to the crates when they arrived there, then ducked their heads around the sides to check for guards. Nothing but a huge open seam in the ground, separating them from a cave on the opposite side, and no crossing in sight.

"Bollocks," she muttered.

"What is it, Gem?" Waters asked over the link.

"Small obstacle."

"Small obstacle? That's like saying I have a small cock. I'd hate to think what you see as 'large,'" Nemo whispered.

"Hey! Open channel, you two," Waters reminded them. "The picture is fuzzy. What do you have *as an obstacle*?"

"Just a crack in the ground," she reassured with a look up above them.

"Crack? Woman, we need to have a talk about your understanding of the English language when we get home," Nemo griped.

"How big is a 'crack'?" Waters asked.

Before Haskell could answer, Nemo did. "Her 'crack' is about twenty feet wide." He glanced up to where she was looking. "Fuck. We're playing *George of the Jungle*, aren't we?"

With the balaclava over her head, she knew he couldn't see her smile, but she felt her body come alive as she looked at him. "Just don't do the yodel as you cross."

For the first time in a long time, this felt fun again. She wondered if it was because he was here with her. As soon as the thought occurred, she shoved it aside. She scrambled up over the crate to the top, a palm to her ass giving her a boost. The crates were bundled together and attached to a crane hook. As she was unclamping the hook, Nemo came up the other side of the pallet to join her. He held the chain steady as she went to the edge of the box to look over the side and into the open seam in the ground. "Piece of cake. You're only going to get one shot when I let go, and this chain swings back, so be ready."

"I'll be ready," he grouched.

Nemo held the chain steady as she backed up the few steps the top of the crate allowed, then gathered momentum with her steps to pitch herself at the impromptu "jungle vine." As soon as she grasped on, her tiny feet catching the top of the hook on the end as support, Nemo let go of the chain and gave her a push for additional momentum.

She swung to about ten feet over the chasm, then headed back his way. Luckily, he had stepped back two steps to be sure to be out of the line of the chain. At the top of her backswing, she pushed with her knees, like when she'd played on the swings as a child, and sailed halfway across the chasm before swinging back again.

On the third swing, she calculated that she probably could have flung off the chain to safety but decided one more round would be safer.

The fourth swing, she cleared the opposite side of the chasm and let go. When she sailed to the top of the arc, she pitched herself into a swan-dive posture, then tucked into a roll as she came at the ground. She hit with a jarring thud, somersaulting end-over-end several times. Her body would definitely hurt tomorrow, but for today, it was all good.

Haskell didn't get to see Nemo's catch of the chain, but he was already hitching a ride on the backswing when she managed to look behind her. Then he was swinging her way. It only took him two swings since the chain already had momentum, plus he had her by almost a hundred pounds, and he was able to just pitch off and land on his feet. He managed to hold onto the chain, although there was a wince when he did, and he looped it around a piece of machinery so that they could use it to swing back across later.

Once he was safely on the ground, she took off for the tunnel on the left, scanning for guards as she went. Nothing. It seemed like too much good fortune for them, which probably meant that it was. Somewhere along the line, something was going to go wrong. She just hoped they weren't going to have to kill anyone in the process.

After they dashed through the tunnel entrance, she stopped and plastered herself to the wall, looking out to see if anyone had come out into the cavern behind them. No one.

"We're in the tunnel. No one in sight."

"Confirmed on our end. While on the one hand, that's good, it doesn't bode well that there are no guards in the main area," Waters grumped.

"Or it means they feel secure in the methods they're using," Haskell offered.

"Have you seen cameras?" TB asked.

"That's a negative," Nemo replied.

"Okay. Heads on a swivel. I'll have Midas try to hack into their system and see if there's a camera system."

"There isn't," Midas jumped in. "One of the first things I looked for. The fucktwats apparently didn't want to invest. But secure in their methods or not, it's still odd that there are no guards in the cavern. I'll crack open their radio channel and see if there's any chatter. These guys don't seem to be terribly high-end, so if there's anything suspicious, they'd likely talk about it out in the open. Stupid criminals, stand up, please."

"High-end or low-end, stupid or smart, keep an eye out," Waters ordered. "Underestimating the enemy is mistake number one on any project."

"Copy," Nemo confirmed. "Okay, Gem. Next stop."

She turned her eyes to him. "This is where things could get dicey. There should be workers down this tunnel."

He frowned. "Not a lot of light if there are workers."

"No," she agreed. "I can't imagine the tunnel would be empty. But maybe they're just not working this vein this shift."

"Doesn't make sense if this is where their rare finds are coming from."

"Unless..." She let the word hang in the air. "What if they found something even bigger in the other tunnel?"

She watched Nemo chew on the thought for a minute and look out across the chasm to the tunnel where the workers had been herded. "What could be bigger than tanzanite and taaffeite in what should be a diamond mine only?" He looked at her. "We need to know what's in that tunnel."

"That's a negative, Nemo," Waters cut in. "Stick to the plan. Get your video proof, get your samples that are a sure thing, and get the fuck out. No time for improvisations."

Haskell held Nemo's eyes with her own. Out of sight of the camera, she reached for his hand and gave it a squeeze. It was understood. Video. Samples. Then, orders be damned, go down that other tunnel. There should be time.

With one last look out into the cavern, they took off down the trackway to their first goal.

37

SEPTEMBER 17, 2022

Nemo

I don't like this at all.

He jogged beside Gem about a quarter of a mile, keeping his eyes open for the both of them.

"Midas, anything?" he huffed out.

"Nope. No chatter. I don't like this at all."

Nemo would have laughed at the fact that his twin was channeling him, but he was too amped up to find the humor right now. "Nothing?"

"Not a goddamn word. I even checked other frequencies to see if they were at least smart enough to move up and down. Dead silence."

"What time are we at?"

"Oh-six-hundred."

Nemo grabbed Gem's arm, stopping her. "Waters, we need to abort."

Her chest heaved up and down. "Nemo, no! It's right up here."

"Gem, this isn't right. They know we're here. They knew we were coming. It's all wrong."

"We need the video and samples!"

Waters came on the line. "Gem's right. You're almost there, Nemo. These guys aren't high-tech or particularly focused. You should see the topside. It's just as much of a ghost town."

"That makes it worse, Waters. In the history of any of our projects, when has there *not* been security of at least the barest kind?"

"I agree," Midas said. "It makes no sense that there's no activity. Traffic to the sex workers is even minimal. Haven't seen anyone in an hour."

"How the fuck do they know we're here?" Nemo whispered. He scanned around. "I'm telling you, Waters. They *know*."

There was a pause. He knew Gem was pissed, but he knew to listen to his intuition. It had saved him many times. Somewhere, he'd seen something that didn't register on his conscious senses, but his brain was processing that they were on someone's radar.

Gem had lost her patience. "Well, while you boys stand around and debate what isn't here, I'm going." She took off.

"Fuck! Gem is proceeding." Nemo followed her.

Waters made a decision. "Go after Gem. I'm calling Medusa and getting her off the ground. Get the video and samples if you can. You see anything that compromises you, get to the surface, with or without it. Use the elevators. Find a place to take cover until she gets here. We're going to bump up the timeline. TB, Steel, and Demon. Proceed now."

"Copy that," came from TB.

"Cerberus, be prepared to make things go boom."

"Waters..."

"I hear you, Nemo."

"This is not going to go well," he muttered under his breath.

When he caught up with her, she was already dragging her finger along three lines in the stratum that were running parallel to each other. "These are the veins," she said, speaking to Waters over the comms. "Diamonds on the bottom. Taaffeite in the middle. Tanzanite on the top." She followed the veins to a dead end. "They've stopped drilling here." She frowned. "I don't understand why."

"Gem, Nemo, I've lost video feed," Midas warned. "Something's interfering with my systems. You need to fucking hurry and get out of there."

She glanced around the tunnel floor. Someone had left a pick behind. She grabbed it and began hacking at the wall. Nemo found another and began to hack about six inches to her right. Unspoken, they worked together to remove a piece of the wall as a physical example containing both veins together.

Gem let loose one last mighty hack at the wall, dislodging the rectangle of material they had been working on. She threw the pick to the floor, stuffed the sample into the pouch at her waist, and followed Nemo at a breakneck pace back through the tunnel.

When they reached the main chamber, Nemo unhooked the chain they'd used to swing across the chasm, then grabbed her. "We don't have time to go single. Hang on, tiny."

She threw her arms around his neck, then wrapped her legs around his waist. Throwing all of their weight into it, Nemo swung them on the chain back across the canyon. With the weight of their combined momentum, it only took two tries to get them across, and that was only because Nemo didn't want to take any chances that he'd crush Gem when he let go. Once they landed, they didn't stop to worry about the chain but ran hell-bent for their climbing gear.

"Nemo!" Gem whisper-yelled. "What about the other tunnel? We need to know!"

Nemo looked at his watch. "No! We've got fifteen minutes, kitty cat. We need to get back up those ropes."

She flipped him off and took off down the other tunnel.

"Dammit! Somebody needs to put a leash on her," he muttered to himself.

He followed Gem to the corridor's edge. He watched her sneak a quick peek inside. Whatever was going on was so far down the tunnel she couldn't see from the entrance. When he caught up to her, all they could see was a curve in the tunnel about a hundred yards down and bright light coming from around that curve.

"What the hell are you two doing?" Waters asked. "I told you to get your shit and get out, not play Sherlock Holmes."

"Remind me of this conversation the next time Kubrick wants to do something you don't want her to do," Nemo sniped.

"Her wanting to jump out of a helicopter is not the same thing," Waters argued back.

"So you're saying I should have let Gem go on her own?"

"Boys! Not the time for this argument. We've got plenty of time, Waters," Gem insisted. "I just want to see what's going on in here that has them ignoring the vein they had been working so hard on and is clearly still producing stones."

"Nemo, finish up, grab her ass, and get out."

There was a harumph on the line from Demon. "Should be easy for him. That's his M.O."

Nemo rolled his eyes. "Really, dude? You're going to bring that up now?"

"If the condom fits."

Gem glared at Nemo. "Both of you, shut up." She waved Nemo to follow her.

Moving quickly and stealthily, Gem and Nemo went down the corridor. As they got closer and closer to the curve, the noise got louder. There were shouts of men—what sounded like orders of an unfriendly sort. They even heard whip cracks, and there were some moans and crying.

"What the hell is going on down here?" Nemo wondered.

"I'm afraid to look, but we've got to."

When they reached the end of the curve, there were two hall-ways of earth. The one on the left was dark. The one on the right took a sharp turn back up into the direction they'd come from.

"Oh. My. God," Gem choked out.

"Am I seeing what I'm seeing?" Nemo asked her.

"What are you seeing?" Waters barked out.

"Kids," Nemo murmured. "They've got fucking kids down here, Waters. Maybe thirty of them, and that's what I can see. All young, maybe eight to ten years of age. Jesus, Waters, we can't leave them here."

"Fuck! Lemme think!"

"We were planning to get the workers out in the trucks, anyway," TB offered over the line. "What's the difference?"

"These kids are going to need a lot of help. They're chained together."

Nemo saw Gem stand up straight out of the corner of his eye. Then he watched her hands go up in the air like she was being held up in a bank.

Oh fuck!

That's when he saw the gun poking into her lower back, right at her spinal column. Nemo stood as well, hands up, and he turned with Gem. Standing behind them was an array of guards with guns pointed at them.

"Well, this sucks," Nemo said in an understated tone.

"Fuck," Gem whispered.

Nemo, knowing he couldn't let the guards know they had a way to communicate with people topside, did his best to make it sound like he was only talking to Gem. "You didn't tell me that your last dozen boyfriends were going to come calling. You'd think they'd have brought flowers instead of guns, at least."

"Shit," Waters swore. "I'm sending TB and Steel in."

Gem tried to warn Waters and the others. "I think, perhaps, it would be better to apologize nicely to them this time rather than run out without so much as a goodbye."

"Boss?" TB asked.

"Stand down," Waters ordered.

A voice not previously heard before—Cerberus—came in. "Was my surprise package delivered?"

Gem apologized. "Leave it to us to come to a party and not bring favors to hand out."

"No party favors are needed, Le Chatte Noire. Your presence is present enough."

The guards parted down the center, and three men in suits passed between them.

The man in the blue suit smiled at Gem. "You're looking as lovely as ever."

"Kent."

Waters swore again. "Kent. As in Leech? Is that Ka-Bar?"

Gem pretended not to hear him. "I see you've made some new friends, Leech." Her eyes roved to two other men who were in black suits. "Hemeda. Pilis. Looking as ugly as ever."

Ka-Bar walked up to Gem, holding her gaze the entire way. He pulled her balaclava off when he reached her. "Did you get what you came for, little black cat? See something good?"

"No," she told him.

Ka-Bar searched Gem's pockets and pouches. He removed the hunk of rock wall from the pouch she had placed it in. Gem had an intense look on her face, one that Nemo didn't quite understand.

Ka-Bar stepped over in front of Nemo, ripping the balaclava off him as well. "Sawyer Newton. This is a surprise, considering you died, what? Five years ago? Six? Both you and your twin, I believe. How interesting to see that those reports were in error. How *ever* did you match up with our little kitten here?"

"Just good luck, I guess," Nemo snarked.

"Hmm. I don't think it's very good luck at all." With the hand holding the balaclavas, he gestured to the guards behind him. Four stepped forward, two flanking the two thieves on either side. "I hope you enjoyed your tour of the mine. Unfortunately, the rest of your visit is going to be far less pleasant." He gestured again to four of the guards and gave an order in Shona.

One of the guards nudged Gem with the muzzle of his rifle. She flashed a look at Nemo, then proceeded the guards out into the main cavern.

Ka-Bar stared hard at Nemo.

Nemo returned his stare. "Was it worth it?" he asked.

"Was what worth it?" his captor returned.

"Abandoning Zahra. Betraying your sister. Never seeing your son."

Nemo swore that he saw a flash of something in Ka-Bar's eyes, but it was gone so fast he couldn't be sure. He did not miss the tic in the man's cheek, however.

"Sometimes choices have to be made."

Nemo berated him, "There are fucking kids down here, and you're killing them."

This time, Nemo did see the flash in the eye, and in his lower peripheral vision, he saw the man clench his fist.

Instead of responding, he turned and headed back up the tunnel.

"He's all yours," he told the Kader brothers. "Remember. Pharaoh wants his prize undamaged. For now," Ka-Bar promised ominously.

The two guards flanking Nemo pushed him out into the cavern and toward a second tunnel on this side of the chasm. He fought their herding, trying to find where they'd taken Gem. She was being escorted up a flight of rickety wooden stairs that had the mine's main wall structure on one side. So that Waters knew they'd been separated, Nemo called out, "I'll come for you, Gem!"

Ka-Bar turned on the first platform. He looked at Gem fighting the two guards as she stopped where she was on the stairs. Then he looked at Nemo down below. "I don't think so, Mr. Newton." He gave a frosty smile, then he turned again and continued up to Gem and the guards, who were once again working their way up the stairs.

38

SEPTEMBER 17, 2022

Haskell

The guards placed her, rather unceremoniously, in what looked like a control room. They had climbed approximately five staircase levels, which appeared to be halfway to the ceiling of the cavern. Once there, one of the guards patted her down, looking for wires or surveillance devices, and he made sure to check extra long at her breasts and between her legs. She withstood it stoically. He also painfully dug into her ears, found the earbuds, and crushed them under his foot.

The second guard pulled a broken-down chair on wheels from in front of a workstation and half tossed her into it once the search was done. Afterward, they both stood on either side of the door, staring at her, rifles across their chests as if they believed she would suddenly spring a weapon out of her skintight shirt and leggings.

Ka-Bar came into the room a few minutes later. "Leave us," he growled. "You can assume your regular schedule."

Without a word, the guards exited the room, and she heard them begin the climb upward to the surface.

Ka-Bar set the chunk of rock on the workstation table, shuttered the large plate glass windows overlooking the cavern, and then perched on the edge of the tabletop in front of a series of dials, switches, lights, and monitors. Microphones on flexible stems sat in front of each chair at the long shelf-table. None of it appeared to have been turned on in ages.

They sat, staring at each other.

Finally, Ka-Bar broke the silence. "No one can hear us."

Haskell hissed at him. "What the fuck, Kent?"

"I didn't have any choice. They had Zahra."

"There's always a choice, asshole! They're kids!"

"They had pictures of Zahra. Proof they had her before I could hide her. I didn't know it was a lie." He cursed under his breath, then began to pace the small space, running a hand through his hair. He turned to Gem. "Have you seen him?"

Gem's anger dropped. "No. I only heard he's healthy, and they're safe."

"Good. It doesn't matter as long as she and the boy are safe."

"Jacques died protecting her," Gem told him. "What happens now?" she asked.

"My orders are to hold onto you. Insurance."

"And Nemo?" she asked, trepidation in her voice.

"Pharaoh Kader wants him. The boys were taking him into the B tunnel. It has a cart that goes to the surface about five miles out. They're transporting him to the old Murphy Mine in South Africa." His look at her was pointed. "He's going to use him as an exchange chip—him for Zahra and the boy."

"Tribe will never trade for him," Gem whispered. Her fear was taking over now.

"I think part of Pharaoh wants that. Either outcome gets him what he wants. They are pissed about something they interfered in a while ago. Not sure of all the details. They were hoping for someone named TB, or the boss, Waters, but they'll settle for your friend, Nemo."

"But you know, and I know, that he'll never let Nemo go."

Ka-Bar shook his head. "No, he won't." He looked out the window at the open cavern where normal activity was resuming now that their quarry had been caught. "They found additional deposits at the Murphy Mine, lower in the stratum. They're planning to blast down farther to access them."

"They're using kids there, too?"

Ka-Bar nodded. "Yesterday, they took half of what we had here down to that mine."

"Explains why the cavern seemed so empty and why the original tunnel was abandoned."

"Yes. They took all of the men they had here as well, save for about a dozen. It'll take them today to get to the mine. I'm honestly not sure how ready that facility is for workers, so they may not reach out right away, but they won't give it more than a couple of days."

Haskell hung her head.

"You love him... don't you?" Ka-Bar asked.

"Yes," she admitted, defeated by the unfairness of it.

"For what it's worth, I am sorry, Haskell."

She nodded. "I know." She pleaded with him. "Ka-Bar, get the hell out of this before it becomes worse for you."

He smiled sadly. "You know I can't leave."

"Why? They don't have Zahra, and they aren't going to get to her! There's nothing holding you to this atrocity."

"But what if they do get to her, Haskell? I need to be here to try and prevent that from happening. Or else be here to prevent the outcome."

She looked at him, swallowing hard. "So the Kaders have turned, then. That's why they want Zahra and the boy. They're going to kill her as a show of loyalty, then raise the boy as a Salieri?"

Ka-Bar nodded. "That's why it was so important to get Zahra to safety in the States. I figured once I got her there, I could contact

Tribe and get her under their protection. That went off the rails almost as soon as I got the photo to Kai." He paused again. "Is she happy with him?"

Gem nodded, her eyes still shiny with tears over Nemo's fate. "Desperately missing you but hopelessly in love with Waters."

He nodded. "Good. She deserves someone in her life like that." Slowly, he rose from his perch and headed to the door. When he got there, he turned his head over his shoulder. "Don't do anything I wouldn't do." And then he was gone.

39

SEPTEMBER 17, 2022

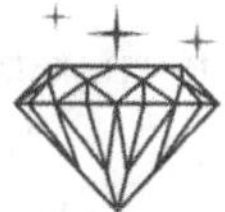

Haskell

This was bizarre. He hadn't restrained her. She thought about his parting words. "Don't do anything I wouldn't do."

Well. That certainly left her open to options. Ka-Bar would pretty much do anything. The man was fearless.

He abandoned his wife and child to the mercies of her family. He's allowing those children to be used and abused, and now he's abandoned you, too. Your little burglar boy is no help, either. What have I been telling you all these years? No man will ever find you worth saving. Just a tiny little tomboy. No man wants that.

"That's. It. No more. Get out of my head," Haskell whisper-yelled. "You know nothing, Da. It's not like if you were alive today, you'd come rescue me. You couldn't. But my brothers would. And Nemo would. He loves me. And Tribe would come out of respect for Nemo, at the very least.

Bollocks, girl. He's never said he loves you, has he? And why would those mercenaries feel any loyalty to you?

"He doesn't need to. I know it. He promised he was all in with me. That's as good as." She sat straighter in her chair. It was as if she'd suddenly found the will to beat back her inadequacies. She remembered what Nemo said. The look in his eyes when he said it. "He promised," she whispered. "And I'm going to listen to his voice, not you. Get out of my head, and don't come back."

Silence.

No echoing cackles, no sharp rebukes, no snarky comebacks. Could her da really be gone out of her head for good that easily?

Gem stood up from the chair and took stock of her surroundings. Ka-Bar had told her there was no one listening in. All the equipment in the room appeared out of working order, so she believed him. She scanned the room for cameras. Nothing. No red lights on equipment she could see or oddities in the ceilings or corners.

The rock she'd cut from the wall was still in the room. She grabbed it and slipped it back into her pouch.

When Ka-Bar had searched her pockets and pouches in the tunnel, he'd found her screwdriver tool, but he hadn't taken it. Why?

Vents! He knew her traffic patterns as well as anyone else who knew her. He'd locked the door on his way out, but it hadn't been to hold her in. It had been to keep her from going out the traditional route, cluing her in that it was being watched. He'd shuttered the window to keep her from breaking the glass and somehow going out the window.

She looked around the room again, but there were no vents at the top of the walls. Stymied, she put her hands on her hips, looking at the ceiling. It was pure rock above her. What the fuck was she supposed to do?

After a few moments of panic, she smacked herself on the forehead. "You idiot!" Immediately, she dropped to her knees and looked at the back wall. In the corner, there was a silver metal airflow unit. "Gotcha!"

In under a minute, she was in the vent. It had been touch and go getting even her tiny frame inside the vent, but she made it. After fifty feet or so, which she assumed was where the metal met the stone wall, there was a sharp bend. Sure enough, the metal opened up into a vertical maintenance shaft with metal rungs going straight up. It was going to be one hell of a climb, and it was going to take a while. Then the challenge would be to get out of the camp and make her way to Beitbridge and the rendezvous point, but she'd get there. Then she'd get to Nemo.

40

SEPTEMBER 17, 2022

Haskell

Exhausted beyond anything she'd ever felt in her life, she gave a shove to the metal grate that was between her and freedom. As soon as it started to rise, someone helped flip it all the way over, and two strong arms pulled her out of the air vent and passed her into two stronger arms. Those arms slung her over their shoulder and took off to behind a small warehouse that housed supplies. They crouched behind some oil drums. "Package acquired."

She was too tired to fight. It had taken her hours to climb the three miles of ladder. She'd stopped more than a few times to rest, but never for long. Every minute she was in that shaft was one more minute that Nemo was in the hands of the Kaders.

She was sliding off the shoulder of whomever had carried her and was now sitting on the ground, leaning against the tin wall of the warehouse. Someone was checking her pulse, then flashing a bright light in her eyes. Hands gently swiped down her body, pressing lightly.

A canteen of water was pressed to her lips. It tasted metallic, but it was heavenly after all she'd been through.

"Roger that. Medusa is on her way. ETA four minutes. Get ready to run like hell."

Gem floated in and out of consciousness until a loud boom sounded not too far away, causing the earth beneath her ass to actually shake. The sound of pounding feet went flying past them, voices in Shona yelling and screaming all around them. Her body was slung up over a shoulder again, and she bounced as whoever carried her ran in the opposite direction toward rotor blades she could barely hear over falling debris and crashing objects. She felt incredibly hot for several steps, then there was the feeling of rain falling on her.

No. Not rain. The drops were too big. In fact, it felt more like a deluge.

The water tower. Someone had blown up the water tower.

Cerberus!

Her body left the shoulder of her rescuer, and she was passed quickly into someone else's arms, then set against the far wall. Several other loud thuds sounded around her, with a yell of "Go!"

"We're in the pipe, gentlemen. Strap in!"

There was a violent rise as if they were being shot out of a cannon. Then, a sharp bank caused her to physically slide across the floor. Arms stopped her slide, then picked her up and strapped her to a bench seat.

A wet, sloppy tongue licked up her face. There was a yip and then a sneeze that covered her in snot. "Scheherazade," she whispered. Her eyes opened, trying to focus. When they couldn't, she sent her hand flailing off the bench, looking for the dog.

The dog's head found the palm of her hand, and she gripped the neck fur tightly in her fist. Scheherazade sat by her side, her muzzle flat on her torso perpendicular to her body.

More water was offered. She drank a few sips.

"Rest, Gem. We've got you."

She didn't know whose voice it was, but there was a soothing hand that smoothed back her curls, which, of course, sprung back to their original position even with the sweat and grime on her. She was so tired. Just a little rest. She'd just close her eyes for a couple of minutes. Regather her thoughts. Then she could get up, and they could go get Nemo.

SEPTEMBER 18, 2022

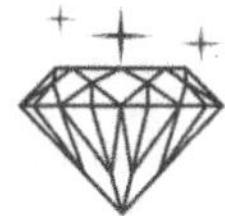

Haskell

"Have you found his tracker signal yet?"

"No. It's like it doesn't exist anymore. I'm trying to boot up his alternate tracker now, but it's going to take some time. We've got to update this shit. Never thought we'd actually have to use it."

"Keep looking, Midas. We'll deal with the rest of it later."

Haskell heard the voices as she swam up from the deepest sleep she'd ever experienced. She tried to shift from her prone position, but her body still felt heavy. A hand smoothed back her hair. She heard herself whimper, but it was as if the sound came from far away.

"The kids?" she whispered.

A cool cloth swiped over her forehead, nose, and cheeks. "Shh. Rest, *colleen.* Your body will know when it's time to wake up. Sleep."

She went back under.

When she woke up again, this time, it was with immediate clarity. She wasn't tired, but she was extremely hungry and thirsty. The bed she was in wasn't very comfortable, or maybe she'd just been in it too long, and her feet felt weighed down.

She looked down at the foot of the bed. "Zade?" The dog's tail thumped against the bed wildly at the sound of Haskell's voice. She slithered up the bed, crawling like an army man on his belly, and then she proceeded to wash Haskell's face with big, sloppy strokes of her tongue.

"Glad you're okay, girl. You missing your daddy?" She stroked the dog's head while it whined. "I know, I know. Me too. We're gonna find him."

"Welcome back," a deep voice said.

The dog didn't move, so the voice clearly wasn't a threat to her.

She looked over to her left. In a chair along the wall sat a man she'd never seen before. Even sitting down, she could tell he was a big man. Probably as big as TB. Muscles on muscles. She couldn't see his face as he kept that in the shadows.

"Who are you?"

"Someone with a vested interest in Nemo."

Haskell felt herself stiffen. "I'm not telling you anything. I don't know you."

The man smiled. "My apologies. A sincere vested interest in Nemo, my employee."

She stared. "You're God."

"In the flesh."

"Shouldn't you be appearing as a burning bush or something?"

God chuckled. "A bit theatrical for my taste. However, like my namesake, I do need you to do something for me."

"Please tell me you're not going to ask me to build an ark," she teased.

"Only if you can tell me what the hell a cubit is. One of life's great mysteries. No, Gem, I need you to lead my people somewhere."

She smiled. Then her face fell. "They haven't found him yet, have they?"

"No. I was hoping you might be able to help with that."

"Murphy Mine, South Africa. Pharaoh Kader has him."

"Thank you, Gem." He used a cane to stand. His movements to the door were stilted, but he managed to move silently. When he reached the door, he stopped. "I know you care for him a great deal, as much as he cares for you. But I ask you to remember your commitment to Mythos. Nemo will be a huge temptation to you to throw everything to the wind for him. To do so, however, would be... inadvisable."

"You don't make decisions for me. No one does but me. It's none of your business what choices I make."

He sighed. "Trust me, Gem. Stay with Mythos. It will make things painful for him, but it will serve you both best in the end."

The door quietly snicked shut. She sat there staring at the wall in front of her, absently stroking through Scheherazade's fur. She had no idea how long it was before the door opened again.

This time, it was TB. "Hey. Glad to see you're up. How are you feeling?"

"Oddly enough, I feel fine. Is everyone here? We need to start planning how to get Nemo back."

"We've been looking. There's been no sign of him. His tracker went dead."

"I just told God where he was. He didn't tell you?"

TB stared at Gem. "How did you tell him? There's no phone in here."

She looked at him like he was crazy. "I told him in person. He was just here." She flicked a hand to the chair.

TB clicked a button on his watch and barked into it, "Midas. Search the cameras. God was just here. He visited Gem. I was only out of the room for thirty minutes, so it can't have been long. And get everybody in here. She knows where Nemo is."

A flurry of footsteps could be heard in the hallway, coming from both down the hall and from downstairs.

"God was *here*?" Midas' eyes were practically bugging out of his head.

"Where the hell has he been?" Demon demanded.

"What did he say?" Steel asked.

"What does he look like?" TB asked.

"How the ever-loving fuck did he get past security?" Waters bellowed at Midas.

The Tribe started arguing amongst themselves.

Haskell stuck two fingers in her mouth and whistled so loud it even hurt her ears. It did, however, get the cacophony of overlaying voices to stop. "Yes, he was here. He didn't offer me a copy of his itinerary. He asked if I knew where they took Nemo. I couldn't see his face because it was in the shadows. And his name is freakin' 'God,' so he probably appeared in a bolt of lightning and left the same way. Now will you wankers please shut the fuck up so I can tell you where Nemo is since he didn't?"

The men were all staring at her. "Sorry, Gem," TB apologized. "We just haven't spoken to him in weeks, and as far as we know, he's never been seen by anyone other than Cherry or Kubrick. Of course we want to know what you have on Nemo."

"And I want to know what that son of a fuck, Ka-Bar, was doing keeping you prisoner." Waters' face was so red she worried he might spontaneously combust.

Midas grinned. "That's a new Kubrickism for the board. I like it."

"Fantastic. I'm glad you're impressed with my woman's ability to swear," Waters growled at him.

"Okay, everyone needs to calm down. Here's what I know. Goons One and Two took me to the original mine's control room. After my earbuds got destroyed, Ka-Bar arrived to talk to me. He told me that Nemo was removed through the second tunnel on the same side of the chasm we were on to get the sample. It has a path to get into it with full-size vehicles. Hemeda and Pilis were taking him to Pharaoh Kader. Have you heard from them yet?"

"No," Waters said. "What do they want with him?"

"They wanted TB or you, but they settled for Nemo." Gem

scowled at Waters. "How long has it been since you pulled me from the camp?"

TB spoke up. "When we lost contact, Cerberus told us to look for an air shaft. Said you'd escape, either alone or with Nemo, and that's how you would do it. You appeared at the top of it almost twelve hours after you were taken. You were covered in dirt and delirious. Dehydrated. Once we had you, Cerberus blew the water tower as a diversion, and Medusa came screaming in on her 'little bird.'" He put the phrase in air quotes with his voice. "That was yesterday. This is the first time you've been aware of anything around you."

"Bloody hell," she muttered. "Why haven't they contacted you yet?" She looked back to Waters, worrying her bottom lip. "Nemo was taken away immediately. He's a bargaining chip. They're going to ask for Zahra and the boy in trade for him. If you don't comply, they'll kill Nemo. If you do comply, they'll kill Zahra."

"Where did they take him?"

"You can't let him be traded. If you do, they'll kill Zahra. They... they've made a deal with the devil."

Tension vibrated throughout the room.

"What do you mean?" TB asked.

"The Kaders have pledged themselves to the Salieri. It's a loyalty test."

"Okay, I'm done with this. Who the fuck are the Salieri? No bull-shit anymore, Gem. You, or someone, needs to start talking now."

Her fingers pinched and unpinched the blanket edge. "Medusa could explain it better, but basically, they're a form of crime family. They have people all over the world, and if it's criminal, they're involved in it. They've been around for centuries, and they have very... specific rules. The Kaders have pledged to murder Zahra in order to join."

"What the fuck? Why does Zahra need to be murdered?"

"Because she's a woman. There are no women Salieri. Men who join the Salieri are forced to remove their mothers, sisters, grandmothers, wives, and daughters from their direct bloodline and forsake their extended family," she whispered.

"What the ever-loving fuck?" Demon bellowed.

"That's beyond barbaric," Steel muttered.

"How do they manage to keep this secret?" Waters asked.

"Their policies, believe it or not, are very similar to Tribe's policies. When Cherry offered me the job way back when, she told me that if I opened that folder and then said no, I would disappear. It was too big of a risk to take when my da needed me so badly. The Salieri work on much the same principle. If you're offered membership and you don't take it, it's a death sentence. Both groups are extremely selective, and both groups do their due diligence and research fully so that they know if someone is worth their effort or not."

"And why are the Kaders worth the effort?" Demon asked.

"The mines," Waters supplied. "Somehow, the Salieri found out about the stones in the mines where they shouldn't be together, and they're going to use the Kaders to get access to them."

"Yes," Gem agreed. "But eventually, they'll use them and throw them away, taking over the mines for themselves until they use up its resources."

"This is all good information, but it doesn't resolve our current issue, which is Nemo," TB pointed out.

Waters held up his hands in surrender. "True. But it does help us know what we're up against." He focused on Gem. "What can you tell us about Nemo's situation?"

"Ka-Bar said that he was being taken to the abandoned Murphy Mine in South Africa."

"Is this another situation like what was going on in the Mzingwane Mine?" Waters asked.

"Yes, and the Kaders are also in control of this illegal mining operation, but it's in its infancy stages. Before they can make that mine pay, they need to blast the veins they found. Pharaoh is going to use the combination of his trade for Zahra and the new mine as his ticket into the Salieri."

Waters snapped into project mode. "Okay, gang, wash, rinse, repeat. Midas, start pulling up anything and everything—"

"—on the Murphy Mine. On it."

"Steel. I need you to check in with the safe house. Make sure everything is good with Zahra and the boy. Double the guard, tighten the rotation, and make sure everyone understands they are on complete lockdown until we give them the signal. No exceptions.

"TB. Get with Cerberus. If it causes blood loss or things to go boom, I want it in working order and ready to be used. Tear everything apart. Clean it. Reassemble it. Make sure it has ample ammunition.

"Demon, get Medusa out of bed and have her get her little bird ready to fly again. Make sure Gem is good to go, get food in her, then put her back to bed to rest up. Then check, double-check, and triple-check the status of our medical supplies. When we get him back, he's likely to be in shit shape, so think about everything that could possibly be wrong with him and make sure we have whatever is needed to treat it, fix it, or heal it.

"Loki and Gilgamesh are working on a plan to get those kids out of Mzingwane. I'll let them know they're going to double down on what we're going to find at the Murphy Mine. Then, I'm going to call Cherry and convince her to get God on the line. Between Loki, Gilgamesh, God, and me, we need to find contacts to help us out. Go!"

The men scattered to their tasks. Waters walked up to Gem's bedside. "Your job is to rest and do whatever Demon tells you to do. We need your help to get him out of this." Waters' face had a strange look on it. "When he comes back, you're both going to have choices to make. Make the right ones."

42

SEPTEMBER 20, 2022

Nemo

KA-THUNK! Chink!

It took everything within Nemo not to make a sound as the belt buckle bounced off his already ripped-apart back, then hit the floor. He wasn't sure which hurt worse, the metal ripping apart new flesh or ripping through the flesh that had already been torn open before, some of it multiple times. It seemed like when these people wanted their pound of flesh, they wanted it literally. Eventually, he'd scream in pain. He wasn't really sure why he was holding out. The outcome wasn't going to change, whether he screamed or didn't. He figured part of it was just the perverse pleasure of not letting them know they were breaking him. They weren't even asking any questions. They were just beating the shit out of him because they could.

He knew Tribe needed time to figure out where he was. When the Kaders had taken him into the second tunnel, they immediately took his watch, pulled out his earbuds, and ripped the gauges out of his ears. He was thankful they didn't think to scan for other piercings. That would have really hurt. Then they scanned him with some sort of device, which located his tracker in his hip. They immediately dug that thing out with what felt like a fork twirling pasta. Then he'd been thrown in an armored truck of some sort and hadn't seen anything until he was let out on the inside of another mine.

If he would just pass out, they'd stop. He'd get a break for a bit. He considered his next action carefully before proceeding. Provoking them would not only get him that break, but it would allow the guys more time to locate him through his second chip.

Contingencies for contingencies. Never gonna tell Waters he's a paranoid SEAL ever again.

"You know," he said during a lengthy pause, "if that's all you and your sisters are capable of dishing out, I could show you a few techniques a torture specialist taught me."

There was a muttered oath in Egyptian, the whistling of the belt slicing through the air, and a burning fire ripped across his shoulder. They had popped both of them out of their sockets before each beating, so this added layer of fire was just extra special.

The next thing he knew, he was lying on the floor, his eyes opening... sort of... to a blank dirt wall. He pulled himself upright into a sitting position, still facing the wall. When he had caught his breath, he used the wall to help him stand, which was no small effort, and then he leaned one shoulder against it. On a silent countdown in his head, he threw his entire body weight on his opposite shoulder against the wall. He grunted as the left shoulder popped back into place. Then he repeated the process for the right shoulder.

Because of his injury at birth that allowed him to pop his shoulders in and out at will, Flame, TB's woman, teased him he had first-hand secret knowledge of what her wolf shifter characters felt like during their change. To be honest, it hurt less than it used to. Or maybe after all these years, he was just used to the pain. Whatever the reason, he'd used it to his advantage many times when he needed to change his body's shape to fit into tight places.

He dared to reach behind him and see if he could tell how bad his back actually was. He hissed in pain at the sting of his touch. When he pulled his hand away and looked at it, it was caked in dirt and blood.

"Well, if I get out of this, it's going to suck recovering from the infection."

"Don't worry, young man," a polished voice behind him assured. "Infection will not be a problem because you're not getting out of this."

"Good. I hate needles, I can't swallow pills, and I'm allergic to antibiotics." Gently, Nemo swiveled around to see who he was talking to. "I thought I'd be talking to one of my new besties, but they must be off braiding each other's hair and having a pillow fight without me. Who are you?"

The man appeared to be in his late fifties. His hair was black, but so black it was clearly colored to cover the gray that most likely was there naturally. He was well built, although certainly not as he would have been in his thirties or forties, and he wore what was clearly a bespoke suit. He pulled his cuffs clear of his gray suit jacket, making a show of checking his cufflinks, and then looked up to introduce himself. "I am Pharaoh Kader."

Nemo called up every piece of strength within him to sit down nonchalantly on the ground. He pulled his knees up, crossing them at the ankles, and leaned his elbows on his raised knees, allowing his hands to dangle in front of them. It hurt like hell to do it, but he refused to show that to this asswipe. They stared at each other for a long time. Finally, Nemo asked, "Don't you want to know my name?"

Kader shrugged. "I was looking for the one named TB. I was hoping for the one named Waters. I have specific issues with both of them. Apparently, I'm settling for you. Who you are is inconsequential, and what you are is merely a means to an end."

"If I'm so inconsequential, why are your two goons smacking me around all the time?"

"Likely, they are bored while we wait. I do not ask because I do not care."

"What do you care about then?" Nemo asked.

The man replied, "Your friends have something I want. They will either give it to me in exchange for you, or you will die, and then I will take what I want another way."

Zahra and Ka-Bar's son.

Nemo chuckled. "But if I'm dead, you'll have nothing to exchange."

Kader smiled. "You will be dead either way, young man. Even if they give me what I want, you will never see the outside of this mine. Nor will your little thief friend back in Zimbabwe."

Okay. Gem's not here. Good to know. The question is, where is she?

Nemo schooled his features and his body language. It wouldn't do to let Kader know that Gem meant anything to him.

"Pfft. That tiny little shit? Not even worth my time."

The man in the suit smiled at him. "I know you would have me believe that is true. However, I also know it to be the exact opposite. My son, Hemeda, told me of your last words to her. Hopefully, she put no trust in them as they were an untruth."

Nemo tried another tactic. "You're wasting your time. My employers won't trade anything for me. When we go out on a job, we know no one is ever coming for us if we're captured or injured."

"Maybe. Maybe not. But what about Miss Dawson? Will they leave her to the same fate? You men, despite your mercenary ways and uncivilized tactics, have a soft spot for women, even ones you have no connection to. If you bring about no results, perhaps a threat to her will."

Nemo laughed out loud. "She means even less to them than she does to me. My friends are already long gone since we missed our check-in. Sorry, Kader. You lose. There's no rescue in the works, and there will be no trade of any kind."

The man continued to smile. "If she means nothing, then I guess we should start our negotiations with her as the prize. We have yet to contact your employer, so yes... I think we'll start with Miss Dawson."

Well, fuck. That backfired.

"Goodbye, young man. If I need to have someone disposed of, I always like to meet them first. Look them in the eye, as it were."

"Well, I guess that's something if you don't have the courage to actually do the disposal yourself," Nemo snarked.

"Oh, I do, and I have. But those days are long behind me. Now I have people for that."

Nemo watched the man leave the room, heard the thud of the door and the clunk of the lock. Now that he was alone, he laid his head back against the wall and closed his eyes, wincing against the pain of his destroyed back.

The team would come. It was just a question of when. He just had to hold on.

His bigger hope was that they were looking for Gem first. Otherwise, if they were looking for him, and she was the one who was on the trading block, they wouldn't get to her in time.

If the Kaders attempted to use torture on her, she had nothing to tell them. She didn't know where Zahra and the baby were. Didn't know much of anything about Tribe, really. And if Waters felt Tribe was compromised in any way, the company had other offices, other corporate shells to work through. Each of the men had their own bolt-holes they could scatter to, as well. He and Midas had several together and apart.

She was a tough cookie, but she wouldn't last long in the face of a beating or, heaven forbid, an assault. His thoughts went briefly to Sarah Miller, Waters' sister, and then he slapped those thoughts away. He couldn't think about that. Not his Gem.

"Please," he whispered. "Please go after Gem first. She's worth so much more than me."

43

SEPTEMBER 20, 2022

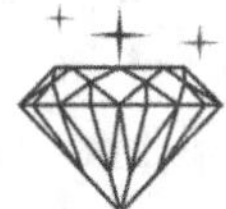

Haskell

"His primary tracker isn't responding, which means they likely found it and dug it out. But I'm having difficulty getting the secondary to activate, and that's buried down deep toward the spinal column. The only reason that wouldn't be activated is if it also had been removed, and that would be fatal." The frustration in Midas' voice was evident.

"If he's in the mine, could the depth be blocking the signal? I mean, we know he's at the Murphy Mine. Is it just that we need to get closer?" Haskell asked.

Midas propped his elbows on the dining room table and ran his hands along his skull. "No. The only thing that might block a signal would be if he were inside a lead box of some sort."

No one responded to the implications of that statement.

Haskell walked up behind him. Instinctually, she put her arms around his neck and hugged him. "You'll find him," she assured him.

"He knows you're looking for him." She wondered if she wasn't trying to convince herself as much as him.

Midas grabbed her arms and gave them a squeeze.

"One hour. Then you get some sleep," she ordered. "TB's good with computers, even if he's not as good as you. He can work on it while you nap. You're not good to Nemo or us if you're too exhausted to think straight."

Midas looked like he was about to argue, but Waters intervened. "She's right, Midas. One hour. Then sleep, a shower, and some food. You've been at this for over forty-eight hours."

Midas replied, "Then I guess I better get back to it."

An hour later, while Midas was sleeping, the rest of the team began to work out a plan for how to get to Nemo. Without a location from his trackers, it wouldn't be impossible, but it would require searching building by building of the compound, and cavern by cavern of the mine itself. Going in blind would be dangerous and take time. Time that maybe Nemo didn't have.

Three hours later, Haskell stood, frustrated and feeling helpless. She'd dragged the table in from the pool deck, and with the help of electrical tape, she'd planned to grid out her kit the way Nemo had in Los Angeles. It wasn't her normal approach, but she'd hoped it would calm her. Make her feel closer to him. Instead, her eyes were blurry with tears she refused to let fall, which also meant that her hands were shaking and unable to tear the tape.

Slamming one hand down on the table, a strangled sob worked its way up through her throat and escaped her mouth. The other hand holding the tape roll went up to her mouth, the back of the hand covering her lips, hoping to keep any further sounds trapped inside. Her shoulders rolled over as she fought the urge to be sick.

A pair of hands reached from behind and to the side, pulling the hand holding the tape away from her mouth. Quiet and low, a voice offered, "Let me help." She looked up into the green eyes of Demon. He nodded with encouragement to her, but her fingers didn't want to let go, as if somehow that meant she was letting go of Nemo. Giving up on him.

"Easy, Gem. Let go. I've got you."

He managed to slip the roll from her grasp, then pulled a long strip of the tape clear from the roll. He gave her the free end, then he walked around the table until he was across from her. After pulling more of the tape clear of the roll to reach all the way across, he ripped off the piece and pressed his end to the edge of the table. He waited, watching for her to do the same.

Meticulously, as if the straightness of the tape made it more likely they would get to him in time, she attached her end of the tape to the table. Together, they smoothed the piece of tape down, edge to center, their fingertips meeting in the middle of the table. She looked up at Demon, and he nodded at her, saying nothing. Then he stood up, started to pull another piece of tape, handed her the end, and they continued the process until the table was gridded out to her satisfaction.

When they were done, she stood staring down at the tabletop.

His voice came from behind her again, and his hands settled on her shoulders. "Better?"

She did feel like she could get air in better. Felt calmer. Her hand smoothed over the tape lines closest to her. "Yes. Thank you," she whispered.

He nodded and made his way outside onto the pool deck. She stared after him, watching as he stood at the water's edge, hands in his pockets, peering down at it. Without her thinking about it, she followed him, pulling the sliding door closed behind her.

Standing next to him, she tried to find the words she wanted to say. "I really do trust you, Demon. I'm sorry if I made you feel otherwise."

He said nothing.

"Who am I to judge what's acceptable, or not, about your... coping mechanism." She cringed at the phrase. By trying to soften the crime, she'd said something equally as judgmental as the first statement. "That came out worse, I think. Look. I guess what I'm trying to say is that we all do things that technically aren't good for us. Midas spends all of his time with Nova, an AI personality. He refuses to sleep, and all he seems to eat, unless we all eat together, is candy and chips. TB closes himself off to everyone except maybe Flame. Even Nemo has his own disaster with his... dating habits. I don't know what else to call them. Hell, I allow my *dead* father free rent space in my head that no matter how good I am as a thief, I'm useless as a daughter."

"You're not wrong about me, Gem. I am a liability to them, but for some reason, I can't force myself to leave them. It has nothing to do with my 'disappearing' if I do, either. Some days, I think it might be better if I did."

"You're not a liability, Demon. The guys don't see you like that."

"They should. I've no excuse for it. Not that there ever really is an excuse."

Haskell knew he expected her to ask why he used, but she wasn't going to. It wasn't her business. She only knew of one person other than Demon who should hear that story.

"Do you know how I know that they see you as an asset? Whatever your motivation for using, it was there before you came to Tribe. That means everyone who mattered knew already, but you're here anyway. If there's one thing I know about your boss, God, is that he never would have approved hiring you if he didn't think you were the best person to do what you do. Waters never would have recommended you to him. The guys wouldn't joke around with you, and I know for a fact that Nemo believes in you one hundred percent. He even told me that he'd rather have you being as you are than working with anyone else." She put a hand on his arm, staring intently at his profile. "Cherry wouldn't be so pissed if she didn't care."

"Don't try to justify it, Gem. You can't. It's weak. It's dangerous. Just because I'm a functional addict doesn't mean I won't screw up."

"No. No, it doesn't. Any of us could screw up for any number of reasons, and we don't use narcotics on a regular basis." She threaded her arm through his and placed her head along his bicep, mirroring his stare at the water as if it had all the answers. "But look at how you choose to handle yourself. When you know you're headed out, you're able to cut yourself off. You *can* do it; you're just not ready yet. When you're ready, you'll stop."

Through clenched teeth, he swallowed tightly. "What if I'm never ready?" The question came out as a whisper, the fear in the question ringing loud.

Haskell squeezed his arm. "I have a sneaking suspicion you're closer than you think."

She felt him shift, so she looked up to find him looking at her quizzically.

"I think you've been ready for a while. There's something you want, and it's so close. The only way to get it is to quit. Unfortunately, you feel unworthy, so you maintain the status quo. You've set yourself up to fail on purpose, but all you're really doing is breaking both your hearts." She patted his arm and laid her head back on it. "Just think about it."

They stood in silence together, contemplating the ripples in the pool from the light breeze. Eventually, he said, "You should know... I promise you—nothing and no one is going to get to you unless it comes through me."

"I'm not worried about me," she told him.

"I know. But you need to know that just the same. And we are not allowing them to get their hands on Zahra. She's safe and in good hands. More importantly, Gem, as long as even one of us is still breathing, we are not leaving him in that mine. I refuse to make promises I may not be able to keep, but I'll do everything until I'm physically no longer breathing to get him back."

She nodded. "I know. He's tribe."

He dislodged from her hold and turned to her. "You still don't get it, do you?"

"I do. Really. Loyalty is everything to you guys."

Demon sighed. He turned his head toward the dining room table, where TB was smiling tightly and talking with someone quietly. "TB! You done flirting with Flame yet?"

TB rolled his eyes. He got up from the table, laptop in hand, and carried it outside to the pool loungers. He handed a pair of earbuds to Haskell. "Encryption is running. Just don't touch any of the keys. She knows that she should close out first, which activates the kill switch on her end." He pulled her to one of the loungers and sat her at the computer. His focus went to the computer screen. "Thanks, princess." He smiled at the redhead on the screen.

She shooed him away with her hands flapping in the camera. "You're welcome, love you, go away while I talk to my new muse. Go play doctor with your medic."

Haskell smiled at the quiet "Eww" she heard from Demon as he went back inside.

TB chuckled. "Add five more swats to the list for brushing me off, little Flame. You're not going to sit for a week."

"Pfft! Like that scares me, Godzilla. Go destroy a city or something. Shoo!"

He was still chuckling as he walked back inside, closing the sliding door behind him.

Haskell turned back to the screen.

"Hi, Gem." Flame's face still had a smile on it, but it had concern in it. "How are you holding up?"

"Umm... okay?"

"Is that an honest answer or a question?"

"To be honest, I'm not sure."

Flame nodded. "I hear ya there. I'm sorry Kubrick's not here. She wanted to be once she heard I was going to be talking to you, but she's in meetings today for her new film."

"I'm not really sure why TB called you..."

"It was actually Demon's idea to have you talk to one of us because he's worried about you, and TB agreed with him that it was a good idea. We've been through some serious crap with our guys, so we understand the worry angle. Mostly, it's because he's worried about you. They all are."

"Worried about me? Why?"

"Because you're Nemo's. He thought maybe talking to one of us would help you see some things differently."

"I'm not sure how I'm supposed to see Nemo being in the hands of a crime lord differently than what it is." Haskell scoffed.

"Oh, no, I didn't mean that. Yes, that's bad. But the guys will have that handled. And you're there to do your thing, so it will all work out." Flame said it as if there was no question of it working out any other way.

"I appreciate your confidence, Flame, but I'm not sure you understand just exactly what's going on here."

The redhead's bark of laughter was jarring. "Oh, hon, I know *exactly* what's going on there. I don't know how much you know about my situation or Kubrick's. Did they share any of it?"

Haskell shook her head. "I know you were targeted by a trafficker. That's it."

"Mmm." Flame bit her lip, clearly thinking about her next words. "I'm not sure exactly what I'm allowed to tell you, but given the circumstances that TB asked me to talk to you, I'm guessing I can share the basics. When I was very young, my parents and I lived on the streets of New York City. When they died, I was taken in by their drug dealer, Gendry. Let's just say he was less of a guardian and more of a groomer."

Pieces of a vague puzzle began to piece together in Haskell's head. Conversations at Tribe and their over-the-top protectiveness of Kubrick, Flame, and Cherry. Past conversations she had overheard with members of Mythos.

"I managed to run away and start a new life. Unfortunately, Gendry wasn't about to let go so easily and tracked me down. He'd connected himself to some sort of trafficking ring, and he was using me as his ticket to move higher up in the organization. I spent months being terrorized from a distance and the better part of two days in a metal box, waiting to be shipped to who knows where. TB and the boys saved my life."

"I'm sorry you went through that, Flame, but I'm not sure what it is that I'm supposed to see differently."

"You."

"Me?" Haskell asked. "I don't get it."

"This isn't about Nemo, Gem. This is about you."

"I'm not following."

She watched Flame scrunch up her face in consideration. "Let me try this approach. Kubrick and me? We know these guys better than they know themselves. They're supposed to be so smart"—she rolled her eyes—"and most of the time they are, like Demon and TB realizing you needed to talk to me, but other times? Let's just say their self-awareness elevators don't always go to the top floor. I'm sure you've seen it with Nemo."

Haskell gave a small smile. "Yeah. His reality of our relationship and my reality don't always mesh."

"Exactly. You and Nemo will mesh eventually, but right now, it's you who needs to be seeing things from another perspective."

"I'm very confused," Haskell admitted.

"You see yourself as an outsider. Separate. I get that. I was in that same headspace for a bit. But after I realized that I was all in with TB, no matter how petrified I was in that box, I knew beyond a shadow of a doubt that he was coming for me. That they *all* were coming for me, including Medusa's boys, because I was tribe, as they call it. You don't have to worry about Nemo because he knows they're coming for him. That they would never ever leave him, but you're not seeing that it applies to you as well."

Flame folded her arms in front of her on her desk and leaned into the camera. "Look. It's simple. You love Nemo, right?"

Haskell hesitated, then nodded. "I didn't want to love him, but..."

Flame giggled. "Yeah, it's difficult not to love the big idiot. I swear, if there's a way to eff something up, that boy's got it down on how. Nemo's heart is as big as his stupid. But without him, TB might never have got his head out of his gorgeous butt over me.

"The point to all of this is... Nemo loves you. He claimed you, loud and proud, to the guys. Now, I'm not going to lie. He made *a lot* of mistakes regarding how he handled that emotional commitment to you the past few years, but the love itself never wavered. And because he loves you so much and so deeply? Those five men he calls teammates will do everything they can to bring him back. Yeah, his boss wants him back. We girls want him back. But for you alone, because he loves you, they are willing to burn the world down so that *you* can have him back. They're the same way about me, the same way about Kubrick, and the same way about Cherry. World. Burning. No questions asked."

Flame smiled at Haskell. "Look around, Gem. Those guys have let you into their world in a way that Kubrick and I can never experience. You were almost one of them, I hear. That factors into this as well. Don't hold yourself off from them. The big lumps will never admit that your inability to connect to them hurts their feelings. Which I get because they are men, and that whole X-Y chromosome thing makes it nearly impossible for them to articulate they even have feelings, let alone that they hurt. Trust them, Gem," she pleaded. "They've got Nemo, and by extension, they've got you, too. You're not alone anymore."

There was a shouting noise from inside the house. Haskell turned around at a knocking sound on the glass door, and TB was standing there, twirling his finger in the universal "wrap it up" gesture.

"Is that Mr. Grumpypants telling me you need to go?" Flame asked.

"Yeah." Haskell nodded.

"Okay. Remember what I told you because it means everything. World burning. Now, go be amazing at what you do. So jealous! Well, not really, but when this is all over, you and I need to sit down with some ice cream and chat. There's got to be a novel in this somewhere about a cat shifter," Flame mused.

Haskell felt the first honest smile on her face in several days. This woman and her shifters!

"Take care of yourself, Gem. And do me a favor. Give TB a smack on the ass for me."

Haskell felt horror spread across her face. "You know he's going to add more swats for that. And I'll probably get a few myself."

Flame giggled. "He wouldn't dare swat you because I can be a jealous witch with a 'b.' As for me, I'll enjoy the extra swats, so no worries there. Just wish I could be there to see what happens when you do it." Flame giggled, winked, blew her a kiss, and cut the connection.

When Haskell stood to go back inside, TB came out and collected the laptop. "We finally got a communication from Pharaoh Kader, so Nova was able to pinpoint Nemo's secondary tracker."

Relief flooded through her. "That's great." He had barely passed in front of her when Gem said, "By the way, I have a message for you from Flame."

He set the computer down and looked at her. "What's the message?"

She looked at him nervously. "I'm kind of afraid to give it to you."

He chuckled and turned back to the table. "No need to be afraid of me, Gem. What could she possibly tell you to tell me that would make you worry?"

SMACK!

TB froze in his slightly bent-over position at the table.

All of the guys in the room were wide-eyed, gazes bouncing from her to TB.

Haskell crossed past him, using Demon as a shield. She looked at TB and shrugged. "Please don't shoot me. I'm just the messenger."

There was a silence that hung in the air for another moment or two, then there was a snort that someone couldn't hold in, followed by a "holy shit," and then everyone exploded in laughter. Except TB.

He turned on her, nostrils flaring, eyes shooting flames. She wondered if maybe she'd made a mistake in trusting Flame. Then she was pretty positive she had when TB started stalking her around the table. Before she could get an apology out, he swooped in, threw her over his shoulder, took her out through the patio doors, and tossed her in the pool.

When she came up sputtering, it was to see Scheherazade standing on the edge of the pool barking her fool head off and all the guys clutching their sides and stomachs, bent over laughing with tears coming out of their eyes. She smoothed the hair out of her face and looked up at TB. Just the one corner of his mouth was tipped up in the slightest smirk.

Haskell grinned. "I told her it would cost her five extra swats if I did it, but she said she didn't care."

"Oh, it'll be way more than five." TB reached his hand down to her to help her out of the pool. She latched on, and with one yank by that single arm, she was up out of the water and standing along the edge.

"Don't be too mad at her," she begged.

"Nah. Gotta love my princess," he said. "She always knows the right thing to say and do in a crisis. Go on. Go get dry. We got shit to do."

Haskell scampered into the house between the men still laughing and rehashing the event, including impersonations of TB's face, and ran upstairs to change clothes.

The tension had been eased. Now they could all get back to work.

44

SEPTEMBER 21, 2022

Nemo

"Well, this is another fine mess I've gotten myself into."

"Shut up, blondie," the dark-haired Pilis Kader grumbled.

"Or what? You'll kill me?" Nemo looked at his current situation—lashed to a timber in the passage and a bomb vest attached to him. "I think that's a given already."

"You have an awful smart mouth for a dead man," Hemeda Kader observed.

"Better smart and dead than dumb and alive."

He knew he was pushing buttons he really shouldn't push, but it'd been way too many days of him missing to think that Tribe wasn't going to need some help finding him. By goading them this way, he hoped he'd distract them so that they didn't tie the knots so tight. Then he'd have a little bit of hope of getting himself free of this nonsense. So far, it didn't seem to be working. He already couldn't feel his fingers from how tightly his wrists were lashed.

There had been a Plan B, but Heckle and Jeckle destroyed that when they dislocated both of his shoulders and then tied his hands behind him.

You'd think they'd get it by now that I can do that to myself. How many times have I put them back in after they've popped them out?

Plan C was dangerous, but it might be his only opportunity to get out of there on his own.

Five minutes later, he was by himself in the barely lit tunnel. He'd been stuck in some weird places over his years as a thief, but this one was probably the scariest. Nemo didn't feel fear often, but he had to admit this was certainly a situation where it was warranted.

He was just about to put Plan C into action and run the risk of bleeding out by slicing open his wrists on the zip ties in order to get out of them when debris started showering down on him. It was just fine grit, but it was annoying, and it burned when it hit his open wounds. "Sonofabitch, that stings!"

"Quit complaining, burglar boy," came a voice from above.

Gem popped out of a fissure about ten feet above him. Right behind her came Steel.

"*Jesucristo*, you're always such a crybaby."

"Gem, what the fuck are you doing down here?"

"Saving your ass, apparently."

"How did you get out of Zimbabwe?"

Sounds of gunfire began in the distance, with muted yells echoing down the passage toward them. Steel suggested, "Perhaps we could save story time for when we get the hell out of here and somewhere safe. I'll work on the right-side ropes, *ojona*."

He cut off to the side and began working on cutting through the restraints.

"What the hell did you just call her?"

"Something I knew would piss you off so that you're too angry to feel the pain when your limbs come free," Steel admitted.

"Cerberus," Gem called over the communications. "We've got a problem. He's got explosives strapped to him."

"Copy that. On my way."

"Great. Now I'm really going to get blown sky-high," Nemo grumbled. Then blood began rushing to his fingers because Steel had cut through the zip ties. "Fuck!"

"Told you," his friend commiserated.

Another body moved itself out from the fissure. "Well, well, well. The fish has truly been fried," Cerberus snarked.

"Shut up, bird brain, or we'll all go up in your pile of ash. Get this thing off me."

Cerberus handed Gem his gun with the silencer on the end. "Fire at anything that comes down that tunnel, love. The rest of Tribe and Mythos are a little busy, so it won't be them."

Steel moved to Nemo's left, cutting away the rest of the restraints. "*Jesucristo, hermano,*" Steel uttered under his breath. "Gem, hold the light."

Nemo realized that Steel had seen his back. "Don't, Steel. It's fine. There's nothing we can do about it right now."

"You can't go back the way we came when you're in this condition."

"What's wrong?" Gem asked. Then she caught glimpses of torn flesh. When she passed the flashlight farther back, she gasped. "Oh my god. What the hell did they do to you?"

"Just some lashes with a belt, kitty cat. I've had worse."

"Nemo, this is more than some lashes with a belt," she hissed. "When we get this vest off, will I be able to see any of your actual back? All of your lovely tattoos..."

"Demon will clean it out and put it all back the way it should be. We have bigger issues right now." Nemo looked at Steel. "You got an extra earbud for me?"

Steel dug into his pocket and pulled a case out, handing it over to Nemo. As Cerberus continued to work on the vest, Nemo proceeded to put his shoulders back into place against the cave wall. Gem winced with both grunts he let out, but he didn't have time to feel bad about it. Then he pushed the earbuds into place and spoke over the channel.

"Nemo online."

"Thank Christ," came TB's voice over the channel, as well as rapid gunfire. "Hurry your asses up down there."

"Waters," Steel started, "we can't come back through the fissure. Nemo's back is torn to shreds. It's already going to be hard enough on him to move through this, let alone scraping his back on the ragged edges of that tunnel. On top of that, the explosives they strapped to him... they did it all with adhesive tape. We're not going to be able to remove it here."

Cerberus explained, "I can dismantle the wiring, but I can't pull it off without taking inches of flesh off him."

"Got it. TB and Demon will make the path."

"Wait. We've got another problem." Nemo looked at Gem. "Remember the tunnel in Zimbabwe?"

She nodded. "Yeah. The kids. They're using them here, too."

"I didn't think it could get worse, but it did. Waters, they've gone all *Indiana Jones and the Temple of Doom*. There's another tunnel here. When you get to the end of it, it's like a frickin' ancient burial ground, with all those slots for bodies. Only problem is, they're not dead bodies in them. They've got kids crawling in there. They're sending them into these narrow human wormholes like we used to get inside Zimbabwe's cavern. But they're all girls. I don't know why only girls, but that's all I saw. Little ones. They're even littler than the kids we saw in Zimbabwe."

"Fuckin' Salieri again."

"Gem?" Nemo asked.

"No time to explain. Waters, I'm not leaving another group of kids behind."

"Loki and Gilgamesh have got it, Gem."

"But—"

"I said, they've got it. We're not leaving them behind, I promise. Nemo, make sure her ass is with all of you coming out of that tunnel."

"You got it, boss man."

At that same moment, Cerberus pulled a wire delicately from the explosive device strapped to Nemo. "Okay, we're clear. Let's get him out of here."

Nemo could barely move. The beating had been restricted to his back, but he was still struggling to move due to poor circulation over the last thirty to forty-five minutes. He hobbled as best he could, one arm over Gem's shoulders, the other over Steel's. The pull in his back from the open and reopened wounds was excruciating, but it was better than being blown up. You couldn't put that back together.

"TB and Demon, have you got them?"

"Elevator doors are opening now."

When they got to the mouth of the tunnel, Nemo had never seen a better or worse sight at the same time. Two elevator doors on the far side of the cavern opened to reveal the team's interrogator in one and the medic in the other. From a far tunnel, Waters emerged with a group of children who seemed to be in distress. Steel, Cerberus, Gem, and Nemo made their way to him, each sweeping up a child or two in their arms and racing for the elevators. TB and Steel kept them covered in case of last-minute appearances from additional guards, but no one arrived.

As the elevator doors closed, Waters updated everyone.

"Okay. Loki and Gilgamesh have the kids in the trucks and are standing guard topside so that when Medusa comes swooping in, you've got cover. These children were the last of them and are in need of medical care. Once you get the last of those kids loaded onto the truck, get the hell out of there."

"Roger that," TB called out.

"Medusa just came up over the horizon," Loki called out over the airwaves.

Nemo couldn't believe what he'd seen over the last few minutes. "I thought this place was barely up and running?"

Waters nodded. "Apparently, that was false. Trucks are going to be a tight fit. Loki, Gilgamesh, and Janus, Mythos' pilot, are full up, but they say they have a place to take them. Hope they've got good resources because there's still enough of a body count to give these kids nightmares for years, let alone their experiences for however long they'd been in captivity. Some of the children looked in much worse shape than others."

When they reached the top of the elevator shaft, Medusa provided air coverage with her helicopter while the team handed the last of the children into the trucks to waiting adults, a couple of whom didn't look to be in much better shape than the kids themselves. With the last child secured, Cerberus, Steel, and Demon each hopped up into a truck, and they took off through the gates of the mine to freedom.

Medusa quickly set the helicopter down, everyone loaded into the bird, TB slammed the door shut, and they were off.

"Scheherazade?" Nemo shouted over the rotors.

"Damn dog wanted to ride with Janus of all people, so Steel's in his truck to watch over her," TB informed him. "Weirdest fuckin' thing. Jumped in that cab with no hesitation, and her damn head was hanging out the window, tongue flapping in the breeze. I swear to Christ, she was smiling."

He grinned. "Her sense of self-preservation disappeared with her puppies." He looked at Gem, huddled on the opposite side of the helicopter. "Come here, kitty cat." He motioned for her to come to him.

"Your back..." she started.

"Don't care. Need to hold you."

Nemo dragged her onto his lap, wrapping his arm around her waist and burying his face in the space between her hair and her neck.

She was shaking so hard her teeth were chattering. She clutched his biceps in her hands. It was too loud to talk, so all he could do to reassure himself that she was fine was to hold her tight and not let go.

He looked up from her shoulders to see Midas in the copilot seat of the helicopter. The relief on his brother's face was crystal clear. Nemo smiled and gave him a thumbs-up. Midas returned the gesture, himself now reassured that his twin was truly back, and returned his focus to what Medusa needed him to be doing.

His sugar cat. His twin. His team. Life was good.

45

SEPTEMBER 27, 2022

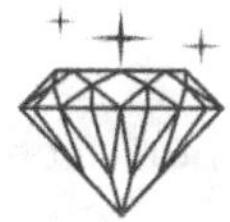

Haskell

"Kaders fled the country. No sign." Midas gave his report from the conference room in Mythos' safe house back in Melbourne, Australia. The team had remained to allow Nemo's back to heal and to try and rout out the Kaders, who had fled as soon as the shooting started.

"Rats fleeing a sinking ship," TB groused, throwing his project folder onto the table.

"Think they went back to Egypt?" Demon asked.

Waters scowled. "If it were me? I'd go underground."

Haskell exchanged glances with her Mythos counterparts.

"Italy," she said softly.

The table looked at her.

"They'll likely be in Italy under the protection of the Salieri. They won't want to give up on those mines just yet. But they'll need to regroup, so it's the most likely place for the Kaders to go."

Waters tapped his pencil against his project folder. It was easily two minutes of quiet before he spoke. "Someone finally going to clue us in?"

Haskell wiggled uncomfortably in her seat, again exchanging glances with Mythos. "That's not my call. I already probably shared more than I should have."

Waters gritted his teeth and ground them together before he spoke. "Well, it's connected now to Ka-Bar, who is also in the wind again, so I think we're now in a need-to-know situation. Somebody start talking."

It was Medusa who spoke, her face inscrutable behind the smoke-tinted glasses she wore. "The simple version is that, as Gem told you, they're an organized crime family. Mythos' entire mission is to shut them down."

"How is it no one has heard of them?" TB asked. "Midas and I have been pretty active on the dark web for years, and we've never heard a whisper of them until Flame was taken."

"And you shouldn't have even heard of it then, but that's moot now."

She took off her glasses and rubbed the bridge of her nose. Gilgamesh got up and went over to a cabinet in the corner and pulled out a bottle of painkillers. When Medusa opened her eyes, she squinted against the light. Loki hit a button on his remote control to lower the light. As the lights went down, her eyes opened wider.

"Holy shit!" Demon whispered from his place across from her.

"Yes, sorry. I know. They're startling until you get used to them."

Medusa's pupils were nearly white, with just the barest ring of mint green around the outside. "It's a rare condition. So rare, in fact, that there's no name for it. Probably some form of albinism." She shrugged. "Sensitive to light, hence the glasses."

"And the colored contacts," TB added, "when you're out in public because they're awfully recognizable."

She nodded.

Steel chimed in, "Hence the name 'Medusa.' People freeze when they see them."

Waters chuckled. "Nice try at distraction, Medusa, but I'm still waiting for information."

She smirked. "Touché." She laid the glasses on the table. "Women are not valued amongst the Salieri. In fact, there are none in their ranks or even in their families."

"They're celibate?" Nemo asked.

"We could only be so lucky," Loki grumbled.

"No, they procreate," Medusa admitted. "But the women are used only for that, and they do not raise the children."

"I still don't understand how people don't know about them, then," TB said. "These women clearly know of them."

"Yes, but... they're not around long enough to share the knowledge." She sighed. "The women are carefully selected for a variety of attributes and characteristics. They are offered a great deal of money to serve as mothers. If they say yes, they live in the ultimate luxury up to the birth of the child."

"And after?" Nemo asked hesitantly.

"They're killed," Loki expelled bluntly. "And if the child is a girl, the child is killed as well."

The men were so stunned they couldn't even swear.

Haskell jumped in, "My guess is that those girl children in the mines were daughters of men they've recruited into their ranks. It's possible adult females are used as additional breeders, but we haven't been able to confirm that. In any case, all of the female line is sacrificed. No exceptions. Now you see why the work is so important." Her eyes went to Nemo, even though her words were meant for the entire table.

"What's next?" Waters questioned.

Loki closed the project folder he'd been given and pushed it toward the center of the table. "Gilgamesh, Medusa, Gem, Cerberus, and I will be taking the children to a compound in an undisclosed location. They'll be provided with food, shelter, whatever they need.

We have counselors and teachers on staff. They will be well cared for and, hopefully, adopted into loving families."

"An orphanage, then," TB sneered.

"Not like you experienced, TB," Loki promised. "It's more like a boarding school. The children are very happy there, but I don't expect you to take that at face value. Haskell can vouch for them, as can any of the team."

"Call it what you want," TB argued. "They're still unwanted children in a facility."

Medusa spoke up. "Except they are wanted. We want them, and so do all the staff who work for us. I... We... will accept nothing less. The children want for nothing, not even affection. If someone applies to adopt, the child must also agree to the process, or they stay with us. And if a child is not adopted, at eighteen, they can choose to leave, with as much support from Mythos as they want or need, or they are welcome to stay at our safe haven until they choose to leave."

"Do you have any who choose to leave?" Waters asked.

"A few," Loki admitted, "but it is rare. Most who leave have met someone and married, so they go to their own homes. The damage for some is too difficult to surmount sometimes, but we continue to try."

Nemo brought up the question he'd been curious about. "The hit on Gem. What are we doing about that?"

Midas cleared his throat. "I was watching the bid. Apparently, The Collector came out of retirement." His eyes looked across the table to TB.

Nemo's head snapped to look at TB, and everyone followed his gaze. Stunned, he asked, "You bid on the job?"

TB nodded. "I figured if I logged in as The Collector and bid on the job, offered a high enough price, no one else could take it."

Nemo floundered. "That's... The risk... The cost had to be huge! Fuck, if that links back to you... Flame? Your..." He caught himself before revealing TB's secret.

"Turns out Nova is really good at creating fake photos. We

provided proof of death to the Kaders. Gem died in the crossfire inside the Murphy Mine."

"I applaud your ingenuity, but what happens if someone ambitious traces the money?" Waters asked, concern on his face. "Identifying The Collector after all this time would be quite the coup."

TB turned his gaze to his boss. "Fourteen accounts, remember? But no one will link it back to me. Golden Fingers over there"—he nodded his head toward Midas—"with the help of Nova, put several additional layers of protection on me, and suddenly, all of my accounts disappeared. Oops."

"That's everything you worked toward for years." Nemo was in awe.

His teammate shook his head. "I just said it disappeared, not that it was missing." TB shrugged with a knowing smile. "As you're so fond of saying, what's life without a little risk? Besides, I owed a favor." His eyes flashed to Nemo. "A life for a life. If I'd lost everything, it would have been more than worth it."

Haskell watched the two men share a moment, and Nemo gave a near-nonexistent nod to his teammate.

"Thank you, TB," she said.

TB gave a single nod and a cocky salute to her.

Loki broke the moment and cleared his throat. "What will Tribe do now?"

"We'll be heading home," Waters claimed. "We'll be continuing our search for Ka-Bar. If you receive more information, we'd appreciate it if you'd share it with us."

Loki nodded. "And we hope you will do the same." He stood at his seat. "We'll be leaving at five a.m."

The Mythos team members stood and began to push away from the table. She looked at Loki. "I'll meet you at the airport in the morning."

He looked at her with a hard expression. Then his eyes flicked to Nemo, who stared back just as hard. When he glanced back at her, he ordered, "Don't be late."

The group filed out without saying goodbye or handshakes.

Once they were gone, Demon whistled. "Those are the weirdest motherfuckers I've ever met. Present company excluded, Gem."

"No offense. They all have some strong past ties to the Salieri, and it's made them a bit darker than most. I'm not technically a member of the team, just a contractor, so I have no connections other than what I've seen and heard, but that's bad enough."

Nemo's fingers were drumming on the table. "Waters, I'm going to take some time. I won't go far."

Waters looked steadily at him. "Keep your watch handy. Don't turn it off."

"I won't."

He got up from the table, Scheherazade following with joy at the thought of a walk. When he pulled the door open, he pulled so hard it went as far back as it could, then slowly began to close on its automatic hinges. Scheherazade stopped in the doorway, looking back at Haskell. Her head tilted, and she yipped as if to say, "You coming?" When Haskell remained seated, the dog chuffed and took off after Nemo. There was silence as the door continued to close.

Haskell sighed. "I'll go after him."

"Gem?"

She knew what question TB was asking, and she shook her head. "I can't. Please understand. This is just too important."

"Maybe it's just best to let him go, then. Kinder to him," Demon intoned, refusing to look at her.

"Maybe. But I can't do that either." She stood and crossed to the door. Turning back to them, she thanked them. "Thank you. For everything. I hope..." She didn't finish the sentence. It was just too hard to speak around the lump in her throat.

She slipped through the door and jogged to try and find Nemo.

When she got upstairs, she flew out the front door, but Nemo was nowhere to be seen.

It was late, and there were few cars in this neighborhood at this time of the night, but the streets were well-lit. There wasn't a single person in any direction.

"Shite. Where the bloody hell did you go?" She looked up and down the street. Running a hand through her hair, she blew out a frustrated breath. This could *not* be how they said goodbye. Not this time.

A seagull landed on the fence across the street. She smiled. "You can run, but you can't hide, burglar boy."

46

SEPTEMBER 27, 2022

Nemo

He was back at the pier, one foot braced on the lowest rung of the wooden fence, leaning on his forearms, hands clasped in front of him. Scheherazade was down in the surf chasing a crab.

This was the exact same spot they'd been before he'd whisked Gem down the beach and made love to her in one of the bathing huts. It had been the hottest sex of his entire life. Not because of where it had been or even what they'd done but because of the woman herself. No one responded like her. No one gave as good as she got like her. No one destroyed him and put him back together like his sugar cat, and no one ever would.

"Fuck," he cursed softly, hanging his head. It was day nineteen. Steel's projection on the bet. His friend was going to lose the bet, which didn't happen often. Nemo had thought he was nuts anyway, but it appeared he wasn't even going to get the thirty days he had put on the board. Tomorrow, she'd be off and running away from him again.

"Nemo?"

His head raised and turned in the direction of the breathless voice. She wasn't smiling, nor was she running to him, so he didn't for one second believe she'd changed her mind and was going to stay.

You didn't exactly ask her to stay, though, did you?

Was it that easy? Just ask her? Somehow, he didn't think it was. This was about saying goodbye since she knew how much her ducking out on him the previous two times pissed him off.

He stood up straight and turned, leaving one arm leaning on the top fence rail, the other dropping down to his side.

She approached slowly until she stood just within his arm's reach, but she said nothing. He could gather her up, hold her tight, and beg her to stay with him.

He heaved a heavy breath. There was nothing else for it.

It's time to stand on your own, Sawyer.

"Do you remember when you asked me why the lift code was zero-seven-zero-five-one-six?" he asked.

"Yes. You said it was the most important date in your life."

"It wasn't an exaggeration. You were the ultimate thief. You stole my heart the moment I saw you. After that first time we were together, I hoped we'd run into each other again one day. I knew, beyond the shadow of a doubt, one night with you was never enough."

His eyes roved her face, noting all the little qualities he loved about it. Her wide blue eyes. The tattoos along her hairline. The tiny hoop nose ring and the labret piercing, balancing out below. Her soft skin. Her plump lips. The dimple in her chin. That rebel curl that fascinated him and defied him at every turn. Just like her.

He let go of the rail and took a single step closer, bringing his hand up to grasp hers. He pulled her close, kissed her palm, then held it tight to his chest. Oddly, he thought he would have to take a big breath to say his next words, but they came out free. Easy. Because they were the only words he could say, and he wanted to say them.

"You're the most beautiful woman I've ever seen, Gem. You're like the statue at the Borghese. You know, the one of Daphne escaping Apollo." His other hand caressed her face as he spoke. "Your skin, all alabaster and smooth. Your curls, wild and untamable. I feel like I'm your Apollo, always chasing, always reaching. But no matter what I do, it's never enough to keep you by my side."

"Is that what you think? That I'm running from you?"

"Aren't you?" he asked. He drew a fingertip across an eyebrow and down her cheek to the corner of her mouth. "Every fuckin' time I get close, you run. Am I right? Are you like Daphne? If I finally chase you down, wear you out, will you freeze and become something other than you are? Something I can only worship from afar?"

Gem's eyes filled with tears. Suddenly, she lunged at him and dragged him by the arms into a half circle so that she was against the wooden pier. "Up!" she told him, lifting her arms so that her hands rested on his shoulders. Immediately, his hands went to her waist, and he lifted her as she did a short jump to set her ass on the rail, a grunt escaping him.

"Am I hurting you?"

"You're destroying me. What do you think?"

"I meant your back."

"It'll heal."

Her legs spread, she pulled him to her core, then tightened her legs to his sides so he couldn't escape. She pulled him tight to her chest, kissed the top of his head, and then pushed him back to look into his eyes. Smoothing her hands over his face, along his hairline, around the shells of his ears, and down his neck, she eventually allowed them to settle on his shoulders. "I love you, Sawyer, but I *can't* stay."

"You still don't believe I love you," he accused.

"No. I mean, yes. I do believe you. I mean, no, that's not why I have to leave."

"Is it the women?"

She smiled and shook her head. "No. Not even close."

"Then what is it?"

She traced the triangle tattoo on his throat. "I belong with Mythos right now. You've seen what the Salieri are capable of. What they're already doing. I can't let that go. I don't want to let it go. I refuse to let it go. Mythos is hell-bent on taking them down, and I need to be there to help." She stopped him from interrupting her. "I know that Tribe will likely be involved again in this mess somewhere along the line, but I don't work for Tribe, and I'm not blind to the fact that you all have other interests and responsibilities beyond the Salieri. With Mythos, they're an exclusive job. No other goal exists."

She sighed and slipped down from her seat to stand between him and the wood beams. "When I was recovering from climbing up that air vent shaft, I had a visitor. It was God. I'd never met him before, obviously, and I never saw his face because he kept it in the shadows. The pain in his voice over not knowing where you were? It was almost as bad as what I imagine Midas was feeling."

Stepping into him, she laid her hands on his chest. "He knew I could very well be willing to throw away everything to stay with you. But he asked me to stay with Mythos. He said leaving would be the wrong choice. For both of us." Her fingertips smoothed the collar of his T-shirt. "He asked me to trust him. To make the *right* choice. Leaving them to be with you would be the worst thing I could do. And," she admitted, "Waters talked to me as well."

He drew back in anger. "Who the fuck are these people to interfere? We supported Waters when he went after Kubrick. We supported TB—"

Her finger pressed against his lips.

He caught her hand in between both of his, pressing his lips to it in desperation. "Please, Gem," he whispered. "I'm begging you. Do you want me on my knees? I'll get on my knees!" Nemo knelt at her feet. "I love you, Gem. I fucking love you, and you're leaving, and all I'll have left are the fucking memories. Memories aren't enough, pretty baby." Nemo clutched her hands, pulling her to him. His arms formed a steel band around her waist, and he buried his head in the softness of her stomach. "I don't want you to go because I want this, Gem. With every part of me."

Her hands threaded through his hair. "Nemo. You didn't let me tell you what he actually said," she chastised.

Hesitantly, he looked up at her.

"He told me that when all of this was done, we both had choices to make, and it was up to us to make the right ones."

Nemo looked into her eyes, searching for something. He knew she was trying to tell him something, but damned if he knew what it was. Then... the light went on in his head.

"No. Fuck! I don't want to do this."

"I know. Making choices is never easy. Not important ones, anyway."

Slowly, he stood to his full height, his eyes never breaking from hers. He slid his hands up to her head. One hand cupped the side of her neck, and the other hand slid down to her hip.

"Gem, I don't know... I can't..." He hung his head. He could feel tears slipping from his eyes.

Her fingers swiped at the tears on his cheeks. "I'm so, so sorry."

When his eyes lifted to hers once more, he knew. There was no choice to make. Letting her go would kill something in him that he'd never be able to revive. "This is breaking my heart."

"Mine too," she admitted.

A tear slid from her eye, and he brushed it away with his thumb. It was then that he knew she understood exactly why this was destroying him.

"Don't cry, pretty baby," he whispered, and he kissed a second tear that fell. "It's not your fault. It's okay. I'm nothing if not adaptable. I have to be because I wasn't lying. I'm willing to accept this because I love you, and it's what *you* need." He tipped his head down, his lips touching hers, opening to her just as he opened his heart.

"Woof!" Nemo felt himself get pushed by two wet, sandy paws, and he almost lost his balance. Both he and Gem broke apart, laughing through their tears at the dog standing on her hind legs, front paws at Nemo's waist, her claws hooked in his belt.

"All right, girl. I'll take her home." He looked at Gem. "She's so bossy."

Sliding her underneath his arm and tucking her into his side, they walked back to their hotel. Her arm curved around his waist, and they watched Scheherazade run in front of them, get to about twenty-five feet, then run back to them, tongue lolling with excitement. Then, she'd repeat the process.

Before they entered the hotel, she stopped him, hands on his chest, his hands around her waist. "You're staying with me tonight, yes?"

He nodded. "Yes. I wouldn't dream of being anywhere else."

He kissed her again, then they turned and walked into the hotel and up to their room.

47

SEPTEMBER 28, 2022

Midas

"Nemo!" He pounded on the hotel door, but there was no answer. "Son of a fuck, Nemo, I know you're pissed she's gone, but we're leaving."

"He's not there, Midas."

Midas turned to see Waters leaning in the open doorway of his hotel room across the hall.

"What do you mean he's not there? Where the hell else would the fuckwitch be?" Midas slammed his hand on the door. "He did *not* go and find some girl, did he? I'll kill him! I really will kill him."

Midas started to storm to the elevator, but Waters got in his path with a hand to the chest and stopped him.

"He made the right choice, Midas. Gem couldn't stay with us."

The computer expert stared at his boss, his molars grinding. He couldn't process what Waters was telling him. Then it hit him. "He's not there, meaning he's no longer *here*? Are you saying he left? With her?"

Waters nodded. He clearly wasn't happy about the situation, but it was clear to Midas that he was resigned to it.

"God warned me the last time we talked that this would probably happen. I gave Nemo my blessing."

"So Nemo talked to you, but he didn't talk to me? What the ever-loving fuck?"

Waters gave a silent chuckle. "No, he did, but clearly, for the first time ever, you didn't check your email."

"I finally managed to get some sleep," Midas groused. "I was in a hurry because I overslept."

"Check your email. Meet us downstairs when you're done. We'll wait. Mythos is letting us use their jet to get home, so there's no rush."

Waters turned and grabbed his bag from by the door, then closed his door and headed for the elevator, leaving Midas standing in the middle of the hallway.

He had no clue how long he stood there before turning and going back to his room. He slammed the door closed, jerked his laptop out of his bag, and opened up his email. Sure as shit, there was a message from his brother. When he opened the email, all he saw was a video icon.

He dropped into the chair, his finger hovering over the trackpad, hesitant to open the file. After a deep inhale and exhale, he finally did.

When the video started, it was to see his brother sitting in his own hotel room in the clothes he had been wearing last night when he left the debriefing. Gem was nowhere to be seen.

"Hey, big bro." He smiled, but it was one tinged with sadness. "You were sleeping when I broke into your room last night, and I didn't want to wake you. I know you haven't slept in days, so you need it.

"Look, I know you're not going to understand why I'm doing this, but... the Salieri can't be allowed to keep doing this. They're too big now. Gem gave me some more info, and... fuck, you wouldn't believe what I've learned. I... have to go with Mythos. Gem is desperately needed by Mythos, so she can't leave, and I can't let her go again. I won't survive it.

"You're the best brother a guy could have, and it's not just because you're my twin. You saved my ass so many times. I know you think I was a shit brother to you, never considering you and what you were sacrificing for me. But I promise you, a lot of the things I did when we were younger were done to protect you. I figured if I took the heat off you, you'd be able to do all the things you were meant to do. Maybe that was the wrong way to go about it, but if I had the chance, I'd do it all the same way again.

"Now? It's time for me to get *my* shit together, and I need to do that on my own. You can't hold my hand anymore or do shit for me so that I don't have to do it." Nemo's genuine smile lit up the screen. "I won't say that you won't have to save my ass anymore because I'm pretty damn sure you will. This isn't goodbye. Part of what I learned... let's just say we'll see quite a bit of each other before long, and my ass will probably need saving big time.

"But, Kash," he said seriously. "This is really important, and I need you to hear me. I have to go because I can't let you keep giving up on your life, your needs, because you're always looking over me. As long as I'm there, you'll keep focusing on me. You're my twin, not my father. You need to start living your own life. You don't need to parent me anymore. I promise. I'll be okay. God and Waters were right. Gem and I had decisions to make, and they needed to be the *right* ones. This is right."

His smile became more sedate again. "I love you, big bro. I'll see you soon." He started to reach toward the computer to cut the video, but then he pulled back. "Oh. Before I forget. Mom still loved me best." He blew a big bubble, let it pop, sucked it back into his mouth, winked, and then he cut the feed.

Midas closed out the email and shut his laptop.

Fifteen minutes later, he was down in the lobby with his bag. All of the men had their wallets open and were handing Steel his money for the bet over Gem and Nemo, trash-talking him as a cheater, somehow having inside information. The man just collected the money and put it away, accepting the insults and saying nothing.

TB handed Midas a cup of coffee. "Everything okay?"

Midas blew on his coffee, took a sip, and tipped his head with a sigh. "It will be. Let's go."

The team of five walked out the lobby doors and headed back to Los Angeles.

Good Enough: The Deadman's Tribe Book 1 – B0CJFSW6LZ

Team Leader, Waters, hires on to consult on a movie about Navy SEALs. Director Kai Serrano not only needs his expertise, but also needs his protection as the men of Tribe Corporation search for her missing brother.

Bad Enough: The Deadman's Tribe Book 2 – B0CTHZPN6Y

Interrogator and all-around bad boy TB has been talking in secret to romance novelist Sylvan Jones about the BDSM lifestyle as part of her research for a new novel. But when secrets from Sylvan's past come back to haunt her, the bad boy is forced into the good girl's real world, and he'll burn the world down to protect her.

Never Enough: The Deadman's Tribe Book 3 – B0CZ339NWF

Thief and playboy Nemo partners up with fellow thief Haskell to trace a cache of conflict diamonds through Africa. Will the playboy have his heart stolen by Le Chatte Noire, or will he resist being caught for life?

Strong Enough: The Deadman's Tribe Book 4 – B0F1RBGWHF

Twenty-six years ago, Cherry's father was kidnapped and never found. Her entire life has been a search for those who took him. After all this time, she finally has a lead. Posing as newlyweds, she and Demon, Tribe's medic, travel to the Caribbean, where they uncover ancient secrets that are tied to his disappearance. Those same secrets now endanger the attraction they've finally decided to explore.

The Lucky Rabbit: A prequel spin-off to the series Six Paths to Justice – B0D777NVR5

A short story in *The Lucky in Love* charity anthology. Cosmos, member and part owner of a BDSM club called The Library, meets a woman who intrigues him more than any other woman has. After a memorable night together, he gets called away on an emergency, and their newfound relationship hangs in the balance. (This story is a prequel to a spin-off series from *Bad Enough*, and will connect to the *Operation Alpha: Police & Fire* world of Susan Stoker.)

Justice for Francesca: Six Paths to Justice Book 1 (Operation Alpha: Police & Fire) – B0DTV65N4V

Tripoli and Fleur's story (seen in *Bad Enough*)

Ethan "Tripoli" Evans met FBI agent Francesca McCabe while she was undercover. When her case exploded around her, she was forced to leave the investigation without notice, leaving him hurt and confused. It's now two years later, there's a murdered woman in his nightclub, and Francesca has been assigned to investigate. Tripoli is not about to allow his second chance to pass him by.

<u>Up Next</u>

Midas's Story: The Deadman's Tribe Book 5
RELEASES OCTOBER 2025!

ABOUT THE AUTHOR

At ten years old, Nicole Craig snuck into a secret box of her mother's books filled with mysteries and romances. Since that day, she has a book (or five) available at all times. At the age of thirty, her husband encouraged her to try her hand at writing. It only took another twenty-five years of teaching high school and a pandemic to do it, creating the types of books she found in that magical box.

Nicole lives in Southeastern Wisconsin. She is a devout Milwaukee Brewers fan, mother of three furry feline children, and married to The One. After twenty-five years as a high school English teacher, she decided to retire to spin fantastic tales, travel, and live the ultimate fantasy: reading a book a day until the end of time.

Please consider leaving a review on Amazon or Goodreads. It's one of the best ways to thank a writer (besides buying their books!) for the work they've done.

Check out her Facebook Reader Group or any of her social media links to get the latest updates on The Deadman's Tribe series or other upcoming projects.

Facebook Reader Group: Nicole Craig's Tribe
Website: https://nicolecraigauthor.com/
Instagram: https://www.instagram.com/nicolecraigauthor/
Newsletter: https://dl.bookfunnel.com/aoslx3defo

ACKNOWLEDGMENTS

The One—I hope your girl, Haskell, brings you joy. I wrote her just for you.

Maddy Opal—For all things Aphmau & MeeMeows! (And quit reading so closely and learning all my secrets before everyone else.)

Jessa Aarons—Thank you for allowing me to stalk you this year, and I've loved getting to know you and your other half. Is there anything left to buy from you yet?

Carolyn Glover—Thank you for your alpha read of *Never Enough* and your British expertise to make sure Haskell sounds as she should.

Rayne Lewis—So glad I can cater to your Smash Penny addiction. The One and I love giggling like twelve-year-olds, cranking the wheel, and having everyone look at us like we're crazy. (They're not wrong.) You are so dear to me. You're my greatest cheerleader, and I'm so thankful you call me your friend.

SJ Higgins, Stef White, Vanessa Esquibel, and Kat Wyeth—Yet again, you make me look good.

Nicole Craig's Tribe—Thank you for being a part of my reader group. We are small, but we are tribe.

My ARC Tribe—Thank you for taking some of your valuable time to read and review my novel. I know it's not an easy job. I appreciate your honest reviews.

To Anyone Who Reads This Book—Thank you. Nemo and Gem (and Scheherazade!), thank you, as well. Please don't be mad at me for my "alternative" HEA.